SERVANT
OF
EARTH

SERVANT
OF
EARTH

SARAH HAWLEY

ACE
NEW YORK

ACE
Published by Berkley
An imprint of Penguin Random House LLC
penguinrandomhouse.com

Copyright © 2024 by Sarah Hawley

Book design by Daniel Brount

Library of Congress Cataloging-in-Publication Data

Names: Hawley, Sarah, author.
Title: Servant of earth / Sarah Hawley.
Description: New York: Ace, 2024. | Series: Shards of magic
Identifiers: LCCN 2024023218 (print) | LCCN 2024023219 (ebook) |
ISBN 9780593819791 (hardcover) | ISBN 9780593818374 (ebook)
Subjects: LCGFT: Fantasy fiction. | Novels.
Classification: LCC PS3608.A8937 S47 2024 (print) | LCC PS3608.A8937
(ebook) | DDC 813/.6—dc23/eng/20240517
LC record available at https://lccn.loc.gov/2024023218
LC ebook record available at https://lccn.loc.gov/2024023219

International edition ISBN: 9780593952986

Printed in the United States of America
1st Printing

To Angela, Julie, Meredith, and Rachel—thank you for a decade of friendship and good books.

AUTHOR'S NOTE

Servant of Earth deals with emotionally difficult topics, including violence, murder, torture, gore, sexual assault (secondary characters), sexual harassment, self-harm, death of a parent after prolonged illness, grief, explicit sexual content, and explicit language.

SERVANT
OF
EARTH

1

THE WINTER SOLSTICE CREPT IN COLD, WET, AND HEAVY with dread.

I looked out at the predawn darkness, tracing my finger over the frosted patterns that coated the exterior of the window. A wintry draft slithered through the gap where the wooden frame had warped with age. As the wind surged outside, a spray of icy rain smacked against the glass.

Another drop of frigid water splatted on my forehead. I yelped, then scowled up at the roof. This leak was new—I'd already been awoken unpleasantly by the one that had formed directly over my mattress during the night—and it was just one more sign of everything wrong in my life. I wouldn't have the money to replace the thatching for a long time, if ever, so I grabbed a bucket and put it under the leak. Soon I wouldn't need to go to the well for my water anymore.

As I straightened, a glow through the window caught my eye. In the distance, a golden faerie light shivered through the darkness. Its path was uneven, made more so by the warped glass. As I watched it move, my chest tightened with worry.

The winter solstice wasn't just the shortest day of the year; it was the day the Fae took yet another thing from humans. A faith that yielded no rewards, prayers that met uncaring ears, a legendary history that had decayed into this disappointing reality . . . We gave the faeries our hopes, and for what? Silence and far-off lights that led nowhere.

And now the Fae—or at least our naïve belief in them—would steal the lives of four young women.

"You don't deserve any of it," I whispered as I watched the drifting orb.

My mother would have chastised me for the blasphemous words. *Only the luckiest and most worthy humans are chosen to join the Fae*, she'd told me eighteen years ago as she unsnarled the tangles in my hair with a wooden comb. It had been another winter solstice morning—a sacrifice year, like this one—and I'd been just shy of turning seven. *Those women are favored above all other mortals, and they live out the rest of their lives in splendor in Mistei, the faeries' kingdom under the ground.*

There was longing in her voice whenever she'd told me that story. She hadn't been chosen for the Fae during the solstice ritual when she came of age. Life had pushed a different fate on her, and there I was as the result: a ragged child held in her equally threadbare embrace, my father long gone and rain dripping through the roof onto the packed earth floor of our hut. Still, she'd passed the fables on to me, as if through hearing them maybe I'd one day be granted the blessings life had denied her.

I didn't believe in blessings anymore.

Another drop plinked into the bucket. I made a rude hand gesture at the distant will-o'-the-wisp, then turned my back on it and began my preparations for the day.

The washbasin still held leftover water from the previous night.

I splashed it onto my face, gasping at the shock of cold. Then I scrubbed my teeth and changed my nightdress for a loose shirt and trousers. The day would be a busy one—it was not only a sacrifice year but the first time I'd be eligible—but I didn't want to miss my favorite morning ritual.

The one-room hut was dark, but I knew the layout by heart. I stepped around the small table and two mismatched chairs that served as a sitting area, making my way to the scarred wooden table by the hearth. Bundles of herbs hung overhead, along with a few withered onions. Anya had given me some cheese the last time we'd gone for a walk together, so I cut off a piece and shoved it in my mouth before grabbing my cloak and heading outside.

The rain had thankfully stopped, but the mossy ground was slick and rimed with overnight frost. The snows would come soon, but we were still in the first month of winter, with its glittering mornings and spats of icy rain. As I rounded the corner of the hut, the wind grabbed at my messy braid, trying to rip the brown curls loose.

The sky was purpling to the east, the blackness of night slipping away. The wood-and-stone buildings and thatched roofs of Tumbledown stood against the lightening sky like crooked teeth, and smoke began drifting from chimneys as the town woke.

The town wasn't my aim, though. My mornings were dedicated to the bog.

Enterra was curved like an hourglass with a longer and wider lower part, and the bog banded the country like a lady's belt, with Tumbledown its buckle. Just north of my hut, the shrubbed land merged into a vast, glassy wet expanse dotted with low mounds of earth and plant matter. Thick fog sprawled across it, obscuring the far side where the land became faerie territory. Dozens of will-o'-the-wisps drifted through that fog, the floating orbs fading as dawn grew closer.

I watched the lights dim and go out one by one, and a familiar sadness settled alongside my lingering anxiety. On solstice mornings my mother's presence felt especially close. Her faith that she could become one of the Fae's favored ones had never faltered. Supposedly the Fae used to travel across the bog to trade with, seek entertainment from, or rain blessings down on humans—and occasionally abduct those they took a liking to—but now the eerie lights that drifted across the wetlands at night were the only sign they even existed.

Loving the Fae hadn't brought my mother any joy. Yet when she'd died eighteen months back, feverish and agonized, her last words had been for them: "Maybe now they will save me."

They hadn't, of course.

I filled my lungs with icy predawn air, willing my bitterness to wait a few hours. The morning was beautiful, and there were treasures to be found. When pink tinged the eastern sky, the last golden wisp disappeared, and I retrieved my net from a hollow log and wound my way out into the bog.

Most people were too afraid to come here. It was easy to get lost and drown; the ground between pools of water was deceptive, and more often than not what looked like solid earth was actually a pit of mud waiting to suck a traveler down. There were legends, too, of knuckers and other Nasties that lurked in the fens and wet places of the world, eager to rend the flesh of those who misstepped.

I'd spent my entire life at the edge of the bog, though, and I never misstepped—nor had I seen evidence of dragons under the water. It had been my haven for as long as I could remember, a place to be alone and free.

I took familiar twisting paths until a stretch of water blocked any further progress. Then I sat on a tussock of pale winter grass, my feet inches from a patch of clover that hid the edge of a pool, and dipped my net in.

"Fishing" was what my mother had called this odd habit of mine, though I privately thought of it as "collecting." My mother's stories had sparked my interest in the border between humans and the Fae, and the bog's secrets had been so tempting that I'd attached a net to a long wooden pole, determined to see what rested at the bottom.

As it turned out, any number of wonders were hidden in the muck and silt. Smooth skipping stones, carved talismans, even coins tossed in by lovers who braved the treacherous paths to prove their courage and commitment to each other. They wished on coppers, hoping the Fae would bless their union. The Fae didn't care, but I certainly blessed them for it. I'd even found what I thought were faerie artifacts before—pieces of faceted glass or strange twists of bright metal. I'd run my fingers over the objects, thinking about who might have crafted them in the distant past and what their purpose had been. Letting the wonder of my mother's stories slip back into me, if only for a few hours.

Something caught at my net, and I grunted as I jerked it free. The object that came up with the muck was brown and misshapen. "Please don't be something disgusting," I said under my breath as I tipped the blob out onto the grass. Artifacts weren't the only things hidden below; there were occasional bones, too, and in a thick, foul-smelling pool deep in the bog, I'd once found a shriveled hand still covered in leathery skin.

When the bog took, it was greedy.

I wiped away the slimy mud. Not a bone, thankfully. Just a rock. I threw it back in with a plunking splash and fished for more.

I was trying not to think about what awaited later that day, but the memory of that severed hand was making me fret about the solstice sacrifice again. The odds of being selected were minimal, but I wasn't the only one eligible this year—my best friend, Anya, was as well, and she was all I had left in the world. Supposedly the will-o'-

the-wisps would lead the chosen women to Mistei, but I'd stopped believing that a long time ago. Probably the first morning I'd fished up a human bone.

I squeezed my eyes shut and focused on my breathing. "This is my place," I said softly. The Fae didn't get to taint everything, and there were still hours left before the ritual.

The rising sun spilled rosy golden light across the landscape, and the fog began to clear. I scooped another stone out of the water and tossed it back. Found a single copper and wiped it dry on my cloak before stuffing it in a pocket. My net didn't pull up anything but thick, slimy mud after that—much of which splattered over my already stained clothes—so I shifted to a different spot and tried again. This time I found a wooden doll the size of my index finger, its face carved with a carefree smile. It had tiny horns that signified it as an Underfae, a type of faerie that was lower in status than the Noble Fae who ruled Mistei.

"Look at you," I whispered, enchanted by the figurine in my palm. This was the sort of treasure I loved most—the kind that made me wonder and imagine. Who had it belonged to, and how had it been lost? It had probably been dropped on accident by an adventurous child from the village, the kind who—like me—had decided to test their mettle on the dangerous paths.

But maybe . . . maybe a Fae child had walked here, instead. Maybe this doll was a thousand years old, a well-preserved remnant of a time when our two species mingled freely and the paths across the bog were clear and well trod.

I tucked the doll into my pocket before I could start speculating about more tragic reasons it might be here. This was already a more productive morning than most, and I considered ending my collecting expedition on a triumphant note. But the low sun sparked off the water and the world felt free and empty in a rare way, so I slid the pole back in. One more try, and then I would pack up and return to the worries and responsibilities awaiting me.

My net met resistance in the thick mud at the bottom of the pond. When I pulled it free, I could tell I'd caught something substantial. I thought it was a rock at first, but when the net emerged from the water, it contained the most beautiful dagger I'd ever seen.

I gasped, pressing a hand to my mouth. The steel blade and wire-wrapped hilt gleamed in the dawn light, and the pommel was capped with a large crimson jewel. Its shine was unnatural: no mud clung to the weapon, and there wasn't a trace of rust on the blade.

My heart pounded as I pulled it from the net. It was heavy, yet the hilt fit my hand perfectly. Had it belonged to some wealthy lady, or even a faerie? The double-edged blade was wickedly sharp, and the scrollwork on the guard looked ancient and arcane. The blood-red stone capping the pommel was the strangest of all. I hadn't seen many jewels in my life, but the few I had seen had been star-bright and faceted. This was a perfectly smooth semicircle, and the dull orb seemed to absorb light rather than reflect it.

I glanced over my shoulder, suddenly afraid that someone had seen me find it, but I was still alone.

This dagger would fetch a fortune. A real fortune, not just the meager coins I earned selling peat and bog-trinkets at market. It would be a life-changing amount of money.

For a moment I let myself imagine a future where I was rich and free. I could leave Tumbledown and its small-minded judgments, find a new place to live where I wasn't known as the herbwoman's wild daughter. No more leaking roof, no more nights where my belly echoed with hunger. No more despair as I imagined my life unfolding just like this, day after day, until I eventually died impoverished and alone the way my mother had. I could become a trader, passing spices and handicrafts between Enterra and other countries, getting to hold and study artifacts that told stories of other legends and other ways of life. Maybe I'd even visit those places someday: cross the western mountains to icy Grimveld and forested Lindwic, then on to other countries I didn't know the names of yet.

Anya could come with me, too—she wouldn't have to marry just to ensure her future. She could take painting lessons, maybe even illuminate manuscripts the way she'd wanted to since she was a girl. We could be new people, unbeholden to anyone or anything but ourselves.

Dreams were nothing but air, though, and real change took more than just hope. Still, my hands trembled as I wrapped the dagger in the folds of my cloak.

I returned to the shore shortly afterwards, unable to focus on anything else.

My hut rose from the mist at the edge of the bog, looking like a boulder with its squat stone walls and inelegant structure. My parents had built the rough house by hand together when they'd first settled here. It wasn't beautiful, but it had stood for over twenty years. Stacks of peat brick—my meager source of income—leaned against the wall, waiting for the next time I could take a full barrow into town.

I paused, considering my options. This dagger was so obviously expensive that I couldn't risk anyone else seeing it. I needed to sell it quickly, and the solstice festival with its crowd of tourists was the perfect time.

I tore a long strip off the bottom of my shirt and wrapped the blade tightly. Then I slid the dagger inside the waistband of my trousers, strapping it to my thigh with the thin leather tie that had secured my braid. My curls sprang free, wild as ever.

There were other things I wanted to sell at market, so I hiked to my secret hiding place: a small cave in a rocky outcropping. The entrance was so short I had to crawl through. Once inside, the space was tall enough to stand in and several body lengths wide.

Every available surface was covered with treasure. Not gold or jewels, of course; if I'd found any, I would have sold them immediately. The objects here were more mundane: simple stone tools, useless household objects, a collection of unusually colored rocks. Each item had been collected from the bog, and each was precious to me. There was the wooden cup that had been one of my first finds. A rusty nail. A chunk of rose quartz. Each object told a story: of the morning when I'd found it, of the people or animals of the unknown past, of the bog and me.

I set the figurine down next to a battered metal cup, then moved to the corner that held things to sell at market. My basket contained a rabbit pelt from my last hunt and some faerie fruit I'd harvested the day before. The blue spheres would fetch a decent price, either from a visiting lady unfamiliar with their bitterness or from the vintner at the top of the hill who would turn them into hallucinatory faerie wine. I grabbed the basket, then headed back towards the entrance.

As I crouched to leave, there was a sharp pain at my right thigh. I yelped. "Damn!"

The dagger must have cut through the bindings. I hurriedly stripped my trousers off, exposed skin pebbling with gooseflesh, then unstrapped the dagger and examined the cut. Luckily, it was superficial: a bleeder, but one that would heal quickly.

The knife edge was clean.

I frowned, inspecting it more closely. Shouldn't there be a trace of blood on the blade? Instead, it shone bright and silver as the moon. I tested the edge gently on my thumb, gasping when it immediately sliced through the skin. My blood slid along the edge of the dagger. Then, as if drawn by some mystical force, it ran *up* from the edge towards a narrow groove in the center of the blade. It sank into the groove like rain into soil.

"How is that possible?" Surely I hadn't seen right. There was no way my blood had just . . . disappeared.

I etched another shallow slice in my thumb, wincing at the sting. Again the blood crawled up from the edge and pooled in the groove before vanishing.

Fae magic. It had to be. What else on this earth could do that?

I shivered.

It had been stupid to cut myself, but the blade looked clean and the wounds were already clotting, and I always kept a few lengths of bandage here just in case. I bandaged myself, then wrapped the dagger in the rough white fabric as well, adding far more layers than should have been necessary. I hesitated before tying it to my leg again. It might be impossibly sharp and potentially magical, but showing a dagger this valuable in my poor village would be more dangerous than keeping it strapped against my skin.

A little pain was worth what it would bring me, anyway. Money, possibilities . . . a future.

TUMBLEDOWN WAS FULLY AWAKE BY THE TIME I REACHED TOWN with my basket. Smoke curled from chimneys, women swept their doorsteps or clustered at the fences between houses to gossip, and children ran around shrieking solstice blessings at one another. Someone narrowly missed me with a bucket of slops they threw into the gutter, and when I dodged, I was nearly run over by the milkman's cart as it rattled over the cobblestones. He always worked at a frantic pace on the major holidays, since the true believers of the faerie faith liked to leave saucers of milk out for any unnatural creatures that might be wandering. Part offering of worship, part bribe to avoid mischief from the less benevolent types of faerie—and a waste of drink and money, to my thinking.

The street market next to the temple was full of visitors from across the country, men and women who peered at us and our rickety stone and wood homes like they were at a menagerie. Tumbledown was famous for being the closest village to Fae territory, so visitors always seemed surprised to realize we were poor. I found their astonishment amusing. We lived in a miserably wet northern clime next to an impassable bog the Fae never set foot across. Why would we be rich? The tourists who flocked to our faerie festivals made up the majority of our town's economy, though, so we let them gawk all they wanted.

I managed to sell the fruit within the first half hour. Visiting ladies went wild for the stuff, which was rumored to help you see faeries. Tonight they'd look with wonder at the will-o'-the-wisps across the bog, convinced the fruit had done its job, not realizing that the residents of Tumbledown saw those lights every night.

The rabbit pelt was harder to sell. I only found a buyer late that morning, and for a price I wouldn't have taken if I hadn't needed to purchase food. *Hunger is the most efficient way to lower one's standards*, my mother had quipped once, back when she'd still had the energy to make jokes.

Hopefully my standards wouldn't need to stay lowered for much longer. I kept an eye out for a buyer who looked wealthy enough to purchase the dagger, but this sale would need to be handled with care. Plenty of people would accuse me of thievery if they saw me holding a weapon that fine.

The crowd hummed with excitement and trepidation for the selection that would happen at noon, which marked the official start of the solstice celebrations. Even the poorest women I passed had taken the time to wash and press their outfits in honor of the holiday. I spared a glance for my grime-encrusted clothes. I should have changed into something nicer, but what did it matter? After the selection I could go home and change into my one decent dress before the main ceremony that night.

"Kenna!"

I grinned at the familiar voice and turned to see Anya rushing towards me, dimples flashing. She started to hold out her arms, then stopped a few feet away, eyeing my mud-stained clothes.

"No need for hugs," I said. "You'd just get dirty, and you look beautiful today."

Anya always looked beautiful, with her cascading golden-brown hair and large hazel eyes. She was tall and curvy, the kind of woman people couldn't help gawking at. In comparison, I was short, thin, and usually covered in mud. "A little wild" was what some of the kinder village women called me; "half feral" was more common. Why Anya had taken one look at me when we were children and decided we'd be best friends, I'd never know, but I was eternally grateful.

"I would normally say the same," she said, looking at my stained trousers judgmentally, "but you didn't make even the smallest effort today."

I stifled a laugh. Anya had called me beautiful plenty of times before, but she made no secret of her dismay over my grubby attire. "There's no need to make an effort. Putting on a dress isn't going to make people think any better of me." I raked my fingers through my tangled curls, wincing when I encountered a long strand of grass. I would definitely be the only woman with grass in her hair during the selection.

"I'm less worried about it being a dress and more worried about the mud splatters. Were you in the bog?"

"Yes. Doing some collecting." The bloodstain at my thigh was small and blended in with the dirt, so I wasn't going to mention it and worry her.

She made a face. "I don't know why you like it out there. What if you fall in and drown?"

"I know where I'm going." Up to a point, anyway. Years of rambling hadn't yet shown me a path all the way across. I nodded at her outfit. "Your dress is nice."

A shadow passed over her face. "I didn't exactly have other options. It is pretty, though." The garment under her cloak was thin yellow cotton, best suited for warmer weather, but it was one of the only dresses to survive the fire that had claimed her house and her parents' lives over the summer. She shook her head. "Maybe some rich man will fall madly in love with me today."

The words sounded sad. Anya was an idealist, believing fervently that a love match was possible and would improve her life, but the kind of husband she found out of financial necessity would likely not be worth having in any other sense.

The majority of women in Tumbledown were married by twenty-five, so both of us were nearing the limits of what was considered acceptable. I was unmarried because I was poor, strange, and undesirable—which was fine by me, since the life of a merchant appealed to me more than that of a housewife—but Anya had had no shortage of suitors over the years. She'd been dedicated to her parents, though. Neither had been in good health, and they'd needed strong young hands to help out around the house. Now that they were gone, she was staying with an aunt who had made it clear Anya would not be welcome forever.

We wound through the market together, looking at the stalls while I kept an eye out for anyone wealthy enough to afford the dagger. I didn't mention this quest to Anya, though—she was the dreamer of the two of us, and I didn't want to get her hopes up about the future until the coins were in my hand. The crowd surged, easily five times what we might expect from a normal holiday, and the mood was one of nervous excitement.

Anya kept up a running commentary at my side. She was smiling, as usual, but there was tension in her cheeks, and her anxiety was evident in the speed of her chattering. My own worry lay heavy in my belly, but of the two of us, I was more likely to stew in silence. When a horse-drawn cart clipped a vendor stand with a loud crack, Anya jumped.

"Hey," I said, pulling up short next to a booth full of woven textiles. "Are you all right?"

She pressed a hand to her stomach as she leaned back against a wooden post. "I'm nervous about the ritual. The thought of going to Mistei is . . ." She shook her head. "Amazing and terrifying all at once. It's not pious of me to say, but part of me hopes we don't get chosen."

Anya lacked my cynicism. Like my mother, she believed the faerie lights would actually guide women across the bog. Still, even if those legends were true and the chosen women lived out the rest of their days in luxury, anyone would be nervous about leaving behind everything they'd ever known.

Fear thickened in my throat at the thought of Anya heading into the bog at night, trusting her life and safety to a children's story. I knew the hidden paths better than anyone, and even I had never found my way to Mistei. I shook my head, dismissing the possibility. "We won't be chosen."

"You don't know that."

"There are hundreds of women here," I said, trying to soothe her. All unmarried women in Tumbledown between the ages of twenty and thirty were required to participate, but women came from all over northern Enterra, either because their hearts were full of naïve faith or because their families couldn't afford to keep them anymore and were desperate for a magical solution. "The odds are low. And if you do get picked, we can run away before the ritual starts."

Anya looked pensively towards the temple two blocks away. It was taller than any other building in town, formed of glittering gray stone that had supposedly been quarried from Mistei many centuries back. The Elder's acolytes were placing yew branches inside a large copper brazier at the top of the temple steps. "Maybe it would be a good thing to be chosen," she said softly. "Maybe that's the way out."

My entire heart rejected the idea, but I knew why she would say that. Being chosen by the faeries would be a way out of her new poverty, a way out of uncertainty, a way out of this reality where she needed to marry a man she didn't love in order to have a decent life.

I didn't believe the ritual brought a fresh start, though, not after the bones I'd found. Maybe the Fae had truly cared about humans once, but no one credible had even seen a faerie in centuries.

"No," I said fiercely. "There will be another way." One that didn't involve losing her to the bog or to some petty household tyrant who would control what she did and where she went and who she was allowed to befriend. Her parents had allowed her to run wild with a half feral bog child; a husband wouldn't be so lenient.

Her smile was small, but her eyes had brightened. "If you say so," she said. Anya the dreamer, taking my word that the future would be happier.

I shoved the fear away. I might not be an idealist, but I was tenacious, and that tended to yield better results anyway. Once the dagger was sold, we'd both have more options.

We walked through the village, and considering the way Anya hovered by my side, I knew she wouldn't leave until after the selection happened. Selling the dagger in daylight might be risky anyway— better to wait until tonight, when the village would be drunk and raucous with celebration.

It was a relief, in a way. There was something comforting about carrying a weapon. Women weren't supposed to unless they were hunting. Was this how men felt? Bold and brave, like no one could hurt them?

We passed a group of tavern louts at the edge of the market, the kind with unsteady steps and wandering hands. One of them whistled as he noticed Anya. "Why don't you come over here? I have something to show you." He cupped himself lewdly through his trousers, and his friends laughed.

Anya's pale cheeks flushed, but she kept her eyes on the ground and walked faster. I stepped between her and the men, baring my teeth.

"Oh ho," one of them said. "The little guard bitch looks feral."

"I couldn't recognize her through the mud."

"At least she doesn't have to worry today—there's no way the Fae want that scrawny ass."

They burst into uproarious laughter. I scowled and kept moving—I was used to men talking like that—but Anya stopped.

"Shut your mouth," she snapped. Her hands curled into tight fists as they laughed louder.

"It's not worth it." I tugged on her arm, hoping she'd yield. This wasn't a fight worth picking, not when Anya was wearing her yellow dress, when she was nervous about what might happen.

She dug in her heels and kept glaring. This was one of Anya's most frustrating—and endearing—characteristics. She never fought for herself, but she always did on behalf of her loved ones.

Anya yielded to my tugs at last and we walked on, leaving the men laughing behind us. Her cheeks had reached fever brightness. "Pigs," she muttered.

"And what do pigs become?" I asked lightly.

Her lips twitched. "Bacon."

"Exactly."

Anya looked over her shoulder one more time, then faced forward again. "Where to?" she asked. "We have a few minutes before we need to gather at the temple."

I hesitated, eyeing the temple's bell tower. There was a fenced yard behind it filled with small stone markers. "She loved the solstice."

Anya understood instantly, as she always had. Her expression softened, and she tucked her arm into mine. "Let's pay our respects."

My mother's grave marker was a crooked flagstone set in an overgrown corner of the yard. Wildflowers would bloom around it in summer, but now it was as unadorned as her life had ended up being. I'd scratched her name into the stone myself, deepening it every few weeks: NEVE HERON.

I knelt in the dirt, placed my hands in my lap, and closed my eyes. I thought of her curling brown hair, the way her smile had flashed bright and quick as a fish in a sunlit stream. Of her laugh, which she always hid behind her hand, and how at night she tried to cry so I couldn't hear it. She'd smelled like earth and pungent herbs, and her fingertips had always been stained yellow and green from her work.

My jaw clenched as I remembered the way she'd pressed those tonic-stained hands to her breast each night as she begged the Fae for a blessing. *Please let me serve you,* she'd whispered. *Let me be worthy.*

An icy wind surged through the cemetery, sending dead leaves skittering across the gravestones. "She loved the Fae," I said, eyes still pressed shut. "And they gave her nothing."

Anya's hand came to rest on my shoulder. "They gave her hope," she said softly.

Hope hadn't gotten her much in the end. Maybe Anya was right, though. I found it hard to believe in a better future without the proof of it in my hands, but my mother had always been full of dreams. When she hadn't been dreaming of Mistei, she'd dreamed of love and a marriage that would leave her happy and comfortable. She'd nearly had it once. My father had been clever and charming, with a laugh like a thunderclap and eyes that sparkled with merriment. He was a traveling merchant who had come to Tumbledown for the Beltane festival. One look into her blue eyes and he'd been lost.

Or so she'd said. It was Beltane, after all, a holiday when people's passions ran away with them, and my mother loved her stories.

I was born less than a year later with the odd amber eyes of my father and the wild curls of my mother. I'd been born on a frozen, moonless night, screaming as if I were furious with the world. Perhaps I had every reason to be.

My father hadn't been as wealthy as he'd claimed, and when his business deals fell through, she'd ended up poor and hungry at the edge of the bog with a man whose charm could never quite make up for the rest of it, and whose patience for having a child and a disappointed wife ran out long before I was old enough to remember him.

I opened my eyes and pressed my fingertips to the cold, rough stone. "Happy solstice, mama," I whispered. "May your spirit find Mistei."

Bells began to toll in the temple tower, a rapid, melodic cadence that only rang out once every six years.

Anya's anxious eyes met mine. "It's time."

2

HUNDREDS OF WOMEN FROM TOWNS ACROSS NORTHERN Enterra gathered in the temple courtyard. Most looked terrified and thrilled at once. Anya and I joined the crowd, and soon we were crammed in so tightly it was impossible to move.

Northern Enterra's faerie rituals were famous, both among true believers and those who considered us superstitious oddities. It was one of the oldest traditions of an old country at the edge of the world. Ocean surrounded Enterra on three sides, while the mountains to the west reached craggy fingers across the northern wilds. That untamed north, all mountains and forest and salt-scoured coast, belonged solely to the Fae.

Enterra wasn't the only country with stories about the faeries or elves or however each region termed them, of course. They lived in wild places: in deep forests and under mountains and on islands in the midst of turbulent seas. But they were as elusive as they were mysterious, rarely interacting with humans. In the south, people had largely abandoned the faith, but Tumbledown and the other villages that clustered near the border were the last outposts of humanity in

Enterra. We saw the lights and passed down the legends; we believed where others might not.

"It's my first winter solstice," a woman near me whispered to her companion.

"My second," was the breathless reply. "Hopefully this time I'm chosen."

I hoped she would be, too, if it meant Anya and I wouldn't be.

The bells stopped ringing, and our village Elder walked slowly up the steps of the temple. The years were wearing him down, but Elder Holman was still the most powerful man in Tumbledown—our priest and mayor in one, keeper of the ancient faith and controller of the town's coffers. He grabbed a torch from an attendant, then lit the yew logs in the brazier.

"Welcome, faithful," Elder Holman said, bowing his white head reverently as the flames soared. "This is a sacred day."

All around the courtyard, families were packed in between pillars, watching nervously. Some held their hands to their lips, murmuring silent prayers—though what outcome they prayed for, who knew.

Elder Holman recited the traditional words, telling the story. When humans and faeries first met at the edge of this bog well over a thousand years ago, they'd viewed one another with distrust. After many years, they had found their way to peace and then to a mingled society. Eventually the realms split again, but both sides decided on a compact to bind the two species together and ensure eternal peace. Every six years on the longest night of winter, four human women would be sent into the bog. The will-o'-the-wisps would light their way across, and the women would become citizens of Mistei, the faeries' vast underground realm. Some would even wed princes, bear their children, and spend the rest of their days in eternal bliss. In exchange, the immortal Fae would keep our country safe, ensuring our prosperity and peace with their magic.

"It is a great honor to be chosen," Elder Holman said solemnly. "And the selection may seem random, but I assure you, the Fae guide my hand from afar. They will adore each and every one of you."

It was more likely the Elder's hand would be guided by the tremors of age, I thought cynically. It wasn't that I didn't believe in the Fae; I just didn't believe they cared about us at all. How could anyone say with a straight face that they brought prosperity to the human lands when so many of us struggled? People were richer in the south, where the Fae were considered an inconsequential legend.

Beside me, Anya stood with her hands clasped to her breast. She looked . . . not entirely afraid, and the hint of excitement in her expression set me on edge.

"We beseech the Noble Fae for help," the Elder said as one of his acolytes brought a large copper bowl forward. Scraps of paper fluttered inside as the breeze threatened to yank them away. "Guide my hands as I make the selection. Help us find the women who will bring you the greatest joy."

The crowd collectively held its breath as he dipped a hand into the bowl. He squinted at the paper. "Nora Martin."

I didn't know the name, which meant she must be from another village. There was movement at the edge of the crowd, and then a pretty, round-cheeked woman was pushed forward. She wore a sky-blue dress belted in orange, and she was beaming like this was the best day of her life. A true believer. At the edge of the square, two people who were presumably her parents clutched each other and started to weep. Nora ran towards them and hugged each in turn, then climbed the steps to stand at the Elder's side.

I exhaled through pursed lips. One sacrifice down. Three more and Anya and I would be free. Then I could find a buyer for the dagger and surprise her with the news that the two of us would no longer be dependent on the mercy of others.

The Elder selected a new paper. "Fiona Key."

This name I knew. Fiona's father was the vintner and better off than most in town, but he had a quick temper and it was common knowledge that he was losing patience for housing an unmarried adult daughter.

Fiona looked dazed. Her hands were clenched white-knuckled at her waist, but she didn't protest at being chosen. As she walked up the steps, her father dropped to his knees, making loud, impassioned pleas to the Fae to take care of his beloved child. His beloved child who, incidentally, looked to be healing from a blackened eye—a purple deeper than exhaustion brushed her cheekbones.

That was the way of some men. Their tongues wagged in an imitation of love while their fists dealt pain. I stroked the dagger's outline at my thigh, thinking about what it might be like to live in a world where women didn't have to depend on people they feared for safety.

As Fiona took her place next to Nora, Anya grabbed my hand and squeezed. I squeezed back, hoping—because I never prayed anymore—that the next two names would be unfamiliar.

A third woman was chosen: Bertha Hollyngworth, also from a village to the south. She looked to be barely twenty, with the sharp edge of starvation to her cheeks and a dress patched together from rags. She mounted the steps with effort, gripping the balustrade for support, though her face glowed with ecstatic happiness.

I bit down on my tongue. They planned to send this hunger-weakened woman into the bog at night? They expected her to follow the dangerous, narrow footpaths that even I, who had grown up beside the bog, only navigated with extreme caution? Say the myths were true; what were her odds of actually following the lights to safety, much less ending up wedded to some impossibly wealthy and handsome faerie prince?

More likely I'd be scooping up her bones in a few years.

I forced myself to take a deep breath. "Almost over," I whispered. One more name and this farce would be done for the next six years.

The Elder unfurled the final scrap of paper. "Anya Hayes."

All sound ceased as black encroached on the edges of my vision.

Then there came a vast roaring in my ears, a sea of hoarse screams that grew in intensity. A pit opened in my mind, and I began to fall. "No," I whispered.

Anya's hands were pressed to her mouth. "It's me," she said past her fingers, eyes wide. "They chose me."

The other women were muttering. "So lucky," one said, and I wanted to spit.

"They can't." My voice sounded like it came from a distance. "They *can't*."

One of the Elder's acolytes pushed through the crowd to reach Anya. He reached for her arm, and I immediately shoved him away. "No," I said, pulse pounding in my temples and my gut sour with terror. "You can't have her."

"Kenna!" Anya sounded startled.

"You can't," I repeated, baring my teeth at the acolyte. "There's been a mistake."

"The Fae don't make mistakes," the acolyte said. He was barely out of adolescence, with sparse fuzz on his chin. "They guided the Elder's hands true."

"No!" My shout echoed off the stone walls of the temple. A scandalized murmur rose behind it as people craned their heads to see the source of the commotion.

Anya's fingers slipped into mine, warm and familiar. "Kenna," she said. "It's all right."

"It's not," I said as my vision turned blurry. "They can't take you. I—I found something in the bog—I should have told you earlier. Once I sell it, you won't need to get married or any of that." A tear slipped down my cheek. "You don't have to go away."

"But the Fae chose me," she said gently. Her own eyes shone with tears, but I recognized the longing in them, too. It was an echo of how my mother had looked every time she'd gazed across the bog. "I have to go, Kenna."

I refused to accept it. "We can run away," I told her. "I'll come get you before the ceremony—"

She shook her head, and her lips curved with a small, sad smile. "This is a way out, Kenna. And more than that. This is . . . It's a blessing."

The word hit me in the chest like a fist. The blessing my mother had died wanting, and here Anya was getting it. And she had too much faith to believe it would end with her corpse resting at the bottom of the bog.

Anya's life and home had burned to ash, I reminded myself as I looked at the growing certainty in her expression. Like my mother losing her husband along with her plans for a loving, stable future— something had to fill that void, and here it was.

"Maybe they'll let me bring you to Mistei," she murmured. "I can ask, once I'm settled in. We won't be parted forever."

I didn't know what to say to that. It wouldn't happen, but how could I rip this shred of hope away from her? So I just nodded, throat tight with grief.

Anya took a deep breath, then turned to face the acolyte. "I'm ready."

I watched her walk towards the temple steps, feeling numb and agonized all at once, like I'd been crushed by a boulder and was losing blood flow to my most essential parts. Anya had been my best friend for as long as I could remember. My *only* friend, really, the sister of my heart. We kept each other's secrets like treasures, and if I had never quite managed to dream for myself, I could sometimes do it for her.

Anya stood in the line of four as the Elder concluded the ceremony, her eyes wet but head held high. The pale winter sunlight picked the gold out of her hair, and the wind whipped life into her cheeks. She was beautiful enough to be a faerie prince's bride, and if anyone deserved a happily ever after, it was her.

This wasn't a dream I could believe in, though. Not after the years of hearing my mother pray to closed and distant ears, not after fishing up pieces of the drowned.

My faith was a bitter one, my hope nearly nonexistent, but I did have a stubborn streak a mile wide and more familiarity with the bog than anyone in Tumbledown. Somewhere in that vast, foggy expanse would be a route to Mistei—and if not Mistei, a path to distant towns and a fresh start. I had a walking stick to test uneven ground and a dagger to turn into coins so I could buy a new future for both of us.

Anya might not believe she needed saving—but I was going to do it anyway.

3

I STOOD AT THE EDGE OF THE CROWD THAT NIGHT, HOOD PULLED over my head. It was full dark, and the air had grown so cold my bones ached. The scent of snow was on the wind, and the bog paths would be even more treacherous once ice settled atop the mud.

The entire village and all our visitors stood in neat rows facing the wetlands, lit torches in their upheld hands. This section of the bog wasn't close to my hut, but I knew it anyway. I'd watched other girls go to their fate here and had tried many routes as a child, wondering which one led to the faeries.

None of them had.

Anya and the other three sacrifices stood at the edge, clad in matching diaphanous white dresses. If they didn't drown, they would likely freeze to death. Fiona wept silently, but Nora and Bertha's faces were alight with excitement. Anya just stared into the distance, expression calm as her thoughts traveled paths I could only guess at.

I'd tried to see her between the selection ceremony and tonight's sacrifice, but she'd been sequestered in the temple and the acolytes hadn't let me in. I'd returned home to eat and grab my trusty walking stick, which I could use to test the ground once we reached uncertain territory.

I may have never found a route to Mistei before, but there had to be one or else the legends wouldn't exist at all. So I would take the group as far as I could on the paths I knew, and then we would figure it out together, no matter how long it took.

Or we'll die together, my mind whispered.

I thought of a crooked flagstone etched with my mother's name and the leaking hut where I spent my lonely days. If I had no one to share this life with, what was the point? And Anya was one of the best people in the world. Better to drown trying to save her than live knowing I could have helped and chose not to.

Elder Holman was speaking, but I didn't pay attention, too busy tracing and retracing the map in my mind. I'd heard the same speech before, anyway. These women were so lucky to be favored by the Fae. So gracious to give themselves willingly for the good of Enterra. The heathens in the southern cities would never know what a debt of gratitude they owed the women of the north, for only through rituals like this did we ensure the Fae's benevolence towards our country.

My pulse thumped in my throat and wrists, and I felt sick with anticipation and fear. The will-o'-the-wisps drifting in the distance seemed to beckon. Their movements had always appeared aimless before—was there a chance they would grow more purposeful tonight?

Bells tolled in the distant village, and the Elder raised his hands. "Live well, my children."

The crowd cheered.

Then Anya and the rest were being ushered forward by men

holding torches. Fire licked towards Fiona's sleeve when she hesitated, and she yelped and scurried forward.

Those torches would travel up and down the border of the bog all night. This was the other aspect of the ritual few people knew about, since few people wandered in the foggy dark the way I had. As a child I hadn't understood why men guarded the shore, but six years ago I'd seen them herd a crying woman back into the marsh and the reason had come clear. The faith couldn't survive being proven wrong—so the Elder and his acolytes needed to ensure no one turned back.

The four women stepped hesitantly into the bog. My muscles tensed as I fought the urge to immediately follow, but they would be safe for a while. People had been wishing on coppers for generations, and these paths were well-known. Once they got into the true dark, though . . .

The white-gowned silhouettes grew ghostly as they moved farther away. I pushed down my fear, my focus narrowing to one thought: *Protect Anya.*

Fiddle music started up, and people began to dance around bonfires lining the shore. I waited until the Elder had turned to speak with one of the faithful. Then I pushed through the crowd and started running.

There were yelps of alarm as hands grabbed at my cloak, but I ripped away. Soon my boots squelched over muddy moss, and after that I was too fast and sure-footed on the narrow trail for anyone to catch up. Not that they tried; it was a sacred night, and most people were hesitant to transgress on a ritual. The Elder would no doubt turn my defiance of the rules into a sermon, probably one in which he invented all manner of nasty ends for me, but who cared? We would either reach Mistei, find a new route out of the bog and settle elsewhere with the money from the dagger's sale . . . or die together.

The path was familiar beneath my feet and the reflected glow of torchlight lit the way, though the light was ember-dim by the time I caught up to the white-garbed figures.

"Kenna!" Anya gasped. She stared at me like she couldn't believe I was real, then lunged forward and hugged me. "What are you doing here?"

"Helping you find a way across." I looked at the other women; they were all shivering and seemed much less certain away from the light and warmth of the gathering. "None of you know these paths. I do, at least to a point. And I have this to test the ground." I raised the walking stick.

"The faeries are going to guide us," Nora said, looking at me judgmentally.

"They're welcome to." I eyed the drifting golden orbs in the distance. "But if they don't . . ."

"They will," Nora said firmly. "You should go back. It isn't right for you to be here."

Anya just looked at me. In the darkness, her shadowed eye sockets seemed eerily hollow.

"I'm coming with you," was all I said.

There was another grumble from Nora, but the others seemed relieved. Anya gripped my hand hard. "I'm glad you're here," she said quietly. "I still don't know how to feel about everything, but it'll be easier with you by my side."

I hugged her again. "I would never leave you. And don't think you can leave me, either."

She laughed, a barely-there chuckle. "Kenna the Fierce," she said, echoing the long-ago warrior's name she'd given me when we were just children at play. "Let's find Mistei together."

The moon was our only companion as we slipped deeper into the bog. The fiddle music receded, echoed by distant laughter. The villagers would celebrate until midnight, feasting and dancing in honor of the solstice.

Nora tried to lead the way at first, but when her foot slipped off a narrow tussock of grass into a pool, she decided letting the person with the walking stick go first might be best after all. Soon the girls were following me like ducklings. Mist swirled around our ankles, and the air was cold and clammy. Someone started crying softly—probably Fiona again—but I didn't look back. All I knew was that Anya was directly behind me, and I would do anything to get us out alive.

I gripped Anya's hand while I led the women along a path I had memorized. I'd chosen this one because it was the most direct route towards the middle of the bog—that seemed a more likely choice than the routes that meandered aimlessly closer to shore. It was comforting to walk hand in hand, but eventually the path grew too narrow and I had to release her. "Careful," I warned. "It's only a few feet wide here. Step exactly where I step."

The moon was full enough that I could make out familiar details. A rotting log. A thick tussock of grass. An intersection where the path split in two.

I hesitated, tapping my walking stick against the spongy ground. I hadn't needed it yet, since these paths were familiar, but we were reaching the limits of my knowledge.

"What's wrong?" Anya asked.

"I don't know which way to pick," I admitted. "I've never found a way back to land besides the path we just walked out on."

"Maybe we can stay here," Fiona said, wiping tears from beneath her bruised eye. "We can sneak back after the celebration ends."

"We can't go back," Nora said, looking scandalized. "The faeries chose us."

Bertha bit her lip; the emaciated girl looked doubtful for the first time as she stared at the drifting lights. Were they moving purposefully towards us? It was hard to tell through the thickening mist. Anya, too, seemed uneasy.

"We can't go back tonight, anyway," I told Fiona. "There will be guards on watch even after the celebration ends." I'd first seen them when I'd been a child too full of excitement to sleep after the revelry—I'd returned to the bog to see the faeries, but instead I'd seen the Elder and his acolytes conferring by moonlight. "And do you really think they'd let us go back to Tumbledown? The Elder wouldn't know how to explain that." I shook my head. "If we can't make it to Mistei, we'll have to find a route that comes out far away from town."

Nora narrowed her eyes at me. "We'll make it to Mistei," she said. Then she reached for Bertha's hand, squeezing it. "We can't lose faith now."

"Let's follow the lights, then," Anya said. "As best we can, anyway."

I'd never been so close to the faerie lights before. They floated in the air around waist height, looking almost like dandelion fluff. One of the will-o'-the-wisps in front of us drifted to the left, then another.

It was better than nothing. "The left path."

The trail forked again and again. Each time I selected the path closest to the lights. They floated within thirty feet of us now, hovering as if watching.

At last we reached the limits of my familiarity with the routes through the bog. I stopped to consider our options, stroking the outline of the dagger at my thigh for comfort.

"Ouch!" The sharp blade had practically leapt to my skin, slicing through layers of bandage and the fabric of my trousers with ease.

"What is it?" Anya gripped my arm.

"Nothing. Don't worry." I could just see the dark stain of blood on my finger.

The ground below me glowed with a line of blue-white light.

I blinked, uncertain what I was seeing. It looked like the slimy trail a snail would leave, but it shone faintly in the moonlight. The line stretched back along the route we'd taken.

I looked ahead, and my heart pounded. The glowing thread wound forward, disappearing into the distance. It was a path, and somehow the dagger had helped me see it. Was Mistei on the other side of that silvery line, waiting for us?

I forged ahead, but the light began to fade. I gripped the dagger again, this time making sure to only touch the hilt through my trousers. The path shone bright as starlight.

A Fae path. A Fae knife. Fae magic.

I turned so my cloak would conceal my actions from the other girls, then loosened my belt so I could reach the dagger strapped to my thigh.

"What are you doing?" Anya asked.

The dagger slipped into my hand like an old friend. I could have sworn the hilt vibrated, a soft greeting like the purr of a cat. I fixed myself up again, then turned to show her the dagger. "It's a knife I found today. I was going to sell it, but I didn't get a chance."

She gaped at the wicked blade in my hand. The scrollwork on the hilt looked otherworldly in the moonlight, and the dark red stone glowed faintly. "That's what you meant earlier," she said. "About having something to sell." Her eyes met mine, and an unspoken communication passed between us. She knew as well as I did how much money something like that was worth, the possibilities it could open up for two poor young women. Yet here we were instead, charging into the uncertain night.

I was glad I hadn't sold it that morning. Anya would still have been selected; at least now it could protect her this way. "I think it was made by the Fae," I said, raising my voice so the others could hear. "When I touch it, the ground glows, like it's showing me the way."

The other women gathered around to look at the dagger, too. I held it tightly, not trusting anyone else with it. What if they dropped it in one of the bog's dark pools? Then we'd be alone out here with nothing but the will-o'-the-wisps again.

When I looked up, I realized the faerie lights were brighter, clearer—and much closer. One drifted within ten feet of us, approaching from the right. Suddenly it didn't look like an orb at all. The thing that approached was a pale, shriveled creature with webbed feet and enormous red eyes, and the light hung like a lure from an antenna on its head.

Its mouth opened to reveal jagged fangs.

A surge of terror swept through my body. I knew, as certainly as I'd ever known anything, that this creature wanted to kill us. The hilt in my hand vibrated with urgency.

Others were closing in on us. "You see them, right?" I asked Anya, my voice sharp with fear. "The monsters?"

Her brow furrowed. "What are you talking about?"

She couldn't see them, I realized sickly. Just like the dagger had shown me a path, now it was showing me the truth beneath the lights. "Touch the knife," I ordered, holding it out.

She reached for the hilt, then pulled her hand back with a shriek. "Ow!" A thin line of blood trailed down her palm. "What was that for?"

A razor-sharp metal thorn retracted into the hilt.

Apparently I was the only one allowed to touch it, and therefore the only one who could see the monsters approaching. The closest creature hissed at me, and a long black tongue darted over its fangs.

Run. The word echoed in my head, cold and metallic, but there was no time to question where it had come from.

"Everyone listen," I said urgently. "We need to run as fast as we can. Whatever you do, stay away from the faerie lights, and only step where I step."

"But the lights are leading us to safety," Nora argued.

"No, they're not." They might have lured us along the correct path until we were far from the Tumbledown crowds, but now they approached with darker intentions. "Just trust me. We have to run."

The nearest monster opened its jaws wider. It ran towards us from the right, its webbed feet skimming over a patch of murky water.

I sprinted over the uneven ground, hoping the blue-white light really did paint a safe path forward. The other girls followed, shrieking and begging me to stop.

A bloodcurdling scream split the air.

I glanced back. Frail Bertha had fallen behind, and now monsters swarmed over her. I heard wet ripping sounds: not fabric, but flesh. The arcing spray of her blood glistened in the moonlight. Nora shrieked, shielding her face from the dark drops.

We ran.

The starry path arrowed across the bog, then turned in dizzying switchbacks. We were running so recklessly it was a wonder I didn't slide right off the path, but terror seemed to lend me extra agility. Anya followed a few feet behind with Fiona close on her heels, but Nora was struggling to maintain the pace. A light bobbed in her wake. The monsters weren't as fast as we were, but they had the advantage of being able to skim across more treacherous sections, rather than being tied to this narrow, winding path. They were closing on us quickly.

Nora cried out, a sound of raw animal pain. When I looked over my shoulder, I saw Anya's terrified face, then Fiona's . . . and then Nora's head tumbling wetly to the ground as her body sagged into the claws of a monster. The creatures began to feed, teeth flashing in the moonlight.

Nora's death might buy us time. I ripped my cloak off and tossed both it and the walking stick aside to lend me speed. The air tore out of my lungs as I ran faster than I ever had in my life. I couldn't hear anything but my own breathing as I followed the treacherous path. The fog was thickening, but the glow of the trail cut through it, and my feet continued to meet solid ground. When I reached another straightaway, I looked back to see how close the monsters were.

Anya was gone.

Not falling behind, not splashing in the water, not surrounded by monsters, not screaming, just . . . gone.

She had been a few feet behind the last time I'd looked. Where was she?

I staggered and nearly fell. "Anya!" I shouted, voice shredded. She couldn't be gone. She couldn't have drowned or been caught by those creatures. She couldn't be . . .

Fiona ran into me, nearly knocking both of us down. "Go!" she screamed, face tight with panic. "Or they'll take us, too."

My eyes darted wildly over the bog. The mist was rising, and I couldn't see Anya anywhere. Lights bobbed as the creatures tore after us with bared fangs. "What happened— Where is—"

"It's too late. Go!"

Too late. No, it couldn't be. It *couldn't.*

But Anya wasn't there anymore, and if she was still alive, she would *be there.* She would never leave me, any more than I would leave her.

The truth settled into my gut and bones, a feeling so heavy and horrible I didn't know how my body could possibly contain it.

"Please," Fiona gasped, tears streaking down her cheeks. "I don't want to die."

Grief nearly choked me, but I forced myself to keep moving. One step after another. Every pound of a foot on the ground was a syllable of her name. *Anya Anya Anya* said the beating tattoo, but I forced it into a different chant: *Survive survive survive.* I couldn't stop.

Couldn't cry. Couldn't hesitate for even a single second or the fanged monsters at my back would rip me apart.

There was a shriek and a splash and then a horrible, keening cry from Fiona. I blocked out the sound of them feeding. They'd be done with her soon, and then I'd be the only one left.

There. Ahead of me. I finally saw a dark line that looked like trees. The path took one last dizzying twist before straightening out into the final stretch that would take me to solid ground.

I was about to find out what was on the other side of the bog.

A sob tore from me as I forced my aching legs to keep moving. As I rounded the final corner, fangs punctured my ankle and I fell. I kicked, striking the monster with my booted foot. It squealed, but then it was back, sinking its teeth in deeper.

This was it.

I still clutched the dagger in one fist. I wrenched free, then rolled over to face the monster. The blade shone sharp and lethal between us, and I felt suddenly certain it wanted to taste the monster's blood.

The creature stopped. Its red eyes widened and its mouth dropped open. Then . . . it backed away.

I didn't stop to question my luck. I pushed to my feet and began running flat out down the final straightaway.

My leg was bleeding. My lungs ached. My soul had been torn wide open. My vision was starting to blacken.

It didn't matter. I wouldn't stop.

So when I burst out of the bog and onto a grassy slope, I couldn't slow for a while. Not until I reached the forest and realized the monsters had stopped at the edge of the bog and were staring after me.

I had made it to Mistei.

I collapsed onto a bed of dead leaves as the strength left my body. My vision was almost completely dark from exhaustion.

I saw two more things before passing out, neither of which made any sense.

The dagger melted and flowed liquidly up my hand and inside my sleeve before I felt it solidify into a spiral around my upper arm.

Then the face of a goat appeared directly above me. The square pupils of its yellow eyes dilated until they almost swallowed the irises.

"Well," the goat said in a raspy, bleating voice. "This is unexpected."

4

I WOKE ON A HARD SURFACE.

I jolted upright, startling the few people in the room with me. No, not people. Faeries. They were tall and unnaturally thin, with moon-pale skin and rainbow hair, and they wore draping purple robes. They stared at me with eerie black eyes: large and liquid, with no whites to be seen.

I sat on a black stone table in a chamber with no windows. The only other furnishing in the room was a gleaming copper tub. My leg stung and my muscles ached from running, but there were no new injuries. These faeries apparently hadn't done anything awful to me while I was unconscious, and I wasn't restrained, either. Because I was a welcome guest?

My emotions tumbled into a chaotic mess. Terror, relief, and then a deep, awful stab of guilt and grief as I remembered that I was the only one here. I'd gone into the bog to help the other women find a path out, but I hadn't led any of them to safety.

I hadn't even witnessed my best friend's death.

Sorrow bit at me harder than any monster could. Tears rolled down my face, and the faerie closest to me recoiled at the sight.

"Get in the tub," it commanded in a chiming voice.

Devastated and frightened, I obeyed the command. My leg throbbed as I limped over to the tub. I hesitated, not wanting to undress before these creatures. Thankfully, they filed out of the room, and I was able to strip and step into the water.

I yelped as blood and mud bloomed on the surface from my submerged calves and feet. The warmth took me by surprise. I lowered myself into the enormous tub, and although it was the most decadent bath I'd ever taken, I couldn't appreciate anything about it.

I just sat there crying.

The door opened and closed again. I whirled, but this time the person approaching me looked human: a woman with a crooked nose, brown hair tied back in a bun, and downcast eyes. She carried a copper bowl and had a towel and a length of gray fabric draped over her arm.

Other humans actually lived here? Had she once run across the bog, too?

"Hello," I said, but she didn't respond. She knelt by the tub and dumped the contents of the bowl into the steaming water. My aches and pains started to fade as a flowery scent filled the air. Had the bowl contained some kind of healing liquid? "Where am I? Who are you?"

She motioned for me to dunk my head.

I did, bewildered by the interaction, and was even more surprised when she pulled a comb out of her pocket and started working on the long tangle of my hair. She was gentle, but each tug hurt—the wild sprint through the bog had created impossible snarls. I closed my eyes and bore it until she finished.

She studied my arm, and I started as I realized my vision of the melting dagger hadn't been my imagination. A silver spiral wound from my elbow to just under my shoulder. The metal had the same unnaturally bright sheen as the blade, and in the very center, positioned on the outside of my arm, was a smooth red jewel.

It hummed against my skin as if greeting me, and I felt a pinprick beneath the jewel. Had it cut me?

The servant cocked her head questioningly, and I scrambled for an explanation. "It was a gift from my . . . father." I wasn't going to let anyone know I had a weapon—assuming it was still a weapon. "I can't take it off."

I swore I could feel the metal yearning for her, hoping for a taste of her blood. Was this Fae magic infiltrating my mind? The woman soaped neatly around the metal, and when she dropped to my forearm, disappointment echoed through me, radiating outward from the armband.

There were more pressing questions than how the dagger had managed to shape-shift or if the impulses I sensed were magic or just a trick of an overtired mind. I asked about Mistei—Were we underground? How far from an exit? Who else was here? What was going to happen to me?—but she didn't answer any of my questions. She just helped me wash and then gave me the towel, laid the swath of gray fabric on the table, and left.

I dried myself and hurried to the table, relieved to find a new, clean dress. As I changed, I was astonished to realize my bruises and cuts had nearly vanished.

The dress fit differently than the gowns I was used to seeing in Tumbledown. Human dresses were modest with high necklines. This one clung to my torso tightly before falling in a sleek flow from my hips. The sleeves belled at the end, and the neckline was rounded just enough to show a hint of cleavage. It was the nicest thing I'd ever worn.

Anya would love it. She had always adored dresses and cosmetics, even after she had grown too poor to afford them.

Reality slapped me hard, puncturing the thought. Anya couldn't love it . . . because she was gone.

My eyes burned, and I dug my knuckles into them. How was I supposed to go on without my best friend? Without my heart-sister?

I'd failed her.

Grief threatened to drag me to my knees, but the door opened again and the faeries returned. They cocked their heads and studied me with those liquid black eyes, like pools of ink against their parchment skin.

They couldn't see me cry. I didn't even know what they were going to do to me.

The faeries commanded me to follow them out of the room. My pulse raced as we walked down a corridor lit by torches that glowed in an array of rainbow colors. There were no windows to be seen anywhere.

I was truly in the mythical underground kingdom of Mistei.

I thought about everything I'd learned about the Fae over the years. Elder Holman had told us the highest-ranking faeries, the Noble Fae, were so beautiful they glowed and possessed magic beyond comprehension. They looked like humans but taller, stronger, and so captivating you could fall in love just by looking at one. They were served by Underfae, who were more likely to have horns or wings or other unusual features and wielded only a small amount of magic. My current eerie-eyed guards were probably Underfae. Worst of all were the Nasties, foul monsters who lived to prey on humans.

I shivered at the memory of the fanged creatures from the bog. That fear was followed by swift, scalding hate.

After what felt like an eternity, the corridor ended at an archway that opened into a huge, glittering chamber. The floor was polished black stone, and the silver walls shone with jeweled accents. Colorful torches flickered throughout the room and glowing orbs hovered in the air, drifting like soap bubbles on a breeze. I flinched at the sight of them, but the dagger vibrated in a way that felt reassuring, and I was relieved to realize they were just lights.

Lining the room were hundreds of the most gorgeous beings I'd ever seen.

The Noble Fae were tall and elegant, richly dressed, and as colorful as butterflies. The shades of their skin varied, but each faerie emitted a faint shimmer, as if they'd been sprinkled with golden powder. These otherworldly lords and ladies wore strange and opulent fashions: velvet robes, dresses light as moonbeams, and brocaded tunics that sometimes reached their thighs and sometimes their ankles. Many of them were armed, too, with swords or daggers in jeweled scabbards. My gray dress, the nicest one I'd ever worn, must look shockingly plain to their eyes—the clothing of a servant or peasant. And indeed, those beautiful, haughty faces looked at me with disdain as my guides ushered me to the side of the room.

A carved obsidian throne rose from a dais at the head of the chamber. Dazzling faeries stood around the dais, but the one sitting on the throne was the most beautiful of all.

He wore a close-fitting violet tunic lined with jewels over silver trousers tucked into shining black boots. His white-blond hair was long and straight, and his cheekbones angled sharply, the lines of his face so precise it seemed as if he had been carved from stone. The cruel spikes of his black crown contrasted with the elegance of his clothing. Rainbow-colored mist wafted around his pale hands, and his power seemed to hover in the air, clinging to my skin like fog.

He looked coldly at a faerie who knelt before him. "Your insolence is unacceptable." The musical tenor of his voice was lined with ice.

"Forgive me, King Osric. It was only a jest." The lord was trembling, his head bowed and hands clasped at his chest.

"A jest aimed at me and uttered in my presence."

"I didn't mean—"

"Silence. I do not find you amusing." The king looked to his left, where a coal-haired male faerie stood. "Take care of it."

The faerie bowed. His face was stern, his skin pale. Unlike most of the Noble Fae in the room, his hair was cropped to his shoulders, and he was dressed simply in a stark black tunic adorned with an opal brooch. A sword was strapped to his waist.

As the swordsman approached, the kneeling lord shook harder, tears leaking from his eyes.

The black-clad faerie unsheathed his sword and plunged it through the other man's heart, then jerked the blade down viciously.

I struggled not to scream as the faerie collapsed to the ground, choking on the blood that bubbled from his lips. The executioner wiped his blade on his victim's tunic and strode back to the king's side, looking politely bored.

According to legend, the only way to kill one of the Noble Fae was to cause severe enough damage that their accelerated healing couldn't fix it quickly enough. The wounded faerie clutched his chest as blood pumped over his fingers in hot gushes. Soon the flow slowed and his struggles turned into weak twitches.

The entire time he lay dying, not a single faerie helped or comforted him. Most of them didn't even watch his last moments.

I had escaped the bog, but I was still surrounded by monsters.

When the dying faerie exhaled a final, gurgling breath, King Osric sighed. "What next, steward?"

"The human, your majesty," a bleating voice replied, and I blinked as I noticed a goat standing on its hind legs near the king. Was it the same goat I thought I'd hallucinated earlier? It wore mauve velvet trousers, a matching coat, and a pair of golden spectacles. It had furry hands instead of front hooves and gripped a tablet and pen as if that were the most natural thing in the world.

The king waved his hand, and my guards pushed me forward. I stumbled towards the center of the room, stopping short of the bloody corpse. I focused on the obsidian floor, trying to control my trembling.

"Bow," the goat bleated. I bowed at the waist, then belatedly tried to switch to a curtsy and nearly fell over. A titter went through the crowd.

"How did it manage to get here?" the king asked.

"She followed the ancient trail, your majesty. It is unclear how she accomplished this."

I dared a glance up. The black-clothed executioner was staring at me with unnerving intensity, and my heart pounded like a rabbit's after glimpsing a hawk's shadow. I focused on King Osric, trying to ignore the killer's dark, piercing gaze. Would he kill me, too? Was he even now imagining my life's blood pouring out?

King Osric tapped his fingers on the arm of his throne, and the colored mist swirled. "Human," he said in my general direction, as if finally deciding he had no choice but to address me, "how did you find the path across the bog?"

"I don't know, your majesty. I just knew where to go." My voice shook. I didn't want to tell him about the dagger. He would take it away from me, leaving me truly defenseless.

He narrowed violet eyes at me. "You knew how?"

"I saw a path, your majesty. It looked like a trail of light on the ground."

Murmurs rose around the room. The king turned his attention to the faerie at his side. "Fae blood?"

The murderer's gaze raked over me. "It must be. But clearly a long time ago in her bloodline."

I flushed at the implication that I looked so terrible no one would ever mistake me for part faerie. Was it so implausible? I was short, but Anya had told me I was pretty—especially when I bothered to scrub my face.

I ruthlessly suppressed the memory of her smile as she'd teased me. I wouldn't break down in front of this cruel court.

The king gestured to a muscular lord who stood with the handful of courtiers allowed near the throne. "What do you think we should do with this human, Prince Roland?"

Prince Roland's snowy white attire was impeccable, and his long brown hair was tied back in a smooth tail. His posture and bearing spoke of rigid discipline, but there was a sadistic edge to his sneer that hinted at something foul beneath that pristine surface. I felt like an insect under his judgmental stare. "Do the same with her as we do with the other humans. Make her serve."

I shuddered. Serve how?

Only the luckiest and most worthy are chosen to join them, my mother had sworn over and over again. How kindly her faith had painted Mistei. How many other humans lived here, and what did they suffer at the hands of these tyrants? Clearly matrimony to a Fae prince and a life of splendor had never been an option.

King Osric sighed. "That's boring."

"If you crave entertainment, you could kill her."

The king laughed. "You're just bitter you didn't win the bet. You thought the redhead would make it farthest."

The redhead. Fiona. Had they been watching us somehow, betting on how long it would take the monsters to kill us? My terror was joined by choking rage. They'd bet on my death and the death of the person I loved best in the entire world. Anya should have been standing here at my side. We should have finished that run hand in hand and collapsed on the grass together, crying in relief.

"Nevertheless," King Osric said, "it is an interesting suggestion. Does anyone agree with the prince?"

Most of the Noble Fae near the dais looked unsympathetic, but one of them was studying me with curiosity rather than disdain: a stunningly handsome faerie with long copper hair and a tunic the red-gold color of flame. He stepped forward, casting a crookedly charming grin at the king. "Well, I won the bet, and I think we should come up with something new to do with her. None of the sacrifices have made it this far in centuries. Could be fun." He turned his smile on me and winked, but the casualness of the suggestion— *come up with something new to do with her*—chilled me.

The king giggled unsettlingly. "You're always interested in games, Prince Drustan."

Drustan bowed. "The fire loves to play."

Every single one of them frightened me—laughing King Osric, bloodthirsty Prince Roland, and wickedly charming Prince Drustan— but the one that terrified me most was the executioner with night-dark eyes, who still hadn't looked away from me. I shivered as I met that penetrating gaze, wondering if I was about to feel his sword plunging through my heart.

"Your majesty," the black-clad killer said at last, "I think you should let this one live."

"Why?" The king looked at him with raised brows, and the fa-erie leaned in to whisper something in his ear. Suggesting he torture me instead?

The king laughed and studied me with more interest. "I've made a decision." He stood, and torchlight glimmered off the jewels lining his tunic. He gestured at the sole female faerie who stood near the throne, a beautiful, ample-figured blond lady with an elaborate crown of braids. "Princess Oriana, I present this human as a gift to Earth House. Specifically, to your daughter, Lara, to serve as her handmaiden as she undertakes the trials."

The courtiers lining the room erupted into laughter as Princess Oriana's mouth pressed into a tight line. Clearly the king had delivered a grave insult by assigning me to serve as a handmaiden in her house. What was Earth House, anyway? The legends said Fae powers were elemental. Presumably that was what the name indicated: the source of her magic. While Drustan's attire evoked fire, Oriana's mahogany gown was embroidered with green vines that wound up the satin like ivy clinging to a tree.

The king sat and waved a hand, dismissing me. I didn't know where to go, though. For a few panic-filled moments I hesitated, not sure if walking straight out would be more of an insult than staying put, but then a warm, furry hand wrapped around my arm.

The goat—the king's steward, apparently—guided me to the side of the room. "I'll deliver you to Alodie. She's the head servant in Earth House. She'll show you where to go."

And indeed, a ghostly pale Underfae with spindly limbs and elongated fingers was walking to meet us. "Come." Alodie's voice was fluting and lovely, like wind over reeds. "We'll get you situated."

I exhaled with relief as we left the throne room, the dead faerie, and all those mocking, cruel faces. I'd somehow survived my first encounter with the Noble Fae.

A stone corridor stretched before me, lit only by flickering torches. Alodie led me down that impossibly long hallway, heading deeper underground towards Earth House and my new position as a servant to the Fae.

5

Y OU'RE AFRAID," ALODIE SAID AFTER WE'D BEEN WALKING
in silence for a few minutes.

"Yes." There was no point in lying. Who wouldn't be afraid?

She glanced at me, and I was struck by the eerie beauty of her face. Long, narrow, and a blue so pale it was nearly white. Her thin frame and fluid movements reminded me of the first Underfae I'd seen, but she wore a serviceable blue dress and her blue-gray hair drifted around her shoulders as if she were floating underwater.

"I understand your fear, but try not to let anyone see it," she said. "You've been given a great honor in serving one of the ladies of Earth House."

"It didn't seem that way when the king announced it. They all laughed."

She smiled slightly. "A great honor for you. A grave insult to Earth House."

"Why?"

"Because humans are considered little more than animals."

I bristled, but she raised a hand to cut me off. "By most," she clarified. "Not by all. I work with many humans. We are all here to serve."

She turned right, and the smooth black stone underfoot gave way to cobbles. Grass emerged from the soil at the edges of the path, and I was astonished to see a few wildflowers. How did they grow here without any sunlight?

Alodie stopped. "Here we are."

The walls were covered in ivy, and the line of torches stopped just ahead of us, casting the path in darkness. "Where are we?"

"The entrance to Earth House." She gestured for me to follow, and as she stepped past the line of torchlight, her posture relaxed. "It doesn't look like much right now, but it's a spectacular sight in the day."

It wasn't completely dark; now that my eyes had adjusted, I realized the arched corridor was lit with faint blue ambient light. The walls around us had changed from gray stone to a smooth material that looked like glass. I ran my fingers along it and yelped.

"Why is it wet?" I stared with shock at the water coating my fingers. The wall hadn't been hard to the touch, either.

Alodie laughed, the sound bubbly as a tinkling spring. "We're surrounded by water, girl. What is your name, anyway?"

"Kenna Heron." I hesitantly touched the wall again. My finger sank through the glossy surface, and it felt as if I had dipped it in a cold river. The current brushed against my skin. "How is this possible?"

"Didn't your human myths tell you about our magic?" Alodie tilted her head curiously. "The separation was not so long ago."

"For us it was." A thousand years, the Elder had said.

"Earth House controls soil, plants, and water—anything found in the ground beneath our feet. This tunnel is the only access point to the house, and it's held in place by spells. Members or guests of

Earth House are allowed through, but the second an unwelcome visitor tries to enter, the water will flood the tunnel and sweep them away."

"Where does it sweep them to?" I felt claustrophobic at the thought of being this close to an enormous amount of water that could come crashing down at any moment. We'd been traveling steadily downward from the throne room for long minutes, which meant we must be far underground. Like being at the bottom of a lake.

"They drown. Death is the punishment for anyone who tries to access a house's territory without permission."

I was sweating by the time we reached the end of the corridor. Alodie pushed open a thick metal door, and I scurried after her, eager to leave the oppressive weight of the water behind.

The room was dark, but when Alodie waved her hand, torches sprang to life around the space, casting a glow similar to the warm light of afternoon.

I gaped at the sight that met us.

Flowering vines covered the pillars and walls of an enormous entrance hall. The floor was packed earth, worn glossy smooth by what must have been thousands of years of footsteps. Trees, flowers, and bushes pushed up from the soil, reaching towards the high ceiling and a distant mosaic that depicted a blue sky and yellow sun. The space was a riot of natural color, and the air smelled of damp earth and growing things.

"It's beautiful," I said in awe.

Alodie smiled. "It is."

Spiraling staircases climbed from the four corners of the room, and arched entranceways on each floor led to unknown corridors. Alodie led me up a winding stair in the back corner. The stone balustrade beneath my hand looked like the knotted branch of a tree, and I marveled at the intricacy of the carving—I could see the grain of the wood, the hints of new buds protruding from the surface, even the tiny bodies of insects.

"So you have Earth magic?" I asked. The Underfae were magically gifted, too, but I didn't know to what extent.

"I have some small gifts with water, but nothing like what Princess Oriana and the Noble Fae wield. I'm an asrai, an elemental type of Underfae. There are asrai in all of the houses, not just Earth, so our abilities vary."

On the sixth and highest level, we entered a wide hallway. It was carpeted in soil, but somehow the dirt failed to cling to my shoes or hem. We passed a line of wooden doors, many of which were carved with incredible natural scenes: tumbling waterfalls, thick forests, and blooming meadows. Alodie led me past a door covered in carved flowers to a smaller unmarked one. On the other side of that entrance was another staircase, this one much plainer.

The room behind the unmarked door was small and simply furnished with a chest of drawers, a narrow bed with a brown coverlet, a wardrobe, and a desk with a looking glass. The walls were painted a soothing blue and illuminated by faintly glowing crystals. The ceiling was covered with crystals as well, although those didn't glow.

"You'll stay here," Alodie said. "Lady Lara's room is through there." She gestured to another door at the side of the room.

Lady Lara. Princess Oriana's daughter and my new mistress. I knew nothing about her except that she was apparently royalty and undergoing some sort of trial.

Alodie opened the wardrobe, revealing an array of simple earth-toned dresses. "This wardrobe will refill itself if you damage a dress, and it will provide any special attire you might need."

A magic wardrobe. Anya would have loved it. I bit my lip hard at the thought. "Thank you, but I still have no idea what I'm supposed to do here. What does being a handmaiden even mean?"

Alodie sighed and gestured for me to sit. There was only one chair at the desk, so I sat on the bed and watched as she folded her long, spindly limbs into the chair. "The Fae houses are each ruled by a prince or princess. Oriana is the princess of Earth House, and her eldest child and heir is Lady Lara. Lara will be undergoing the immortality trials soon, and it's customary for every candidate to have a special servant who attends to their needs during this time. The king selected you."

"Immortality trials?" I grew more confused with every piece of information she gave me. "What are those?"

She pinched the bridge of her nose as if staving off a headache. "The trials happen when young Noble Fae come of age," she explained patiently. "They become eligible at age eighteen, but the trials are held whenever there are enough candidates to compete—usually every decade or so. The trials test key Fae virtues. If a young faerie succeeds, they are granted immortality and the full use of their magical powers."

I'd known the Noble Fae were undying, whereas Underfae lived elongated but ultimately mortal lives, but I hadn't realized they didn't possess their full magic or immortality until adulthood. There was so much our legends had left out. "What if they fail?"

"It can go very poorly," she admitted in a hushed voice. "If a candidate does not succeed, they will gain immortality but be stripped of all magic. Those faeries are usually cast out by their families and become servants. And sometimes . . ."

"Sometimes?"

"If the failure is bad enough, the candidate dies."

So my mistress was about to be tested, just as I had been tested earlier tonight. Prove yourself or perish.

"How will I serve Lara during the trials?" I'd barely survived my own test. How was I supposed to help a Fae lady survive hers when I had little knowledge of this world or how to be a proper servant?

"Bring her food. Help her dress. Accompany her to functions and ensure she has everything she needs. When the trials begin, you may need to participate in a small way."

Now I was the one who felt a raging headache coming on. I looked at the door that separated my room from Lara's. Would my new mistress be kind? Considering the reactions I'd received in the throne room, I doubted it.

It was too much to process. The flight through the bog, the audience with the king, and now this new position helping a royal lady undertake a life-or-death test . . .

Alodie sighed at my expression. "It won't be easy. Just try to make it look easy."

Don't show fear. Make it look easy. The picture her warnings painted matched what I'd seen at the Fae court as those beautiful monsters had sneered at me. The Noble Fae lived for power and thrived on exploiting weaknesses.

"When do I start?" I asked dully.

She eyed my exhausted face. "Sleep for a few hours. Lara is out with friends. When you hear her return, you may go to her door and see what she needs—food, help undressing, or anything else. There's also a bell beside the door that she can ring if she needs you."

"Won't I startle her if I just appear at her door?"

Alodie looked like she was stifling a wince. "By now she'll have heard about you. She won't be surprised."

Her tone told me the lady wouldn't be happy, either.

I HADN'T THOUGHT I'D BE ABLE TO SLEEP, BUT EXHAUSTION dragged me under seconds after Alodie left. I didn't even remove my shoes before lying down. My last thought was surprise that the crystals on the wall were dimming on their own, as if understanding that I wanted darkness.

I woke to the sound of slamming drawers in the next room.

I sat up, rubbing the sleep from my eyes. My room was now lit with a pale yellow-rose glow that reminded me of dawn. The light emanated from the crystals in the ceiling, mixing delicately with the soft white gleam of the crystals that had sparked back to life on the walls. Did the faerie lights mimic the sky outside? If so, I had slept for more than a few hours, and Lara had come home much later than expected.

It was tempting to pull the covers back over my head and lose myself to unconsciousness. Being awake meant being afraid. It meant remembering with every heartbeat that Anya was gone.

Another drawer slammed. I stood and tried to finger-comb my hair and smooth the wrinkles out of my dress but eventually had to admit defeat. My first impression would not be a tidy one. I took a deep breath before rapping on the door firmly.

There was no response.

A cowardly part of me hoped my new mistress didn't want to see me. I knocked again. "Hello?"

"What?" came the angry reply.

I hesitantly turned the knob and peered inside. "Lady Lara?"

A statuesque faerie stood in the center of the room. She was stunning, with long, waving black hair, berry-red lips, and hooded brown eyes. The effect was somewhat ruined by the scowl slashing across her face. "Well? What do you want, human?"

"My name is Kenna, and I'm your new handmaiden."

"I've heard." Her voice was flat and furious.

I mustered my courage. "I've come to see if you need anything."

Her mint-green gown hissed over the packed earth floor as she stomped to her dresser. Her room was far more elegant than mine and about four times the size, with a carved wooden screen that separated the sitting and sleeping areas. Half-visible past the screen was a four-poster monstrosity of a bed draped with gauzy green fabric. The furniture was carved from golden wood, and the walls were covered with pink-flowering vines.

"I don't." She yanked her earrings out so forcefully I winced, then threw them on top of the dresser. "Get out."

She didn't need to repeat the command. I backed out with an awkward curtsy. "Ring the bell if you need anything." I shut the door behind me.

Something shattered against it.

I blinked at the door, heart pounding. I had a feeling that bell would stay silent for a long time.

Not knowing what else to do, I explored my room further. There was another door in the back, perfectly flush with the wall. I pushed the edge hesitantly, then jumped back as it clicked and swung open.

Inside was a bathing chamber with a deep copper tub fed by pipes leading into the walls. One entire wall was taken up by a marble counter topped with an enormous mirror. I trailed my fingers over the glass in amazement. Every mirror I'd ever seen had rippled and distorted my reflection, but this was smooth as a still pond.

My face looked gaunt. I reached up to my cheeks, pressing my fingers against sun-freckled skin. I hadn't eaten well for a long time, but I'd never seen the evidence of it so clearly before. In contrast to the thinness of my face and frame, my hair looked enormous, a wild, curling brown tangle that fell to my lower back.

Anya had loved my hair. She'd told me she'd have traded her own wavy tresses for it in a second, and I'd told her she was crazy. Tears blurred my eyes at the memory. It felt like her ghost haunted my every step to make sure I never forgot her . . . or how I'd failed her.

Now that I'd recovered from my initial horror, the full force of grief washed over me. I sank to the floor, clasped my face in my hands, and wept.

I don't know how long I sat there. Long enough for the light emanating from the ceiling crystals to grow brighter. Long enough for my eyes to ache and my knees to stiffen. Eventually I took a few deep breaths and scrubbed at the salt trails on my cheeks. There would be time for mourning later. Maybe in the dark the next time I lay down to sleep. Maybe every night for the rest of my life. Now, though, I needed to focus on survival, which meant pulling myself together, purging every sign of weakness from my appearance, and beginning the search for an escape route.

Everything I'd seen so far had convinced me I needed to escape Mistei. I didn't want to spend my entire life in servitude to a species that hated humans. I would perform my duties for as long as it took to find a way out, and then I'd start a new life somewhere far away from the Fae-human border.

My knees cracked as I rose, and I winced. The earth floor hadn't stained my dress, which must be faerie magic as well. I turned the faucet handles above the deep sink and a stream of warm water came out. I washed my face, rinsing the evidence of my grief down the drain.

To my surprise, the end of the counter held not just a pitcher and glass but cosmetics and ointments. I sniffed the bottles, wondering which ones were soap and which were scent, then tested them until I found one that frothed in my hands. There were bottles beside the tub as well, presumably for washing hair.

It was unimaginable luxury. Servants in the Fae court lived better than anyone in Tumbledown did. I applied a few drops of a liquid I had identified as honeysuckle perfume to the insides of my wrists, as Anya had told me fine ladies did, then combed my hair, wincing as I worked through the knots. The cosmetic boxes had small carvings on their lids: the graceful line of a cheek, a pouting mouth, an art-fully depicted eye. I selected two at random, applying a small amount of rouge to my cheeks and a pale blue shimmer to my eyelids.

I hardly recognized the woman in the mirror. My amber eyes looked more alert, the redness from crying diminished by the ice-blue shimmer. My cheeks shone with a healthy glow. With my hair smoothed by yet another ointment, I looked clean, neat, and pretty.

The wardrobe provided me with a blue dress, which thankfully had sleeves loose enough to hide the dagger still wrapped around my bicep like jewelry. Once fully attired, I set out to explore my new surroundings—and start looking for a way out.

The house teemed with activity. I tried not to gawk at the Under-fae I passed while descending the servants' staircase next to my room, even though they openly stared at me. Servants filed in and out of corridors and hurried up and down the stairs bearing trays and boxes. There were more elegant asrai, their hair varying shades of blue and gray, as well as small, soil-colored beings that only reached up to my knee and carried brushes or fireplace pokers—brownies, presumably. Their exposed skin was crusted with lichen, and their black eyes were bright and curious. I whipped my head around at a whisper of movement in the air and saw a tiny pixie, no larger than my longest finger, darting past on gossamer-thin wings. Elder Holman had told us about pixies: they were supposedly be-nevolent and brought luck and health. Their darker counterparts were sprites, which delighted in mischief.

The pixie hovered beside me, studying me with round eyes. She was delicate and beautiful, with blushing ivory skin and a tuft of dark green hair. She flitted away before I could speak.

I emerged in a corridor on the bottom floor. From one direction came the sound of clattering dishes, and from the other came splash-ing and a few high-pitched giggles. A communal bathing room, perhaps, or a laundry facility. More Underfae gathered here, but my attention was grabbed by a woman hurrying by. Now that I'd noticed the twinkling sense of magic that emanated from even the smallest faeries, there was no mistaking this drab woman for anything but human. She looked to be in her fifties, with graying hair and melancholy eyes.

I approached her. "Hello. You're human, right? My name is Kenna. What's yours?" I extended my hand, but she stopped in her tracks and stared at me in shock. Her hands fluttered in the air, then dropped to her sides, as if she was overcome with emotion. She didn't respond.

The silence was growing awkward. Was there a taboo about humans speaking to servants of the Earth lords and ladies? "I was wondering if it's fine for me to look around. Do you know if we're allowed to leave Earth House?"

Wide-eyed, she nodded and pointed down the hall.

"Thank you." I walked away with feigned confidence. When I glanced over my shoulder, she was still staring after me.

I was relieved to find Alodie in the main hall. She smiled at me. "How is Lady Lara?"

"She has not required anything of me," I said carefully.

"That bad? She'll accept it eventually. She has no choice."

"Well, until she does, I wanted to explore a bit." To find out whether there were any convenient exits I could slip through unnoticed. "That's allowed, right?"

"Yes. You are not a prisoner." She smiled apologetically. "You can't go aboveground, though. All the exits are warded to prevent anyone from leaving without the king's permission."

Not a promising start. "But I'm free to go anywhere within Mistei?"

"You can visit the public spaces, but you can't enter any other house's territory without permission."

"How many houses are there?"

There was a slight hesitation before she answered. "Five total. The others are Fire, Light, Illusion, and Void."

Interesting. The Elder had said the Noble Fae could grow plants, summon fire, even turn day into night, but I hadn't realized those abilities depended on what faction they allied with. There was so much to learn. "And where are their territories?"

A brownie tottering under a pile of boxes called Alodie's name, and she raised a hand in acknowledgment at the frazzled-looking Underfae. "Be there in a second!" Then she returned her attention to me. "I'll draw you a rough map of where the entrances are later today. Until then, just be cautious."

I didn't want to be cautious. I wanted to get out of here.

Alodie must have seen it in my face, because she rested a fine-boned hand on my shoulder. "I'm sure being underground feels strange and restrictive to you," she said softly, "but Mistei is enormous. There's plenty of room to explore. Some say there's no end to how deep you can go." She paused. "Though I wouldn't recommend exploring too far down, or you'll run into the Nasties."

Plenty of room. Sure. "So I'm not a prisoner, but I can't go outside or visit other house territories, and I shouldn't go too far down."

She looked sympathetic. "I understand this is new for you, but you'll grow accustomed to it. Once you settle in, I doubt you'll miss the outside world at all."

I silently vowed never to settle in.

6

I HAD TO BOLSTER MY COURAGE BEFORE ENTERING THE WATER
tunnel. Alodie was right; it was beautiful during the day. The rays
of sun that speared down from above lightened the water to a vibrant
turquoise, and fish swam on all sides. Some were ordinary species
I'd caught near Tumbledown, but others were exotic and colorful,
their scales gleaming like jewels. The lake bed stretched away in either
direction, punctuated by outcroppings of rock and drifting plants.

It felt surprisingly peaceful considering how quickly the water
could kill an intruder, and I remembered how Alodie's shoulders
had lost their tension the moment she'd entered the tunnel. As a
school of sparkling orange fish darted up to investigate me, I felt certain I was welcome here, a bone-deep comfort so abrupt and foreign
it must have been part of the house's magic.

I tried to retrace my steps from the previous night, but soon I was
hopelessly lost. Mistei wasn't a golden castle in the middle of a cavern as my mother had believed—it was a huge labyrinthine city, and
with no sky above to show me the position of the sun or stars, it all
looked the same. The corridors were far brighter this morning, lit by

torches and the same embedded ceiling crystals that had reflected dawn's light into my room this morning, but it still felt oppressive. Normally I'd be collecting treasure in the bog right now, not trapped deep underground.

My heart clenched at the thought of my collection. I'd never even gotten to show Anya the doll I'd found.

The pain of that realization felt like glass embedded in my chest, drawing blood with each heartbeat. I knew from losing my mother that grief had countless small traps like this—not just the big ache of missing someone, but the small cuts of memories or wishes. People vanished all at once, but the things you wanted to tell them or do with them or show them didn't.

After an hour of walking, I accepted I would never make it back to the throne room. I'd taken a wrong turn somewhere, and this path spiraled upward. I stayed on the main slope rather than investigating the doors that beckoned to the right and left. Most were closed, but occasionally I caught glimpses of empty chambers, cozy sitting rooms, or libraries. There was even a row of small shops where Underfae hunted for fabric, glassware, and jewelry.

The path widened as it climbed. Torches flickered in elaborately carved sconces, and the ceiling crystals beamed down the brilliant light of midday. Near the top of the slope, the crystals disappeared and only torches lit the path forward, their reflected light shimmering off the obsidian walls.

The ramp leveled out, and a wide room opened before me. Forbidding stone statues lined the sides, and slicing through the middle of the room, blocking any further advance, was a curtain of fire.

"Amazing," I whispered to myself, staring in awe at the vast, crackling sheet of flame.

As I walked closer, one of the statues turned its head to look at me. Not a statue, I realized with a start. A gargoyle-like Underfae.

The creature was charcoal-colored with a ridged brow, twisted horns, and heavy wings. Its back was stooped, and as it stepped towards me, its front claws trailed against the floor, making an eerie scraping sound that lifted the hair on my arms.

I turned to make my escape . . . and ran directly into another gargoyle.

Its eyes burned with rage as it gripped my wrist, its claws digging into my skin. "Trespassers must burn," it said in a voice like boulders tumbling down a mountain.

Then it began dragging me towards the fire.

"Please let me go," I begged, trying to pull away, but the gargoyle wouldn't be deterred. It yanked on my wrist, forcing me to stumble behind it or be dragged.

The fire took up my entire field of vision, an enormous, writhing wall that stretched to a distant, smoke-blackened ceiling. Sweat poured down my face and my skin tightened under the onslaught of painful heat. Soon that heat would grow agonizing, and if the gargoyle tossed me in . . .

Death by fire would be excruciating.

"I didn't mean to come here. I don't even know where I am. Please!"

The gargoyle snarled and shook me. I went limp, trying to slow its progress by burdening it with my full body weight, but it muscled forward as if I weighed nothing at all. I kicked at it and scrabbled against the floor, begging for my life as its claws drew blood from my bruised wrist.

Heat battered me as the flames drew near. The dagger was writhing down my free arm, pulsing in time with my frantic heartbeats, but whatever it meant to do wouldn't happen fast enough. We were only feet away from the fire now. The gargoyle gripped my shoulders, preparing to push me in.

"Stop."

A clear male voice sliced through the crackle of flame. The gargoyle stopped instantly.

"Release her."

It unhooked its claws from me, and I shoved away from the fiery wall. I crashed to the floor . . . and found myself staring up at a bemused-looking Noble Fae.

It was Drustan, the rakish and impossibly handsome prince who had winked at me in the throne room. This close, I could see streaks of crimson, blond, and black in his copper hair, so like the shifting colors of the flames behind me. He wore a loose red shirt tucked into tight black trousers, and a rapier hung from his golden belt.

Amusement flickered in his eyes, which were gray like ash. "Already getting in trouble?"

I scrambled to my feet and curtsied, glancing over my shoulder to make sure the gargoyle hadn't pursued me. Thankfully, it was slouching its way back to its post. I returned my attention to Prince Drustan, struggling to talk past the fear that still clogged my throat. "I got lost. Please forgive me. I'll go now."

He stilled me with a hand on my left arm. "Wait."

On my other arm, the dagger shivered against my skin. Its frenetic pulsing had slowed, and now I couldn't tell if the tremor was a warning or just the dagger's way of letting me know that Drustan was powerful. What would he do to me? Wherever I was, I had clearly trespassed.

Prince Drustan was taller than me by a full head. He touched my chin with surprisingly hot fingers, nudging my face up. I struggled not to look away from the power reflected in that gaze. Magic emanated from him in rippling waves, and the air around him looked distorted. "Do you know where you are?"

Maybe it was foolish to admit ignorance to one of the Noble Fae, but what else could I do? "No, my lord. I mean, my prince."

He smiled, revealing even white teeth. "That's a good thing. Otherwise I'd ask why Earth House is sending spies to Fire territory."

Fire was one of the five Fae houses. I remembered Alodie's advice and winced. *You can't enter any other house's territory without permission.* Only an hour into my explorations and I had already broken a fundamental rule—and nearly paid for it with my life.

"I didn't realize." I tried to back away, but he held my chin firmly. "I knew the Fae wielded elemental magic, but I only just learned about your houses."

Drustan looked surprised. "Really? Your leaders didn't tell you about Mistei?"

"They did, but a lot can be forgotten in a thousand years."

"For humans, I suppose that's true." He let go of my chin at last, but this time I resisted the urge to retreat. I'd shown enough weakness already. He cocked his head, studying me. "So you ran across the bog to a place you know little about. Why? It didn't look like you were even chosen for that ritual."

Sweat beaded on my forehead and my palms were damp. His expression was pleasant, but this encounter felt dangerous. I couldn't pinpoint exactly why, but my body knew something my mind didn't yet. "To save a friend," I said through a thick throat. If he'd truly been watching, he knew how that had ended.

He waited for several seconds as if leaving me room to offer up more, but I didn't owe him Anya or my grief. Finally, he nodded. "You risked your life to help someone else. An admirable trait. What is your name?"

"Kenna, my prince. Kenna Heron."

Those gray eyes were still fixed on me; I wondered what thoughts moved behind them. "Well, Kenna, I can appreciate a noble sacrifice." His smile slid towards a smirk. "And I bet quite a bit of gold on you making it the farthest, so there's no reason to sully that victory now. Let me walk you back to safer territory."

Relief rushed out of me on an exhale. Whatever his reasons, the prince was being merciful. "Thank you, my prince."

He turned, then beckoned for me to follow. I had to jog to catch up with his long strides, but with every step away from the fire my sense of relief grew. As we approached the ramp, a few servants appeared. They were similar in appearance to Alodie, but their red hair crackled with electricity and their eyes glowed like embers. Fire asrai. They bowed deeply in deference to the faerie at my side.

He clicked his tongue after we passed them. "I've asked them not to bow when we're in house territory. Or at least not to bow so low—they're going to tip over if they're not careful."

"Why wouldn't they bow?" I asked. "You're a prince." Even Elder Holman had expected people to bow to him, and he'd been nothing but a small village leader. Drustan was immortal royalty.

"I don't particularly enjoy protocol. It too often creates an atmosphere of fear rather than engendering loyalty."

Another Underfae curtsied as we descended the ramp.

"Then why do they still bow if you've asked them not to?"

"I rose to the position of prince a few decades ago, which is a short time in Fae memory. The servants have not overcome old habits yet." He smiled at me. "But I'll convince them eventually."

This wasn't what I had expected from a Fae prince after witnessing that brutal scene in the throne room. He was charming, and he didn't speak to me like I was a servant. Still, my nerves prickled with apprehension. As we wound our way down the ramp together, I could hardly breathe from the nearness of him, the unnatural heat of him. I was both afraid and enchanted. I wanted to leave his presence as soon as possible, yet part of me protested at the thought.

The Elder had been right about this characteristic of the Noble Fae: one look and a human could be entranced.

"Are the leaders of the other houses as casual about protocol?" I dared to ask, struggling to conceal my nervousness in the face of all that beauty and power. "In the throne room it seemed otherwise."

He laughed, sharp and hard. "Not in the slightest. I'm doing my best to make Fire House a less restrictive place, but the others adore their protocol." He eyed me consideringly. "Though I hear Blood House was more aligned with my personal preferences, back when they still existed."

"Blood House?" Alodie hadn't mentioned that ominous-sounding one.

He pressed a finger to his lips. "Quietly, if you please. It's actually best for servants not to speak that name at all if you can help it. Not in other company, at least."

Whether his chattiness was on a whim or had some other unknown motivation, I needed to seize every scrap of information he offered. "Forgive me, my prince. I just didn't know there was a sixth house."

He was still looking at me with that assessing quality to his gaze. "Your knowledge is severely lacking."

"Yes."

After a long pause, he sighed. "You're going to blunder into trouble if you don't know this history. Well, more trouble than you already have." He beckoned me closer, then lowered his voice to just above a whisper even though there was no one nearby. "Fire, Void, and Blood rebelled against King Osric some five hundred years ago. Before I was born," he clarified at my wide-eyed look. "Fire and Void saw the error of their ways, but Blood did not. The house was eliminated."

The stark words sent a shiver through me. "And the other houses supported the king?"

"Illusion and Light have always supported him, but Earth is neutral in all conflicts. It's a point of pride for them but deeply irritating to Osric."

Maybe that was why the king had liked the idea of insulting Princess Oriana and Lady Lara. "What are the powers of each house?" I pressed, hungry for more information.

"You're a very curious woman." The corners of his lips pulled upward again. He didn't seem to be able to go long without smiling, though it was impossible to tell if his show of good cheer was genuine. "A useful trait."

I just raised my eyebrows, silently asking again.

"The houses are paired into opposing twins," Drustan said, relenting. "Earth controls the terrestrial elements, and Fire controls anything in the natural world beyond that. Flame is our favorite, thus the name, but we have some power over air, wind, and weather as well." He lifted a hand, and fire crackled over his fingertips before vanishing.

"Void House controls darkness and emptiness. They can eliminate light and create monsters from nothing but the night air. They can rip holes in the universe that will crush a faerie into nothingness. Their opposite is Light, which, as you can imagine, casts light. Their second great power is that they are mostly immune to the magic of others—they will quickly see through an illusion and are more resistant to mystical fire. They prefer to fight their battles with weapons and brute strength."

He must have seen my shiver, because he leaned down to whisper the next words, his hot breath painting the curve of my ear. "Void House wears black, and Light House wears white. I'd stay away from both, if I were you."

I remembered the calculated coldness of the black-clad killer who had suggested giving me to Earth House as an insult. He must be from Void House, while Roland, the sadistic prince who had suggested killing me, hailed from Light House. "What about Illusion?"

"Illusion can change what the mind perceives. They can cast images and make you hear and feel things that aren't real, and they use manipulation and trickery to get what they want. The king was the Prince of Illusion before he took the throne. Now he is king of all Mistei, and there are no princes or princesses in his house." I wondered at the flatness of Drustan's tone, but his expression revealed nothing.

"And Blood?" I asked.

Someone was coming up the ramp—another asrai who stopped and curtsied at the sight of us. Drustan nodded at them in acknowledgment. Once we were past the Underfae, he took my left arm and pulled me aside. His fingers were long and strong, and the heat of his touch sank through my sleeve. The prince leaned in to whisper in my ear again, and though I braced myself for that puff of heat and the nearness of his lips, a quiver went through me anyway.

"You really should be careful about when and how you say that name," he said. "You earned me a lot of gold last night, so I'm giving you an introduction to Mistei in exchange, but others among the Noble Fae won't tolerate a servant speaking about the lost house. And you never know who might be listening in the shadows."

Unease crawled down my spine. Torchlight danced over the obsidian walls, and for a moment it seemed as if the stone was alive and breathing. Still, it seemed hypocritical for Drustan to tell me about Blood House with one breath and then admonish me for my continuing curiosity with the next. "You're the one who brought them up," I pointed out, staring at him in steady challenge. "My prince."

He grinned, and my heart pounded in response. "Not just curious but bold. I knew the second I saw you that you were the strongest of the lot, no matter how short you were."

I scowled at the cavalier mention of the other women. "How were you watching us run, anyway?"

"King Osric casts an illusion on the wall so we can watch the hunt. He finds it entertaining."

My eyes burned and I looked away, clenching my fists to contain my rage. My nails inscribed sharp arcs of pain into my palms. "Entertaining? The others died."

I could feel him watching me. "They always do," Drustan said, but his tone was softer this time. "Except for you."

We had reached the bottom of the ramp, and I breathed a sigh of relief as the obsidian walls were replaced with gray stone. We were back in the main tunnels. "I can find my way from here," I said. *Maybe.* His presence was too unnerving, too stimulating, and I needed distance to clear my mind. I curtsied. "Thank you."

When I rose, his expression was deadly serious. "I meant what I said. Stay away from Light and Void. And Illusion, for that matter."

I raised my brows. "But Fire is perfectly safe?" My near demise said otherwise.

"Fire is . . . open-minded, shall we say. We have friends in many places throughout Mistei."

It was a subtle offer, I realized. To be a friend of Fire House. The problem was, I didn't know what that meant.

I nodded, eager to get away so I could think in peace. "Thank you again, my prince."

"On the note of protocol," he said, "hearing 'my prince' every other sentence gets tedious. Calling me Drustan would be inappropriate in front of other Noble Fae, but I have no qualms about hearing my name in more . . . private contexts." He winked at me, and I flushed. "And my friends are afforded certain privileges."

Again he gave that word—*friends*—a slight weight. The dagger twitched against my arm again, matching the quivering unease that filled me. Prince Drustan was charming, but I got the sense this conversation hadn't just happened because of a prince's whim. He'd been testing me somehow, not just educating me.

I curtsied. "I'll keep that in mind."

His gaze seemed to burn into my back long after I'd left him behind.

7

LARA REFUSED TO SEE ME.

I'd been too unsettled to explore further after the incident at Fire House, so I'd returned to see if she needed anything. My hesitant knock only resulted in a barked "Go away."

What was I supposed to do if my mistress didn't want a hand-maiden?

Part of me was relieved not to have any duties, but I wasn't a fool. In order to survive long enough to escape, I needed to succeed as a servant. Besides, every pause gave an opportunity for grief to catch up with me again—better to stay busy and save my tears for the lonely hours of the night. I returned downstairs, determined to ask Alodie for another task.

Alodie wasn't in the main hall anymore. Instead, Princess Oriana stood there, breathtakingly gorgeous and abundantly curved. She was talking quietly with a cheerful-looking young faerie who wore a single yellow rose pinned to his blue tunic. The teenager's wavy brown hair had golden streaks that matched Oriana's blond tresses, but his brown eyes were the same shape and shade as Lara's. This must be a younger brother.

The Noble Fae all seemed to have frozen into immortality looking like they were between twenty and thirty years of age, so it was odd to think that Oriana could be this boy's mother. It would be an adjustment, being unable to guess family relationships on a glance the way one could in the human realm. For all I knew, Oriana was thousands of years old.

I tried to retreat, but Oriana noticed me immediately. "You." She pointed a stern finger at me. "Come here."

I approached and curtsied. Thankfully, this one didn't wobble too much. "Princess."

She studied me with grim resolve, as if I were an unpleasant duty that must be undertaken. She wore a twisting wooden crown and a forest-green dress, and her hair was plaited into thick braids that wound around each other to the middle of her back. The hazel of her eyes reminded me of Anya's, and a pang went through me. "This is the human," Oriana told the teenager.

He smiled, and a dimple popped out on one cheek. "I gathered that."

"Forgive me if I intruded," I said. "I was seeking Alodie to find out if she has any tasks for me."

Oriana's eyebrows rose. "Hasn't Lara given you enough tasks to fill your time?"

I phrased my answer as delicately as I could. "She does not require my assistance, my princess."

"So she's being a brat," Oriana said flatly, and the boy guffawed. I almost choked. I stared at her, unable to respond.

Oriana sighed. "Lara has always been sensitive to criticism." She snapped her fingers, and I twitched at the sharp sound. "Come."

The boy smiled at me before leaving the hall, and I followed Oriana up the spiraling staircase. She marched to her daughter's door and pounded on it.

"What?" was the testy response.

"Open the door."

The door opened a few seconds later, and Lara stepped aside as the princess swept in. I trailed along behind, not knowing what else to do.

Lara glared at me as I positioned myself in a corner. Her black hair was down, and she wore a rumpled turquoise nightgown. "I don't want the human here."

"Yes, that's apparent." Oriana settled onto a plush couch, motioning for Lara to take the brocade-upholstered chair opposite. They stared at each other. The familial resemblance was subtle, but I found it in the angle of their arched brows and the shape of their noses.

The silence drew out. Lara shifted uncomfortably in her seat.

"This human," Oriana finally said, "was gifted to you by King Osric himself."

"I don't want her."

"You have no choice. He is the king."

Lara looked at me with hatred. "The others have been taunting me about it. How I'm so weak I need a human servant. It's humiliating."

"It's only humiliating because you allow it to be. If you didn't care what they said, it wouldn't matter if your servant was human, Underfae, or Nasty."

"I have to care what they say. Aren't you always telling me I can't look weak?"

"Yes. And by rejecting this gift, you are making it clear to everyone at court exactly how humiliated you feel. You're confirming what they already think."

Lara flopped back in her chair, exhaling heavily. "I hate this. Why does the king dislike me so much?"

"It's not just you," Oriana said. "It's all of Earth House. He hates that we're neutral and have never taken his side. He sees it as weakness, so he delights in testing us. You must be stronger than that."

"So I just take the insult? Accept it when everyone laughs?"

"Yes."

Lara looked at me again. I tried to keep my expression calm and my body relaxed, even though I hated the way they discussed me like an object, not a person.

"How does that prove my strength?" Some of the anger had faded from Lara's expression.

"By acting with confidence despite the insult, you imply that you are above it, that you are so worthy you don't need to be concerned about a human assisting you in the immortality trials. By holding yourself in a position of respect, you teach others how to treat you."

I listened intently, wondering if there was a lesson in this for me, too. I'd always told myself it didn't matter how others perceived me, but appearances were everything to the Noble Fae. If you appeared confident, you were confident. If you appeared powerful, you were powerful. So when I had reveled in appearing dirty, feral, and defiant to cover up my miserable life and my hundred petty fears, everyone in Tumbledown had assumed that was who I was, and no one had bothered to look any deeper.

Lara sighed. "What if the trials require something she's incapable of doing?"

At least she was calling me "she," instead of "the human" or "the insult."

"They won't. Even the king would not sabotage a contestant so much. But I've been thinking about how we can use this to our benefit. We've been so focused on viewing the king's gift as an insult that we failed to appreciate the advantages it brings."

The calculating look in Oriana's eyes made me nervous. What did she mean?

"What advantages?" Lara asked derisively. "You see her."

I bit my cheek, determined not to say anything rude in response. I knew what they saw when they looked at me: a small, unkempt, inferior being. I could work on the unkempt part, but there was only so much I could do about the rest.

"Exactly." Oriana cast me an appraising glance. "Many areas of Mistei are warded against Noble Fae and Underfae. There's only so much a traditional servant could have done to help you, only so many risks they could have taken. But a human can risk more, and no one will think twice about her because humans aren't considered a threat. They're physically weak, they have no magic, and most of them have had their tongues cut out. Who would they speak with, even if one of them somehow gained the courage?"

My stomach dropped. *Tongues cut out.* That explained why the humans I had met so far hadn't spoken to me. The thought made me want to vomit. If I hadn't been assigned to Lara's service, would the Fae have done the same to me? Mutilated me to prevent my voice from being heard?

"Your handmaiden will spy for us," Oriana continued. "She will learn everything she can about what the upcoming trials will entail. She will explore deeper, darker places than would have been possible otherwise."

This sounded very bad. I shifted nervously, and Oriana's gaze shot to me. "You will do everything you can, human," she told me in the sharpest tone I'd heard from her yet, "to ensure Lara succeeds. Anything. There are no limits."

She truly meant it. Anything up to and including murder would be acceptable in her eyes if it helped her child win.

"Yes, my princess." It was the only answer I could give.

"Earth House is more merciful than most, but even our mercy has limits. If you fail to assist Lara or if you cease to be useful, we will punish you accordingly. You will be sent below to live as the lowliest servant—if I don't decide to have you executed."

A chill wormed down my spine as she shifted her attention back to Lara. With her commands and threats delivered, Oriana was apparently done with me.

"Have the human assist you," she told Lara. "Take her to every event so she can listen for information about the trials. And no matter what, don't show any weakness—or there will be consequences."

LARA AND I STARED AT EACH OTHER AFTER ORIANA LEFT.

She looked just as mired in dread as I felt. Why? She wasn't the one under threat of getting her tongue cut out . . . but then again, I shouldn't forget that she, too, risked death if she failed the trials.

She was young, I remembered. Somewhere near my age. I kept thinking of the Fae as if they were all ancient and powerful, but Lara wasn't. It had been hard enough growing up in the human world—what must it have been like to grow up in the terrifying Fae court, where any weakness invited punishment?

I would do anything to escape, whether that meant playing the perfect servant or becoming Oriana's spy, and if I couldn't escape before the trials began, I would help Lara succeed for the same reason. I wouldn't just be preserving my own life, though. Brat or not, Lara was afraid, and she was in danger.

In that moment, the way I saw my mistress began to shift. Despite her harsh attitude, despite the vast gulf between our stations, we had become reluctant allies in the same fight.

"Can I bring you anything, my lady?" If we were to be allies, I needed to start building a truce with her.

She opened her mouth, then stopped as if reconsidering whatever she was about to say. "Water," she said at last.

There was a pitcher and glass in her washroom, as there had been in mine. When I returned, Lara accepted the glass silently.

"I'm sorry." I didn't know what else to say.

She drank, then closed her eyes and tilted her head back with a sigh. "I don't want your pity."

The sharp edges were still there. It would take time for her to accept me, if she ever did. She wasn't throwing things, though, so I counted this as progress. "Can I do anything else for you, my lady?"

"There's a lunch I need to attend. Help me get ready."

Such simple words, but I didn't even know where to start. "I've never served a lady before," I told her, figuring honesty was required if we were going to get along. "What do you need me to do?"

She rolled her eyes and gestured to the wardrobe. "Pick an outfit."

I opened the doors and suppressed a gasp at the cascade of fabric that poured out. Most of the gowns were the blue, green, or brown that were so common in Earth House, but a few were pink, cream, or yellow. I trailed a hand over smooth satin, rich velvet, and a fabric so light and sheer it fluttered with every shifting air current. What would a lady wear to lunch? It was all so outrageously beautiful that I had no idea what to choose.

I grabbed an ivory dress at random. The bodice was studded with tiny emeralds, and the skirts fell in a cloud beneath a green satin belt. The sleeves were fine mesh dotted with more emeralds, the fabric so thin it looked like spiderwebs. I held it up, and she looked at me as if I were insane.

"That's a ball gown," she said flatly. "This isn't a ball. This is lunch."

I cringed. "Of course." I put the dress back and raked through the others, finally finding one that didn't look as overwrought as the rest. It was dark green with long sleeves and a scooped neck, and the skirt was covered with black netting. The overall effect reminded me of pine trees in a dark forest—evergreen needles alternating with shadow. I showed it to her, and she nodded.

I helped her dress in silence, quickly learning that the outfits rich ladies wore were unreasonably complicated. There were underthings she had to point me to, and once I'd draped the satin over her full figure, I needed to tighten a seemingly infinite number of laces until the gown accentuated every curve.

I stepped back and appraised her. She looked incredible, the green making her olive-toned skin seem to glow and the neckline highlighting breasts I could only aspire to. "Perfect," I dared to say.

She cast me another withering look. "Cosmetics?" she asked acidly. "Hair?"

I started sweating. I had encountered cosmetics for the first time this morning. And hair—how did one do a lady's hair? I thought of Oriana's complex braids and almost whimpered.

I ushered Lara into the washroom in silence, casting a frantic eye over the dozens of bottles and boxes on the counter. I looked at the inscribed tops, organizing them into areas of the face. Lips, cheeks, eyes. Then I started peeking inside them. There were so many shades—an array of reds and pinks for the lips and cheeks and infinite variations of the rainbow for her eyelids. What was I supposed to do with these?

As I pawed through them in near panic, she sighed. "You don't know how to use makeup, do you?"

"No, my lady."

She bustled over and started collecting boxes and brushes from the untidy heaps I'd made. "I can tell by how terribly you applied your eye shadow."

I flushed. Had I applied it incorrectly?

"Here." Lara indicated that I should watch. "Do the eyes first." She lined her eyes with a brown pencil, then smudged deep green eye shadow along her lash line. It looked exactly like what I had done, I thought bitterly, but then she took a lighter pigment and blended it in until faint glimmers of green rose all the way up to her eyebrows.

Oh. Yes, that looked better than what I had done. I compared our faces in the mirror. Now I could see that my blue eye shadow was both asymmetrical and too severe.

Her dark lashes were short but naturally thick, and she brushed an inky pigment over them that emphasized them even more. She used a cloth to clean up stray green powder that had fallen on her round cheeks, then patted on a shimmering coral blush. Then came a cream that deepened the natural berry tone of her lips, and finally she brushed glittering powder from her forehead to her chest, careful to avoid getting it on her dress.

I blinked at her transformed face in the mirror, awed at her skill. She was naturally beautiful, but now she looked unearthly. That innate faerie shine intensified the shimmering colors, and I was reminded of the flashy, glimmering fish that swam around the tunnel entrance to the house.

"I'll be sure to practice," I told her.

"Please do." She returned to the main room, sitting at a vanity that held a looking glass whose gold frame had been fashioned to resemble tree branches. "I used to have the cleverest asrai servant. She was brilliant with cosmetics and hair." She cast me a bitter look in the mirror. "They sent her to a different family after the king gifted me with you." Her emphasis on the word *gifted* told me she still saw me as anything but a gift.

"I'll learn."

I brushed out the midnight length of her hair. The texture of it reminded me of Anya's—soft with a natural wave. Another prick of grief stung my heart as I thought about how Anya and I had braided each other's hair while sharing town gossip. I'd learned a few simple hairstyles from her—one of those would have to do for Lara. I started braiding her hair above the ear, planning to loop the braid over her head and fix it behind her other ear with pins, leaving the rest to flow freely down her back.

"Are there many families in Earth House?" I asked. I hadn't explored the entirety of the house yet, but it seemed vast and I'd seen many Noble Fae wandering the halls or lounging in sitting rooms while the servants rushed around.

"Yes," Lara said. "My mother's bloodline is the strongest, but there are other Noble Fae families with similar powers."

"Did your father come from one of those?" I concentrated on pulling more hair into the braid.

She was still for a long moment. "Yes, though I barely knew him." I immediately realized I had made a mistake. "I'm sorry."

She sighed, apparently taking mercy on me. "My father was Oriana's second consort, and she only chose him a few decades ago. That's why Selwyn and I are so young compared to the heirs of the other houses. My father died shortly after Selwyn's birth."

Selwyn must be the cheerful-looking teenager I'd encountered earlier. "I'm sorry," I repeated, meeting her eyes in the mirror. "My father abandoned my mother and me when I was only a few years old. I grew up without one as well." Perhaps this shared pain would be our first common ground.

Her expression gentled. She nodded, silently acknowledging my confession.

The braid was turning out better than I had expected. I was nearly done, and so far it was only a little crooked. I scrambled for another topic of discussion. "So you and Oriana have the same magic?"

That quickly, the softness in her expression vanished. She looked as if I had insulted her. "I only have a little magic," she said in a biting tone, "because I haven't undertaken the trials yet."

I winced. Apparently I had reminded her of another way in which she felt inadequate. "Of course."

I finished the braid in silence. She studied it in the mirror, blatant skepticism written on her face. "It's simple."

"It's a simple dress." Not to me, of course, but she nodded as if accepting the logic and rose from her chair.

"Come." She snapped her fingers as if I were a dog, just as her mother had.

"Where are we going, my lady?" I asked as politely as I could manage.

"Lunch at Light House. Do not embarrass me, or I swear I will have you removed from my service, no matter what Oriana says."

Our moment of camaraderie was over. I followed her to the main staircase, resisting the urge to roll my eyes. She needed a small victory—I supposed I could understand that. So I played the cowed servant and followed in her wake, trying to look docile.

It wasn't until later that I remembered what Drustan had told me. *Stay away from Light House.*

8

THE ENTRANCE TO LIGHT HOUSE WAS SITUATED ON WHAT must have been one of the uppermost levels of the vast underground city. My legs were shaking with fatigue by the time we'd finished climbing a succession of marble steps and emerged into a hall lined with pillars. Lara wasn't even winded—faeries were apparently more resilient than humans.

My eyes hurt at the radiance. The floor was white, the walls were white, the thick pillars that marched in lines down the chamber were white. Bright orbs of light drifted above, and torches and crystals flooded the space with brilliance. The stone beneath my feet was veined with gold.

"Are we going inside the house, my lady?" I wondered what horrible trap lay in wait for the enemies of Light House. Earth House drowned unwelcome visitors, Fire burned them . . . what would Light do?

"Of course not," she said under her breath. "We'll be in one of the outer chambers for entertaining guests."

I breathed a sigh of relief.

A white-and-gold-clad servant emerged from a door at the far end of the hall. He glowed as if lit from within, and white feathered wings sprouted from his back. The hem of his snowy robe rippled around his feet. It was only when he drew close that I saw he had no mouth whatsoever, and his eyes were orbs of liquid gold.

The glow around him was partially caused by a circle of light that tracked him as he moved. I looked up to see where it was coming from. Eight enormous glass lenses had been set into the walls near the ceiling, and unnaturally strong faerie light poured through all of them to collect in a moving pool beneath his feet.

I'd seen what the boys in Tumbledown had done with an anthill and a fragment of glass. Was this how Light House defended itself? By intensifying that light until it burned through any intruders?

The servant stopped. *Welcome, Lady Lara.* The deep voice sounded inside my head. I jumped, but Lara didn't seem alarmed by the mental communication. *Please follow me.*

He led us to a nearby door, and I was relieved when the light didn't follow. It had stopped at the last pillar some ten feet away and gone no farther.

The room was full of Noble Fae.

I followed Lara for a few paces, then stopped after she gave me a cutting look. I retreated to the wall where other servants stood with bowed heads and clasped hands and adopted the same position, sneaking glances at the magnificent room.

It was like standing in a cloud. The floor felt soft beneath my feet, and puffs of mist drifted at ankle height. The bottom half of the walls glittered like snow in sunshine, and the top half faded into the pure blue of a clear winter sky. A golden chandelier easily twenty feet in diameter illuminated the room.

The Noble Fae glittered, too. They wore elaborate clothing in colors I now recognized as belonging to the five houses—the natural tones of Earth, the purple and rainbows of Illusion, the red and orange of Fire, and the harshly contrasting white and black of Light and Void. Lara joined a male faerie who wore a brown velvet jacket a few shades lighter than his skin. He bowed to her, and she smiled at him.

I had the sudden feeling someone was watching me. I looked around stealthily—and met eyes with Prince Drustan, who looked resplendent in a gold tunic highlighted in crimson. He was engaged in conversation with two faeries from Light House. He grinned, and I looked away hastily.

Someone else was watching me, too. The cold faerie from Void House, the killer who had been the cause for my current position as Lara's servant. He looked like death in a long black coat held together by silver clasps, and the same opal brooch from yesterday was pinned to his chest. He was speaking to another member of Void House, but his eyes held mine.

A trickle of fear skated down my spine. This had to be the Void prince. Everything about his watchful pose and frigid gaze spoke of barely restrained power.

His attention moved on, and I was able to breathe again.

A bell rang, and the faeries gathered at a long dining table. An array of dishes appeared on the snowy tablecloth. The smell of roasted meat was mouthwatering; I hadn't eaten anything since yesterday, too dazed by my new surroundings. I watched jealously as Lara lifted a spoon of steaming soup to her lips.

"Makes you hungry, doesn't it?" The soft whisper came from my left.

The charcoal-haired Underfae standing next to me was also stealing a peek at the table. He was a few inches shorter than me and wore the red-and-yellow livery of a Fire servant. His skin was ash gray, and his irises were black with a hint of flickering orange fire.

I was wary, but he smiled at me so contagiously that I couldn't help smiling back. "Are we allowed to talk?"

"No. But that never stops us."

Indeed, down the line I could see other servants whispering softly together, barely moving their lips. To my surprise, they spoke freely between houses—Illusion speaking to Fire, Light and Void sharing some piece of gossip. It was a sharp contrast to the table before us, where the Noble Fae sat in segregated clusters according to house.

If the servants shared information with one another, maybe I could start learning more about the immortality trials now. "I'm Kenna," I said.

"The human who made it through the bog, right? My name is Aidan. I'm a Fire sprite."

Weren't sprites supposed to be tiny and evil? This one was much larger than I'd expected and seemed perfectly pleasant. I was willing to bet that, once again, the human legends had been wrong. "Nice to meet you. How did you hear about me?"

"Gossip travels fast between servants. Congratulations on surviving."

I'd been so overwhelmed that I'd hardly had time to dwell on the memory of that frantic sprint for survival. It welled up now, an echo of visceral terror sliding through my veins. The dagger winding around my arm pulsed and pricked my skin, taking a small amount of my frantically coursing blood. Once again, I swore it sent me a feeling or thought. *We won*, it seemed to whisper. My heartbeat calmed, and I breathed deeply.

"The humans don't know," I said. Perhaps it was a risk to share my own confidences, but I needed to start building relationships. Besides, Aidan had greeted me with interest and friendliness, when so many of the faces around me looked hostile. "They don't know that it's just a game for the Fae. They think the humans are welcomed here and given a better life."

Aidan winced. "I heard the solstice ritual once really did exist for the purpose of uniting the two species. But at least since the king's been on the throne, it's turned into entertainment."

"How long has he ruled?"

"Eight hundred years."

It was impossible to comprehend being ruled by the same king for that long. What were the Fae rules of succession? Did he have no heirs and no desire to relinquish the throne?

There was something else that had been bothering me. "How did all the other humans get here if no one ever makes it across the bog?"

"The king sends scouts out periodically to abduct them." Aidan gave me a sympathetic look. "Sometimes for their beauty, sometimes for their strength, sometimes on a whim."

A whim that tore out tongues and forced people into servitude. I'd never imagined that sort of evil.

The doors opened, and the Noble Fae rose as four purple-liveried soldiers bearing curved blades marched in. King Osric came after them, followed by more soldiers. As the king entered, the Noble Fae and servants bowed. I scrambled to follow their example, dipping into a curtsy so deep my legs shook.

King Osric stopped at the front of the room, a glittering vision in a full-length tunic of opalescent silk. His pale hair hung straight down his back, and once again rainbow mist drifted around him. He would have been the epitome of delicate beauty were it not for the cruel black crown adorning his head.

Hate filled me. This faerie was the reason Anya was dead. His *whims* ruined lives.

"Welcome to the first event of the trial season," he said.

I stiffened. Was this the first trial already? What was Lara supposed to do? What was *I* supposed to do?

"There are nine candidates here today. Please stand."

Lara stood, along with the brown-jacketed faerie she'd been speaking with earlier. In addition to the two Earth candidates, there were two wearing white, one in orange, two in black, and two in purple.

Surprisingly few candidates, considering Alodie had said the trials were held every decade or so. Maybe this was one thing Elder Holman had gotten partially right. He'd claimed faerie births were rare—one reason why the women offered on the solstice were so important. He'd never outright said they were meant to be breeding stock, but it had been implied.

The idea hadn't sat well with me even before I'd come to Mistei and learned the truth. Now revulsion twisted my stomach—at the Fae, at Elder Holman, at every lie and perverse belief that had led me here.

"Soon you will undertake our kind's most difficult tests," Osric continued. "Six trials will be held over the coming months, each dedicated to a particular house and each designed to test a specific Fae virtue. At the end of the trials, we will learn which candidates are worthy of an immortal life and the gift of magic."

I was relieved to realize this was just lunch, not a trial. It was interesting that there were six trials but only five existing houses; perhaps this tradition was the only thing that remained of Blood House.

"I hope you will all be worthy." The king's eyes lingered on the two Earth candidates. "But I know you won't be."

Lara's gaze fell to the floor. I bit the inside of my cheek, wishing I could speak telepathically to her the way that Light servant had spoken to us. *Don't let them see*, I would say. *Lift your chin high. Fight the bastards.*

"The trials begin in one week. In the meantime, let us celebrate." The king grabbed a glass of wine from a servant and raised it. "To your success."

The king left after the toast, and conversation started up again as soon as he was gone. The Noble Fae finished the meal in a buzz of excitement and stood from the table as music began to play. The used dishes vanished, along with the table.

"Do you know anything about the trials?" Aidan whispered.

"No, do you?"

He shook his head. "I'm manservant to Edric." He nodded at the Fire candidate who was currently conversing with Drustan. "I've only served him for the last few months, and before that I was a household servant. I've never even witnessed the trials."

I suppressed my disappointment. "Maybe Prince Drustan can tell him about them." And then Aidan could tell me.

"About Fire's trial, maybe. But not about the others."

"Why not?"

"No one can remember the specifics of past trials. It's part of the magic. Once the trial season ends, the memories just vanish."

I gaped. "What?"

"It's true. The magic is very old and very powerful. The house heads only know the details of whichever trial is associated with their house this year."

I almost missed Lara's upraised hand and the snap of her fingers. Aidan's elbow in my ribs alerted me, and I rushed over.

Lara held out her empty glass, barely looking at me. "More wine."

The two candidates she stood with—male faeries from Illusion and Light—watched avidly as I curtsied.

"It really is foul, isn't it, Garrick?" the redheaded Illusion candidate asked loudly as I headed for the sideboard.

"An insult to the eyes," Garrick agreed. The Light candidate was tall and broad-chested, with short, curling brown hair, pale skin, and a heavy jaw. The collar of his white tunic was as stiff and sharp as a blade. "What would happen to a human handmaiden in Illusion House, Markas?"

Markas grinned. "I'm sure someone would have fun with her. I can't imagine Light House doing the same, though. You're all so serious."

Garrick smirked, but the look in his brown eyes as he studied me was chilling. "We don't tolerate inferior beings in Light House."

My hands trembled as I refilled Lara's glass, but I forced my face into a calm mask before returning to her.

"My lady." I curtsied deeply and handed her the glass.

"That will be all."

"I'm not surprised the king gave it to you, Lara," Garrick said. "Everyone knows you're the weakest candidate. A human would be the only suitable handmaiden."

My entire body stiffened as I stalked back to the wall. My cheeks heated with rising anger. I wanted to lunge at him, to bare my teeth and snap as I had at the bullies in Tumbledown. To strike him.

Aidan winced as I resumed my place with stone-faced dignity. This time I didn't lower my head in submission. I kept my chin raised, my eyes fixed on Lara as she suffered through the escalating taunting.

"No wonder your father died," Garrick told Lara as Markas giggled. "He was weak, too."

Lara recoiled as if she'd been struck. "That's enough, Garrick," she said, the words assertive but the tone wavering.

Garrick wouldn't be deterred. "At least he won't see you fail. Perhaps his death was a mercy, to save him from the shame." He glanced at me, then blinked as if startled to see me glaring at him. "Look at it." He elbowed Markas. "It looks like a rabid animal."

My display of defiance had gained the attention of others, as well.

The Void prince looked at me with a faint smirk. Drustan, too, was watching. There was a gleam in his eyes, as if he approved of my anger.

Appearance is everything, I reminded myself, doing my best to relax my face and unclench my jaw.

My gaze lingered on Garrick for a second longer, and then I let my eyes drift away, as if I no longer found him interesting. At the same time, I formed my fingers into a rude gesture against my skirts.

The hiss of his indrawn breath was audible. I smiled and ducked my head again.

Lara stormed over a minute later and snapped her fingers. "We're leaving."

We exited the party to the sound of cruel laughter.

LARA DIDN'T SPEAK TO ME FOR THE REST OF THE DAY, OTHER than a curt order to have food sent up to her rooms for dinner.

I went to the kitchens to deliver the order and eat a small meal, then began acquainting myself with my temporary home. Earth House was cozy but not claustrophobic. The ceilings were tall, and greenery sprang up in every corner. Occasionally I stepped over a babbling brook or passed pools where ladies bathed while servants combed or oiled their hair. It felt like being outdoors, and I relaxed as my feet sank into moss and loamy soil. I'd noticed that many faeries didn't wear shoes within the house; maybe I would try that tomorrow.

Eventually I found a comfortable room carpeted in grass. Sumptuous pillows were piled around a pond coated in water lilies, and brilliantly colored birds chirped from the branches of an overhanging tree.

I was sitting at the edge of the pond, dangling my feet in the water, when Lara's younger brother, Selwyn, found me. He still wore a yellow rose, although now it peeped out from his pocket.

I scrambled to my feet, curtsying as he approached. "Forgive me, my lord. I don't know if I'm allowed to be here."

He smiled. "You're allowed to be in any of the public areas unless asked to leave. Please, sit back down."

I hesitantly sat on a tussock of soft grass and was surprised when he lowered himself to a pillow on the opposite side of the pond. We stared at each other across the water.

"I heard you were rude to Garrick at the luncheon," he said. "He's Prince Roland's nephew, you know."

Oh, wonderful. I'd insulted Light House royalty. "He was taunting Lara."

He nodded. "I know. He's like that to everyone. I'm happy you did it."

"You are?" The response wasn't what I'd expected from the young Earth lord.

"I'm sure my mother wouldn't agree, but I like that you stood up for Lara." His dimple popped out. He looked charming and sweet, so unlike the other faeries I'd met. Then again, he looked to be sixteen years old at most—perhaps he hadn't acquired a sadistic streak yet.

"I didn't do very much."

"Yes, but you have to understand that we never do *anything*. Earth House is all about neutrality, poise, and appearances. We never glare or act rude." His frustrated tone indicated he frequently received the same lecture Lara had about acting above the insults of others. He trailed a finger through the clear water. "I'm tired of it."

I didn't know what to say in response, so I looked into the pool. Curious orange fish had emerged from the depths to investigate the ripples.

"I'm worried about Lara," Selwyn said after a long pause. "The trials are supposed to be really hard. Candidates fail every time."

"I'm sure Lara will do fine." Maybe.

Selwyn looked at me pleadingly. "Can you help her?"

"I'm going to try."

"My mother said that because you're human, you'll be able to help in unexpected ways. Has she said anything to you?"

"Yes, we discussed it." No need to mention his mother's threats—or the fact that I had no idea how much information I'd be able to uncover.

He smiled, obviously relieved. Apparently the boy had more faith in my ability to help Lara than I did. "I'm so glad." He stood, brushing off his trousers. "Anyway, I just wanted to say thank you. My sister's . . . well, she's all I have." Looking embarrassed by the confession, he quickly walked away.

I smiled as I watched the darting fish, touched by the odd encounter and by Selwyn's obvious affection for his sister. I'd thought the Noble Fae were all awful, but he'd seemed almost like a human boy, all idealism and gangly limbs. And if he loved Lara that much . . .

Maybe I should try to get to know her better.

After a few final moments with the birds, the fish, and the gentle lap of water against my toes, I rose, sighing. It was time to venture back into Mistei to learn more about my surroundings. My resolve to escape hadn't wavered, and I needed to educate myself about the city's geography as quickly as possible.

I now knew which corridors led to Light House and Fire House, and Alodie had shown me roughly where the entrances to Void House and Illusion House were so I could avoid those as well. But there were hundreds of other options, a seemingly infinite splintering of paths. I chose one at random. The dagger, still disguised as an armlet, hummed as we headed deeper underground, but the sensation felt encouraging, so I kept walking.

After long minutes on the sloping path, the light dimmed, the torches growing redder and the crystals above darkening until the ceiling spoke of twilight. I'd passed plenty of faeries at the start of my explorations, but the farther down I went, the emptier the corridors became. Eventually the walls became mottled gray-and-black stone, like a snowstorm at night, and the air grew heavy and stale. I was the only person in the corridor.

A stone archway opened on my right. A snarling beast with enormous fangs had been carved into the capstone, and the room beyond was pitch black. I shivered at the cold emanating from it and started to walk past, only to be stopped by a stinging pain on my arm.

"Ouch!" I shoved up my sleeve to glare at the dagger armband. The red jewel pulsed faintly. "Do you have to keep doing that?"

Yes, came the faint reply.

I started. That had definitely been a voice in my head, not just an impression of feeling or instinct. It was metallic and genderless and echoed as if coming from far away. The same voice that had told me to run in the bog.

I tried to suppress my shock. "Why? What are you?"

Whatever I wish. The metal shifted, and at first I thought it was just the flicker of torchlight on steel, but then I realized it had liquefied and was now writhing snakelike up my arm. It flowed from my shoulder to my neck. I raised my hands, frightened as it wrapped around my throat, but then it solidified into a necklace. The red jewel was positioned precisely in the hollow of my throat.

"Are you some kind of faerie?" I asked. What if it was one of the Nasties?

No. It seemed amused. *Different.* It sent me an impression of magic made solid, power strong enough to be alive.

"Why do you keep cutting me?"

I drink.

"Why?"

It is my way.

It wasn't an answer, but the necklace . . . dagger . . . armband . . . seemed disinclined to share more specifics. "Does it have to be my blood?"

If you won't feed me other blood, yes.

The answer sent chills through me. "Are you going to kill me?" I asked hoarsely.

No.

The answer was vehement. I swallowed, feeling the heavy shift of the jewel at my throat. "How long will you stay with me?" Was this a permanent situation, or was it looking for another host? I liked carrying a weapon and it had helped me through the bog, but now that it was speaking . . . now that it was regularly consuming small amounts of my blood . . . I didn't know.

The dagger didn't answer, but it flowed back down my arm and settled into the familiar spiral around my bicep, as if sensing my discomfort at having it wrapped around my throat. Apparently it could take whatever form it wanted—or perhaps whichever form *I* wanted. It would turn into a dagger again if that was what I needed.

It thrummed in agreement, and I knew it enjoyed being a dagger best of all. Flashes of violence rose in my mind—blood spraying, warm and rich and so very delicious . . .

I shook my head to dispel the vision, feeling disturbed. I started heading back down the path, but the dagger bit me again.

"Stop that!" I glared at it.

Then I heard it. Footsteps, coming from the path behind me. The dagger was warning me about someone.

I ducked into the pitch-black room. The alternating black-and-white stone tiles beneath my feet, barely visible in the reflected glow from the corridor, were carved with more nightmarish monsters. The stale air held a faint hint of spice. I braced myself, but nothing moved in the blackness.

The footsteps drew closer. I edged back until I was cloaked in darkness.

It was the deadly Void prince and another black-clad faerie. Based on their matching dark eyes, pale skin, and the raven's-wing sheen of their hair, they were probably related, but while the prince projected cold menace, his longer-haired companion gave an impression of ferocity and barely leashed violence. His movements were sharp and restless, and his hand hovered over the hilt of his dagger.

". . . would be foolish," the long-haired one was saying.

"Regardless, Fire has made its decision," the prince said calmly. "We must—" He paused, stopping dead in the corridor. His head snapped to the side, and he looked into the room. I held my breath, suddenly terrified he could see me. Could Void faeries see in the dark? Was that one of their talents? I cursed myself for not asking Drustan.

"What is it?" The long-haired one started turning to look as well, but the prince smoothly ushered him along.

"Nothing. Sometimes I swear that hall echoes with ghosts."

The long-haired one laughed. "If only ghosts could wield swords."

"Let's talk about the labyrinth," the prince said as they disappeared from view. "We're almost prepared . . ." I strained to hear the rest, but his voice faded into nothingness.

I waited for long, anxious minutes until I felt sure they weren't coming back. My neck prickled with unease, both at what I'd overheard and at the yawning blackness behind me. Whatever this echoing room was, with its ghosts and cold air and the subtle hint of spice, I couldn't let anyone know I'd come here.

Never, the dagger agreed.

9

ORIANA WAS VISITING LARA WHEN I BROUGHT HER BREAKfast the next morning. I deposited the tray on a table and curtsied, but when I started to leave, Oriana stopped me. "Stay. I'm almost done." She frowned at Lara. "As I was saying, I'm disappointed in your comportment yesterday. You should have remained for the entire event."

"They were only going to insult me more," Lara said sullenly.

"You must be hard as stone. Treat their insults with the disinterest they deserve."

Lara sipped from her mug of tea, casting me a glance. I could tell she was embarrassed that I was witnessing this scolding.

"Do better, and don't forget that your actions reflect on all of us. I will not allow you to humiliate Earth House." Oriana swept out of the room, and the door clicked shut behind her.

Lara's posture sagged, and she stared blankly at the far wall.

I moved the breakfast tray closer to her. "Here. Eat this while I choose an outfit."

She obeyed, eating slowly as if rote actions were all she could

manage. I felt a wave of pity. She must feel like a constant disappointment to Oriana.

"What events are you attending today?" Maybe I could distract her.

"A party," she said distantly. "And then a formal dinner."

Two outfits to plan. Two hairstyles. I didn't know if I could manage it, but I would try my best.

I selected a chestnut-brown dress for the party that fit tightly in
the sleeves and bodice but flared out into voluminous folds. The
hem and neckline were lined with sapphires and emeralds, and the
wrists were draped with delicate blond lace.

Lara let me dress her in silence. I ushered her into the bathing
room, where I fiddled with cosmetics until I found a combination
that might look good with the dress. She held still as I applied sweep-
ing brown-and-gold eye shadow and pink lipstick. It didn't look as
good as what she had done yesterday, but it would do.

Anya would laugh uproariously if she could see me now, I
thought as I brushed Lara's hair. She had been the one interested in
beautiful things. She would have been rolling on the ground with
hilarity as she watched me trying so hard to fit in to this opulent
world.

I blinked back tears, then realized Lara was watching me in the
mirror. "Forgive me."

"Tell me," she commanded.

Her hair reminded me of Anya's. Not the color—Anya's had been
golden brown—but the length, wave, and shine were similar. I
brushed Lara's hair gently, wishing with all my heart that Anya were
here with me. "My best friend died. When we ran across the bog."

Lara's expression softened. "I'm sorry."

A tear rolled down my cheek at the simple kindness, but I dashed
it away. "I can't help thinking about her. She would have been much

better at all of this than I am." I waved the brush to encompass the clothes, the makeup, everything.

Lara was silent as I started on the hairstyle. Today I'd do three simple braids that met at the back of her head with the rest hanging loose.

"My older brother is dead," Lara finally said. She raised a hand to cut off my sympathy. "I never knew him. He was the son of Oriana's first consort, and he was . . . He died the year before I was born. But he had already passed the trials. He was meant to be the next prince of Earth House, if Oriana were ever to relinquish the position. He would have been much better at all of this, too." She laughed bitterly. "Even Selwyn would have been a better choice for the heir, but he's only sixteen and I'm twenty-three, so it falls to me."

I braided her hair carefully, grateful for the gesture of trust. "So we are both ill-suited for our positions." When she didn't respond, even to snap at me, I smiled at her in the mirror. "That's why they'll never expect it when we succeed."

After a few moments, Lara smiled hesitantly back.

THE PARTY WAS HELD AT FIRE HOUSE. I PRETENDED NOT TO KNOW where we were going as Lara and I ascended the spiraling ramp. As had happened at Light House, we stopped short of the fiery hall itself, instead turning into one of the rooms near the top of the ramp.

The walls were lined with iridescent velvet that shifted from crimson to gold depending on one's position in the room, and the ceiling had been painted to resemble billows of smoke. Faeries stood around small tables, sipping flaming beverages and nibbling at small plates of food.

Aidan cast me a quick grin as I squeezed in next to him at the wall. "Welcome to Fire House."

"It's beautiful." The aesthetic was simple and elegant, the main decoration provided by those mysteriously shifting walls. Flames danced in an enormous fireplace at the back of the room. "So what is this event?"

The sprite rolled his eyes. "Same as the others. They talk, they eat, they insult each other in various witty ways."

I stifled a laugh. "You seem disenchanted."

"Let's just say I miss the days when I didn't need to attend these gatherings."

I studied his master, the sole candidate from Fire House. Edric was slim and charismatic, with dark skin and a cloud of inky hair. Rubies glittered on his fingers as he illustrated some point to the admiring ladies gathered around him. His crimson tunic reached to his polished black boots, and firelight played across more rubies sewn into the garment.

"Is Edric ready for the trials?" I asked.

Aidan looked at me with affront. "Of course. He's brave. He'll do well."

I bit my lip, wishing the same could be said of Lara. "Is the first trial the Fire trial?"

"I don't know." Aidan glanced back at Edric. "I assume not, since he hasn't mentioned anything to me."

We watched and listened as the Noble Fae glided around the room, greeting one another with false smiles. Three of the candidates gathered nearby, and I could tell by their gowns that they hailed from Void, Illusion, and Light.

"Which virtue do you think you'll do best at, Karissa?" the Light candidate, a willowy brunette, asked.

"Hedonism, of course." The Illusion candidate dimpled. Karissa's red hair was darker than the male Illusion candidate, Markas's—his was coppery, but hers gleamed the same crimson as the walls. "And of course you will excel at cunning, Gytha."

Gytha laughed. "Of course. Also at hedonism, I dare say." She smiled poisonously at the Void candidate. "I'm not really sure what your strengths are, Una."

Una smiled back coolly. Her black hair was braided in a thick plait to her waist, her dress bore no ornamentation, and she hadn't bothered to apply any cosmetics—not that her sharply beautiful features or glowing russet-brown skin required augmentation. "Yes, I prefer not to be so obvious," she said with delicate emphasis, casting a dismissive glance over Gytha's overwrought ivory gown.

I suppressed a snicker.

Gytha and Karissa left after that, arms linked and heads bent together as they shared what I presumed was some piece of malicious gossip. With no one else to talk to, Una drifted around the room. She stopped beside the Void prince and the long-haired faerie I'd overheard him speaking with last night. She didn't seem intimidated in the slightest by them.

"Who are they?" I asked Aidan, nodding at the midnight-hued trio.

"You really don't know?"

"If I knew, I wouldn't have asked."

"That's Prince Hector, Lord Kallen, and Lady Una of Void House. They're siblings—Hector is the eldest, Kallen the second, and Una the youngest and a half-sibling." He paused, then lowered his voice even further. "They had other siblings a long time ago, but they were all killed during the rebellion."

The rebellion five hundred years ago, the one that had been the end of Blood House. I matched his whispering tone. "Did Hector and Kallen . . . participate?"

Aidan shook his head. "They were born after the rebellion. Their father, the previous Void prince, was spared after he bent the knee. Hector has no children, so Kallen is his heir."

"Hector seems close to the king," I observed, remembering how he'd been standing to Osric's left when I'd first arrived. Now that I recognized house colors, I realized his opal brooch was a tribute to Illusion House and the king.

Aidan cast me an odd glance. "You must be thinking of Kallen. The long-haired one is Prince Hector. He rarely visits court. I'm actually surprised to see him today."

I looked back at the trio, reassessing my earlier judgment. The long-haired, fierce-looking brother was Prince Hector? He must be exceptionally powerful, considering how terrifying his younger brother was. Kallen had brutally murdered someone in front of hundreds of Noble Fae without changing expression; what was his older brother capable of?

As if sensing my stare, Kallen looked at me.

I dropped my eyes immediately.

"Careful," Aidan whispered. "They call Kallen the King's Vengeance. He spies and kills for the king, and they say nothing goes on in Mistei that he doesn't know about. Some servants say you shouldn't even think about him or he'll know it and appear out of thin air."

I shivered, thinking of how he had stared into the blackened chamber I'd been hiding in. "That seems unlikely. Right?"

Aidan chuckled. "They aren't gods, you know."

Diverted by the talk of gods, I realized I knew little about Fae religion. In Tumbledown, we'd worshipped faint, inaccurate memories of the Fae—the echoes of something that now, laid bare to my sight, I knew hadn't been worthy of worship at all. "Do the Fae worship any gods?" I asked, wondering what these vain, violent, terrifying creatures would hold sacred.

"No. We worship the magic itself," Aidan said. "More specifically, we worship the six Sacred Shards it originally came from. You'll see the Shards depicted in artwork throughout Mistei—they're rumored to have fallen from the sky long ago."

I hadn't noticed yet, but I would look for it. "Six Shards, six trials, six virtues." Six years between sacrifices of innocent human victims, too. "What are the virtues?" I asked past the flare of anger at the thought of the solstice ritual.

"Courage, discipline, cunning, strength, hedonism, and magic."

I wrinkled my nose. "Hedonism doesn't sound like a virtue."

"To the Fae it is." His eyes flickered like embers. "Don't tell me humans have forgotten how much we revel in trickery and pleasure."

How exactly did they plan to test hedonism, and did I have to watch? "Our village Elder chose to omit the part about pleasure."

"The human world sounds dull."

I considered the gorgeous room before me full of duplicitous, dangerous faeries. "I suppose it is." It certainly seemed that way now—a place of poverty and small-minded people. Then I thought of the glorious pink wash of sunrise over the bog, the open sky, and the scent of growing things. The wonder I'd felt after finding unknown relics. The simple pleasure of spending an afternoon with a friend.

I couldn't tell him I wanted to go back. That would show weakness. So I thought of Lara and pasted a bored look on my face.

"It won't work, you know," Aidan said.

"What won't?"

"Trying to pretend you don't miss it." His dark irises were now almost entirely overcome with flame, and his face shone with crafty intelligence rather than his usual geniality.

"Why is that?"

He grinned, and the intensity immediately drained out of him. "Sprites have a small gift, but a very useful one. We can sense secret desires." His gaze returned to Edric, and I wondered what he'd learned about his master over the last few months.

"What do you do with that information?" Could he sense my plan to escape? Or did he simply know that I missed the human world?

"Whatever we like. Mischief, for some. Making bargains. Or simply using the information to better know the people we're close to."

"What do you *specifically* use it for?" I was growing tired of faerie evasion.

He chuckled. "I like you. You don't talk around things. You ask what you want to know."

"And do you answer?"

His smile was so bright it eased some of my wariness. "I don't use it for anything. I just like to know people. Although if I were to sense something dangerous to Fire House, that would be a different matter."

My secret desires had nothing to do with Fire House, so I felt safe there. I returned my attention to the party, watching Lara fake a smile at something Gytha was saying. The other Light candidate, Garrick, watched their interplay with a sneer on his face, then interjected with some cruel witticism that made Gytha laugh and Lara flush.

"You faeries certainly make it hard to trust," I told Aidan.

"Good," he said. "It's dangerous to trust down here. Protect yourself and those closest to you and stay wary."

I felt like I'd seen three different Aidans in only two days. The cheerful servant, the tricky sprite, and the cynical voice of caution.

What was I to make of this odd Underfae? "You seem . . . complicated."

His snort was loud enough to attract the notice of nearby nobles. He looked down instantly, suppressing his chuckles, although his shoulders still shook.

"What's so funny?"

"You. You're very straightforward by Fae standards. It's a rare trait."

I was getting accustomed to faerie insults. "You mean I'm simple."

"Oh no, not at all. You're complicated in a different way." Those fiery eyes met mine again. "It should make the next few months interesting."

Edric snapped his beringed fingers, and Aidan sprang to attention. "One more thing," he whispered. "The first test is Void. The trait is courage. And knowing them, it'll be conducted in complete darkness."

He winked at my shocked expression and walked away.

I WAS DESPERATE TO ASK AIDAN MORE ABOUT THE FIRST TRIAL, but the party concluded soon after that, and Lara and I made our way back to Earth House.

"Well?" she asked as we entered the water tunnel. A kaleidoscope of fish darted around us. "Did you learn anything from the other servants?"

"I did, actually." I had no idea why Aidan had changed his mind and told me about the first trial, but he had. Because he liked me? Because it amused him? "The first test is Void and courage. It will likely happen in complete darkness." I thought back to the conversation I'd overheard yesterday between Prince Hector and the deadly Lord Kallen. If Void's test was first . . . "I heard something about a labyrinth, too, but I'm not sure if that's related or not."

"Oh, Shards," Lara said. The faerie equivalent of a curse? "It probably is."

Rather than heading to her room, she stopped at a different door carved to depict a pine forest and a cascading waterfall. She knocked, then beckoned for me to follow her inside.

This room was even larger than Lara's, and for a moment it didn't seem like a room at all. Living trees lined every wall, their branches twining together to form a verdant ceiling that mirrored the lush grass underfoot. The furniture—a variety of sturdy oak desks, dressers, and velvet-upholstered chairs—seemed oddly out of place, as if the pieces had been dropped into a forest clearing by a whimsical hand. A behemoth of a green-curtained bed loomed from behind a folding screen.

Oriana sat at her desk, writing. She looked up as Lara entered. "Did the party go well?" she asked.

Lara sat on a deep-cushioned couch. "It did. Gytha and Garrick are vipers, but you already knew that."

"Did you react?"

"No, I was perfectly stoic. Kenna heard some interesting gossip, though."

Oriana's gaze flicked to me, and I curtsied. "I heard that the first trial will be Void and courage, and that the test will likely be in total darkness."

"And?" Lara prompted.

"A separate conversation I overheard mentioned a labyrinth."

Oriana's indrawn breath was audible. "Of course," she muttered, discarding her quill pen and turning to face us fully. "Void House has always delighted in extremes."

I had no idea what they were talking about. I glanced at Lara, but her attention was fixed on her mother. "If it's the Labyrinth of Chaos, I don't know much about it. Only that it's pitch black and supposedly impossible to escape."

"It can't be impossible or no one would ever have passed the test. Assuming this is the same test they've done in previous years, of course. I don't know."

Because her memory had been magically erased. I supposed it made sense—if the trials happened every decade or so and the Fae lived forever, they would quickly run out of new tests.

"The Labyrinth of Chaos is a legend," Oriana explained. "No living faerie outside of Void House has ever been inside it, at least that we can remember. It's where they once executed their prisoners. They would release them at the edge of the labyrinth with no light or supplies and tell them to find their way out."

Lara leaned forward. "That doesn't sound impossible. Some of them must have survived."

"Perhaps. There are two things that make the labyrinth so difficult, though. One of them is Void's love of chaos. The labyrinth isn't orderly. There are no patterns. Every path you take will be different— a different angle, a different width, a different length or slope. From above, it would probably look like nothing but abstract scribbling. It will be hard to remember where you've come from."

Lara grimaced. "What's the second thing?"

"There are monsters in the labyrinth. Flesh-eating Nasties. The only way to escape is to find the exit before the Nasties find you."

Silence fell over the room.

"Oh," Lara finally said.

Oh, indeed.

10

THE DAY WASN'T OVER YET.

King Osric was holding a formal dinner, and unlike previous events, this one would include most of the Noble Fae. That meant thousands of eyes on Lara.

I stared at her unbound hair with dread.

She'd already applied cosmetics herself, claiming it was too important to trust me with. Now she sat impatiently waiting for me to craft a hairstyle worthy of the king.

"All I know how to do is braid," I said in a small voice.

She made an exasperated noise. "Just braid it and pin it up."

Everything I did was a mess. The braids sagged or the hair pulled out of them or they jumbled together like a tangle of snakes. I was near tears an hour later, and we weren't any closer to being done.

Lara snatched the brush and pins from me. "Give me that," she snapped. She yanked aggressively at the knots I'd created, then bound her hair up, fixing it with a small band before braiding the hair into sections. "Here. Do it in three plaits. Then wind them around, pinning as you go."

Somehow, between the two of us, we wrestled her hair into an enormous bundle of braids on the back of her head. I was panting with exertion by the time it was done.

"Please start practicing," Lara said as she rose. "I'm honestly embarrassed for you."

She was wearing the ball gown I'd initially chosen for the Light House lunch. The ivory satin fell in decadent waves to her feet, and the emeralds lining the bodice glittered with every movement. When I'd tried to select a simpler dress, she'd informed me that ball gowns were appropriate for formal dinners because dinners always concluded with dancing. I had a feeling I'd never understand all the rules of the Fae court.

She looked at my sweat-stained dress and tangled hair. "Make yourself presentable."

I tried. The wardrobe in my room provided an evergreen gown with half sleeves decorated with embroidered vines. I bound my hair into a simple bun, using what must have been a thousand pins to keep it in place. When I returned, she inspected me from all angles. "It'll do."

When we emerged, Oriana complimented Lara's gown while Selwyn pretended to gag behind her back. Lara suppressed a smile at her brother's antics and swept down the stairs. As I followed, I wondered how she managed to look so elegant all the time. Did young Fae girls practice that precise angle of the head, that swaying stride? I wanted to look elegant, too.

Anya would have laughed at that sentiment, maybe even harder than she would have laughed at my attempts to apply cosmetics. She'd always been naturally graceful, though—her chin had often tipped in that same angle Lara had mastered, like she was a queen without a court.

Oh, Anya, I thought sadly. *I wish you were here.*

We passed the throne room and descended a wide ramp into a cavernous space. It was shockingly enormous, at least ten stories tall, and I could easily believe the entire Noble Fae population of Mistei would fit inside in their many thousands. Natural stone columns rose to the distant ceiling, where an array of stalactites hung like teeth.

The clink of glasses and the murmur of conversation echoed off stone. Hundreds of round tables had been set up within that vast chamber. The tablecloths displayed the colors of the five houses, and crystal glasses winked under the illumination of floating faerie lights. A dais in the center of the room held a table draped in opalescent lace, and the candleholders atop it were shaped like six jagged stones in red, purple, green, orange, black, and white. A depiction of the Sacred Shards, presumably.

Servants lined up between the tables, their eyes politely downcast. I was dismayed to realize Lara's table was situated in the very center of the room, mere feet from the dais. There were nine place settings, one for each candidate. I joined the line of servants, nodding to the unknown Void servant next to me. Aidan stood farther down the line, but I couldn't force my way in to stand next to him with so many eyes on us.

Within minutes, every table had been filled. Once again, the noble houses were segregated. It gave the chamber the appearance of a patchwork quilt—here a patch of onyx, there a cluster of shimmering violet. Other than the candidates' table, the only table with any variety was atop the dais, where the king sat with the house heads and Lord Kallen.

Underfae in purple livery dashed around the room bearing wine and water. It seemed my job as handmaiden was to stand as stiffly and quietly as possible, ignoring the ache in my feet as I waited for Lara's snap. A decorative servant rather than a useful one, an accessory she could coordinate to her gown.

Jugglers with mirrorlike skin and eight arms apiece moved between tables, the dozens of balls they threw shining like tiny suns. Hundreds of glittering pixies flew in formation above, creating graceful patterns in the air until the room was aglow with motion and light.

A feast shimmered into existence on the tables, and I stifled a gasp at both the magic and the opulence. There were dozens of varieties of roasted birds, some with fans of bright feathers still attached. They alternated with tureens of soup, soft cheeses, bread so warm it steamed, and mounded salads topped with berries. I watched Lara take small bites of everything, my stomach grumbling in envious want.

The bounty was already more than the assembled guests could possibly eat, but an ululating horn announced the arrival of another course. Entire roasted stags and pigs were carried in on long poles, the ends braced by straining servants. The meat glistened under the faerie light, succulent and juicy. More servants set up stands beside the tables in which to slot the ends of the poles, and then a troop of muscular Underfae with bared bellies and small, bat-like wings arrived beside the meat, bearing two swords apiece. They began an intricate, swirling sword dance, and with every spin, slices of meat dropped onto waiting plates.

The manservants and handmaidens had stopped all pretense of looking at the floor, and we watched avidly as the dancers increased their pace. The deadly steel flashed so quickly that soon I couldn't track the dancers' movements. I was aware only of long arcs of silver as the faeries danced a web of violence over the room.

When it was over, each carcass was stripped to the bone.

The Noble Fae had watched the performance with mild amusement or indifference. I supposed every novelty grew stale after a few centuries, but I remained shaken by the artful play of blades. I wanted to move like that: like silk and lightning, like elegant death.

Learn, the dagger purred in my mind.

And who will teach me? I thought back at it, wondering if it could hear. The blade seemed amused but didn't reply.

The dinner plates were replaced by sumptuous desserts. Each candidate received a different one, as if the cooks had accounted for the individual tastes of every faerie in attendance. Lara's dessert consisted of a pastry so light it seemed to float. A dusting of sugar and a pool of red sauce decorated the plate around it. As she punctured the pastry with her fork, cream oozed out. She mixed each bite of pastry with the sauce, and her eyes closed blissfully at the first bite.

Dessert. That was a concept I'd never had the chance to grow overly familiar with. It could be found at some formal events in Tumbledown, like weddings or festivals, but my mother and I had rarely had the luxury of considering anything but our most basic needs. I desperately hoped someone was saving the leftovers and that the servants would get to sample them.

King Osric stood, drawing every eye. Conversation and the clink of silverware faded.

"Welcome, friends." His magically amplified voice echoed through the room. He smiled, and I was struck again by how beautiful he was. His silver doublet was topped with a froth of lace that stretched to his chin, and his tight-fitting trousers were of shining amethyst satin. With a rainbow of jewels on his fingers and glittering powder in his pale hair, he looked like a delicate, exotic dessert himself—except for the brutal crown. "Tonight we celebrate the first immortality trial, which will occur in only a few days. Let us raise a toast to our candidates. May they bring glory to their houses."

The Noble Fae raised their glasses. Every glass now contained dark red wine, rather than the variety of beverages they had been drinking before.

"These formal dinners bring me joy," King Osric continued. "It's not just the sight of so many of my subjects gathered in one place, but also what these dinners represent—our commitment to work together for the good of Mistei. We have diverse gifts but one history. It is only together, united under my rule, that we can be truly strong."

He paused, one hand extended in a dramatic orator's pose as he drew out the tension. As his hand dropped, Osric sighed. "I regret that not everyone agrees with this sentiment."

I heard the creak of heavy doors opening, but I couldn't look away from the king. He captured my attention utterly, and I had the unsettling sensation he would know the second my gaze wandered. A flickering white light veined with swirling rainbows emanated from him, intensifying until his entire body was encased in it. He glowed like a star, but I could still see that beautiful, stern face as he fixed his attention on whoever was approaching.

"Behold," he said. "The enemies of Mistei."

A procession of faeries was making its way between the tables. In front were two winged guards dressed in white, each wielding a razor-sharp axe. Just like the servant who had greeted us at Light House, these had no mouths, but their eyes were pure white, rather than gold. Each wore a single bloodred jewel on a chain around their necks.

I stifled a gasp as I realized what followed behind.

Eight prisoners of varying species shuffled forward in a line, their wrists bound to a shared chain. As they mounted the steps to the dais, an anguished cry sounded from somewhere behind me, only to be cut off immediately. The king's lips curled.

"Yes, it is shocking." He stared in the direction of the cry with a wicked smile. The blinding glow of his skin had dimmed to just a hint of radiance. "Shocking to understand that after so long, there are still those who wish to tear this kingdom apart."

My stomach sank. Something awful was about to happen less than twenty feet from me.

Five of the prisoners were Underfae. They wore tattered gray robes, so I couldn't tell which houses they had once belonged to. Perhaps that was the point; once you betrayed the king, you no longer belonged anywhere. Three of them were asrai, although their coloring ranged from black to golden, rather than Alodie's pale blue. One was a female sprite, and the last was a short faerie whose gossamer wings identified him as a sylph.

The other three, though, were what drew my attention.

I knew instantly that two of them were Nasties. One had the flat head and flicking tongue of a snake, albeit one ten times larger than any snake I'd ever seen, but its long body also possessed arms. Pale ooze dripped down its scales to pool on the floor. The other Nasty looked like a naked man from the neck down, but his skin was burnished brick red and he had the horned head of a bull. His eyes were positioned at the front of his face like a predator's, and they shone with cunning.

The final prisoner was Noble Fae. His posture was straight and tall under the shapeless robe, though his sternly beautiful face was shadowed with exhaustion. The glimmer of his complexion seemed dull in comparison to the rest of the Noble Fae, as if it had been muted by some ordeal.

Osric turned to Prince Hector of Void House. "This is one of yours, I believe."

Hector studied the prisoner coldly. "I disavow him."

"And yet he belonged to your house when he was overheard wishing for my death."

"I had no knowledge of this."

"Normally the prince of a house would be tainted by association. Do you know why I will choose to believe you this once?"

Hector crossed his arms and looked at the king with an expression that veered dangerously close to boredom. "Because I speak the truth?"

King Osric smiled. "Because Lord Kallen was the one who informed me of his treason."

Hector glanced at Kallen, but the King's Vengeance sat in stony silence, seemingly unconcerned at having betrayed a member of his own house. "We are loyal to you, my king," Hector said, returning his gaze to Osric. "If I had known, I would have told you first. There is no mercy for traitors in Void House."

Osric clapped his hands, and the cracking sound made me twitch despite my determination to remain stoic. "Excellent. Then the honor of executing this one shall fall to you."

Somewhere a faerie began weeping.

After a pause that set the hairs on my arms upright, Hector stood and bowed. "It is a privilege, my king."

I braced myself for violence. The prince would stab the traitor, or perhaps behead him . . . but all Hector did was stand before him, sword sheathed.

"You should not have spoken," he said. "You know the laws."

The prisoner nodded once and bowed his head.

A dark circle appeared in the air to the prisoner's right, and another blossomed to his left. I squinted, trying to understand what they were. They started small, the size of a coin, but quickly expanded. They gave me chills. It felt like a fundamental piece of the world was missing, as if a hole had been torn in the air and something black and suffocating showed through the rip.

The two expanding spots reached the prisoner at the same time. He screamed once as he was ripped completely in half. Each half crumpled, compressing with horrifying rapidity until the pieces were sucked inside the holes. Even the violent spray of blood hung in the air for less than a blink before the darkness consumed it.

As abruptly as they had appeared, the holes vanished.

There was nothing left of the faerie. My ears rang with his

scream, but I couldn't tell if it was my shock or if his cry still echoed through the cavern.

What *was* that power?

I stifled the urge to vomit as I remembered the awful ripping sound as his body had been torn in two. His blood had floated in the air like sparkling rubies before vanishing forever, and now there was nothing of him to bury, nothing for the now-wailing faerie somewhere in the crowd to mourn over.

Hector raised a hand, and the crying cut off instantly. His hand shone white and unblemished; no trace of the murder he had just committed remained on those elegant fingers. His face hadn't even changed expression. He calmly took his seat, picked up his fork, and ate a bite of chocolate cake.

The king laughed. The hair on my neck rose as his laughter rolled through the hall, light and musical, lasting for so long that even a few of the faeries on the dais shifted uncomfortably in their seats. Osric was insane, I realized. Or if not insane, so far removed from humanity—if it could be termed that—that he truly found joy in this moment.

He raised his glass. "A toast! To the annihilation of the unworthy."

The assembled Fae drank. I watched the bloodred liquid swirl in Lara's glass as she set it down. Her fingers were trembling, but she hid them in her lap, and her face remained calm. Across from her, the Light candidate Garrick was studying the line of prisoners with a look of sick anticipation. He returned his attention to Lara's carefully blank face and smirked.

"More wine." Every glass on the table was abruptly filled to the brim. Osric laughed again. "For the servants, too. Let us all drink together."

A cup hovered in the air before me, and I took it numbly.

"Drink," the king commanded.

We drank.

The wine was richer than any I'd tasted before. Beneath the familiar tang were hints of cinnamon and pepper, but the aftertaste contained a horrifying coppery note. I choked it down.

"Prince Drustan." The king gestured lazily, his rings glittering in the light. "There are seven criminals left. Surely you can eliminate one for me?"

A muscle flexed in Drustan's jaw as he folded his napkin carefully. "Of course. It would be an honor." The Fire prince rose, looking so bored I wondered if I had imagined that ticking muscle.

He approached one of the asrai. It was over almost instantly. A pillar of white-hot flame rose from the ground, swallowing the faerie whole. She died without screaming, leaving a pile of ash and bone fragments behind.

Drustan returned to his seat with the same casual air Hector had assumed, but he didn't touch his dessert again.

The other house heads followed, and each death was a horrifying display of power and brutality.

Oriana looked mildly amused as she pulled a green bracelet from her wrist and tossed it at an asrai. Not a bracelet—a vine. It latched on to the prisoner, elongating and winding around him with stunning speed, binding his arms to his sides as it sent new tendrils snaking over him. At first I thought she would suffocate him, but what she did instead was far worse. The vines tunneled *into* the faerie's body, winding through every limb while he screamed, and then they tore him apart into small chunks.

Unlike Hector's method of execution, this one was slow, and it left plenty of blood behind. Ruby liquid dripped off the dais and pooled on the floor, and spatters of it painted the sky-blue silk of Oriana's ball gown. She frowned as if disappointed a favorite dress had been stained before returning calmly to her seat.

We raised our glasses.

We drank.

Roland, Prince of Light, took the sprite. When he raised his hands, a light flashed on the dais, so bright I had to look away, so bright that even with my eyes squeezed shut I felt it against my skin. It took several seconds for the afterimage to fade enough for me to see what had happened.

The sprite's eyes overflowed with blood instead of tears as she stumbled forward with outstretched arms. He'd blinded her. Roland laughed as she staggered, as if this was a game they were playing, that of the hunter and his helpless prey. Then he grabbed one of the guards' axes and cut off her head. It fell to the floor with a wet thud.

We raised our glasses.

We drank.

I didn't know what any of the faeries had done to deserve this, other than the Noble Fae who had wished for the king's death. Was that all it took to be declared a traitor? Expressing a single doubt about the king or his rule?

There were four victims left—the two Nasties, the sylph, and a final asrai. The Nasties looked furious, but the two Underfae trembled in sheer terror.

Would each house head have to kill again? I braced myself, wondering if the murders would be the same or if there were other ways for them to kill. Could Oriana drown a person from within with her water power? Could she bury them alive? How would Roland murder if he used his powers alone, rather than taking a life with his hands?

"It seems the bulk of the work has been left to me," King Osric announced. "I'm grateful for it. It's always a pleasure to fight for my kingdom. Let these lives serve as a reminder of your king's strength and the price of treason."

His skin glowed, and wisps of iridescent magic twined around his fingers. His hair lifted as if he stood within a lightning storm, each pale strand glittering. "Unchain them," he told the guards.

The guards didn't move, but the shackles fell from the prisoners. The two Nasties immediately bolted, the sylph launched into the air, and the asrai ran, only to slip and fall in a puddle of blood. The king laughed as she scrambled away, smearing crimson across the floor.

What was he doing? The prisoners were fleeing, the bull-headed Nasty so fast he was almost out the door. I desperately wanted them to escape, Nasty or not. It didn't matter what they had done; nothing could be worth this torment.

King Osric raised his hands, and the prisoners stopped. They didn't freeze in place; rather, they blundered around as if lost in a darkened room. The bull-headed Nasty ducked and spun, growling as he fought an unseen assailant. The sylph screamed and dove as if trying to escape something. I waited for him to stop, but he kept flying, down, down, down, until he crashed into the dais with bone-shattering impact.

The two Nasties were fleeing again, but this time they ran towards the dais. The asrai had stopped trying to escape; she lay dreamily in the pool of blood, moving her arms and legs through it the way I'd once made Fae shapes in the snow with Anya.

Osric was casting illusions and showing each of them something different. He was changing their perception of where they were, who was around them, and where they needed to go.

The winged faerie wept as he dragged his broken body over the floor, and I wanted to weep, too. I was going to vomit if I had to watch this much longer. There was so much blood; the scent of it hung thick in the air.

At the high table, Oriana still looked bored, although she gripped her wineglass tightly. Hector continued eating his cake, but Kallen stared straight ahead with unfocused eyes, as if even he didn't want to take in the details of this slow execution. Drustan glared at the king's back, smoke rising from his clenched fists. Only Roland seemed to share the king's enthusiasm for the kill; his mouth curved in a vicious grin. The smile was mirrored by his nephew, Garrick, the sole candidate at Lara's table who seemed pleased by the violence.

I understood why Fire, Void, and Blood had rebelled. To destroy a tyrant who laughed at butchery, who had held the throne for centuries by mercilessly eliminating any challengers, even those with no power to defy him at all.

The performance must have been nearing its end, because Osric had gathered all four back on the dais. They looked at one another, but I knew they were seeing whatever he had chosen to show them.

Osric flicked his fingers, and they tore each other apart.

Maybe he had shown them soldiers coming to kill them. Maybe he had forced them to envision themselves trapped underground and clawing through the dirt for air. I didn't know what they saw, but they used their hands and claws, ripping, shredding, screaming.

The last one standing was the bull-headed Nasty, who calmly walked to one of the guards, grabbed an axe, and cut off his own arm. He bled out silently.

"Four drinks," King Osric crowed, raising his glass as the Nasty slumped at his feet. "And then it's time for dancing."

I FLED THE CAVERN, SOBBING.

I was going to vomit. *Not yet not yet not yet*, I silently chanted. I hadn't passed anyone but a few startled humans carrying baskets of linens, but anyone could be watching in the public spaces.

The dancing had started almost immediately after the massacre. Moments after we finished our final toast, the blood and gore had vanished, along with the wineglasses and tables. The Noble Fae began mingling as the chairs were whisked away as well. Then delicate, lively music floated in from above, played by winged Underfae with flutes and lyres.

I had managed to escape shortly afterwards. Lara had taken one look at my face and jerked her head, clearly dismissing me to compose myself. She had looked shaken, too, her eyes damp, but she'd taken a few deep breaths, downed an entire glass of wine, and pasted a smile on her face before accepting an invitation to dance. Her first partner had unfortunately been Garrick, who had commented on her reddened eyes before clutching her hand so hard I worried he would break her bones. Despite Garrick's insults and cruel grip, Lara had managed to remain composed. I knew she'd been aware of Oriana watching and judging the entire time.

I wasn't capable of faking calm after what had happened. Bile rose in my throat. So much blood. So much pain.

The dagger nipped at my arm, jolting me back into my own skin. I swallowed heavily. I didn't have a destination in mind, but the blade did, and I followed where it urged. Soon the torches dimmed to red, the temperature dropped, and a faint spicy scent drifted through the air.

We had returned to the pitch-black room where I had hidden the previous day. I bolted inside and immediately sank to my knees. My stomach heaved, but I hadn't eaten much today, and all that came up was a thin stream of acid that burned my throat. I moaned and dropped my head to the ground, panting and crying.

The darkness no longer seemed frightening but comforting, like a blanket wrapped around my shoulders. The most horrifying thing I'd ever seen hadn't been concealed by darkness but performed under bright lights in front of thousands. My fear of an empty room was laughable in comparison.

I thought of my mother as I wept, of her desperate, optimistic faith in the Fae. She'd died with a prayer on her lips, and for what? These monsters had been the object of her dearest hopes, but they were nowhere near worthy of it.

I sat upright at last, wiping away tears and snot. My hair had fallen loose during my run, and tendrils of it clung damply to my temples and fell in heavy tangles down my back. My green gown was wet with sweat. I wouldn't be presentable when I returned to the cavern, but maybe if I stood in a corner no one would notice.

"Why did you come here?"

I shrieked and scrambled farther into the room at the unknown male voice. "Who's there?" I couldn't see anything in the darkness around me, and no one was silhouetted in the doorway.

"Quiet." A tall figure edged into the pool of light from the hallway, and I recognized Lord Kallen of Void House.

I recoiled. "You followed me." My heart was pounding so hard I thought I might faint, and my legs shook too badly for me to rise.

"Not precisely." He sank into what he probably meant to be a nonthreatening crouch just inside the room. It only reminded me of a predator readying to pounce. "I warded the doorway so I would know if you decided to go exploring again."

My stomach dropped. "You saw me." He could see in the dark after all, which meant this was it. He would accuse me of trespassing or eavesdropping and send me to the king for execution, assuming he didn't kill me himself. Then it would be me fleeing through pools of blood while the Noble Fae watched.

"I did." He studied me with midnight eyes, head slightly tilted. "So why did you come here?"

After a hesitation, I decided on a partial truth that left out the dagger. "It felt safe and quiet. I thought no one would find me if I had to be sick." I laughed bitterly. "Clearly I was wrong." I shoved hair out of my face and lifted my chin, determined to regain some composure. He'd startled me badly, but that was no reason to forget Oriana's lesson about maintaining appearances.

"You did well, you know. At the dinner."

"I don't know what you mean."

"You didn't let them see this." He gestured at my tear-streaked face. "That's the hardest thing to learn, even for young Fae."

I had to be very careful. Faeries were masters of trickery. Kallen might seem sympathetic now, but I'd seen him kill without hesitation, and he had reported one of his own house members for treason. "I'm not used to violence like that. My lord."

"Imagine watching it four times a year, every year, for eight hundred years. That's how long some of the older faeries, like Roland, have been witnessing it."

"Prince Roland didn't seem upset." The most diplomatic way I could put it.

"He wasn't upset eight hundred years ago, either," he said. "Which is another lesson—immortality can change many things about someone, but the core stays constant."

I didn't understand why he was teaching me lessons. Was it a trick or an honest and bizarre desire to help me, just as Prince Drustan had decided to help? Maybe Lord Kallen had bet gold on me, too. I sighed and asked the question outright. "Why are you telling me this?" Aidan would have laughed at my bluntness.

Kallen shrugged. "I don't particularly wish to return to the dancing. Besides, I'm curious about you. It's rare for humans to exhibit even a small amount of magic. Extremely rare, considering our species have lived apart for a thousand years."

"I don't know why it happened." It wasn't precisely a lie. The dagger had shown me the path through the bog, but I didn't know if that would have happened to anyone who carried it, or if the dagger had chosen to help me. "I never had any powers before." Also not a lie, although it contained a glaring omission: I still had no powers whatsoever.

Right? I asked the dagger silently. *No Fae blood?*

No Fae blood. It seemed amused by the question.

"Perhaps the stress brought it out," Kallen said.

"Perhaps. Why don't you want to return to the dancing?" If he wanted to question me, I would question him right back.

The red torchlight from the hallway caught his face at an angle, bringing out sharp cheekbones, a straight nose, a mouth that gave away nothing. A hard face to read. "Maybe I'm a bad dancer," he said.

"Do you enjoy it?"

"The dancing or the bloodshed?"

"Either."

"I rarely enjoy dancing. The bloodshed is a hard necessity."

Of course. He was part of the king's inner circle, and I couldn't afford to forget that. He was a spy, pursuing information in every corner, which was probably why we were having this conversation. He likely wanted to hear what I'd experienced in Earth House so far, what I thought about the king, what sort of magic I'd conjured in the bog, and whether or not I would be able to do it again.

"What is this place?" I changed the subject to avoid accidentally revealing my thoughts about King Osric.

"You're very bold." His voice was an even baritone, as controlled as the rest of him. "Even most of the Noble Fae don't dare question me."

Drustan had commented on my boldness, too, had even seemed to enjoy it. "Who better to question than the King's Vengeance?" I asked with more confidence than I felt. "You probably know everything."

His lips curled. "I see you've been learning about me. What else have you learned?"

"Nothing."

"Come now. Tell me what you know and I'll tell you what this room is." He sounded casual, but I could tell he was interested in the answer.

"You are the second child and heir to Void House. Hector is the eldest and Una the youngest. She's competing in the trials. That's it. Oh, and I was told you appear whenever someone thinks about you, so I should try never to think about you."

It was a risk to take that flippant tone, but it paid off when he smiled slightly. Maybe if I amused him, he would let me go. "I'm afraid the gossips give me powers I don't possess," he said dryly. "You are free to think about me whenever—and however—you wish."

Curse faeries and their insinuations. I hoped he wouldn't notice my blush in the darkness. "Your turn," I said.

He looked behind me as if tracing the outlines of the room, but even if I opened my eyes as wide as I could, I still couldn't penetrate the blackness. "This is the entrance to the sixth house of Mistei. They fought against the king hundreds of years ago and lost and were wiped from memory."

Blood House. A chill went down my spine. If any of them had survived, they likely would have reveled in tonight's carnage. "Is there a trap in the room?"

"Guarding the entrance, you mean? No, not in this room. This is an antechamber before the entrance hall. There's a large archway behind you. I wouldn't explore beyond it if I were you."

"What happened to them? The house that rebelled." Remembering Drustan's cautioning, I didn't say the name aloud.

Kallen's mildly friendly expression faded into his usual cold mask. "Don't ask that again. If the wrong faerie overheard, you would be in trouble."

"Aren't you the wrong faerie?" I dared to ask.

His jaw clenched. "You're a human and new to this world. You get one warning." He rose gracefully to his feet. "Go back to the cavern. Don't return here, and don't ask too many questions. You may not find future conversations so pleasant."

I scrambled up far less gracefully, spitefully thinking that he must have a high opinion of himself if he assumed this conversation had been pleasant. "Thank you for the warning, my lord," I said stiffly. *And for not killing me*, I didn't add as I curtsied. Then I brushed past him without a second glance.

It took me a long time to retrace my steps and find the cavern. By the time I slipped back inside, the gathering was far smaller.

Lara was hovering near the wine, but she strode towards me the instant she noticed my return. She belatedly remembered to snap her fingers in command when she was a few paces away. She was drunk, I realized as she came to a swaying stop in front of me. "What took you so long?" she whispered heatedly.

"I was sick."

"I am so bored," she said loudly enough for nearby faeries to overhear. "I'm going home."

"Yes, my lady." I ducked my head gratefully.

We returned to Earth House in silence. Her face was tight, her mouth clamped in a thin line as if suppressing the words that wanted to burst out. It wasn't until we were back in her chamber that I felt comfortable enough to speak.

"Are you well?" I asked.

"Of course." She tugged her earrings out and threw them violently onto the desk. "Why wouldn't I be?"

I wasn't sure how to approach this conversation. I knew she had hated every second of the executions, which was why she was currently drunk, bitter, and going to bed early rather than dancing with some handsome Fae lord. "I found it upsetting."

"You're a human," she said flatly. "I'm not."

She reached back and started yanking on the ties to her dress. I stepped forward to help, but she shook her head. "I can do it myself," she snapped.

She couldn't, though. Every pull on the narrow ribbons was making the tangle worse. She hissed something under her breath, then looked over her shoulder, gaze fixed somewhere to the side of me. "Can you . . ."

I bit my cheek against the urge to say something rude. Whether she wanted to admit it or not, she was upset. My own hands were still shaky as I dug my short nails into the knot and pulled on the ribbons. I loosened the lacing on the entire back of the dress, and then Lara stepped away and stripped the gown off, leaving it in a heap on the floor.

She opened her mouth—then closed it again. No thanks for my assistance, apparently. Clad only in her undergarments, she sat down at the vanity, staring at herself in the mirror. Her eyes were reddened and full of misery.

"Should I—" I reached for the hairbrush, but she shook her head.

"No," she said, just as vehemently but softer this time. Her eyes abruptly welled up, and two tears streaked down her cheeks. She made a distressed noise, then closed her eyes and pressed her fingers into them as if trying to shove the tears back in. Her shoulders shook as her mouth opened around near-silent sobs. "Don't tell my mother," she gasped.

My heart broke a little for her then. "I would never."

She nodded but still didn't remove her hands from her face. "I usually don't— I've never— I *hated* that."

There was a painful lump in my throat. No wonder Lara was so snappish and mistrustful; she didn't even feel safe crying in private after watching eight people be butchered. "I did, too," I said. "It was . . ."

She nodded even though I hadn't finished my sentence. "It was."

"Do you want to talk about it?" I hesitantly offered. I wasn't even sure *I* wanted to talk about it.

She shook her head. "I just need to . . ." She sniffled. "Alone."

She wanted me to leave, and honestly, I was glad of it. My stomach felt sour and hollow, my mouth tasted awful, and there were horrors echoing in my head. Still, I didn't feel right abandoning her. At a loss for what else to do, I went to the bathroom to fill a glass of water. "Drink this before you sleep," I said, placing it on the vanity. I didn't know if faeries felt ill the morning after drinking, but it would hopefully help her feel better anyway.

She nodded, still hiding her face in her hands. "I—" Her breath hitched. "Water will be good."

Not quite a thank-you, but close. "Good night, my lady."

"Good night, Kenna," she whispered.

I returned to my room, closing the door on the quiet sound of her sobs.

I couldn't sleep for hours. Every time I closed my eyes I saw the carnage—piles of bodies and ash, shredded chunks of faerie, and that thick pool of blood. The few times I slipped into sleep, I found myself jolting awake, heart pounding, convinced there were corpses in the room. The crystals on the walls brightened each time as if letting me know that I was alone and safe. After my third panicked awakening they stayed lit, and with the room illuminated in soothing blue light, I was finally able to fall asleep.

My last thought before I drifted off was simple. *I have to get out of here.*

11

As the void trial drew near, I helped the other servants of Earth House prepare. We cleaned and polished until every inch of the house gleamed. Delicious scents wafted from the kitchen at all hours as the Fae celebrated the beginning of the trial season.

The festive atmosphere seemed discordant to me. How could the Fae have moved on from those grisly executions so quickly? Did they truly not care, or had the executions been happening so frequently for so long that they no longer let the sight affect them?

I was even more eager to escape Mistei after that awful dinner, so I continued my hunt for an exit whenever I had a spare moment. My legs ached from the miles I'd walked, but between the exercise and the hearty Fae food, I was growing stronger. I'd found countless fascinating and secret places: bare stone alcoves hidden behind tapestries, sloped chutes for the adventurous to slide down as a shortcut between levels, a ballroom whose walls, floor, and ceiling were composed of unbroken sheets of mirrored glass.

Now that I'd grown accustomed to being underground, I appreciated how many novel ways the Fae had found to bring light to what should have been a dark, oppressive place. There were the ever-present torches and the ceiling crystals that mimicked daylight, but some rooms were lit with more exotic objects: jagged mounds of pink stone that glowed from within, fireplaces large enough for horses to stand in, even luminescent nets of what looked like spider silk draped across the ceiling.

I encountered Prince Drustan near the throne room during one of my expeditions. He was speaking with another member of Fire House, but his gaze lingered on me as I passed. Soon he caught up to me. "Good afternoon," he said.

I looked up at his handsome face and lively eyes, trying to forget that a few nights ago he had burned a faerie alive. He'd had no choice; I knew that, just as I understood that he had made her death as fast as possible. Still, the sheer power contained in his body was terrifying.

"Good afternoon, my prince. I hope your house is well."

"My people are excited for the trials. As are yours, I imagine."

My people. The Fae would never be that. "Yes, the atmosphere does seem oddly celebratory."

"They should celebrate. It's rare to have so many parties and events, and it's even rarer for anything to surprise an immortal. No one knows what to expect. Besides, four of our holidays happen during the trial season: Imbolc, the spring equinox, Beltane, and the summer solstice." He glanced sidelong at me as we turned down an empty corridor. "I suspect you'll enjoy Beltane in particular."

We'd observed the same holidays in the human world, but I had no doubt Fae celebrations were far more interesting than the dancing and storytelling in Tumbledown. The wicked edge to Drustan's smile made me wonder what, exactly, he thought I'd enjoy about Beltane.

"I still don't understand why you all forget what happens during the trials," I said, voicing a doubt that had been nagging at me. "Surely someone must write down what happens so they can check later."

"Believe me, many have tried." He smiled ruefully, as if he had been among them. "Even the words vanish from the paper they're written on."

"So the magic you worship, the six Sacred Shards, just . . . erases memories? Are the Shards alive?"

"All magic is alive. And yes, the Shards obscure our memories once the trials end."

"What does it feel like?" I was nervous about the prospect of my memory being erased by a sentient rock.

"It doesn't feel like anything. You wake up one morning and it's as if the specifics are hidden behind foggy glass. We remember the parties and balls and the excitement, but details about the tests themselves are indistinct."

Fascinating. "But you know what will happen during the Fire trial, right?"

"Yes, the Fire Shard shared the details with me."

The Shards could communicate? That was . . . strange. But then I remembered the dagger curling around my arm and the impression it had given me—of magic so powerful it could shape-shift and speak—and the idea didn't seem so preposterous after all.

We turned down another corridor and strolled past a series of mostly empty rooms. I had no idea where we were going anymore; the moment he'd fallen into step with me, I'd forgotten my original intentions. I kept my strides confident, not wanting to look foolish.

I didn't know why he'd sought me out—probably just boredom— but I shouldn't waste this opportunity to learn more about the Fire trial for Oriana and Lara. "Were you surprised by it, or is it something you expected? How difficult will it be?"

He raised a mocking eyebrow. "So many questions. Don't think I'll share any secrets that will help your mistress."

I scowled. "I'm just curious how it works."

"I'm sure. Lara's the heir to Earth House. Don't you think she'll succeed without your help?"

I bristled at the doubt in his tone, even though it reflected my own privately held skepticism. "I have every faith in my lady."

He hummed, and my eyes were drawn to his lips. "There are some Fae who think Earth House's long-standing neutrality has made it weak."

I tore my gaze away from that generous mouth. Why was he baiting me like this? "I'm sure that's not the case."

His gray eyes widened, and despite my irritation, I found myself unreasonably captivated by the curve of his long auburn lashes. It was as if every inch of him had been crafted by a sculptor with a taste for sensual detail. "Is that so?" he asked. "Is Earth finally shedding its oh-so-boring neutrality?"

The conversation was taking a turn I didn't understand. I stopped in my tracks, not bothering to hide my annoyance. We were alone in the corridor, and besides, he had enjoyed my boldness before. "You deliberately misunderstand me."

He reached towards me, and I held my breath as he hooked a finger in one of the curls that had sprung loose from my braid. He drew it out, studying the dark coil. "Perhaps I do. Or perhaps you misunderstand them. It's a hard line to walk, and one that has done Earth House no favors over the centuries."

"Please speak plainly, Drustan." I used his name deliberately—a challenge of the power dynamic between us, a reminder that he'd invited this bluntness from me.

His eyes snapped to mine and held for long seconds. I refused to blink or look away. He dropped the curl, and the flashing smile he gave me held a crackle of flame in it. "It's dangerous to speak plainly. You should know this by now."

"Yet here I stand, perfectly well." I lifted my chin, trying to ignore the hot trembling his nearness had sparked in my belly. "I've been told it's refreshing."

"Then I will share a small thought with you, one blunt truth in honor of yours." His voice dropped so low I could barely hear him. "Earth House cannot maintain its neutrality forever. Eventually King Osric will decide not to tolerate it any longer. He grows bored without an enemy to fight. I wonder if Oriana has considered that."

My skin prickled. "Are you telling me Earth House is going to be attacked?" I whispered. If so, why was he telling me and not the princess?

He shrugged. "I know of no such plans. I simply consider the long view, as most Fae do. Our history is complicated, but it tends to repeat itself. There will be a reckoning eventually."

"Why tell me this? What do you expect me to do?" I had the sense our entire conversation had been designed to lead to this revelation, but I didn't understand why.

"I don't *expect* you to do anything," he said. "I merely think you're in an interesting position, close to some powerful members of Earth House. As I've told you, Fire House has many friends. Oriana and Lara could be among them—as could you." He trailed a finger down my cheek, leaving tingling heat behind. "I hope you remember that if you hear even a hint that Earth House may reconsider its position."

He strolled away, leaving me dumbfounded behind him.

12

THE NIGHT BEFORE THE VOID TRIAL, I WOKE TO A GENTLE knock on my door. When I opened it, Alodie was standing on the threshold. She was swathed in a hooded cloak, and the pale blue of her face and hands looked ghostly in the shadowed corridor.

"Get dressed," she said. "Wear something dark."

I complied, surprised to see that the wardrobe had provided me with black trousers and a shirt instead of a dress. Where exactly were we going?

I followed Alodie downstairs in silence. As we walked, the crystals overhead sparked with the barest light needed to see our immediate surroundings, then doused after we passed. "I have something to show you," she said as we reached the ground floor, "but you must swear never to speak of it to anyone but Princess Oriana, Lady Lara, Lord Selwyn, or myself. If you try to betray this secret, you will die. Is that clear?"

I blinked at the steel in her normally soothing tone. "Very clear."

She led me to the room I'd spoken with Selwyn in, where a willow tree shaded a still pond. The birds were silent as she pushed aside the hanging branches. I ducked under, and then we were enclosed in a cave of greenery, mere feet from a blank stone wall.

Alodie passed a hand over her chest and a golden object appeared in her fingers. A key, attached to a chain around her neck.

She held the key out to me, and I gingerly accepted it. As my fingers closed on the metal, the glowing outline of a door appeared in the stone wall. When I gave the key back, the glow disappeared. Alodie brushed the key against the wall rather than fitting it into a lock, but it worked all the same. The wall swung inward, revealing a staircase leading down.

I followed Alodie down the steps, cursing softly when the door shut behind us and we were left in complete darkness. A faint golden light sputtered to life. The key shone like a miniature torch in Alodie's hand, casting ominous shadows under her cheekbones that gave her face a skeletal aspect.

"This is Earth House's greatest secret," she said. "All throughout Mistei, deep within the ground and hidden between the walls, are tunnels that no other house has access to. They don't even know these tunnels exist. We don't know when they were formed or why, but it's rumored the Earth Shard was responsible."

On either side of the narrow staircase was nothing but empty space. I tried not to think about the drop that awaited if I slipped.

"This is why Earth House is neutral," Alodie continued. "The princess's ancestors began using these tunnels long ago to collect information about the other houses. Earth House came to be revered for its wise counsel and uncanny understanding of what motivated others, and soon the princes and princesses of Earth were treated as honored advisors to the Fae kings and queens. They stayed neutral to protect this secret, but also because its use taught them the value of neutrality. During a war every side believes itself to be correct.

Someone must stand apart and view Fae history with impartiality, or history will only remember one side of any conflict."

We reached a rough stone floor. Water dripped in the distance as Alodie led me into a damp passageway. "The only places in this kingdom where these tunnels do not go are within or beneath the other houses' territories, since the Shards protect the sanctity of those spaces," she continued. "That means we have access to the throne room, libraries, ballrooms, studies, and almost anywhere else we might want to eavesdrop. The entrances cannot be found by any magic other than that of the keys, which were forged so long ago they have fallen out of even Fae memory. There are four keys in total. Oriana, Selwyn, and Lara each have one. Oriana's eldest son, Leo, had the fourth key, but I have guarded his key carefully since his death. It is now yours for the duration of the trials."

"Why?" It seemed like far too much responsibility for a servant.

"Lara needs help," she said, worry entering her eyes and voice. "More help than the princess ever expected her to need. If she fails in the trials, Earth will lose the small amount of position it still has in the king's eyes—which is a very dangerous place to be."

True as it may have been, the way she said that bothered me. If Lara failed, she would either lose her magic or die. Why wasn't that everyone's first concern?

The vaulted ceiling was slimy with moss, and soon we reached an underground river. Crystal lights dotted the walls at intervals, casting a buttery glow over the oily-smooth water. A small boat was tied to a post on our side of the river, and Alodie gestured for me to hop in before joining me. She cast off, using a paddle to expertly maneuver us into the middle of the flow.

I eyed the water. The Elder had said that whenever water grew too dark, a knucker was sure to be lying in wait, all coiled scales and hungry fangs. "Is there anything to worry about down there?"

It took Alodie a moment before she understood the question. "You mean Nasties?"

"Knuckers or kelpies or . . ." I trailed off, thinking of the lantern-lure monsters that had chased us across the bog, their webbed feet skimming the water's surface. "Will-o'-the-wisps?"

"No. With a few exceptions, the Nasties are all sequestered in much deeper levels of Mistei, and none of them have ever had access to the Earth tunnels." She seemed to understand where my thoughts had gone, because she released the paddle to press a long-fingered hand to mine. "The ones you saw above—those are to protect Fae territory. King Osric doesn't allow other Nasties out without permission. If they were to violate his orders, his soldiers would execute them."

I nodded, swallowing the lump in my throat. Then, embarrassed by my fear and not wanting to dwell on that horrible flight across the bog, I returned to the topic at hand. "So how will these tunnels help Lara?"

Alodie released my hand and grabbed the paddle again. "I told you the tunnels go everywhere in Mistei except within the other houses," she said, stroking the blade through the dark water. "That includes anywhere the trials will be held."

"You want me to help her from down here."

Alodie nodded. "Most of the time you can help by spying from the tunnels and learning whatever you can about the upcoming trials. I can tell you where the princes often linger in case they disclose important information. For the Void test, however, Princess Oriana has planned something different. She was able to learn the precise location of the Labyrinth of Chaos. These tunnels lead directly there."

I put the pieces together. "You want me to join Lara in the labyrinth."

"Yes." Alodie's voice was calm but unyielding. "She cannot afford to fail. With both of you in the labyrinth, and with you connected to the secret exit by a cord, you will be able to help her navigate out successfully before disappearing back into the tunnels."

Cold dread crept through my veins and balled in my stomach. "You want me to accompany Lara through a pitch-black labyrinth and help her cheat to pass the test, all without being noticed by the other candidates or eaten by ravenous monsters."

"It won't be easy," Alodie said apologetically, "but there's no other choice."

I remembered what Oriana had said, that they could risk more with a human servant than they could have with an Underfae. I was small and unremarkable. The wards throughout Mistei had mostly been designed for faeries. I'd even proven myself adept at navigating difficult paths during the solstice ritual.

Most importantly, I was expendable.

No one would miss me if a monster ate me while Lara escaped. And if I were caught, it would be the princess's word against mine—assuming she let me live long enough to be questioned. Oriana could throw me to the Nasties and no one would care.

Alodie secured the boat at a dock that appeared on our right and hopped out with her usual grace. I teetered less elegantly at the edge before she grasped my arm and tugged me forward.

The tunnel sloped sharply upward, the ceiling so low we had to crawl in places. Eventually we reached a small cavern, inaccessible save for the path we'd just taken.

Alodie removed the necklace and gave it to me. "Place it around your neck and let the key fall over your heart."

When I did, the key vanished as if it had turned to mist and seeped into my skin. I couldn't even feel the chain anymore. I waved my hand over my chest and the necklace reappeared. Another wave and it vanished.

Whether the key was in my hand or hidden beneath my skin, I

could still see the glowing outline of another door in the cavern wall. I approached it hesitantly. "Should I go in?"

"Not now. Void House may still be preparing. Tomorrow night."

I pressed my ear to the stone, straining to hear anything that might give me an idea of what waited in the maze beyond. All was silent.

Then, as if summoned by my curiosity, a low, keening howl sounded on the other side of the door. I jerked back, sweating. "I can't do this. I'll die in there."

"You have no choice."

She was right. The princess had told me what would happen if I failed to help Lara: a far less comfortable servitude or death. Right now I had free access to the public areas and a reason to be in many of the more exclusive spaces as I accompanied Lara to parties and balls. This key gave me access to so much more, which meant more opportunity to look for an escape route. I still had a tongue and the wits to use it. I had an offer of friendship from the Fire prince, should I need help. All that would vanish if I refused to do this.

A prick on my arm reminded me of one other thing I had, and the thought of it loosened some of the tightness in my chest. The dagger had frightened away the Nasties in the bog. Maybe it would frighten these ones as well.

I took a deep breath, calming myself. "All right. I'll do it."

THE VOID TRIAL FELL ON IMBOLC, WHICH WAS A QUIETER HOLI-day than most in the human world, dedicated to setting intentions for the coming year. It was a lesser holiday for the Fae, too, beginning with a period of contemplation in the morning before a formal lunch held within house walls. The afternoon was filled with music. I didn't know the songs—didn't even know the language a few of them were sung in—but the haunting melodies were so beautiful they made me weep.

There was no avoiding the anxiety that hummed beneath my skin, though, which grew more intense with every passing minute. It turned to outright dread once we left Earth House for a pretrial dinner near Void House. In honor of the hosts, everyone in attendance wore black. Anticipation hung heavy in the air, nearly as potent as the scent of roasted meat.

After dinner, King Osric raised his hand, commanding silence. The king, too, wore black, although his long midnight cloak glittered with iridescent stars. The outfit suited his heavy crown much better than his normal attire. He finally looked like the tyrant he was.

"The first trial commences in two hours," the king said. "As you know, we honor Void House tonight, and the dark Shard has chosen the nature of this trial. Prince Hector has informed me that this test of courage will be conducted in the Labyrinth of Chaos."

A chorus of gasps told me not all of the candidates had been privy to that information. Lara, thankfully, did a credible job of looking shocked. The Fire candidate, Edric, merely lifted one dark brow and crossed his arms; he wasn't surprised, since I'd shared Oriana's suspicions about the labyrinth with Aidan during a recent lunch as thanks for the sprite's initial clues. Una and the other Void candidate, a faerie named Wilfrid, didn't change expression at all.

"The labyrinth has ended the lives of countless criminals and traitors over the years," the king continued. "The walls are warded against the use of magic, and there will be no light whatsoever available within the maze. You will need to find your way out as quickly as possible while avoiding the labyrinth's most infamous danger: the vicious and bloodthirsty Nasties who feed on the fallen."

The king definitely had a flair for the dramatic, and by the sick smile on his face, he enjoyed the terror he was causing. I tried to block out the emotional impact of his words and focus only on the details provided.

"You have five hours to escape. After that, you will be considered to have failed the test. If you fall behind, though, there is one more way to redeem yourself—or a way to further your lead, if you manage to escape the labyrinth quickly." Osric snapped his fingers, and a waiting manservant stepped forward and draped something over the king's outstretched hand: a simple black belt with two gauzy scarves hanging from it. "Each candidate will wear one of these belts. There are tokens attached at either side." He slipped one free from the belt and held it up. It was about the size of a handkerchief, with a silver medallion attached to one corner to weigh it down. "The Shard will also take into consideration who is in possession of the most and least tokens at the end of the trial."

Garrick and his Illusion crony, Markas, relaxed at this information. They were the brawniest of the candidates, and I knew from their frequent bullying of Lara that they would enjoy the chance to take tokens from the others by force.

Lara's tense posture told me she was terrified, though. So was I, to be honest. It was one thing to navigate unknown tunnels in the dark; I was used to that sort of questing. It required patience and an attention to detail I'd been perfecting since childhood, the ability to remember directions and mark my steps on a mental map. The Nasties had been my biggest concern, but I'd told myself that if we were quiet and quick enough, they might not catch us.

If we had to contend with not just Nasties but strong, competitive Noble Fae for whom this trial was a matter of life or death . . . I didn't know how we would manage. I wouldn't be faster or stronger than any of them, and Lara likely wouldn't be, either. If we ran into another candidate, it was unlikely Lara would be able to keep her tokens.

King Osric clapped his hands. "Those are the rules. Now, the candidates will be escorted to chambers where they will change their attire and wait for the trial to begin. Prince Hector will lead spectators to the exit from the labyrinth shortly before midnight. May the Shards give you courage."

I smiled at Lara as she was escorted away by a black-winged Underfae, willing her not to panic. She would perform better if she entered the maze in a calm state of mind.

I wouldn't be with her for the next portion of the evening. None of the manservants or handmaidens would be, for fear we would arm the candidates with supplies to help them escape. This suited me, as I needed the extra time to prepare for my own covert entry into the labyrinth.

The wardrobe provided me with exactly the outfit I needed. Tight but flexible black trousers, a long-sleeved black shirt, and shoes ideal for running. I braided my hair and slipped the tail down the back of my shirt, then pulled a loose hood over my head that covered everything but my eyes. I looked like a walking shadow. The dagger curled into a thick bracelet around my wrist, high enough that it was hidden by my sleeve but low enough that it could easily slip into my hand if needed.

Perhaps I didn't need to take such care with my appearance when there would be no light to see by anyway, but I wasn't going to take any chances. The Nasties that lived there navigated through the darkness somehow; I couldn't assume their eyes were the same as mine.

I tied a round wooden box to my ankle, tugging at the string protruding from it to make sure the spooling mechanism within was working smoothly. I'd been astounded when Alodie had told me the small box contained enough string to last even if I walked in circles for days, rather than the five hours allotted. It was smooth and fine, barely wider than a hair but strong enough that I couldn't break it. Nasty spider silk, she'd said, procured at great cost. Once I had accompanied Lara to the opening of the labyrinth, I would be able to follow the thread back to the secret door.

I added a leather pouch to my belt just in case I was able to grab another candidate's token. With that, I was ready.

I retraced the route Alodie had shown me and waited in the cave, unsure how close it was to midnight. Alodie had told me I would be able to hear voices at the main opening to the labyrinth due to the way the rock had been carved. Once the king announced the start of the trial, I would enter. The candidates had been taken to other entrances around the maze—official Void entrances, unlike this secret cave— and would start at different positions equidistant from the exit.

With nothing else to do, I traced patterns in the dirt and tried to let my mind go blank. When that didn't work, I went over the steps of my plan again. Once inside the labyrinth, I would tie the loose end of the string to an iron ring at the base of the wall, presumably used to restrain prisoners. Alodie had seemed confident it would be there, so I would simply have to trust her. Then I would move as quickly as possible to find Lara. The labyrinth wouldn't be silent, Alodie had assured me—there would be Nasties roaring at the very least, and possibly other sounds meant to disorient prisoners. Under cover of that noise, I would make a specific trilling call I'd practiced for hours the night before, one of Earth House's secret codes. Once I heard a response, I would follow the sound to wherever Lara was.

Then we would stumble around in the dark together.

Not stumble, I corrected myself. We would explore. That sounded more deliberate. We would protect her tokens carefully and move as quickly and quietly as possible through the maze, using my string and natural memory for patterns to guide Lara out. I'd distract any enemies who appeared as we headed for the exit. Then Lara would emerge victorious, and I would follow the string back to freedom.

Simple.

Nothing to worry about at all.

I grimaced.

Strange howls came from within the labyrinth, although now that I knew the stone around the labyrinth had been carved to amplify sound, I realized the Nasties were likely farther away than they sounded. Still, I would move away from any howls that sounded too close.

Long minutes passed, time enough for my breaths to slow and my agitated heart to calm. I closed my eyes, mentally preparing myself for the utter lack of light.

"It's time," a voice announced from seemingly just above me.

I jumped, all pretense of calm lost as my heart took off at a gallop.

It was the king, speaking to the assembled spectators. "The candidates stand at entrances around the labyrinth, guarded by servants of Void House. They will be released into the labyrinth in less than a minute. Then we will have five hours to see who emerges victorious—and who doesn't emerge at all."

Was that the clink of glassware? When the king announced a toast, I rolled my eyes. The only thing he seemed to love more than speeches or murder was making toasts. "We will drink and revel until dawn. Here's to the first trial. May it be an interesting one."

The crowd's laughter echoed off the stone as they drank with him.

I pushed to my feet, shook out my stiff legs, and summoned the key. I clutched it tightly, staring at that glowing entrance.

No choice, I reminded myself.

I pressed the key against the door, which swung open to reveal a darkness so thick not even the light of the key could cut through it. I vanished the key, took a deep breath, and walked into the labyrinth.

13

THE DOOR SWUNG SHUT, SEALING ME IN.

Blackness.

The lack of light was tangible, a heaviness against my skin. I opened my eyes wide, straining to see anything, but it was as if I'd been struck blind. In the absence of sight, my hearing seemed amplified, and I shuddered as screeches and wails echoed from every direction.

This was the void the Fae had named their house after. A nothingness so profound that the absence had formed its own identity. A terrible, unfathomable beast opening its maw.

I managed to find the ring in the wall by fumbling. I knotted the string firmly, then knotted it again just to be sure. I couldn't afford to have that knot slip.

Listening didn't give me any hints as to which direction to move in, so I stepped away from the door . . . and walked straight into a wall.

I hissed, rubbing my forehead, then turned to the right. The corridor was narrow enough to trail my fingers along both sides at once.

As I walked, I marveled at how smoothly and silently the string un-spooled behind me, periodically testing the tension to make sure it was still attached to the ring. Eventually I stopped testing and trusted my knot work. The thread unspooled with barely any pressure, so I didn't have to strain against it, and with the box attached to my an-kle, it lay low to the ground where hopefully no one would trip on it. If they did, they'd probably think it was one of the chaotic tricks of the maze.

I made the trilling sound Alodie had taught me but heard no re-sponse. What if I never found Lara? Would Oriana cast me out or kill me?

I walked faster, trusting that my fingers would find a wall before my face did. Eventually they met open air. My fumbling explora-tions revealed two choices. Turning right would keep me close to the exterior of the labyrinth, so I chose the left-hand path towards the heart of the maze. I knelt and snagged my string under a rough edge of stone at the corner, creating another anchor point.

As soon as I stepped into the new corridor, my feet slid out from under me. I cursed, gripping the wall to stay upright, then gingerly crouched to touch the floor. Slick, mossy stone met my fingertips, a whisper-thin layer of running water slithering over it. The hazard convinced me I was heading in the right direction, since Void House would make escape as difficult as possible.

I pressed my back to the wall, inching along with sideways steps until the passage finally widened and the floor roughened and dried out. It was now impossible to touch both walls, so I kept my hand on one. I ignored the periodic openings that appeared beneath my fin-gers, hoping that cutting a straight path inward would help me find Lara quickly.

I kept trilling. Sometimes the trills were met with befuddled squawks, and once by a deep rumble that echoed through the floor.

I stopped making noise for a few minutes after that, until whatever malevolent presence had been nearby had vanished.

Finally, maybe an hour into my explorations, I heard it: a raw, keening trill like the call of some bloodthirsty bird. I headed towards the sound, knees shaking with relief.

The darkness was getting to me. So far I hadn't encountered anything terrible, but it was only a matter of time. If they were like the monsters in the bog, these Nasties wouldn't strike right away. They would circle, prolonging the tension so they could get as much enjoyment out of the hunt as possible.

It took long minutes to find Lara. I took several wrong turns into rooms with no outlets and once began losing elevation on a sloping ramp. At last, the trill was close enough it had to be within twenty feet, and I heard the slide of a shoe over stone.

"Lara?" I whispered, hoping desperately it wasn't some other candidate who had figured out the code.

"Thank the Shards." She was there in seconds, fumbling for my arm. "It's so horrid in here."

"Have you met any candidates? Any Nasties?" We couldn't afford to talk much, but it was important to know if there was anywhere we should avoid.

"Nothing." Her shiver passed into me. "I thought there was something near me once, but I held still and it moved away."

"Tokens?"

I heard her patting her belt. "Still there."

"Then let's hurry." Since Lara and I would be at a disadvantage in any conflict, speed was our only hope. "We'll get through this."

Lara let me lead, and we explored in silence, linking hands to ensure we were never separated. I carefully only gave Lara my left hand; the dagger on my right wrist had stirred at the presence of another person and was vibrating hungrily.

Quiet, I thought at it. Then, reconsidering, *Or stop shaking over her, at least. It would be helpful to know when anyone else is nearby.*

The dagger grumbled, but the tremors did indeed stop—after it nipped me. I flinched at the small sting, wondering how many scars I'd end up with when this was over.

An eerie wail came from down a corridor, and Lara jumped; when it faded, she squeezed my hand as if sharing her relief with me. It made me think of Anya, how we'd clasped hands in the bog. The two women were so different, but sometimes I swore there were echoes of Anya in Lara—in a tilt of the head, a sigh over a pretty dress, a squeezed hand as we explored in the dark. Reminders of what I'd lost.

I forced Anya from my thoughts. She wasn't here; Lara was. If my focus wavered, we both stood to lose even more.

My strategy was to cover as much ground as possible, plotting our overall trajectory as best I could on my mental map. It wouldn't be perfect by any means, but at least I could maintain a general sense of what direction we were heading in and where we should explore next.

As promised, there seemed to be no logic to how the labyrinth was laid out. Wide, smooth-walled tunnels alternated with paths so narrow we had to edge through sideways. Some curved in long arcs, while others bent at sharp angles. The floor alternated between rough pavers and slick, mossy stone.

A few times we heard growls, and once an ear-splitting roar from what must have been only a few tunnels over. Each time we hurried in the opposite direction from the sound, and none of the monsters followed us.

During one of these strategic retreats, we reached an archway that led into a warren of cramped corridors. I barely fit beneath the ceiling, but Lara had to stoop to avoid hitting her head. We wound through the maze-within-a-maze, encountering dead ends more often than not. This route had to lead somewhere, though—it felt distinct to me, like a new section of the labyrinth, and the ground sloped gradually upward. It even smelled different, like dust and stale earth.

Thirty minutes later it was clear I'd been wrong. The wall in front of me was unyielding, with no hidden opening to be found. "Dead end," I told Lara, trying to suppress my panic. "And we've tried everything else."

We had wasted a dangerous amount of time in a section with no outlets. Now that I knew there was no escape, the lowered ceiling and narrow passageways made me feel claustrophobic. We retraced our steps quickly.

The dagger pulsed against my skin as footsteps sounded ahead of us.

I drew Lara into a tiny side chamber, barely more than an alcove, and pressed a warning finger to her lips. Someone else was exploring these tunnels. The only way to escape would be to sneak out after they passed and hope they were so stymied by this impossible maze that they wouldn't follow for some time.

The footsteps came closer. They sounded substantial, like someone wearing boots. Lara and I both wore flexible shoes that whispered over the floor, but whoever this was had enough confidence in their fighting abilities that they hadn't felt the need to opt for stealth.

The footsteps slowed as they passed. I felt a faint disturbance in the air directly in front of my face.

Lara shrieked.

I leapt into the passage to tackle whoever it was, but rebounded off stone, bruising my hands. The pound of running footsteps receded towards the entrance to the low tunnels.

I reached for Lara. "Are you all right?"

She gripped my arm, fingers digging in. "The tokens," she gasped.

I fumbled at her belt and then felt the floor, but she was right. The other candidate had stolen both tokens. I swore. "Come on."

We passed under the archway a few minutes later, finally reaching the main tunnels again. I tugged her after me, heading in a direction we hadn't pursued yet. We splashed through a small stream before reaching a ramp that led sharply downward. My shoes were soaked through and I skidded on the smooth stone, barely managing to keep my balance.

A furious, inhuman scream sounded directly ahead of us. We sprinted back up the ramp as heavy claws scraped over the stone behind us. Winter-cold breath puffed across my ankles.

I tripped at the sudden flattening of the ramp and tumbled into the main corridor. Lara landed on top of me, knocking the wind from me. I braced myself for the puncture of fangs or claws . . . but nothing happened.

We lay in a panting heap, ears straining, but the monster had seemingly disappeared.

Someone else had been drawn by the sounds, though. Again I heard heavy footsteps from a distance, and the dagger rumbled hungrily as whoever it was approached.

This candidate couldn't do anything to hurt Lara's chances now that her tokens were gone. They also didn't know there were two of us working together.

"Stay here," I whispered. "When the footsteps get close, make a noise."

I moved a short distance away and braced myself for a fight. Lara whimpered, and the footsteps stopped before turning in her direction.

I lunged, crashing into a tall, muscular body, and grabbed every fluttering token I could from his belt. He spun with a snarl, but I skipped away on silent feet, then crouched against one of the walls.

He would expect me to run as far and fast as I could, which hopefully meant he wouldn't expect to find me on the ground mere feet away. I held my breath as the faerie stood motionless, no doubt listening to figure out which way I'd gone. Something scrabbled against stone in the distance, and he took off running.

I returned to Lara and handed her the tokens. Four total. She tucked them into her belt.

I sat back, wondering where to go next. The only outlets nearby led to the low-ceilinged maze, the monster-infested ramp, or the same tunnel an angry faerie had just sprinted down. We had no good options, which meant we had to decide on the lesser of two evils—an unknown candidate who was currently looking for us, or the monster lying in wait below?

I knew my preference: head after the candidate and hope we didn't run into him again. I was too afraid of whatever icy creature had almost attacked us.

I frowned.

This was a test of courage, and the least courageous option was to run away from the monster. Besides, it hadn't followed us past the top of the ramp. Was that because it only guarded a small patch of territory—or because it had been trying to deter us from exploring further?

I hurriedly explained my suspicions to Lara—that we needed to always choose the path that required the most courage, which meant heading straight towards any horrible noises. She was silent, thinking it through. "That sounds awful," she finally said. Her voice trembled. "But it's exactly the sort of trick I can imagine them playing. The trials have to directly test a specific trait, and right now we're mostly testing speed and sense of direction."

The more I thought about it, the more correct the answer seemed. "We have to try it. I don't know how much time is left."

She took my hand, and I felt the faint vibrations of her terror as we started back down the ramp. My heart pounded so frantically the monster could probably hear it.

When we reached the bottom of the ramp, a low growl sounded. We stopped, listening. The scrape of claws on stone started again, drawing nearer. The air chilled, and a gust of frozen wind hit my face, as if something enormous had exhaled.

I gathered all my courage and kept walking. Lara trailed a few steps behind, clearly willing to let me test the theory first so she would have time to escape if I was wrong.

The growl morphed into an angry scream. I flinched as talons scraped the wall directly above my head, breaking loose chips of rock that sprayed down on us like hailstones, but I didn't slow my pace.

More screams, more horrible noises, more gusting frozen air. The Nasty was mere feet away; the prickling awareness of its proximity crept over my skin.

It didn't attack, though.

Triumph bubbled through me. The next time claws scraped over rock, I didn't jump. Those claws could have torn me in two, but they hadn't. The monster was allowing us to pass.

Eventually the sound of the Nasty faded. We walked onward, listening. When a howl rose from our right, we headed towards it.

Again and again we chose the path that sounded the most dangerous, making our way through a gauntlet of screams and roars. Nothing attacked us, and we didn't once encounter a dead end.

The darkness around us lessened, and I could just see Lara's outline beside me. She squeezed my hand. "We're close." She sounded like she might cry.

The end of the tunnel danced with firelight from the revelry going on outside. My eyes weren't accustomed to even that small illumination, and I winced.

I stopped. "You go alone from here."

Lara hesitated, clearly afraid of walking even that final stretch alone, but finally she let go of my hand, which had started to go numb from her tight grip. "I'll see you at home," she said before running towards the light.

I was already moving back into the maze, but I heard a cheer go up as she emerged.

The route back was much easier. No monsters growled at me, since I was moving away from the exit, and I had the string as a guide. I removed the box from my ankle and held it, pressing a clever button in the side that wound the thread back onto the spool as I went. With the string pointing the way, there was no need to feel around, and soon I was able to move at a near-run.

I slammed directly into a broad chest.

I yelped and jumped backwards, almost dropping the box, but someone's hard hands wrapped around my upper arms. Another candidate—an exceptionally tall one. "Who's this?" My heart sank as I recognized Garrick's cruel voice.

If he got the chance to examine me, I was doomed. I was too short to pass for Noble Fae, and if he discovered the box and cord in my hands, it would become blatantly apparent someone was cheating. I did the only thing I could think of—I hissed and let out my best impression of a Nasty's bloodthirsty howl. He jerked away, and I seized the opportunity to kick him, knocking him into the wall. He swore and reached for me again, and this time I raked a clawed hand down his face. Flesh accumulated under my nails as he screamed.

I seized a token from his belt—it would serve him right to lose one—and started running. He stumbled after me, shouting and cursing, but I was too fast and sure-footed. I spooled the string up desperately, skidding around corners at a breakneck pace.

My feet encountered a patch of wet, mossy stone and I crashed to the ground, hitting my tailbone hard enough to bring tears to my eyes. I sobbed, half in pain and half in joy at the realization that I was back in the slippery corridor I'd first encountered hours ago. I crawled, hardly caring as water soaked into my trousers and stone abraded my hands. One more turn brought me to the exit.

I unknotted the string from the iron loop with shaking hands and summoned the key. When I tumbled out into the cavern, the key's golden glow sparked back to life. It was blindingly bright after so many hours of darkness. I closed my eyes and lay on the ground, tracking the soft red afterimage on the backs of my eyelids.

Lara and I had succeeded.

I RETURNED TO EARTH HOUSE, CHANGED INTO MY DRESS FROM earlier, and made it back to the throne room in time to view the closing ceremony for the first trial. I'd hoped to reach Lara in time to hand her Garrick's final token, but when I arrived, the nine candidates already stood facing King Osric. Many, like Una and Lara, looked triumphant, but a few appeared dejected. Not everyone had made it out in time. Garrick's fists were clenched in rage, and stark red lines streaked across his face where I had clawed him. He had five tokens on his belt. Five instead of six, because his final token rested in a pouch at my waist.

"Congratulations on completing the first trial," King Osric said. "Here are the results."

The goatlike Underfae who served as the king's steward, whose name I'd learned was Pol, recited the finishing times and how many tokens each candidate had collected. Una was the fastest, but she'd finished with only the two tokens she'd started with. The other Void candidate, Wilfrid, wasn't far behind. It was suspicious, since I'd learned at least one member of Void House could see in the dark, but the Shards supposedly ensured a level playing field. Lara had been one of the slowest to complete the maze, but her four tokens stirred a murmur of disbelief from the crowd. To my delight, Garrick hadn't completed the maze, although his five tokens were the most collected by any candidate, which would count for something in the final reckoning. Two of the nonfinishers had no tokens whatsoever: Karissa, the crimson-haired Illusion candidate, and, to my dismay, the other Earth candidate, Talfryn. He was well-liked in the house.

"Garrick," the king said after the results had been announced, "you are the only candidate with an odd number of tokens. Did you drop one?" A few laughs greeted the question, most emanating from the Void contingent.

Garrick scowled. "I was attacked, your majesty."

"By one of the candidates? None of them have your missing token."

"By a Nasty. It clawed me and stole my token."

King Osric laughed, but this time the Void contingent didn't join in. Hector and Kallen looked at each other with narrowed eyes. They'd known the Nasties wouldn't attack during this trial. Hopefully they would assume another candidate had clawed Garrick and the token had been lost in the confusion.

Kallen abruptly turned and scanned the crowd. I looked away, adopting an expression of boredom.

"I can sense it, you know," a voice whispered in my ear.

I jumped. Drustan stood beside me, looking down at me with raised brows.

"Sense what?"

"The token in your pouch."

My heart pounded on a surge of fear. He knew I'd been in the maze, which meant he knew Lara had cheated. "I don't know what you're talking about."

"You forget that I'm a prince. The strongest faeries are sensitive to magic, and that token is steeped in Void magic. You'd better get rid of it before someone else senses it on you."

"Why are you warning me?" I whispered. "Why aren't you turning me in?"

His jaw clenched as he looked at the candidates. "I dislike Light House," he said with quiet venom, and then his face relaxed into a smile, as if he'd suddenly remembered the mask he needed to wear. "Almost as much as I admire defiance."

I nodded and started to leave, but he caught my arm, his fingers burning through the thin sleeve. "Remember what I said about Fire House's friends."

I slipped out of the throne room, hoping no one would notice my departure. The entrance to Earth House was a long walk away; I would be better served by finding one of the hidden doors to the catacombs. Luckily, there were several nearby.

I was just outside a door, preparing to summon the key, when footsteps sounded behind me. I turned, and my heart sank.

Kallen stood ten feet away, watching me.

I curtsied. "My lord."

The King's Vengeance strolled towards me, and I resisted the urge to clutch the pouch that held the stolen token, as if by gripping it I could hide it from his gaze. My feigned nonchalance didn't fool him, though. His eyes ran over me leisurely, stopping at my waist.

"You've committed a crime." The calmness of his voice sent shivers down my spine.

"I have?" Maybe if I pretended ignorance . . .

"You were in the labyrinth. I can sense it on you."

"No, I wasn't—"

He cut me off with a slash of his hand. "Don't lie to me, or you will greatly regret it. Tell me."

I swallowed hard. He was right; I couldn't lie to him, not with Void magic on me. I could only hope for his mercy. "I was in the labyrinth," I admitted.

"You took something."

I nodded, wondering if I was signing my own death warrant. He held out a hand, and I opened the pouch with trembling fingers and laid the token in his palm.

He studied it. "How did you get into the labyrinth?"

I couldn't betray the secret of the catacombs, but what else would he believe? "I snuck in before the trial started."

"The labyrinth was well guarded. I find it unlikely that you made it past the sentries."

I shrugged. "No one ever notices humans. I waited until they were distracted and crept in."

"If I find out you lied to me," he said, menace filling that dark velvet voice, "it will go very badly for you. You have one more chance to tell me a different story."

I spread my hands helplessly. "I can't tell you anything else. I snuck in. That's it."

The token still rested in his hand, the fabric draped like the wings of a dead bird. He watched me for a few more excruciating seconds, then closed his fist around the token and placed it in his pocket, as if marking the end of his questioning. "You could be executed for this."

An icy chill rippled over me, followed by pinpricks of panicked sweat. I waited, trembling, for my sentence.

"Do you want to be executed?" he asked when I didn't respond, as casually as if he were asking what time it was.

"No, my lord." Not that it mattered. He had all the power in this situation, and he knew it.

Dark eyes skated over me consideringly. "I propose a bargain."

Relief at avoiding death was followed by fresh anxiety. A faerie was a very dangerous creature to bargain with. They lied as easily as they breathed and charmed as easily as they killed. "What sort of bargain?" I asked, hoping the cost of survival wouldn't be too high.

"I will get rid of this token, and I won't tell the king what happened tonight." He paused, watching me process this absolution. "In exchange, you owe me information."

"What sort of information?" What would the King's Vengeance want from a human servant? Didn't he have other, more successful spies? What could possibly be worth a favor of this magnitude?

"Every piece of information you can give me. What Earth House discusses behind closed doors. What Drustan keeps whispering in your ear." He smiled sardonically at my startled blink. "Oh yes, I've seen him speaking with you. You're a strange choice of companion for a prince."

"He finds me entertaining," I replied, feeling defensive. "And he bet on me at the solstice, so he's invested in my well-being."

"Perhaps that's what he says, but everything he does is designed to further his own goals. If you get any hint of what those goals might be, you will tell me immediately."

I was well and truly trapped. If I refused the bargain, he would have me executed. Better to agree now and find a way to feed him just enough information to keep him happy without betraying Lara, her family, or Drustan, who had been kinder to me than he had any reason to be. It would be a very difficult line to walk.

Still, better to walk that line than to have my journey end right here.

I nodded. "I will tell you anything I learn."

Kallen smiled, but no mirth reached his cold eyes. "When you have information, go to the antechamber before Blood House. Wait there until I arrive, no matter how long it takes."

I nodded, silently vowing to go there as infrequently as possible.

As if he'd read my mind, he said, "If you don't show up there often enough, I will come looking for you." He stroked a cool finger down my cheek, and I suppressed a shudder of disgust at the touch. "And, Kenna . . . believe me when I say you don't want that."

14

LARA AND I BOTH SLEPT UNTIL EARLY AFTERNOON, SINCE the revelry hadn't ended until after dawn. Lara had been ebullient when I'd helped her undress after the celebration. "Did you see their faces? They didn't believe I could do it."

I'd smiled, even as a small, uncharitable part of me thought, *You didn't do it. I did.*

Then she'd gripped my hands. "Thank you." She'd given me a genuine smile, and my resentment had dissipated at that simple sign of gratitude.

Her good humor continued that afternoon. When she'd finally rung for me, all she'd requested was that I have the kitchen send up a tray. The rest of the day was mine to do whatever I wished with. What I wanted was to keep sleeping, but there was no way I would squander an opportunity like this.

I set out with two specific goals. The other human servants couldn't speak out loud due to the Fae barbarity that had seized their tongues, but I'd realized they communicated with one another in some sort of sign language. The fluttering hands of the woman I'd met my first day in Earth House had been my first hint, and since then I'd seen others employing the same motions. I planned to visit the human levels and ask them to teach me. The second goal was to continue exploring the catacombs. Perhaps I would see or hear something useful, like information to feed Kallen or details that would aid my eventual escape.

The human levels were very different from the Fae levels.

They were deeper underground, and I emerged from a staircase into a narrow hallway with a low ceiling and uneven cobbled floor. There were no crystals to simulate daytime; guttering torches provided the only illumination, the walls above them blackened from centuries of flame. It smelled like smoke, sweat, and excrement.

There were no closed doors down here, only open archways. I passed countless workrooms where men and women sewed, polished silver ornaments, scrubbed pans, sorted grains and lentils, ironed, folded, and cleaned. It seemed the more menial household tasks were delegated to humans rather than Underfae, although that couldn't always be true; there were Underfae in Earth House who cleaned, ironed, and folded as well. Maybe Oriana didn't want supposedly inferior human hands touching her linens.

I received a few curious glances, but no one approached. It was eerily quiet without normal servant chatter, but hands flashed everywhere and occasionally a laugh or grunt broke the silence.

The workrooms gave way to chambers filled with rows of tiny beds stacked one atop the other. There were no doors here, either. Was it a subtle exercise of Fae power, stripping the humans of their right to privacy?

It felt like walking through an animal's burrow: dark and claustrophobic, the air foul. I felt ill after only a few minutes. The faces I passed were haggard and many bodies were stooped with age or the effects of hard labor, but despite the grim surroundings, many wore smiles and animated expressions as they signed. People finding joy in one another despite the circumstances.

Then I heard faint sobbing from down the hall.

I followed the weeping, curious. In one of the rooms, a woman sat on a bed with her arms wrapped around her knees. Her reddish-brown hair hung to the floor, shielding her face. Beside her sat an elderly woman who rubbed her back comfortingly.

"I'm afraid," the woman whispered.

I jolted in surprise at the words, and both women looked up like startled rabbits.

"Forgive me for intruding," I said, raising my hands disarmingly. "I wanted to meet other humans."

The old woman looked at me suspiciously, but the younger woman—who I could now see possessed a beautiful pair of brown eyes—seemed struck with wonder. "Did they just release you from the king's brothel, too?"

Brothel. The word was a fist to my stomach. I tried to keep pity out of my voice. "No, I'm a handmaiden in Earth House."

The woman sat straighter, brushing tears off her cheeks. "I've heard about you. I had a visitor on the solstice." Her voice faltered on the word *visitor*, and I knew what she meant. "Why didn't they cut out your tongue?"

"I have to talk to my mistress. Why didn't they cut out yours?"

She flinched. "Because it was needed."

Oh. I winced at my own thoughtlessness, the unintentional cruelty. "I'm so sorry," I said. "I didn't even know there was a brothel down here. I don't know anything about the other humans. My name is Kenna, by the way."

"I'm Triana." Triana gestured at the woman who still rubbed circles on her back. "This is Maude. She's been here the longest of anyone, and she came from the brothel, too."

Maude's fingertips were stained a familiar green and yellow—she must be an herbworker, turning plants into potions and poultices. The ache of sorrow below my breastbone deepened. In summer it would be two years since my mother had passed, but sometimes small things like this would remind me of her and then grief would rip over me like a sudden gust of wind.

I pressed a hand over my heart and bowed my head. "It's nice to meet you both. As nice as it can be in the circumstances, anyway."

Maude's expression softened, and Triana's lips curved in a melancholy smile. "Our lives have taken a turn, haven't they?"

"How long have you been here?" I asked. Maybe I should have left her to her grief, but her eyes were brighter now, and she looked as interested in talking to me as I was in talking to her. "And where did you come from? I'm from Tumbledown."

"Oh, Tumbledown! I've been there. I lived in Alethorpe, and I was stolen from my bed eight years ago." Triana shivered. "An Illusion Underfae was looking for women. The king likes variety."

Alethorpe was a village a day's ride from Tumbledown; it was possible I'd seen her at a long-ago festival. Here was proof of what Aidan had told me: that the king abducted humans on a whim. Fresh fury filled me at the thought, and I let it push aside the sorrow. Anger was easier to feel.

I looked at Maude. "I don't speak your sign language yet; I'm sorry. But were you also from Alethorpe?"

She nodded, mouth turned down and the weight of years in her eyes.

"The Elders never told us any of this," I said, hating those village leaders nearly as much as I hated King Osric. "What the Fae are truly like, what they do to people." Instead they'd filled our heads with empty dreams. All that talk of blessings and how the Fae whispered in their ears and guided their hands . . . Had they known the cruel truth, or had they been as ignorant as the rest of us, inventing their own authority?

The latter, I'd bet. And the Elders would never be the ones who paid the price for their own lies. It was paid by people like Triana and Maude, like Anya . . . even people like my mother, who had given her best years to faith and died praying for a salvation that never came.

"I was a true believer once." Triana's mouth twisted bitterly. "Would you believe that at first I was happy to be stolen away? I thought I was going to be showered in riches. That maybe the Fae had seen something in me no one else ever had." She dipped her head, hiding her expression behind her hair. "They saw something in me, all right."

Maude made a soft noise in her throat and stroked a stained hand over Triana's hair.

"Was everyone down here stolen from their beds the same way?" I asked.

"Yes, for the most part. Usually because they were beautiful or particularly strong. But others were brought here as babies."

At first I thought I'd misunderstood her—the idea was too abhorrent. "Did you say *babies*? Why?"

"Who knows? Probably to train them as servants from birth."

A shiver raced through me. "I can't imagine growing up here."

Triana smiled sadly. "I suppose we were lucky in that sense. At least we know what the outside world looks like. There are some down here who have never seen the sun." She patted the open portion of the bed beside her. "Come, make yourself comfortable." Maude nodded, echoing the invitation.

I sat, grateful for the hospitality. "You said they released you from the brothel?" I asked hesitantly.

"Yes." Triana drew a steadying breath. "I'm too old to appeal to them anymore. Most of the Noble Fae like their whores young and . . . unblemished. At least for a while." Her shoulders curled inward at the words, and Maude made another soft noise and wrapped an arm around her.

Everything about this was sickening. "So you'll become a servant now."

"Thankfully, yes."

I frowned, remembering the heartbroken sound of her weeping echoing down the hallway. "You said you were afraid, though. What are you afraid of?" Wouldn't cleaning and mending be better than whatever she'd endured in the brothel? There was a world of difference between choosing to trade one's body for coin and being forced to—not that I imagined the Noble Fae compensated humans for their suffering.

"It's silly." Fresh tears seeped from Triana's eyes. "I wanted this for so long and I told myself any sacrifice would be worth it, but now that it's finally here . . . I'm afraid to lose my tongue."

I recoiled. "They're still going to cut it out?" I should have expected it from the Fae, but still—the barbarity was shocking.

"Tomorrow morning. Underfae from Fire House will cut it and cauterize the wound, and then I'll be like everyone else." She shuddered. "It's still better than the brothel."

"I'm so sorry. I can't imagine." For all that I was a prisoner, my life underground was practically paradise compared to what Triana had experienced, and I felt guilty at the thought. "Do you know sign language?"

"A little. We were kept separate from the other humans, but we learned some. Maude's going to teach me more."

I hesitated, wondering if I could ask to join those lessons or if my very presence would remind Triana of what she had lost—of what I was still in possession of purely by chance. "May I join you sometimes?" I asked. "I'd love to get to know you and learn sign language."

Triana looked at Maude. "What do you think?"

Maude studied me with dark, penetrating eyes, then nodded.

Triana smiled. "Then yes."

AFTER THANKING MAUDE AND TRIANA PROFUSELY, I LEFT, NOT wanting to intrude on Triana's sorrow any longer.

I'd noticed a flickering secret door in the corridor, but I left via the main stairwell in case anyone was watching. Other stairs led to deeper levels where more humans lived. I wondered how many people were housed here. Hundreds, at the least. A shocking number of people to have been stolen from their beds without the human world noticing, but then again, I'd heard occasional stories in Tumbledown about people disappearing: presumably lost to the bog, runaways, or murdered.

I found another entrance to the catacombs a few levels up and slipped inside before pulling a piece of parchment and a pen from my pouch. My mental map wasn't enough, considering how many levels and corridors wound through Mistei, so I'd started documenting my discoveries. I sketched the layout of the human section.

It would have been easy to get lost in the catacombs, but two things worked in my favor. One was that I would always reach the underground river eventually, which I could then follow back to Earth House. The other was that there were so many openings—both traditional doors and peepholes for spying—that I was likely to find an exit in a familiar location. Nevertheless, I made sure to document my route as I set off down the tunnel.

This section of the catacombs was rough-hewn, and I walked

carefully, the glowing key illuminating my path as the tunnel sloped upward. Eventually that light was joined by illumination from a small hole in the wall. I squinted through it, wishing I could study the peephole from the other side to see how it had been hidden from sharp Fae eyes. Perhaps it blended into a wall decoration.

The tiny hole looked out on a corridor near Fire House. The torches shone red gold, and the crystals in the ceiling were warm with late afternoon light. A cluster of laughing children darted past.

I hadn't seen many children in Mistei. The candidates were the youngest faeries at court or any of the formal dinners, and while there were children in Earth House, they didn't often go exploring. Probably because the royal court was dangerous even for full-grown faeries.

There were other openings nearby, so I continued investigating, peering through peepholes and pressing my ear against cracks and hidden doors. Most conversations I overheard were light, the topics ranging from fashion to the trials to the upcoming spring equinox celebration. I kept moving until I found a small stained glass window set at eye level. The sharp-edged design depicted a bonfire, and light from within the room cast shards of color over the corridor.

I squinted through the distorted glass, trying to determine which room this was. There were shelves along the walls—a library or study. Three figures leaned over a desk in the center of the room, two wearing pale clothing and one in dark red, but I couldn't make out their features.

I pressed my ear to the glass, straining to make out the faint words.

"That display was more sickening than usual." The voice belonged to Drustan.

"It's always sickening," an unfamiliar female voice replied.

"Usually there aren't quite so many to kill, though. His tolerance for dissent is diminishing. Soon it will be illegal to even think something negative about him."

"We should watch our words," another male voice said. "Lord Kallen is said to have spies lurking in every corner."

I winced.

"I warded the door, and if there was magic in this room, I would sense it. Even Kallen's sight has limits."

"Still, perhaps temper the words used to discuss our dear king. We want to show you the roster."

Drustan sighed. "Very well. His depravity won't last for much longer, anyway."

The conversation stopped, replaced by the rustling of paper and a few murmurs too low to make out. Though I strained to see through the warped glass, it was impossible to tell what roster they were reviewing or who the other two speakers were.

My heart raced, and I felt a bit sick. Drustan had not only criticized the king but implied his days were numbered. That was treason, and Kallen would definitely want to hear about it.

"What about Beltane?" the female faerie finally asked loud enough for me to hear. "Do we want to make connections?"

"No," Drustan said. "Too much risk. Osric has allies in Grimveld."

"Elsmere is about to gain new leadership, though. Young and untested, possibly malleable."

"You always hear the most interesting rumors. I wish you'd tell me where."

"Some secrets are mine to keep."

I wasn't entirely sure what they were talking about. Grimveld was a country to the northwest of Enterra, across the mountains we called the Giants' Teeth, after a legend so old all but the name had been forgotten. In Grimveld's icy plains, it was rumored day and night each lasted six months. They were said to have Fae, too, who wore ice as armor and rode creatures spun from snow. Elsmere wasn't a place-name I'd heard before, though, nor did I understand what Beltane had to do with anything.

"It's a decent suggestion," Drustan said, "but young and untested isn't what we need, and the bonds between us were never strong."

The other male faerie spoke up then. "Outside forces will also have outside opinions."

"True," the lady said.

"Besides, Kallen is always whispering in ears at these events," Drustan said. "If they're malleable, he'll have molded them before we can even make an introduction."

More soft, indistinct murmurs followed, then more rustling paper. Eventually a door opened and closed, and after that nothing moved in the library.

I felt cold, shivering from more than just the damp chill of the corridor. Even without understanding the specifics of what they had discussed, I knew that conversation had been a significant one. Kallen was expecting a report from me soon—what else did I have to give him?

I wasn't willing to betray Drustan, though—especially if he was plotting against the king.

15

THE SUCCESSION OF PARTIES AND DINNERS PROGRESSED, and the days blurred as I served Lara, assisted Alodie around Earth House, and visited Triana and Maude. My twenty-fifth birthday came and went, too, not that it mattered. What was the point of celebrating when the only two people who would have cared were both gone? My mother would never again make another tiny fruit loaf and sing off-key, and Anya would never again pretend to be annoyed that I had leapt a whole year ahead of her. Human time held little meaning in Mistei, anyway, so I shoved down any feelings about that milestone and dedicated myself to my eventual escape.

I spent every free moment exploring the catacombs, looking for a way out while listening for news about the trials. I was growing familiar with the places where the most elite faeries gathered to drink, trade barbs, and gamble on pointless bets. I'd even discovered a passageway beneath the throne room, an eerie, lightless corridor through which sound echoed from above. I could never stay there for long; every conversation I overheard was cruel, every joke vile, and sometimes the jokes were accompanied by screams. A trap-door glowed from the roof above my head, and every time I walked beneath it, I had a horrible vision of it swinging open and revealing me to King Osric's bloodthirsty gaze.

Since no one was inclined to share secrets in the throne room, I focused my attention elsewhere, lurking in the walls of nearby li-braries and sitting rooms. In some places the passages between rooms were so cramped I had to inch along sideways, and I tried not to imagine what would happen if I got stuck.

My greatest breakthrough came one afternoon when my explora-tions coincided with a gathering of the Illusion and Light candidates in a richly appointed parlor. I could see them through a peephole—Garrick and Gytha from Light House shared a couch, while Karissa and Markas paced as if unable to stay still.

"Come on," Gytha said. "Just a hint." She looked sleekly elegant, with her brown hair twisted into a bun and a snowy satin gown drap-ing in perfect folds to the floor.

Karissa laughed, a sound as pretty as wind chimes. Her purple velvet dress was bound by a sash of iridescent silk, and with her red hair cascading in wild curls to her waist, she was as vibrant as Gytha was austere. "Do you really think I would share anything? You fin-ished the labyrinth, Gytha. I didn't." Her gaze slid to Garrick. "Of course, I'm not the only one who failed."

"Oh, did I fail?" Garrick asked. "I seem to recall emerging with the highest number of tokens. How many did you collect, Karissa?"

Karissa's cheeks reddened. "Even more reason not to share what I know with you."

"We could share what we know about the Light trial in ex-change," Gytha said.

"You go first."

"That's hardly fair. Your trial's next."

"You're all beating me in this competition, including Markas, and he's an idiot. It's more than fair."

Markas scoffed but didn't defend himself.

Gytha laughed. "Very well. You know Light values discipline. Our test will be one of control. The ability to master your body even while your mind is compromised."

"Compromised how?"

Gytha shrugged. "That's all I can say." It was clearly not all she knew, given the smug look she exchanged with Garrick.

Karissa sighed dramatically. "That's hardly enough information to go on."

"Too bad," Garrick said. "Your turn."

Karissa smirked. "Oh, I think not. Come, Markas." She started to walk away, but Garrick was on his feet before she'd gotten more than a few steps. His hand banded around her arm, jerking her to a stop.

"Don't think you can renege on the deal," Garrick said. His fingers dug into her flesh.

"It wasn't good information," Karissa said, jutting her chin defiantly even as tears sprang to her eyes from his manhandling.

Garrick shoved her into the wall and slammed his hands on either side of her head. "Try again."

Gytha was watching with amusement, and even Markas looked on with an air of cruel satisfaction. Apparently house loyalty only went so far when there was humiliation or violence to be enjoyed.

Karissa's shoulders slumped with defeat. "I was just joking," she said sullenly.

Gytha arched one perfect brow. "Then you're as funny as you are intelligent. Come on, Karissa. You know you don't have the sophistication for these kinds of games."

"You're such a bitch, Gytha."

"At least I'm a competent one."

Garrick wrapped his fingers around Karissa's throat, and she held her hands up in surrender. "Fine," she said. "Illusion's virtue is cunning, so expect it to test your wits."

"How?" Garrick didn't release her.

"Through a series of riddles and puzzles, all of which must be solved within an allotted time period."

"What sort of puzzles?"

"I'll tell you if you tell me how our minds will be compromised."

Garrick's fingers tightened around her throat. He squeezed, smiling as Karissa scrabbled at his fingers, then finally let go. "We'll see you at the trial," he said.

The two Light candidates left the room.

Karissa glared after them, then turned on Markas. "You should have defended me."

He shrugged. "You should have known better than to challenge Garrick. It isn't my fault you're a fool."

"I know how much you love licking Garrick's boots, but I need to gain standing after the Void trial."

"And you think going against him is the way to do it?" Markas shook his head. "No one goes against Garrick. He's first in line for Light House."

Karissa's brow furrowed. "I thought Roland's brother was heir. The youngest one—Lothar? I thought he gained the position after Roland killed Garrick's father."

Wait, Prince Roland had killed one of his own brothers? And Garrick was still loyal to him?

"Not anymore," Markas said. "Garrick was boasting about it just last night. Said Prince Roland finally saw who was worthy. Garrick is in, Lothar is out."

"That makes no sense. Lothar is centuries old; he's respected at court. Garrick is . . ." She wrinkled her nose as if smelling something foul. "Garrick."

Markas shrugged. "Maybe he's lying. The point is, neither of us can afford to go against him. If you want to gain standing, you should try to do better in the trials."

Karissa made an outraged noise and raised a hand to slap him. Markas caught her wrist, then laughed when she tried to scratch him with the other.

The two Illusion candidates kept bickering as they left the room. I, however, felt giddy with delight at my success. Princess Oriana had been making it clear I needed to produce more information about the upcoming trials or face consequences, and I'd finally come up with something.

I told Lara about the conversation that night as I did her hair.

She made a face in the mirror. "I'm terrible at riddles. Selwyn loves them, though. Maybe he has a book I can read."

"Are Fae riddles difficult?"

"Difficult and dull. They're usually terrible poems from centuries ago that reference inside jokes about dead kings."

"That sounds awful."

"It is. I'm actually less worried about the Light trial. I'm getting better at looking bored all the time, so if all I have to do is hide whatever I'm thinking or feeling, it shouldn't be too bad."

Lara was being more candid with me every day. It had started after the formal dinner—probably because I hadn't told her mother about the crying—and the Void trial seemed to have strengthened that tentative bond between us.

"I wish I knew what they were going to do to your mind," I said. "Knowing Light House, it's probably going to hurt." I shuddered at the memory of Prince Roland's glee during the executions.

Lara grimaced. "I suppose you're right. I've never understood why they're so sadistic."

I pinned a braid into place atop Lara's head, then tucked a yellow blossom into it. "I heard they're immune to magic."

"Mostly, yes. They're resistant to it, at least—Illusion might trick one for a few seconds, but not forever. Even Oriana's vines would struggle to burrow into them. That's why they provide the king with jailers and executioners, because they can't be fooled or harmed by the other houses."

I thought of the winged guards from that horrible, bloody dinner, the pure white of their eyes and the smooth skin where their mouths should have been.

"Not that anyone can kill with magic without the king's permission," Lara continued, "and it's very draining to use the power like that, but it was more common before the rebellion. Light does fight with magic sometimes, but they prefer weapons. It's so primitive."

Like humans, I didn't say. "How often do the Fae fight? Surely battles aren't that common."

"There are minor fights between houses fairly frequently, or even between families in the same house. The last time we had a real war, though, was the rebellion. Oriana says it was gruesome." Lara surveyed my handiwork in the mirror. "You're getting better at this. Find a necklace, and then I'm ready for dinner."

I hunted through her jewelry box. "Do you actually enjoy these dinners?"

"Not really. Everyone's so competitive that all they do is insult each other. Garrick and Gytha love telling me I'm going to fail."

Garrick and Gytha seemed to enjoy tormenting everyone. "Do you have to pass every test to succeed?" If so, Karissa and Talfryn were already doomed.

"I don't think so. The judgment's based on cumulative performance, but no one knows how the magic decides." She waved the thought away and stood. "Let's go."

I stood next to Aidan that night, watching Lara converse with the other candidates at a small dinner hosted by Illusion House. Markas and Garrick were seated together, and Gytha and Karissa seemed to be allies in bitchery again. All four of them insulted Lara frequently.

Lara was right—she had gotten better at looking bored. I could tell when a taunt had found its mark, though, by the clenching of her fingers and the occasional twitch of an eye.

"She's doing well," Aidan said. "She surprised everyone during the first trial."

"She's tougher than she looks."

"Edric certainly isn't underestimating her anymore."

The Fire candidate had performed well, finishing the labyrinth on time with two tokens. As Edric threw his head back and laughed at a joke from Gytha, Aidan gazed at him fondly.

"You care about him, don't you?" I asked.

"Very much."

How unfair that the candidates faced possible death when they had friends and loved ones who worried for them. What would Aidan do if Edric failed? Where would he go? The scales between us were even, but if I could prevent him from losing someone he cared about . . .

"Illusion's test will be puzzles and riddles," I whispered. "Light is discipline, so controlling your body when your mind is compromised."

He glanced at me in surprise. I shrugged. "Consider it repayment." For taking a chance on me before the Void trial.

"But you've given me three pieces of information now, and I've only given you one."

"Better come up with more, then." I winked, and Aidan chuckled.

Lara lingered for private drinks with the other candidates, so I headed back towards Earth House alone. I took a different route than normal, one that was less direct but meandered past some interesting rooms. One hallway was lined with alcoves containing marble statuary, life-sized depictions of Noble Fae lords and ladies so realistic they looked ready to draw breath. The corridor air shifted in one of the strange breezes that drifted through Mistei; as the torchlight guttered and the shadows deepened, I imagined stone eyes shifting to watch me, stone hands clenching around weapons.

I shook my head at my own foolishness, then paused by the statue of a beautiful lady wrapped in roses, telling my heart to calm.

Footsteps sounded in the hall behind me. I spun, then felt relieved when Prince Drustan appeared. He was smiling and relaxed-looking, his garments shining bright as the torches. "Good evening, Kenna," he said, coming to a stop beside me. He nodded at the statue. "I see you've found the first Earth lady, Princess Clota."

A distant ancestor of Princess Oriana's—I'd heard her name mentioned in the house. Her marble face was round, her figure lush, and a carved cascade of water seemed to pour from her upraised hand to pool at her feet. I wanted to ask who the other statues depicted, but Drustan had followed me here from dinner and there was undoubtedly a reason for it.

Looking at his easy smile, I remembered what I'd overheard: *His depravity won't last for much longer.*

My relief shifted into a sparking uncertainty. Nervousness—or perhaps anticipation—prickled through me. "Good evening, my prince," I said, curtsying.

He raised his auburn brows. "Are we formal this evening? I thought I made my preferences clear."

"Only in private and when it comes to your friends," I pointed out. "I'm a mere servant, and we're still near Illusion territory."

Whatever his game, it was a dangerous one, and I was as wary as I was curious.

His smile widened, and that crooked grin scrambled my thoughts and sparked heat in my lower belly. It was a smile that invited confidences, confessions . . . intimacies. "And here I was hoping we were closer than that, Kenna."

My cheeks heated at the way he nearly purred my name. Curse him for being so attractive—he muddled my head, made me feel hot and foolish. I looked around, but the hall was empty except for the statues in their shadowed recesses. Drustan didn't seem worried about eavesdroppers, though his voice was pitched low enough not to carry.

Well, I preferred plain speaking anyway. "Me, specifically?" I asked just as softly, hoping my blush didn't show in the low light. "Or someone placed advantageously in Earth House?"

His eyes flared slightly, then trailed over me. "When you ask questions like that, the answer is definitely you, specifically."

He was standing too close. The heat emanating from him warmed my chest, my belly . . . lower. He looked breathtakingly perfect with that chiseled face and clever eyes and the Fae-bright glimmer of his skin—as unreachable as a star for a mere mortal, as *untouchable*—but oh, how I wanted to touch him. A few copper strands hung loose from his tied-back hair, and my fingers twitched with the desire to tuck them behind his ear.

I struggled for rational thought. "I'm not sure I understand what you mean by that, my prince."

He leaned in, breath ghosting over my cheek. "Call me Drustan. And I think you do understand, Kenna." He pulled back just enough for our eyes to meet. I fell into those gray irises, molten silver in the torchlight. "Bold but clever is a rare combination."

My heart wasn't working properly. Neither were my knees,

which wavered. I clenched my fists in my skirt as if that would keep me standing upright. "I wish faeries would just say what they mean instead of talking around it."

Drustan let out a surprised-sounding laugh, then straightened. "Not as much as I wish humans listened to the meaning between words." He dug his teeth into his plush lower lip as he studied me. "Have a good evening, Kenna."

He was going? I barely understood what had happened, but my entire body longed for him to stay. Still, I had my pride. "You as well." I dabbed a tongue to my lip. "Drustan."

His lashes briefly veiled his eyes. Then that smile tipped up again, crooked and sensual and hiding meanings I could only guess at. He walked away and turned the corner, leaving me feeling breathless and electrified.

"How interesting."

I leapt backwards at the unexpected voice, pressing a hand to my chest as my shoulders slammed against the wall.

The shadows in an alcove at the end of the hall seemed to shift, and then a faerie walked out, tendrils of darkness trailing after him. Lord Kallen, whose face was as cold and still as a marble statue's.

My pulse leapt frantically as he approached with measured footsteps. Hunting me slowly, like he knew there was nowhere I could run, no way for me to outpace him or hide. He could see in the dark and coil in the shadows like a snake; where could I go that he wouldn't find me?

And then there he was, standing before me the way Drustan just had, except there was no heat coming from Kallen's skin and his eyes spoke of black ice.

"Lord Kallen," I said, fumbling a curtsy.

"Are you fucking the Fire prince?" he asked.

I flinched at the crude word. "N-no, my lord."

"Hmm." His gaze traced over me. "You will be soon, I'll wager. He's never set his sights on anything he cannot have." A secret smile touched his lips. "For the most part."

Did Drustan have his sights set on me? The thought was intoxicating, but not something to contemplate in the presence of the King's Vengeance. He was saying it to draw some reaction out of me. "I'm on my way back to Earth House," I said coolly. "If you'll excuse me."

I tried to move past him, but he gripped my wrist. Not hard, but not soft, either. Unyielding. "What were you two speaking of?"

"I—I don't know," I stammered. "He told me this statue was Princess Clota. He said he'd like for us to be closer. Then he wished me a good evening, and that was it."

"That was it," Kallen repeated. He didn't look like he believed me.

There were meanings between Drustan's words I hadn't pieced together yet, so no, that wasn't it, but I wasn't lying, either. "I think he enjoys toying with me," I told Kallen. Also not entirely a lie. "I'm a curiosity."

"The human who made it across the bog," he mused. "A drop of Fae blood and a large quantity of courage. I do see why it's intriguing."

The dagger shifted slightly on my arm, and I nearly startled again. I was so used to my permanent jewelry that I sometimes forgot it was there. I'd tried to take the cuff off for a bath once, but the metal had turned liquid and raced over my skin while nipping and projecting annoyance into my mind. Eventually I'd given up, deciding to worry about it later.

The dagger's movement gave me some comfort. If I was in true danger, it would surely protect me. I took a deep breath, fumbling for that courage Kallen had so oddly complimented. "I wish you wouldn't find me intriguing," I said honestly.

There was a crack in his solemn expression, the slightest twitch of his mouth. "Most people share that sentiment." He paused. "Most people don't say it to my face, though."

"May I leave, my lord?" I asked with as much politeness as I could manage. "I have duties to undertake back at the house."

"No, you may not," he said with none of the same politeness. "You haven't given me any information." His fingers flexed on my wrist. "And I don't like to be kept waiting."

A quiver raced through me. Sweat gathered at the small of my back and beneath my arms despite the chill of the corridor. Here it was, the payment coming due. What did I have to offer?

"I heard Garrick is the new heir to Light House," I said. "The candidates were discussing it."

Kallen's face remained impassive. "Garrick assumes an outcome that isn't settled yet. What else?"

"Else?" I asked. "Is that not enough?"

"For the weeks you've spent lurking in corners at court events? No, it's not enough." He tipped his head, making the midnight silk of his hair shift. It brushed his shoulders, straight and sleek as a raven's wing. "Come now, Kenna. One more piece of information and I'll let you leave."

It was as hard to think around Kallen as it was around Drustan, though for different reasons. Drustan made me flustered with want, but right now fear was making my mind race in too many directions. Drustan's grin might hide secrets, but Kallen didn't smile at all . . . and I suspected his secrets were far worse.

There was one thing I could offer, though its origins would need to be obscured. "I overheard something at a party," I said. "Someone mentioned a place—Elsmere? They said it had a new ruler. Or was about to."

His eyes widened. "Who said that?" he demanded. It was the strongest show of emotion I'd seen from him yet.

"I don't know." I thought of the pale figures through the stained glass of the library window. They wouldn't have been members of Light House, since Light was allied with the king. More likely it had been a Fire lady wearing a pastel yellow gown that was impossible to differentiate from ivory through the colorful glass. "A Light lady," I lied. "I don't know her name."

"What did she look like?"

"She had . . . brown hair?" I hazarded, figuring that would encompass the largest number of people. I was dropping false clues, but I didn't want him to actually follow them anywhere.

"Is that a question, or are you telling me?"

"She had brown hair," I repeated. "Light skin. It was an offhand comment, and I don't remember the rest of the conversation. The word just caught my ear because I'd never heard of Elsmere before."

He stared at me for a few more agonizing seconds, then released my wrist. "That will suffice for tonight."

I breathed a silent sigh of relief and cupped my wrist in my other hand, rubbing it not because it hurt but because I wanted to wipe away the memory of his touch.

His dark eyes dipped to my wrist, then back up. Torchlight flickered across his face, making his cheekbones and nose seem sharp as blades. "Until next time, Kenna."

The shadows in the alcove across the way darkened and thickened, then started crawling across the floor towards us. I stumbled back, pressing myself against the wall as the tendrils wound around Kallen's ankles, up his legs, and around his torso, wrapping him in a cocoon of night. The last to vanish were his eyes, which still watched me.

A breeze rippled the hem of my dress. When the light in the corridor returned to normal, he was gone.

16

T HE ILLUSION TRIAL ARRIVED FASTER THAN I WOULD HAVE
believed. It had been a full month since the Void trial, but
time had passed so quickly it felt like a week.

The trial would be held during a ball that night. Lara pored over
one of Selwyn's riddle books as I pinned her hair into a braided crown.
Her gown was gorgeous. The bodice was the color of spring grass and
covered in delicate evergreen netting, and the plunging neckline was
lined with alternating diamonds and pink silk rosebuds. The same netting was draped over the top half of her frothing skirts, the fabric gathered at intervals with more rosebuds. She looked like spring incarnate.

In contrast, I was wearing the same green dress I'd worn to the
king's murderous dinner. It was a functional garment, not one designed for beauty. For a moment I imagined wearing silk and jewels
instead. It was an odd fancy, but now that I had access to cosmetics
and dresses, I found myself appreciating them more. While once I
had embraced my reputation for being half feral, my time at the Fae
court had allowed me to sample a different way of being. It was far
more appealing than I ever would have guessed.

The loss of Anya grew more distant with each passing day, but the pain of her absence was sharp in moments like these. I could imagine her teasing me for wanting to wear a fancy dress. "I thought dresses were for the unimaginative," she'd crow, spitting my old words back in my face. "I thought you wore trousers to be original." I would tug on her hair, and she'd laugh and tweak my nose and then challenge me to a race that she would, of course, win, being nearly a foot taller than me. Then she'd claim her victory prize—a detailed description of my dream dress, down to the last stitch.

Lara cocked her head and smiled into the mirror, and something in the movement reminded me of Anya, too. "I like it," she said. She stood and smoothed out her skirts, then pressed a hand to her stomach and took as deep a breath as the bodice would allow. "Time to solve some riddles."

Selwyn was waiting for us at the bottom of the stairs. "You look terrible," he told Lara as she swept into the hall.

"Don't be jealous of the adults, Sprout." *Sprout* was the nickname she called him when Oriana wasn't around. "Isn't it already past your bedtime?"

He scowled. "I don't know why you bother dressing up, anyway. Do you actually want to impress the king? Everyone knows—"

"Selwyn," she said firmly as Oriana approached. "Thank you for complimenting my dress. Have a good night."

As Selwyn stalked out, Lara shook her head. "Teenagers."

THE BALLROOM LOOKED LIKE PURE MAGIC. THE MIRRORED CEIL-ing, walls, and floor reflected color and light into infinity. Garlands of flowers hung from the ceiling, and gleaming marble statues stood at ten-foot intervals around the perimeter. Hundreds of faerie lights drifted above the crowd. The Noble Fae wore their finest attire: elaborate, glittering gowns and long, formal tunics slit high at the sides to reveal black trousers and polished boots. It was warm inside the crowded room, and the faeries kept themselves cool with bejeweled fans that matched their outfits. They fluttered like a cloud of butterflies.

Lara snapped open her lace fan and strode in confidently as I faded back into the group of servants. We weren't positioned stiffly at the walls today. Instead, we would wait on our masters hand and foot, providing them with refreshment and repairing any rips in their attire caused by the dancing.

It was strange, wonderful dancing. Couples alternated between synchronized, elegant movements and pacing in intimate circles, one hand gracefully outstretched, the other nestled at their partner's waist in a way our village Elder would have frowned at. Occasionally ladies partnered with other ladies while lords danced with lords— also something the Elder would have frowned at, but the Fae were open to love across gender boundaries. It was sensual in a way I hadn't realized dancing could be, the promise of physical touch mixed with coy aloofness.

Lara danced with both ladies and lords, and I was surprised to realize not all of them were from Earth House. In fact, many of the couples twirling across the mirrored floor were from opposing houses. I asked Aidan about it on my way to fetch a glass of wine for Lara.

"Mingling between houses is a tradition during these dances," he told me. "It's not exactly forbidden at other times, so you do see cross-house friendships, but the dances are one of the only places where it's actively encouraged. It's good to remember we're all citizens of Mistei."

Drustan danced with an endless succession of beautiful ladies, his head tipped back in laughter more often than not. His copper hair was tied back, highlighting the strong planes of his face, and he looked gorgeous in a shimmering scarlet tunic accented with embroidered flames. I watched him, riveted by the athletic grace of his movements.

I averted my gaze when I realized Aidan had noticed me staring. It was no use, though.

"The Fire prince certainly draws the eye." Aidan looked amused. "I've always wondered . . . does he burn as hot in the bedroom as he looks like he would?"

I flushed. "Stop talking nonsense."

His smile expanded into a brilliant grin. "There's no shame in looking, dear Kenna."

I hurried away before he could tease me further.

I brought Lara several glasses of wine, alternating them with punch so she could retain her wits. I'd just started to wonder if the trial would happen at all when the music stopped. Silence fell as the king stood from a transparent glass throne at one end of the room.

He wore a blinding white tunic edged in violet, and diamonds glittered over each sleeve like frost on a frigid morning. "Welcome to the second trial," he said.

I waited with bated breath, ready to leap into action to help Lara. Assuming I would be able to help. With so many curious eyes on the candidates, she might have to undertake this challenge alone.

"Your next test is one of cunning and intelligence. Each of you will find a bracelet around your wrist."

Lara's eyes widened in surprise as she beheld her new silver bracelet topped with a small purple box. The other candidates looked equally startled as they inspected their own.

"There are several clues for each candidate in this room. The bracelet is the first clue. Solve each one by midnight and follow the instructions they provide." He clapped his hands and resumed his seat.

For a moment the ballroom remained still and silent, staring at the king. Was that it? Surely there were more instructions.

King Osric just smiled and gestured for a servant to bring him wine.

Well. At least I would be able to help Lara by looking for clues and potentially solving a few of the puzzles. I met her panicked gaze and nodded reassuringly.

The contestants scattered like leaves in the wind, scrambling to the edges of the room to investigate their bracelets as the dancing resumed.

I slid a hand into my pocket, wrapping it around a smooth piece of bark just smaller than my palm that would help us cheat in this trial. Lara and I needed to communicate somehow, but it would be dangerous to be seen passing notes or speaking too much. Princess Oriana had provided a solution in a matching pair of bark strips that were enchanted to share whatever messages were written on them. With Lara's rudimentary Earth magic, she could inscribe messages on her bark, which I would then read on mine before slipping away to write my responses in pen. We would be able to communicate from across the room, and Lara wouldn't even need to remove the bark from her pocket to send a message.

I waited until the wood warmed under my fingers, then stepped behind a statue and pulled it out.

Thin incised lines showed two views of a box with a hinge on one side and an ornate keyhole on the other. Each side contained a circle labeled with a letter—*R*, *G*, *O*, *P*, *B*, and *W*. Beneath the drawing she'd written:

It's locked. Jewels on sides are house colors.

So the letters indicated red, green, orange, purple, black, and white. This was clearly some sort of puzzle box. I frowned and wrote suggestions below the diagram.

Press jewels.
Pull jewels off to see if key is behind.

I slid it into my pocket and watched as Lara surreptitiously pulled her bark out, hiding the motion behind her flicking fan. She returned it to her pocket and began fiddling with the bracelet.

My bark warmed. She had wiped both her previous message and my own away, and now new words appeared:

Purple clicked but box didn't open.

I thought back to the diagram. The purple jewel was situated beneath the hinge, and the side with the keyhole was red. Why would it click but not open? Did she need to push the purple jewel while inserting a key on the red side? But if the box was the first clue, where would she even find a key?

The purple gem was clearly part of the solution, so I focused on that. Purple was the king's color, representing Illusion. Many of his courtiers wore it tonight, and the servants wore purple-and-silver livery as well. Could one of them have a key?

Purple represented Illusion . . .

The answer hit me like a thunderbolt. Illusion magic proved that appearances could never be trusted.

There was no key.

I scribbled hastily:

Push purple and open from hinge side.

Lara tinkered with the box, then squealed in delight when it popped open. The hinge had actually been a handle, and the true hinge had been hidden in the elaborate keyhole. She pulled out a folded scrap of paper.

I meandered around the room, waiting for my pocket to warm. It wouldn't do to lurk behind statues all night. Eventually I felt the glow of magic, and when I was finally able to look, I understood Lara's consternated expression.

Petals fan out from buds
Roses blooming from green leaves
Behind the garden are secrets

Was there a garden somewhere in the ballroom? Flower garlands draped from the ceiling, but none of those contained roses. Maybe this was a snippet of a famous poem, in which case I had to agree with Lara's assessment that old Fae poems were terrible. Had one of the dead kings grown flowers? Was there a faerie joke about roses?

I strolled the perimeter, studying the statues that lined the walls. They looked like luminaries from ages past, some with crowns or scepters, some in elaborately carved gowns. There were even a few Underfae depicted, which surprised me. It seemed long ago Mistei had been more egalitarian.

Eventually I completed my circuit of the room and had to accept that there were no flowers or gardens depicted on any of the statues.

Very well. Rose and green were also colors. I scanned the room for outfits that matched that color scheme, like Lara's own gown, but there were far too many.

Perhaps the clue was less obvious and had to do with one of the other words. *Petals, fan, buds, roses, blooming, green, leaves, behind, garden, secrets.* If I eliminated anything having to do with non-existent flowers or gardens, that left me with *fan, behind, secrets.* *Secrets* undoubtedly indicated the answer to the puzzle, which I would presumably find *behind* whatever object the poem pointed to. That left only *fan*.

Fan.

I studied the crowd again, searching for green and rose, but this time I focused on accessories, not gowns.

There. A dark-haired lady in a shimmering violet gown with a scalloped neckline. She stood alone at the edge of the dancing, watching the crowd and fanning herself lazily. The silk fan in her hand didn't match her dress: it was spring green with pink roses clustered in the center.

I passed behind her on my way to the refreshment table and saw a line of writing along the edge of the fan, but couldn't get close enough to read it without attracting attention.

I brought Lara a glass of wine. "Rose fan and Illusion dress," I whispered, then curtsied and spoke more loudly. "Do you need anything else, my lady?"

Lara's eyes roamed over the ballroom and found the Illusion faerie. "No, I have everything I need."

A few minutes later, Lara casually meandered towards the lady. She bumped into her and apologized, then gestured appreciatively at the fan. The lady smiled and showed her the front and back, then slipped a piece of paper into Lara's hand.

I watched the dancing while waiting for Lara's next message. As always, my eyes were drawn to Drustan. He moved elegantly across the floor, the slits in his swaying tunic revealing flashes of leg. I slid an appreciative gaze over the muscular thighs revealed by his well-tailored trousers. If only his tunic was shorter so I could see the curve of his buttocks, too . . .

When I dragged my gaze back up to his face, I realized he was watching me. His lips were pressed together in suppressed mirth, and he raised one teasing eyebrow. I blushed wildly and looked away, mortified that I'd been caught ogling him.

Thankfully, the next message arrived then. I ducked into the washroom to read it.

Fan said Nidhug the Unlikely. He's the 3rd statue from the end, the big one with the ugly crown, but I looked and nothing's there. She also gave me another ridiculous poem.

The words on the bark vanished and were replaced with more.

*When snow's upon the green green grass
Earth sleeps alone but never dies
Beneath the icy winter blast
Seeds lie waiting to arise
But what if winter stayed, alas!
The season will not compromise
The frigid sleet, the lakes of glass
And where you kneel on once green grass
The king in ice will sit and sigh
That once a House existed nigh
But now the blooms are dead and lost
Even Earth must bow to frost*

A shiver went down my spine at the ominous little poem. Was it some kind of warning? A promise that Earth's time as a house was coming to an end? Lara gave a little shrug when I reentered the ballroom. Her face was tight with worry.

I couldn't think what the clue meant. There was no grass in the ballroom, nor was there snow or frost, which meant this was a metaphor of some sort. I kept walking, scanning outfits and accessories for winter motifs and hoping the answer would come to me.

Perhaps she needed to look for something cold. The air was

warm from the press of bodies, so I returned to the refreshment table. There was ice in the punch bowl, but nothing that looked like an answer to a riddle.

I met Aidan there. "How's Edric doing?" I asked quietly.

Aidan winced. "Not well. Lara?"

"She solved two clues, but she says the next one is completely nonsensical." I hesitated before deciding I might as well ask the next question. "Were there any kings of winter in Fae lore? Someone who controlled ice, maybe?"

He stared at me suspiciously. "Did she tell you what the clue was?"

I couldn't tell him the truth. It was one thing for servants to share relevant information before the trials, but it was another thing entirely to admit to cheating during the test itself. "No, but when I brought her wine, she was muttering something about a winter king. I was curious if it was a clue."

"Don't ask anyone else that. You can't be seen helping her or it'll go very badly for both of you."

"Of course." I tried to look chastened. "It was foolish of me."

Aidan clapped my shoulder sympathetically. "It's hard to see them struggle, isn't it?"

"I'm afraid for her." *And for me.*

Aidan's eyes danced with the faintest flicker of embers. "There are no kings of winter that I know of." When I looked at him in surprise, he sighed. "We both know you were just going to keep poking around until you found an answer. So stop right there and let Lara figure it out herself."

I smiled at him. "Of course. Thank you."

Hours passed while I turned the poem over and over in my mind, wondering what I'd missed. The dancing continued unabated, the spins getting less elegant the more wine the Fae consumed. It would be midnight in less than an hour, and Lara and I were still stuck with two clues and no answers. The statue of Nidhug the Unlikely hadn't yielded anything so far and seemed to have no relation to the poem at all, which meant there was at least one more clue to solve after we deciphered the poem.

I started silently listing words from the poem in case one of them would spark a thought. It had worked for the last clue, after all. *Grass, winter, seeds, sleet, lake, glass, ice, Earth, frost.* Two categories of words: Earth House imagery and winter imagery. Since Lara was from Earth House, were those words supposed to be about her? If so, what did winter represent?

I considered the verbs associated with Earth imagery. *Sleeps, lie, arise, kneel, bow.* Sleeping and lying were out of the question for this ball, but she could conceivably kneel, bow, or arise. *Sleeps, lie,* and *arise* belonged to the first part of the poem, which described a typical winter, and I had a feeling the answer lay in the second part of the poem and the unending winter that would destroy Earth. Was she supposed to kneel before the king in ice? Bow to frost?

King. Glass. Ice.

King Osric lounged on a glass throne, his attire as blindingly white as snow. Heart hammering, I drifted along the wall towards the throne until I was close enough to see the details of his clothing. The diamonds on his sleeves weren't lined up evenly but organized in clusters. There was no mistaking the pattern.

Snowflakes.

Earth must bow to frost.

The answer made sense, given what I knew of the king. The poem was a subtle threat, a promise that one day Earth House would perish at Osric's hand—something Drustan himself had warned me about. As for what Osric wanted Lara to do, I was sure he would be ecstatic to have Earth House's heir kneel at his feet in supplication. He took any chance to humiliate Princess Oriana.

Lara was near tears when I brought her a fresh glass of wine. "I can't figure it out."

I hadn't written my instructions down, knowing Lara would need convincing. "Kneel before the king," I whispered.

"What?" Her eyes widened.

"I think it's what the clue means. Kneel, and maybe he'll give you a new clue. Or maybe there's something on the floor."

"That's embarrassing," she hissed.

"We have fifteen minutes left. It's this or nothing."

I left before she could argue further.

She approached the throne at last, jaw clenched and hands fisted in her skirts. The conversation around her died, replaced by curious stares.

King Osric looked at her as if she were an insect. "Yes?"

Lara swept her skirts out and sank into a low curtsy that transitioned elegantly into her kneeling before him. Murmurs rose at the gesture of obeisance. "My king." She looked up at him with remarkable aplomb. "I would like to thank you for this marvelous ball, and to remind you of my utter fealty to you."

King Osric's laugh echoed around the room, silencing all other conversation. "A lady of Earth on her knees—what a delight. Your mother should learn such charming manners." He glanced triumphantly at Oriana, but the Earth princess knew how to control her emotions and seemed utterly disinterested in the proceedings. Osric returned his attention to Lara. "Rise. Your gesture finds favor tonight."

Lara rose and curtsied again before backing away from the throne. Her cheeks were flushed more deeply than usual as she approached me. "I tore my hem," she said loudly, then whispered, "It was there."

I knelt before her and pretended to fuss with her skirt. "What?"

"There was writing on the back of the throne. I could see it through the glass. *Stand beside gold.*"

It was reckless to talk directly, but we were running out of time and no one was close enough to listen in.

"What does that mean?" And what did it have to do with Nidhug the Unlikely, our other clue with no resolution?

"I think I need to be standing somewhere at midnight."

"Is anyone wearing a gold tunic? Or maybe it's another one of the statues—is anyone in Fae history known for being golden?"

Lara shook her head helplessly. "I don't know my history that well."

I rose. "Let's look for anything that might fit that description."

I moved through the crowd, searching for anything golden. Unfortunately, many of the Fae wore gold, either as the main color of their garments or as accents. Lara examined the statues on the other side of the room, searching the plaques at their feet for a relevant name.

We had mere minutes left. A few of the other candidates were also hurrying around frantically, which was a relief, at least. But where were the rest of them?

I noticed a still spot in the middle of the dancing. It was Garrick, looking relaxed as he spoke with a beautiful lady. He didn't move, despite the couples spinning around him. Una stood twenty feet from him, craning her neck as if examining the decorations on the ceiling. A few other candidates stood throughout the room, some examining statues, some chatting casually in the middle of the floor. The dancers moved around them as if they weren't there. No wonder I hadn't seen them before; they'd been hidden by the whirl of skirts.

They were all lined up precisely with various statues along the wall.

I retreated behind a statue and scribbled on the bark.

I think you have to stand in line with two statues.
Nidhug is one.

The answer came back quickly.

We need to find a statue that relates to gold.

Lara hurried towards Nidhug, and when I looked at the clock I realized why. There was only a minute left. She wouldn't be able to investigate the other statues and make it back to her position in time. She looked at me pleadingly.

Something gold, something gold . . .

If Nidhug was one position marker, the other needed to be on an adjoining wall. The back wall didn't contain anything gold, only more marble statues.

Then I saw it. A statue of an asrai writing in a ledger. Piles of carved marble coins were heaped around her feet. Unable to shout the position to Lara or write on the bark in full view of the ballroom, I walked towards the statue, jerking my head for her to follow. A bell began chiming midnight. If Lara wasn't there by the time the last stroke rang . . .

I stopped exactly in line with both Nidhug and the statue of the faerie counting her gold. The final stroke chimed just as Lara reached my side. As the sound faded, we were bathed in illumination. A cluster of faerie lights had congregated above, leaving most of the room in darkness.

I darted away, leaving Lara standing alône. Around the room, other faerie lights marked the positions of candidates who had successfully solved their puzzles. Only three had not: Talfryn, Karissa, and Edric.

Aidan looked devastated when I reached his side. "He can't fail," the sprite said.

Impulsively, I gripped his gray hand and squeezed it. He squeezed back, but his eyes were fixed on Edric's dejected face.

King Osric rose. "Congratulations to the six who completed the challenge. Each candidate needed to stand in a specific place at midnight. One clue told them their first position marker: a single statue in the ballroom. The other clues directed them to take certain actions that would lead them to the final clue." He grinned wickedly at the crowd. "Some actions were delivering wine to someone or dancing with a stranger." *Or kneeling on the floor,* he didn't say. I resented him all the more for revealing how innocuous the other actions had been in comparison. "The final clue led them to another position marker. Both together would reveal the exact place a candidate needed to stand."

The assembled faeries applauded politely.

"Now dance. Drink. Celebrate. The second trial has concluded."

Aidan was still gripping my hand when the music resumed.

"Edric can still pass," I said. "One trial isn't enough to stop him."

He swallowed. "I know. But if he died, I . . ." He shook his head.

I was touched by the depth of feeling on his face. "I'll help you however I can. We know a little about what Light House will expect. Which test is after that?"

"Fire. He should do fine on that one." He shrugged apologetically at my quizzical look. "I can't tell you anything about that one or it will ruin the test. Just know that Lara doesn't need to prepare and it won't be unpleasant."

Void, Illusion, Light, Fire . . . "Then it's just Earth and Blood, right? I don't know what the Earth test is yet, but I'll let you know if I learn anything. Who oversees the Blood trial?"

"I don't know." He grimaced. "The Blood trial worries me most of all. The magic can run the trial without a house head, but that means there's no gossip to collect about what's going to happen."

"Can we ask anyone what sort of test Blood House would have favored?"

His ash-gray skin paled. "Absolutely not. We're already skirting the edge of propriety by mentioning the house at all, even if it's just related to the trial. The only ones who speak of them anymore are the Nasties, which should tell you everything you need to know about their reputation."

I watched the dancing while I considered what he'd said. If no one would speak about the house except for the Nasties . . .

I shivered. There was only one choice.

17

I PEERED DOWN THE STAIRWELL, WONDERING IF I WAS THE greatest fool ever to live.

Was I really about to seek out the Fae's foulest monsters to ask them about the Blood trial?

The stone steps were uneven, and there were no torches to light the way. It looked like the entrance to a cave. Would there be any illumination down there? If not, I'd need to return to the upper levels to grab a torch. I didn't want to use the key where someone might see it.

Not that the key could provide anything but its golden glow down here. The Nasties lived below even the human quarters, and I hadn't been able to find any hidden Earth tunnels that went that far underground yet. Thus, the direct approach.

I clenched my hands, digging my fingernails into my palms. The pain helped ground me. I reminded myself that I had my wits, a decent amount of speed, the protection of Earth House, and a mystical dagger. Surely that would be enough.

I braced myself against the walls on either side as I descended.

Soon the light of the corridor above had receded to a faint glimmer. Just when I thought I wouldn't be able to see my steps anymore, a bluish light appeared below, like the diffuse gleam of sunlight through water.

The stairs ended in a pillared hall lit by glowing blue moss that grew up the columns and crawled over the ceiling. Three archways yawned in the wall opposite the stairwell. The left-hand opening was pitch black, and the air emanating from it was icy. The middle archway was illuminated by the same blue light as the main chamber, revealing a cobbled path. The right-hand opening led to sharp rocks lit by a fiery red flicker.

I chose the middle opening and the terrain I would be fastest on should I need to run. The path led into another cavern lined with luminescent moss. Milky-white stalactites and stalagmites reached towards each other, and the sound of dripping water echoed off the walls. Something small scuttled behind a rock as I approached, but the dagger barely twitched against my arm, so I assumed it was mostly harmless. As I passed, I saw three beady red eyes, a furred snout, and a hairless forked tail. The Nasty equivalent of a rat.

The path wound through a series of similar caves, and the deeper I went, the stranger the surroundings became. I passed pools of still water, glittering black crystals, and towering monoliths, all lit with that faint blue glow. A footbridge with no railing arced over a fast, narrow river; as I crossed it, a green fin breached the surface, followed by the thrash of a scaly tail that sent water splashing over the front of my dress. A knucker?

Yes, the dagger replied, squeezing my bicep hard. *Don't fall in.*

"I'll do my best," I muttered, relieved when my feet met solid ground again.

The next cavern was filled with snow-white grass that reached to my waist. I brushed my hand over the silky fronds; as they moved under my touch, grass stirred elsewhere in the cave. Something was approaching quickly from the right, sending ripples through the grass. The dagger vibrated in warning and took form in my hand. When I raised the blade menacingly, the motion stopped.

"Better stay like that," I whispered to the dagger. It quivered in agreement.

Throughout the cave system, smaller paths arrowed away from the main thoroughfare, but I had no desire to explore them. The path I was on was wide and well lit—it had to lead somewhere important.

At last I emerged in a chamber almost as large as the cavern where the king's dinner had taken place. A strange, cylindrical building rose in the center. It was continuous with the black stone above and below, as if it had been carved from the rock when the cavern was first formed. Twisting pillars rose to the ceiling, and balconies punctuated each level. The doorways and windows were wide enough to accommodate the stretch of wings.

The path splintered ahead of me, weaving a dark web throughout the space. Other exotic features dotted the landscape: carved monoliths depicting monsters, enormous stone benches, even a gnarled oak tree that rose over another patch of bone-white grass. The bark glittered, and as its leaves rustled in one of the inexplicable winds that scoured Mistei's corridors, tinkling music echoed through the vast chamber. Not wood and leaves at all, but stone.

Here, at last, were the Nasties.

They stood in clusters, sat on benches, and gazed into pools. They flew, crawled, and slithered. They were as varied and brilliant as the Noble Fae and Underfae, but twisted, as if their beauty had been distorted in an imperfect mirror.

There were tall Nasties with humanlike bodies and the heads of deer. An enormous golden snake with three ruby eyes. Tusked animals with six legs and wiry fur covering their muscled bodies. There were even Nasties whose faces looked gorgeously Noble Fae–like above their contorted bodies and sharp claws. Nightmares flew overhead, crimson-scaled beings with the backwards-jointed legs of animals but the torsos and heads of humans. Twisting horns sprouted from their foreheads, and their membranous wings reminded me of bats.

The murmur of voices mixed with hisses, snarls, and chimes. Not all the words or sounds were recognizable, and I wondered if they'd developed a common tongue to speak with the more monstrous creatures, those whose mouths didn't work like mine.

The sound died as hundreds of eyes focused on me. I felt their malevolence like a thickening of the air.

The dagger pumped with urgency in my hand. "I know," I told it. My body tingled with the knowledge that I was weak and an outsider—potential prey to these horrors.

The nearest cluster of Nasties broke apart as they approached me. I was being surrounded. I kept my spine straight, trying not to let my fear show. Illusion shaped reality in Mistei—perhaps feigned confidence would protect me.

The Nasty in front of me inhaled deeply. It was mostly feline in form, with a whiskered muzzle, pointed ears, and a swishing tail, but its arms and legs were wholly human beneath a layer of silky black fur. There was a white blazon on its chest, and I remembered Elder Holman saying that black animals, especially those with a single white mark, might be shape-shifters from the other realm. *And Fae creatures often have unnatural hungers,* he'd warned.

The Nasty smiled, revealing sharp fangs.

Sweat dampened my dress. "I'd like to visit whoever is in command down here," I said with false bravado. The king was theoretically in command everywhere in Mistei, but surely the Nasties had their own hierarchy.

"Why?" the Nasty asked in a rumbling voice, stepping closer.

"I'm from Earth House. I have questions."

The circle around me continued to tighten. "Earth House has no business down here."

"I have business down here." I brandished my weapon. "Stop where you are."

The Nasty didn't stop. "I wonder how your blood will sing on my tongue," it said, licking a fang.

I held my ground despite the fine trembling that started in my legs. "I'll kill you if you try to find out." I had never killed anyone before, but just because this Nasty sounded human didn't mean it was any less of a monster. I could do it if I had to.

Movement flashed to my left. An enormous serpent, striking with stunning quickness. I barely had enough time to move the dagger between us before it knocked me over. It followed me down, the blade embedded in its scales.

Yes, the dagger exulted, and I felt an echoing pulse of sick joy in my veins as the jewel on the pommel glowed red. The serpent's eyes dulled as it fell to the ground, its formerly strong body shriveled and dry.

The dagger had completely drained it of blood in only a few seconds.

I hid my shock and shoved the snake's corpse off me, rising to my feet. I raised the dagger, ready for another attack, but no one approached. Instead, they backed away, looking wide-eyed at the weapon in my hand.

A keening sound started to my right. One of the tusked, piglike Nasties collapsed to the ground, head bowed. Others joined it.

Were they grieving? It made me sick to think of them mourning a friend the way I had mourned Anya.

They were monsters, I reminded myself. They didn't feel that deeply. "Which way?" I asked the catlike Nasty, trying to hide my nausea and discomfort.

It pointed silently at the citadel in the center of the chamber. Creatures scurried out of my way as I mounted the steps to the monumental front doors and walked into a vast entrance hall.

Before I could step more than five paces inside, a short, wizened creature with pointed ears and skin gray as granite rushed up, bowing and motioning for me to follow. I might have believed he was an Underfae, but something unsettling twisted beneath his skin, like worms burrowing. He led me down a few labyrinthine corridors, then stopped before a door that had been hammered out of silver. He opened it, ushering me through.

The room was lit by candles. It was intimate compared to the entrance hall, with checkered black-and-white floors and more hammered silver lining the walls. A loosely woven ivory tapestry covered one entire wall, and before it was a stone altar. A nude female faerie stood behind the altar, visible from the waist up.

She was beautiful in a terrifying way, with milk-pale skin, jet-black hair, and round eyes the color of fresh blood. Her ruby lips gleamed wetly in the flickering candlelight. On either side she was protected by a line of winged guards, the same type I'd seen flying above.

"Why have you come here, human?" Her voice was smooth and caressing, but it gave me the sensation of something skittering over my skin.

Time to speak the words I was never supposed to speak. "I'm seeking information about Blood House."

"Is that so?" She cocked her head. "How curious. Will they not tell you above?"

"It's forbidden to speak of Blood House above."

By the look on her face, she already knew this. "So you have sought out the Queen of the Nasties in the hopes I will defy Osric and tell you whatever it is you need to know."

A queen? Osric definitely wouldn't approve of that. My pulse accelerated with rising fear. "I was told only the Nasties had the courage to speak of Blood House. Your majesty."

She laughed, and the hairs on my neck rose. The sound dug into me like whisper-thin needles. "You are correct, of course. You seem familiar with blood already, though." She glanced significantly at the dagger in my hand, as if she knew about the snake I'd killed. "Do you really need us to tell you more?"

Would she put me on trial? Execute me? "Your subject attacked me," I protested, gripping the hilt tighter. "I have the right to defend myself."

"If you were fast enough to kill him, he did not deserve to live." She flicked a hand dismissively. "I am curious about that dagger, though. Where did you get it?"

"I've always had it."

"Liar."

"It's the truth. It belonged to my father."

"Will you give it to me in exchange for information about Blood House?"

The dagger shuddered so strongly the vibrations shook my bones. I glanced around for danger and realized several of the winged Nasties to my right stood closer than they had a few seconds ago. Each wore a belt bristling with knives, and their black breeches cut off at the knee, revealing taloned feet that could easily disembowel me.

"Perhaps," I lied, trying not to panic. "Just tell me this—what did Blood House hold sacred? What trait would they seek to test in others, and how might they test it?"

"You presume much, demanding answers from Queen Dallaida without offering something in exchange first." She smiled widely, and now I could see that there were no teeth in that gaping mouth.

There was something else behind those crimson lips, though, something black and glistening . . .

"Queen Dallaida," I said, shifting my weight towards the exit, "I mean no disrespect, but it's a simple question. Hardly worthy of a dagger like this."

"A simple question with a complex answer. Here is the easiest part of it. Blood valued strength."

I knew strength was one of the sacred traits, but it wasn't enough to help me guess what the trial might be. "What kind of strength? Physical? Did they value violence?"

"All forms of strength." She flicked a pale hand, and the winged soldiers began advancing towards me. "Did you know the Dark Fae—the Nasties, you call us—used to swear fealty to Blood House? After the other houses banished us for being too foul to look upon, Blood welcomed us because we were strong. You, however, are weak."

She was going to try to take the dagger by force. I began sidling towards the exit, trying to keep an eye on all my enemies at once. There were two guards standing in front of the door—I might need to kill them to escape.

I'd never killed anything other than animals. I could tell myself the snake I'd slain had also been an animal, despite the intelligence in its eyes, but these winged Nasties definitely weren't. Monstrous, yes. Animal, no.

I would do whatever I had to in order to survive.

One of the Nasties hesitated as he studied the weapon in my hand, but at a barked order from Queen Dallaida, he moved to intercept me. He, too, held a knife, but the shiver of the blade told me he was trembling.

Were they that afraid of the dagger? I knew it was magical, but to inspire a reaction like this . . .

A metal disc protected the Nasty's chest, polished so smooth I could see the echo of my terrified face in it, but his arms, legs, and wings were unencumbered. Vulnerabilities to aim for—if I was fast enough.

The Nasty lashed out. I leapt to the side, barely avoiding the cut of his knife. I feinted high, then sliced low, severing the artery in his thigh. He collapsed as the dagger thrummed in delight, jewel glowing red. The other guard fell just as quickly, and the queen shrieked.

I glanced back and saw Dallaida rounding the corner of the altar to chase after me. For a moment it seemed she was nothing but a disembodied torso floating through the air, but then I saw the scuttling mass of black below. Her moonbeam-white torso was supported by eight segmented legs. Now that I could see the bulging abdomen that began below her navel and the horrid legs scrabbling against the stone, I realized what the ivory tapestry behind her was. An enormous web.

I fled, leaving the queen shouting behind me.

The granite-skinned steward was still standing in the entrance hall. I expected him to attack, but instead he stepped aside and bowed deeply. As I burst out of the front doors, hurtling past clusters of startled Nasties, wingbeats sounded as the queen's legions took to the air. One of them dove at me, but I spun in time to strike a glancing blow against its hand.

It was enough. The dagger drank, and the monster fell out of the sky. A forbidden thrill sizzled through me, as if the dagger and I were one being reveling in the kill.

The Nasties around me exclaimed at the murder. Some reached out to apprehend me, but others bowed. It was bewildering and horrifying, but I couldn't ponder the contradictions now. All I could do was run, dodging the strikes of winged soldiers and sidestepping anyone who attempted to detain me.

My breath sawed in my throat as I retraced my steps. The grassy room flashed past, and then I was sprinting over the narrow footbridge. Another attacker swooped towards me, and I ducked and nearly fell into the river, teetering at the edge of the bridge for a breath-snatching moment. The Nasty's wing tip skimmed the water as it tried to correct its course, and a dragon head broke the surface, opening a jaw full of needlelike teeth before clamping down on the wing and dragging the Nasty underwater.

My lungs burned, and terror pounded through me. I kept running, pushing myself to my limits as I passed monoliths, crystals, and ponds. More moss, more stone, more of the cobbled path, and behind me the pounding steps and sharp wingbeats of my pursuers.

One of them landed in front of me. He held a wickedly hooked blade, and his smile revealed fangs. "Aren't you quite the omen?" he asked.

I ignored the strange words and ran straight towards the Nasty. His golden eyes widened as the dagger in my hand glowed, flush with victory and starving for more. He abruptly shifted form, red scales melting into black feathers, and took to the air again as a small hawk. My dagger sliced through the place where he had been standing.

My legs felt ready to give out, but I was nearly back where I had started. The crooked stone steps were the most wonderful thing I'd ever seen, and I fled towards them with a cry of relief.

Something slammed into me from above and behind, knocking me down. I turned over, wincing at the pain in my knees and hands, and looked up at my winged attacker.

This Nasty was dark crimson, with dripping fangs and eyes like onyx. Her ears were pierced with silver, and her tail was cruelly barbed. As I shoved myself to my feet, that barb arced towards me. I lunged on instinct, knocking the Nasty to the floor and landing on her chest. Before she could recover, I drove the dagger deep into her eye socket.

Black, acidic blood sprayed me, burning the skin of my face and neck. Forbidden pleasure rushed into me through the blade's hilt as the creature shrieked and fell silent.

The other monsters halted in their tracks. They looked at me like *I* frightened *them*. Maybe this had been a general in their forces and they wouldn't proceed without her. Or maybe they had realized, as I just had, that I wouldn't hesitate to kill every last one of them.

It didn't matter. I fled up the steps, listening for sounds of pursuit, until at last I tumbled out into the blessed safety of the human levels.

I DIDN'T RETURN TO THE NASTIES AFTER THAT DISASTROUS EXPE-rience.

The only thing I'd learned about the Blood trial was that the house's favored trait was strength—something I no doubt would have learned soon anyway. It was frustrating to have failed, but I knew better than to attempt a mission like that again. The price had been high, and it would be even higher the next time.

I'd murdered five Nasties. I'd gone from a woman who hunted for sustenance to a woman who killed in self-defense.

It had been my life or theirs, so I didn't feel guilty about killing them, precisely. What I did feel guilty about was the pleasure I'd felt while doing it. That pleasure had come from the dagger via our strange emotional bond, but knowing that didn't make me feel any better about it.

What was done was done, though. Obsessing over it wouldn't change anything.

While I didn't descend too far underground after that, I did visit the human levels frequently to learn sign language from Maude. Triana and I had learned the basic alphabet and were working on common words and phrases. It was fascinating—the structure of the language was different in some ways from how I spoke things aloud, and nuances of meaning were delivered via facial expression, mouthed words, or the position in which the person's hands were held in relation to their body.

During my first visit after the amputation, Triana had been pale and weak. The Underfae had shaved her head before removing her tongue, and she'd looked like an entirely different person. Recently, though, she'd started smiling again. We had to go slowly in both speaking and listening, with plenty of missteps, but she was able to tell me she enjoyed her new work. "No Fae," she'd signed when I'd asked what she liked about it.

I could understand her relief. I hadn't seen the brothel yet, but it was only a matter of time before I encountered it during my explorations. What horrors would be revealed through those spy holes?

I'd been bringing Maude and Triana food from the Earth kitchens in payment for lessons. Swallowing was difficult for them without tongues, so I chose soups, sauces, and food that could be easily positioned in the mouth with a finger so they could chew thoroughly before swallowing. Even with the extra I brought, Triana looked a little thinner every week. When I mentioned it, she shrugged. "Little food," she signed slowly. "But better than brothel."

"What did you eat there?" I asked, signing clumsily while I spoke out loud. She'd let me know she didn't mind if I asked about the brothel. Maybe it helped to share some of what she'd experienced.

"Good food. Rather be hungry."

I understood. She'd been kept like a prize animal before: fed fine food, dressed in silks, then sold to any and every buyer. She ate less now, but her eyes were brighter and she held her head high. Her circumstances, grim as they were, were proof that no one owned her that way anymore.

They owned her in different ways, of course. She wasn't a prize animal, but she was still Fae property. All humans were property, including me.

If someone else ruled Mistei, would that still be the case? I considered it after the lesson. If King Osric were deposed, would the humans be freed? The Noble Fae would no doubt still want to be served, but maybe things would improve, especially if faeries like Drustan, Lara, and Selwyn had the power to shape the future. Maybe the humans could become paid servants like most of the Underfae. Maybe they could return home if they wished to.

I imagined that future as I climbed towards the higher levels. I'd start collecting wages from Oriana's deep coffers of faerie gold. Since the magic wardrobe kept me clothed and the kitchens kept me fed, there would be no need to spend any of it. When I had enough, I would leave Mistei and buy a house in a village far to the south. I'd make friends there, perhaps take a lover. Become a trader and travel across the mountains to Grimveld to see the six-month sun, then down to Lindwic with its vast lakes and tangled forests. Then back to Enterra and the home I'd made for myself.

The idea was so sweet it caught in my throat.

A better future required more than just hope, though. Right now, all I had were my choices. I would choose to keep fighting for that future, and my actions, not my dreams, would determine my fate.

When a cluster of Noble Fae appeared ahead of me, Drustan in their midst, I made a choice. I waited until the prince noticed me, then turned and walked into an empty room.

If anything was going to change in Mistei, Drustan would be part of it.

He wandered in ten minutes later. He looked artfully disheveled this morning, his bright hair hanging loose around his shoulders and his white shirt unlaced at the chest to reveal pale skin lightly tinged with gold. As the door shut behind him, he waved his hand, and a shimmering orange curtain of magic blanketed it. A ward.

"I take it you wanted me to follow you," he said. "Otherwise I have no idea what we're doing in here."

"It's been a while since we've chatted."

His eyes wandered over my face and down to the minimal cleavage my practical blue dress exposed. "I'm delighted, although normally humans don't summon princes for casual chats." His voice was a smoky purr, and he gave the word *chats* the slightest emphasis.

I ignored the heat that washed over me at the insinuation. "So you're allowed to approach me whenever you wish, but I'm never to approach you? I'm not sure that's how friendship works." My pulse raced at my own boldness.

The skin beside his eyes crinkled as he smiled. "Then we are friends."

I took a deep breath. Here it was—my statement of intention, the beginning of a long series of choices and actions to bring about a better future. "Yes. I wanted to tell you that we are friends."

With those words, I bound my cause to his.

He approached me slowly, like a stalking cat. "And do you have any information for a dear friend?"

"I went to see the Nasties."

He stopped, ash-gray eyes widening. "You what?"

"I wanted to learn more about Blood House."

"That was very foolish. They're dangerous, Kenna."

I shivered at the pleasure of hearing my name on his lips. "I know. But I wanted to ask them about the Blood trial."

"Still trying to help Lara, I see. Careful with that."

"You already knew I was helping her," I dared to say. "Anyway,

I didn't learn anything. The Blood trial will test strength, but I don't know how."

"So if you didn't learn anything interesting about the Blood trial, what exactly are you here to tell me?"

I didn't know how to articulate my decision: that if he was plotting an uprising against King Osric, I would help however I could for as long as I remained in Mistei, whether that was one day or many years.

My mother and Anya had been the dreamers; I was the one who always wanted proof. My faith in anything tended to be shot through with cynicism. But Mistei could not continue the way it was, in sadism and suffering, and I couldn't continue like this forever, either. If I read Drustan's intentions right, this was at least something tangible to believe in, even if the act of believing frightened me a little.

So. If Drustan was defying the king, I would, too. I would fight by his side.

Such words were too dangerous to speak out loud, so I gave him the piece of information I thought he might appreciate. "There's a spider woman down there named Dallaida. She's calling herself the Queen of the Nasties. I thought that was interesting, since the Nasties already have a king."

"You met Dallaida?" He looked scandalized. "And she didn't eat you?"

"I run fast." I deflated as I realized this wasn't helpful information at all. "I'm sorry. I didn't realize you already knew about her."

"Dallaida has been unofficial leader of the Nasties for a century now. It is news that she's taken on the title of queen, though. She must be feeling confident that the king's days are nearing an end." His tone was so casual he might have been talking about what he'd eaten for breakfast, not regicide.

I curtsied, wondering if he would try to recruit Dallaida. "That was all I had to tell you. As a friend."

His hand rose to my face, gently gripping my chin. "Thank you for your friendship, Kenna. It's incredibly important to me, and you'll help countless others as well. I promise you, Mistei is going to change for the better."

I swayed when he released me, and his wicked smile told me he'd noticed my unsteadiness. His gaze dropped to my lips and lingered for long, hot seconds before he backed away.

After he'd left, I couldn't help but wonder what this information-sharing "friendship" would turn into. I respected him, and he seemed to respect me. Our interactions were spiced with teasing, humor, and undeniable heat. We both wanted a better world.

Was Kallen right about Drustan's intentions towards me, despite our vast difference in station? Because if the Fire prince wanted more from me than just an alliance . . .

Well, I wanted more, too.

18

ARTH HOUSE ON THE SPRING EQUINOX WAS MAGICAL.
We'd been cleaning and decorating for days, and as I followed Lara into the main hall that morning, I marveled at the transformation. The already lush garden was covered in a riot of flowers, enormous blooms in every shade of the rainbow that had sprung from the seemingly infinite well of Oriana's magic. Chains of prisms hung from the ceiling, reflecting light and color in every direction, and the air smelled like planting days in the fields outside Tumbledown.

Lara looked like a spring dream. Her black hair hung loose and waving to her waist, topped by a crown of yellow roses. More roses lined the hem of her flowing green dress, and she wore a gossamer cape dotted with tiny diamonds.

I wore a green dress today as well, with short, filmy sleeves that required the dagger to twine around my ankle rather than my arm. A simple crown of daisies topped my loose hair. It had been a long time since I'd left Earth House without my hair constrained in a tight braid or bun, and I marveled at how silky it had grown after repeated applications of Fae hair tonic. My skin, too, had grown smoother and softer since I'd arrived, and my thin frame had gained welcome curves. Between the food, the exercise, and my new love for cosmetics, I looked less like a ragged peasant every day and more like one of the fine ladies who visited Tumbledown for the faerie festivals.

The spring equinox was Earth House's special holiday, and the theme was renewal. All week, servants had been repainting the walls and collecting old furniture and clothing in piles. The discarded items would be burned aboveground, Alodie had told me, as a symbol of starting over.

That was the part that most excited me. We were all going aboveground today, even the servants, and learning that had put fresh kindling on my smoldering dream of leaving Mistei. It would be my first time out in the fresh air since I'd been captured three months ago, and I planned to make the most of it by looking for places to hide and the best routes to take back towards the bog in preparation for whenever I was able to escape.

And if that opportunity for escape presented itself today? I hesitated while studying myself in the mirror, thinking about my unspoken vow to Drustan. I wanted to help him overthrow the king. But I hadn't known during our last conversation that even the servants would be allowed outside today. There was so much danger in Mistei, and not just from the king and his cruel court. Kallen and Oriana both expected my fealty in different ways, and each had promised dire consequences should I fail. Eventually the balance of my conflicting obligations would come tumbling down.

I wasn't a dreamer by nature, not when there was a more tangible option. And besides, I was just a human servant. Drustan had resources I could never dream of. He didn't truly need me.

My stomach felt oddly hollow at the thought.

Before the equinox revelry, we had to attend a ritual to "renew the ward." It was held in the throne room, and I was pleased to see the other houses had adopted Earth's colors for the day, just as they had adopted Void's color for the first trial. A sea of green, brown, and blue greeted me, and almost every faerie had flowers in their hair.

King Osric wore a tunic of palest blue and a long white cloak studded with opals, looking once again like a king of ice—deliberately, I was sure. He wore no flowers, just his crown.

"Welcome." He gestured to the gathered crowd, highlighting the opals that shimmered at his wrists and fingers. "The spring equinox is a time of renewal and rebirth. One thing we renew every year is our pledge to commit no violence against the throne."

He beckoned, and the four house heads stepped forward. They had each bared one arm—Oriana because her diaphanous sapphire dress only had one sleeve, the others by rolling their sleeves up to their elbows. Osric descended from the dais to join them, completing a circle in the center of the room. I hadn't noticed it before, but the outline of a crown was engraved in the floor between them.

At the king's snap, a servant rushed forward bearing a purple pillow with five knives on it. Each house head grabbed a knife and held it above their exposed forearms. The king intoned something in an unknown language, and all five cut deeply. Their blood poured out, combining in the indented outline of the crown. Once the streams had mixed, the blood sank into the stone and disappeared. A rush of power shot through the room and blew my hair back from my face.

Everyone was silent as the house heads applied cloths to their quickly healing wounds. King Osric grinned as the servant bound his arm. "Safe for another year. Fire, Earth, Void, Light, and Illusion offer no violence to my person. Now onward to the celebration!" He clapped his hands, and the crowd dispersed.

I tugged on Alodie's sleeve. "What was that?"

"The renewal of an old spell," she murmured as we followed the

SERVANT OF EARTH   217

crowd out. "After the rebellion, King Osric had it inscribed in the stone that no member of the surviving houses would commit violence against him. They can still attack one another, but trying to use magic or physical violence against the king will cause the person assaulting him to die. The ward is renewed every spring equinox."

My heart sank. "So he can't be hurt by anyone?" I didn't dare say the word *killed* out loud.

"Exactly." She nudged me. "Praise the Shards for his safety."

"Praise the Shards," I repeated, understanding the silent warning. Even speculation was punished here.

The realization that Osric couldn't be deposed by violence was disheartening, but surely there were other ways to limit his powers.

In a few hours it might not matter to me anymore, anyway.

We reached a spiraling staircase. Normally it was warded and guarded by Illusion soldiers, but today that restriction had been relaxed. My pulse raced as we climbed, passing levels I'd never seen before—rooms filled with low couches and smelling of sweet incense, rows of upscale shops lined with jewels and silks, and corridors with mysterious barred doors. Eventually the stairs ended at an archway where an enormous metal door had been pushed open to reveal a sunny green landscape.

My eyes smarted as we emerged on the side of a large hill. Mistei's lighting crystals were a poor approximation of the sun's brilliance. As tears poured down my cheeks, I ducked my head, not wanting anyone to see. It wasn't just the brightness that affected me—the air smelled fresh and familiar, and songbirds sang in the trees.

The grass was thick and dotted with wildflowers. About twenty feet away at the top of the hill, a large bonfire had been built out of furniture. I could see the bog beyond the forest below, much farther away than I had expected. Tumbledown was a barely visible smudge in the distance.

I felt a sad longing for my village, as miserable as it had often been. Life had been simpler there. No conflicted loyalties, no bloody banquets, and though the path of survival I'd walked had sometimes felt narrow, it had never been as narrow as the one I walked in Mistei. As wind kissed my cheeks, I thought of sunrise over the bog and my mother's herbs hanging from the rafters and Anya and I sharing a meager cheese picnic, and my heart hurt.

A simpler life was in my reach again, though. I was outside at last.

Faeries poured out into the sunlight from doors dotted over the hill. I looked around, wondering what surrounded us other than the bog. The lake covering Earth House's entrance sparkled in the light, and vast swaths of forest spread into the distance, with grassy hills poking their heads up at intervals. To the north and west the hills rose into mountains, culminating in the snowcapped peaks of the Giants' Teeth. On nearby slopes, smaller bonfires were being built by Noble Fae and Underfae who hadn't been invited to the king's celebration. Soon every hill resembled an island in a sea of trees, each with its own separate populace.

I grabbed a glass of wine for Lara from one of the refreshment tables. The pale liquid sparkled like distilled sunshine. It was warm up here with no trees to shade the sun's rays, and the cold feel of the glass in my hand was a pleasure. I delivered the wine to Lara, then retreated to study the layout of the space. Faeries were already dancing around the unlit bonfire while fiddlers played lively tunes, and I was surprised to see Noble Fae dancing with Underfae and servants chatting and laughing with their masters. It seemed class lines were blurred on the high holidays. Aidan stood at Edric's side, sipping wine and grinning as if Edric were the best thing he'd ever seen.

My heart ached at that, too, and I cursed myself for the sudden and unwelcome development of a romantic streak. Was self-pity and a longing for impossibilities truly all I was capable of feeling? It was a day for action, not emotion, and I had an escape to plot.

There were so many faeries milling about and the slope of the hill was so long and unobstructed that it would be difficult to slip away unseen. Better to wait until later when everyone was drunk. I wandered away from the group and peered towards the forest below.

A shadow fell across my path. I turned, shading my eyes, and saw Drustan.

The Fire prince was beautiful in Earth colors. Forest-green velvet set off his flaming hair, which he'd left wild and free. I laughed at the chain of daisies in it—a mirror of my own.

"You laugh at a prince?"

I shook my head. "I laugh at a friend who looks very fetching in flowers."

He grinned. "So I've been told. What are you doing over here instead of enjoying the party?"

"Just admiring the view." I tried to sound casual. "I never knew what was on the other side of Fae territory."

He gestured at the expanse of forest and mountain. "All of that is Fae territory. Mistei is longer and deeper than you can imagine—I don't even think we've charted all of it. But a long time ago we lived aboveground as well. Even in those mountains."

"Do you remember it?" How old was he, anyway?

"No. We've lived entirely underground since the rebellion."

"Why?"

"Because it's easier to control people when they have no way to escape," he said bluntly. "Back when things were more . . . open . . . we were free to leave or live outside the city. Now, though, it would be too much territory to protect. It would be hard to keep the population nearby if they didn't want to stay. A cave, though . . . A cave makes a nice prison." His mouth thinned, the line of his lips bitter.

"And so one of the most marvelous Fae cities in the world turned into something it was never meant to be."

I stared at him in shock. I knew everyone lived underground and that the king's permission was required to leave, but I'd never realized . . . "The Noble Fae are trapped here, too?"

"Ever since the war. No one can escape."

I touched his sleeve, and he looked down at my hand, his jaw tightening. "I'm sorry."

He nodded in acknowledgment, then smiled with forced joviality I didn't believe for a second. "This looks so open, doesn't it? Like a person could just wander off and never be seen again." He paused, gaze boring into me. "You should know, though, that the entire base of this hill is warded against escape. The only way anyone leaves and survives is if the king gives special permission and alters the wards."

I moistened my lips, suddenly certain he'd seen right through me. "Interesting."

So I wouldn't be escaping today. For a moment disappointment threatened to drown me, but I forced myself to let go of today's hope and focus on tomorrow. I hadn't explored all the Earth catacombs—it was possible there was a secret exit. A way past the king's wards and out of this beautiful prison.

"Now, Kenna the Curious, I think it's time for you to dance." Drustan grinned, and the smile was less forced this time. His restored good cheer did wonders for my own, and I turned my attention towards enjoying the party. If I couldn't escape, at least I could have a good time.

Still, I wasn't sure about dancing. I followed him back to the celebration, protesting the entire way. "I don't dance. Not well, anyway. Not like faeries do. Human dancing is mostly just holding hands and spinning in circles." I was babbling, but it would be mortifying to trip in front of the elegant Noble Fae.

He placed a hand on the small of my back, as if planning to push me into the melee.

"Oh, please don't throw me in there. I'll fall over and be trampled to death."

"I won't let you fall." His voice was a hot whisper in my ear. I was shocked when the hand at my waist pulled me towards him, and his left hand scooped up my right. "Grab my shoulder."

I did, wondering dazedly if this was actually happening. Was the Prince of Fire actually dancing with a human servant? No one seemed surprised by the sight, but I still felt embarrassed. "I am far below your station," I hissed as he guided me into the dancing.

"That's one of the main points of this festival. We're encouraged to mingle, to remind us that we're all Fae. Or, in your case, Fae-adjacent. I'm sure the king would like that remedied, but the tradition is so old no one even remembers when it began. Now hush."

He spun me expertly through the crowd, whispering the steps in my ear until I caught on. Then we danced in silence, twirling to the fiddle music, around and around and around.

A wave of heat washed over me, and the crowd cheered as the bonfire lit up, a bright conflagration that reached towards the heavens. I looked at Drustan with raised brows.

He laughed. "I can do two things at once, you know." He leaned in, pressing his mouth against my ear. "I'd love to show you sometime."

I squeaked at the insinuation and stumbled, which made him laugh harder, and then he spun me one last time as the tune came to an end. He bowed, and I barely remembered to curtsy. Then he winked and grabbed a new partner, and someone else offered me their hand.

To my surprise, it was Pol, the king's goatlike steward. He was surprisingly graceful for someone with hooves, and we danced a jig that left me breathless and giddy. Another partner grabbed me when he left, then another and another. I caught a glimpse of Lara through the crowd, tossing back her head and laughing as she spun in the arms of a lady from Void House.

I curtsied as the latest song ended, then fanned myself and started making my way to the refreshment table. If everyone else was drinking wine, I might as well.

A firm hand caught my elbow. "Dance with me." The words weren't a question but a command.

I looked up at Lord Kallen and swallowed. I couldn't refuse, so I nodded, tensing as he laid a hand low on my waist and carefully cupped my fingers. This dance was slower, an elegant glide that was a simpler version of what I'd danced with Drustan. I didn't want to stand too close to Kallen, which left me in the uncomfortable position of standing at arm's length and staring straight into that unyielding face.

I'd tried not to look too closely at him before, but now I had no choice. He wore a deep brown tunic, nearly as dramatic as his usual Void attire, and shimmering lightning filled the opal brooch on his chest. His customary frown was absent today, revealing full lips and flashes of white teeth. His lashes were thick and long, a sooty black that contrasted with his pale skin, and I was surprised to realize his eyes weren't black, after all, but a deep midnight blue. He was flushed from the exertion of dancing, his shoulder-length hair was tousled, and a sheen of sweat glistened in the hollow at the base of his throat.

It was unfair for the Noble Fae to be so beautiful, I thought bitterly. Their outsides ought to match their rotten insides.

"You haven't come to me with more information," he said as we slowly circled the bonfire.

"I didn't think anything was important enough to tell."

"I get to decide what's important and what isn't. What were you discussing with Drustan earlier?"

Was he always watching me? "He told me everything out there is Fae territory, even the mountains, and that some faeries used to live aboveground. I thought it was interesting."

"He seems to enjoy playing the tutor. Has the Fire prince been paying you any other special attentions?" The words *special attentions* were given a hint of derision, and I stiffened but held back a sharp retort.

"No," I said firmly. *But I'd like him to.* "And he hasn't told me much of substance. Mostly he enjoys being witty, and he finds it amusing to teach me odd bits of Fae history. He told me this festival is egalitarian, for instance, which explains why you're dancing with me."

"I see. How is Earth House reacting to Lady Lara's unexpected success in the trials?"

I blinked at the abrupt change in subject. "Oriana is pleased, of course. Lara grows more confident every day. They hope for similar success in later trials."

"Are you still helping her?" He asked the question lazily, but there was steel in his gaze.

"No," I lied. "Though I pass along gossip if I hear it, of course."

"Good." He paused to sharply guide me out of the way of a drunkenly spinning couple. "Mistei is different from the human world, Kenna."

I didn't like hearing my name falling from his lips. "I am aware, yes."

"If you give too much of yourself down here," he continued in an odd tone, looking down at me intently, "you risk losing everything. Because no one will ever return that loyalty. You'll give and give and end up hollow . . . or dead. Remember that."

I didn't understand what he was talking about. My forehead furrowed as I looked up at him. "My lord?"

"So what gossip have you heard and passed along to Lara?" he asked, ignoring my confused inquiry.

What a strange person. Then again, the Fae all seemed to love being cryptic, and trying to parse their words was often a waste of time. "I've heard the Light test is about physical control, but I don't know anything beyond that."

"Is that why you visited the Nasties? To gossip?"

A shiver crawled down my spine. How had he known? Maybe he really did have spies in every corner. "Yes," I admitted, knowing I couldn't pretend otherwise. "I heard they were the only ones who would speak about . . . a certain house I'm not supposed to speak about. I didn't learn anything."

I wouldn't tell him about Dallaida styling herself a queen. He would tell King Osric, and then the king would destroy her. As nice as that sounded, any enemy of the king's was an ally of mine, and if Dallaida felt confident enough to challenge him, she should have the chance.

"I'm amazed the Nasties let you live." Kallen spun me dizzyingly, and I stumbled before he pulled me closer to stabilize me. His hand was hard on my waist, preventing me from pulling away. I was inches from his chest, my breasts almost brushing him with every inhale.

I tried to suppress my flush. I knew what this was. He was trying to keep me off-balance, disconcerting me with forced intimacy, trying to intimidate me with his beauty and his power. One of the games the Fae so loved to play.

The weakness of the Fae was that they expected everyone else to play by the same rules. I stopped trying to pull away and instead looked up at him and smiled. "I find the Fae are perpetually surprised by what humans can do," I said. "You'd think they'd start learning."

He snorted as the song came to an end, then leaned in, his breath brushing my ear. "Happy equinox, Kenna. Next time don't wait so long to tell me what I want to know." He strode away, leaving me dizzy and relieved behind him.

I made my way to the wine immediately, declining offers to dance from Underfae and Noble Fae alike. I grabbed a glass and drained half of it.

The wine was light and sweet, bursting with crisp apple flavors and a hint of melon. I closed my eyes as it traveled down my throat, cooling as it went. When I opened them again, the world looked different—the colors more intense, the sunlight laced with glitter. My heart beat in time with the music, and I felt the ancient power of the earth beneath my feet, as if I were part of the soil.

As I finished the glass, a pleasurable lightheadedness swept over me. This was Earth House's special blend, crafted in cellars deep below the residential quarters. The only time the other houses got to taste it was on the spring equinox, and it was widely seen as one of the best parts of the holiday. I could see why the Fae loved it so much—I'd never tasted anything so incredible.

I grabbed a second glass and made my way to the edge of the dancing, waiting until Lara's shining black hair flashed by. As she completed a turn, I lifted the glass in the air. She grinned and nodded. When the song ended, she grabbed the glass, drank the wine in a few swallows, and returned to the revelry. I would have joined her, but my new wine-enhanced sight made simply watching an incredible pleasure. The gowns swirling by took on the look of leaves in the wind, and the grass pulsed with life.

Lara laughed, and I watched with affection as she grabbed a new partner. The Noble Fae all had an ethereal luster to their skin, but she was surrounded by something more, a trace of Earth magic glistening in the sunlight like an aura. It was a pale reflection of Oriana's brilliant golden gleam, but it made her seem alive in a way no one else around her was.

Anya had loved dancing, too. She'd been around Lara's height, and for a moment I could pretend Anya spun through that crowd, alive, well, and happy.

I exhaled a deep breath and blinked away the illusion. Lara returned—her face rounder than Anya's had been, her hair raven instead of golden brown, her features entirely her own.

In the glow of the wine, I made a decision.

I'd been comparing Lara to Anya for too long and finding Lara lacking. I'd been longing for a reality that would never come to pass because I couldn't stand that both my mother and my best friend were dead and I was alone. It wasn't fair to Lara or to me.

Dreams were nothing but illusion. They obscured sight of what actually existed. All those moments I spent imagining Anya were moments I didn't see Lara. All those times I wondered what Anya would do in my situation were times I wasn't thinking about what *I* would do.

I inhaled deeply. When I exhaled, I breathed out Anya's ghost at last.

19

W E WOKE AT DAWN TO PREPARE FOR THE LIGHT TRIAL.
It had been a week and a half since the spring equinox, and Lara had spent that time practicing meditation and physical exercises. I'd joined her for some of them, although the combat training she'd undertaken with Oriana had been beyond my capabilities. Even without her immortality, Lara had a level of endurance and strength I lacked.

Despite all that preparation, Lara was grim as I dressed her in a shapeless white robe. Her hair was unbound and her feet bare per Light House's instructions.

"Are you all right?" I asked as I brushed her hair.

She blew out a breath. "What if they torture us? What if that's the test?"

I could see from the shadows beneath her eyes that fear had kept her up all night. I ran my hand over her hair soothingly. "If it was that awful, I doubt many faeries would pass the test. It might not be pleasant, but it can't be too horrible."

"The labyrinth was horrible."

"But the monsters didn't actually attack you," I pointed out. "They wouldn't risk your lives like that."

She buried her face in her hands. "I think I'm a coward."

"You aren't." I put down the brush and knelt beside her chair, waiting until she looked at me. "It's normal to be afraid. Maybe that's what they're testing—how to be afraid and do your duty anyway."

"What if I can't?"

"You can," I promised. "You won't be alone. I'll be there with you, and if there's anything I can do to make it easier, I will."

"How do you stay so calm?" Lara looked almost angry. "You never seem upset."

It was jarring getting a glimpse of how she viewed me. Realizing that she, a Noble Fae lady with magic and money, heir to a great house, saw traits in me she coveted.

"A lot of the time I'm not as calm as I seem," I said. "Remember how sick I got after the dinner? But sometimes . . ." I trailed off, feeling uncomfortable. I didn't like showing others my vulnerabilities, but Lara needed help. Maybe I needed help, too—the comfort of knowing my secrets rested with someone else, and it wasn't just me carrying these burdens.

I met Lara's eyes in the mirror. Not hazel, but the brown of fresh-tilled soil. A new possibility rather than one already lost.

"I've experienced some bad things," I told her. "My father left when I was very young, and I grew up in poverty. There were weeks when we barely ate." My throat hurt more with every word, as if it wanted to clench until no more truths could escape. "My mother grew sick, and the illness took her slowly and painfully. She passed nearly two years ago, and then it was just me. Except I had one friend, so close we were almost sisters." I took a deep breath, feeling the echo of too many hurts. "She was chosen on the winter solstice, and

I followed to help her out of the bog. But she died behind me, and I never even looked back."

The expression in Lara's eyes was horrified . . . and sympathetic. She nodded slightly, encouraging me to finish the story.

"You think I never get upset," I said, "but that's not it at all. Life can be so painful. During the worst moments, all you can do is focus on one second at a time. You focus on staying alive. You make it your only goal, and you forget everything before or after." The choices, not the dreams. The fight, whether hope existed or not. "It's hard, but that's the only way I've ever been able to get through."

Lara grabbed my hand and squeezed. "Your life is better now, isn't it?" she asked in a small voice.

I blinked back sudden tears. What a terrible, complex question. "Better in many ways," I said. "I have food and shelter, and I enjoy working for you. I'm learning things I never could have imagined. But . . . I'm not free."

Lara withdrew her hand, looking hurt. "None of us are free."

"I know. Which is probably why none of us are happy."

She bit her lip and looked away.

The crystals on the ceiling pulsed—a time warning. The Light trial was about to begin.

"Come on," I said, standing and reaching out a hand to help her up. "We'll take it moment by moment."

WE JOINED THE OTHER CANDIDATES OUTSIDE LIGHT HOUSE. THE servants were given simple wooden boxes, which we carried as we trailed the candidates up a spiraling staircase.

We emerged at the edge of a sunlit courtyard atop a rocky hill.

The marble floor glittered as if strewn with diamonds. Roland, Prince of Light, stood opposite the entrance with King Osric, and Noble Fae onlookers lined every side.

"Welcome," Prince Roland said. "The Light trial tests control and discipline. You are to bear whatever happens in stoic silence. Walk to the center of the courtyard." He beckoned, and the candidates stepped forward.

Karissa yelped, and Lara winced. Smears of red followed each step as she limped forward. I frowned, wondering what had hurt her, then realized that every glittering spot on the marble was a piece of broken glass.

"Lie down," Roland said when the candidates had reached the center.

Lara's robe was far too thin; the glass would cut right through it. But she lay down with grim determination and didn't make a sound as she stared at the achingly blue sky.

"Servants." Roland snapped his fingers. "Place the boxes at your feet and open them. You will withdraw a vial of orange liquid, then walk to the candidates and pour it into their mouths."

There were three vials within, each the size of my thumb—orange, purple, and black. The orange liquid glittered in the sunshine the same way the glass shards did. Whatever this was would undoubtedly hurt.

I took a deep breath, preparing myself, then pulled the tie out of my hair as I rose, leaving my curls to tumble free.

I made my way towards Lara and instantly realized I had chosen the wrong footwear for this trial. My thin slippers weren't suited for walking on broken glass. I struggled to keep a straight face as the glass cut into my feet. Other servants were limping as well—except for those from Light House, who wore thick-soled boots.

I knelt by Lara's side, trying to avoid cutting my knees. "Open your mouth and drink," I whispered. As I leaned forward, my loose hair formed a thick curtain that obscured my face and hands.

The vial was small. I surreptitiously tilted it to my mouth, swallowing half of the potion before I gave her the rest.

It burned like fire in my throat. I met Lara's wide eyes and nodded at her in encouragement, then retraced my steps as quickly as I could. My feet stung, but that pain rapidly faded in comparison to the potion's effects. Lightning bolts of white-hot agony forked through me, radiating out from my throat and gut. I took my position in the line of servants as my eyes blurred.

We stood in silence for what felt like forever. Even a half dose of the poison was excruciating, as if I'd swallowed fire. It knotted my stomach and covered my vision with a red haze. It stabbed knives into my temples and beat fists against the backs of my eyes. My hands trembled as I bit down on a scream. When my sight briefly cleared, I saw a few of the candidates writhing in agony—but Lara stayed still.

Eventually the pain receded and the haze cleared. I breathed deeply, focusing on the trickle of sweat down my back and the feel of the ground beneath my throbbing feet.

"The second vial," Roland commanded.

This one was iridescent purple. I could guess what it did.

Lara's eyes were filled with tears the second time I approached. Again I took half of the potion before giving it to her. "Illusion," I whispered.

I returned to the servants' line, only dimly aware of the prick of glass beneath my feet. After the pain potion, those cuts didn't sting so much.

My mind disconnected from my body.

I was back in the bog, spongy peat beneath my bare feet and grass brushing my legs. For a moment I was wildly happy to have escaped

Mistei, but then the path gave way beneath me, and I was sinking into an infinitely deep pit of mud. The liquid forced its way up my nose and down my throat, filling me completely, drowning me, killing me . . .

I clenched my fists and breathed, despite the urge that screamed to hold my breath and keep holding it. *It's not real*, I told myself. *Not real. Not real.*

I walked across a misty battlefield, clutching the dagger as I splashed through ruby puddles. The jewel in the hilt glowed brilliantly, and I could sense the gallons of blood it had drunk. More blood painted my face and hands and dripped from my mouth, and we were both so glad of the taste . . .

A monster stood in front of me. It was ten feet tall, with eight arms and two wolflike heads. Its fangs dripped with gore, and each hand bore claws as long as my forearm. Long enough to decapitate me if it got close enough. It howled at the sky and then bounded towards me, impossibly fast.

I ran and ran and ran and ran . . .

Some distant part of me was aware of the shell of my body standing stiff and silent on a field of white. The gap between my body and my mind felt insurmountable, but I focused on a chant in defiance of Illusion's lies.

Don't move. Don't move. Don't move.

I lay at the bottom of a lake. The water was murky, but the light of day slanted down enough to illuminate my surroundings. Fronds of some water plant drifted around me like hair.

Something plunged into the water above, a struggling mass I recognized as a woman. Her long white dress dragged her down. She was wounded, great clouds of blood billowing into the murk. As she neared where I lay in the mud, she finally saw me. Her hazel eyes widened as her brown-gold hair tangled in the lake grass. She flailed and screamed, terrified of me but unable to escape.

I tasted the copper tang of her blood in the water, and I didn't once blink as Anya kicked and convulsed and finally stopped moving, her eyes still fixed on my face with a look of horror.

Don't scream. Don't scream. Don't scream.

I was standing in a white courtyard once more, my nails digging into my palms, my mouth clenched against a cry.

"The third vial."

I knelt and opened the box with shaking hands, reeling from shock and horror. Was I back in the real world, or was this a hallucination, too?

Was that actually how Anya had died, drowning bloody and alone?

I stumbled upright with a vial of black liquid clenched in my fist and walked automatically towards Lara, my body remembering its duties even as my mind struggled to tell reality from illusion. I fed Lara half of the black potion before remembering I needed to drink some of it to spare her the full effect. I lifted it to my lips but hesitated as her eyes darted frantically, as if she couldn't see me anymore.

If orange had been Fire and purple had been Illusion, this would be Void. Talfryn let out a moan and thrashed his arms after he swallowed the potion, and Karissa's hands clutched at the marble as if she were trying to keep herself in place.

I kept the vial clenched in my fist until I stood beside the other servants. While everyone watched the candidates, I bowed my head and tipped the final bit of potion into my mouth before letting the empty vial fall into the open box at my feet.

It was instantly dark.

Not just dark. Black. Empty. An absence of light so profound it sank shadowy tendrils into my lungs with every breath.

Silent, too. I floated in an endless void, free from the constraints of the world, lost in a dark dream. I couldn't tell up from down or if

I was truly floating or frozen in place or falling down an infinite well. My internal sense of direction spun wildly out of control, making me dizzy. I wanted to flail my arms to regain balance, but instead I held perfectly still, or what I imagined still to be in the absence of all other stimulus. It didn't matter if I was upside down or if I fell. All that mattered was this moment and my control over it.

There was a deep, creeping horror that came with the loss of everything. It wound around me, slid into me, pulled apart the threads that made up my being. People weren't meant to survive this place. It was as if the universe had been wiped clean and this was the black that had existed long before the stars.

I drifted in that cold, empty place for what felt like an eternity, long enough that I began to wonder if I had died. Was this what the afterlife was? Was I relieved to be here or angry?

Light flooded back in, so bright I winced as tears streaked down my cheeks.

I was still standing among the other servants in the sunshine, still staring at the candidates on their beds of glass.

"Rise, candidates," Prince Roland said. "The trial will end as soon as you leave this courtyard."

The candidates struggled to their feet, many of them swaying. Karissa fell back to the ground with a faint cry, slicing her knees on the glass. Lara looked towards me as if I were a candle in the window on a stormy night. She walked slowly, testing each step, but she didn't fall. At last she reached me, and I slipped my arm around her back, supporting her as she sagged.

There were no celebratory meals or dances. Just Lara and I stumbling back to Earth House together, a trail of blood behind us.

20

EVEN WITH FAERIE MEDICINE, MY CUT FEET TOOK DAYS TO heal. Lara was walking properly within a day thanks to her Noble Fae resilience, but I remained miserably propped in bed, reading books and hating Light House with a passion.

Alodie took over my duties with Lara, making sure to check on me every time she came upstairs. Lara came to visit often, too, sitting on the edge of the bed and telling me all the court gossip. We didn't talk much about the trials except to speculate about what Fire's hedonism trial would entail. She refused to tell me what visions she'd seen in the Light trial, but then again, I didn't tell her what I had seen, either. I wondered if I truly had halved the pain and trauma for her or if the potions had been potent enough that the quantity consumed didn't matter.

I still didn't understand my hallucinations from Illusion's poison. My best guess was that I'd been confronted with my fears: the bog betraying me, Nasties pursuing me, and my best friend dying in front of me.

It had been horrific, but I understood the purpose of the test.

Could a faerie maintain their composure while injured, disoriented, or frightened? They encountered so many awful things over their centuries of life. A certain toughness was required.

Lara's brother Selwyn visited me a day into my convalescence and sat hesitantly by my bed. It was the first time we'd spoken one-on-one since our conversation by the pond.

"Thank you for helping Lara," he said. "She told me what you did."

I smiled at him. He teased Lara whenever he could, but Selwyn truly cared for her. "I was happy to."

He tugged on a lock of his gold-streaked hair, his brown eyes unusually solemn. "The trials sound so awful. I don't want to go through them."

"You'll do well. Lara tells me you're very smart."

"Maybe." He sounded doubtful. "I don't know why it has to happen at all, though. The whole system is cruel. Why do any of this?"

He reminded me of so many teenagers I'd known. Of myself, too. At some point every child grew old enough to understand the world wasn't fair. My realization had come much earlier than Selwyn's, but then again, I'd grown up in crushing poverty. He had been raised in luxury almost entirely within the walls of Earth House.

I wondered why he was confiding his doubts in me, then realized that the Noble Fae probably weren't sympathetic to these types of questions. They valued strength and abhorred weakness. As a lowly servant wrapped in bandages and confined to bed, as well as a complete newcomer to their world, I was the embodiment of weakness. Maybe that made me safe in his eyes.

"I don't know," I told him honestly. "A lot of things in life aren't fair, but all we can do is get through them as best we can and try to make the world better. Lara will succeed, and so will you. You're braver than you realize."

He blushed and ducked his head. "Thank you. You, too."

He left a single yellow rose on my desk before leaving, and it cheered me up every time I looked at it. Not all Noble Fae were cruel. Perhaps idealists like Selwyn really would make the world better.

When my feet were finally healed, I headed out into the city. As soothing as Earth House's greenery was, I needed to stretch my legs and get a sense of everything that had happened while I'd been convalescing.

I had begun viewing the tunnels and chambers differently since my conversation with Drustan on the spring equinox. Mistei was just one city, albeit a magnificent one, in what had once been a vast and populated Fae territory. The Fae must have been so proud of it, of the craftsmanship required to carve these endless rooms and the magic that gave it life. The entire underground city was a testament to creativity, complexity, and extravagance. Visitors had probably come from other lands to gawk at it, and young faeries would have moved to Mistei from their aboveground homes, hoping to make their fortunes in its twisting subterranean streets.

Now, though, it was a beautiful prison. I missed the sunlight after only a few months—how must the Fae feel after centuries without it? How did Drustan, who had been born after the rebellion, feel on those rare instances he glimpsed the outside world?

I hadn't seen Maude and Triana in a while, so I headed there first. Triana was off on an errand, but Maude greeted me, looking unusually worried. Before I could speak, she slipped a note into my hand, shaking her head and shooing me away when I asked what it was.

I found an empty but well-lit corridor that housed an entrance to the Earth tunnels—ever since seeing Kallen melt into the shadows, I always checked for any alcoves or dark spots before using the key.

The note was written in a sharply tilting but graceful hand, in ink so dark it seemed to swallow the key's light.

Find out what Drustan knows about Prince Hector.
Immediately.

My hand shook as I tore the note into tiny shreds and dropped it into the pocket of my dress. I knew who had sent it: Kallen, who apparently tracked my movements so closely that he'd known I was receiving sign language lessons from Maude. Having her hand me the note was a reminder of his power . . . and my vulnerability.

Why was Kallen asking about his own brother? What had happened while I'd been abed? I'd never seen Drustan and Hector together outside of formal events or even heard the princes discuss each other. I'd heard Kallen speaking about Drustan, though. *Fire has made its decision*, he'd told Hector outside Blood House's antechamber.

They'd been discussing something foolish. What had it been?

I feared I knew the answer. Drustan's thinly veiled hints, probing questions, and offhand comments had centered on a common theme: that King Osric was corrupt and potentially not long for the throne. Did Hector and Kallen want to prevent a coup?

I wouldn't betray Drustan's revolutionary leanings, but I needed to give Kallen information or he would punish me. I didn't doubt his ability to follow through on his threats.

The game I was playing, if it could even be termed a game, was dangerous. Illegally assisting Earth House in the trials. Promising friendship and information to Drustan. Spying for Kallen on behalf of the king. Three completely opposed missions, and if any faction found out about any of the others, I was as good as dead.

My own mission was simple: stay alive long enough to escape or see a new king rise.

I WENT LOOKING FOR DRUSTAN, WANDERING PAST THE THRONE room, the entrance to Fire House, the library where I'd once spied on him, and a variety of other rooms where the Noble Fae liked to gather, but he wasn't anywhere to be found. Perhaps he was within Fire House. Most of the Noble Fae mingled in common areas during the day, but it wouldn't be unusual for him to take lunch or meetings in his sanctuary.

I lingered near Fire House for a long time, waiting for him to appear. Kallen had said "immediately," which meant I was running out of time.

Somewhere below, a door slammed.

The sound came as a faint reverberation in the floor. I thought it had come from farther down the spiraling slope, so I walked in that direction, wondering what levels were below this one and how to get there. I hadn't seen any indication of a staircase leading to lower levels from this part of Mistei, which meant either the floor below me was accessible from much farther away or there was a hidden door.

I was still halfway down the ramp when the wall opened up just before the next curve. Drustan stepped out, and the wall closed behind him.

I turned around and pretended I had been walking up the slope the entire time. When he appeared by my side, I jumped as if startled. "Oh! I didn't hear you."

He smiled, but it was strained. A long scratch marred his cheek. "I'm very stealthy when I want to be."

"You're hurt." I reached a hand towards that seeping mark, stopping before I touched him.

"It's nothing." And indeed, the wound quickly faded, leaving only a small streak of blood behind. He wiped it away.

I was jealous of the speed with which he healed. Lara would heal like that, too, once she gained her immortality. I, however, had feet marred with permanent scars from the Light trial.

"What are you doing here?" Drustan asked.

"I was wondering if you could provide me with some information."

He smiled like a lazy cat, and my stomach fluttered. "Is that so? Come with me, then. Friends don't share information publicly."

He led me up the ramp and into a small, plainly appointed chamber that looked like a study or sitting room. As the door closed, the orange glimmer of a ward sparked around its edges.

Drustan leaned against a wooden desk in the corner and crossed his arms. "So?"

My fingers twisted in my skirts. The room was small enough that I was excruciatingly aware of his nearness and the heat rolling off him. "I saw Prince Hector watching Lara before the Light trial." It was the most plausible lie I'd been able to concoct on such short notice. "The way he was watching her made me nervous. What can you tell me about him?"

Drustan's eyebrows shot up. "Hector? That frigid bastard? I can't imagine what he'd want with your lady. He normally likes them a little less noble. A little more . . . defenseless."

The words left me cold. "You don't mean . . ."

"Hector is dangerous," Drustan said flatly. "He's cruel and calculating. He will do anything to further his own interests, so if he really is watching Lady Lara, I recommend you advise her to stay well away from him."

"His own interests? What do you mean?"

Drustan seemed to weigh his words. "You know Hector, Kallen, and Una are the only children of Void House, correct? All the other heirs were killed in the rebellion before the previous Void prince, Dryx, swore fealty to the king." His mouth twisted. "As did my own father and mother. The three recommitted themselves to Osric and were spared to settle the unrest in their houses."

"Both you and Hector are princes now, though."

"My father died during an ill-fated duel with Roland thirty years ago." Drustan's jaw clenched, and I remembered his scathing hatred of Light House, which he'd used as a reason to help me hide the evidence of Earth House's cheating. "My mother didn't want to go on without him and threw herself on the king's wards."

"I'm so sorry," I said, horrified by the revelation.

Drustan shook his head. "It's past. But Dryx didn't die with the same honor as my father. He was murdered in his bed, soon after Una was born."

"But Void House is inaccessible to outsiders."

He raised his eyebrows, waiting for me to make the connection.

"You're saying Hector killed his own father?" As a woman who'd never known a father, I found the concept repulsive. How could Kallen stand to look at his brother?

"Unproven, of course, and a servant was ultimately executed for it. Hector did not grieve his father's passing. He took the title of prince and came one step closer to the throne."

"King Osric rules Mistei. What difference does it make if Hector is a prince?"

Drustan pushed off the desk and walked towards me. "That's a good question, but you're a clever woman. You know the answer."

My breath came faster as he approached. "You're saying Hector wants to become king."

"There are many who tire of King Osric's tyranny and plot to find a way around the wards that protect him. Unfortunately, not everyone agrees on who should rule next."

I looked up at him, wondering what emotions were concealed behind that casually amused mask he so often wore. "That's treason."

Drustan winked. "Good thing I'm talking about Hector, then."

My heart pounded as I considered the implications. Hector wanted to overthrow the king and take his place. Kallen was seeking information about his brother, or at least about what Drustan knew about Hector. Kallen was King Osric's assassin and spy. Hector and Kallen were descendants of a house that had once attempted a coup. Osric had killed their siblings. Hector had killed their father.

It was an impossible tangle of loyalties and betrayals. Was Kallen trying to stop his brother . . . or help him?

Fae politics were so complicated, every feud and resentment shaded with the memories of past centuries. Faeries rarely forgot, but did they forgive? Or did they view everyone around them only as tools to be used to achieve their goals?

My mouth was dry. "When will Hector make his move?" I asked. Surely no one could be worse than King Osric, but if the Void prince was as cruel as Drustan said, Mistei might escape one tyrant only to suffer under another.

"So many questions." Drustan stepped even closer. Perceptive gray eyes studied me, and I wondered if he could see straight through to my heart and mind, to the things I wanted and dared not express out loud.

I cleared my throat. "I am often accused of being curious."

"It's interesting that I am so often the recipient of your curiosity," he mused. "Do you have no one else you turn to with questions? There are many others who could have told you about Hector's reputation."

But not about his possible coup. "I—I hadn't considered asking anyone else." I winced at my stammer. I was awkward and obvious; he'd see through me in a second. "You've been very honest with me, my prince."

"So formal." He took another step towards me. "And yet I told you to call me Drustan."

He was a foot away, so close I could grip his velvet tunic in my fist and pull him towards me. The possibility sent heat washing over me as anticipation coiled low in my belly.

"Drustan." I managed the single word before lapsing into silence, unable to prompt my brain into coming up with anything else. As my eyes drifted from his sly smile to the strong line of his throat, I wondered what he would taste like.

A throb started between my legs, pulsing with forbidden want.

Drustan grinned, quick and savage. "I think you enjoy seeking me out, Kenna, and I think you know exactly why."

"I don't. I mean, I enjoy your company, but—" Oh, I was just making it worse. I trailed off, staring at him with wide eyes.

He cupped my cheek. "You've always been honest with me, too," he whispered. "Don't stop now."

His other hand snaked around my waist, and then he pulled me into him and pressed his lips against mine.

Oh.

His mouth was hot and soft, and he tasted like smoke and spice. I moaned as his tongue pressed into my mouth, then kissed him back with all the heat in my body. My movements were clumsy, but he angled my head and kept the lead, teaching me the way of it.

I'd kissed a few village boys before. It hadn't been anything like this. Those had been uncomfortable mashings of lips and teeth, usually abruptly begun and just as quickly ended—an urge or a curiosity or a liberty taken, nothing to pursue.

This . . . It was like drowning in melted chocolate. Like sinking into a feather bed after a warm bath. I could feel myself dissolving, pieces of my soul falling into him with every lick and suck.

Then he bit my lip, and my awareness slammed back home. My body ached for his. My stomach was tense, the sensitive parts below throbbing with need. I gripped his neck and tugged him closer, pressing against him, needing something, anything, to ease the ache building deep inside.

He snarled against my mouth and gripped my hair to hold my head in place. In response, I raked my nails down his back and was gratified when he shuddered.

"Like holding lightning," he breathed against my lips before setting in again. He kissed me hard, his tongue and lips and teeth consuming me, his hands holding me so tightly they felt like brands against my waist and scalp. I was panting, completely out of control. I'd never felt like this before. Never dreamed . . .

As suddenly as it had begun, the kiss ended. He pushed me away from him, breathing hard as he stared at me with molten eyes. "You should go. Unless you want to finish this now."

My pulse hammered. Did I want to finish this now? I'd wanted him for months, but now that he was looking at me with the same lust, the reality of it was intimidating.

"I—I—" I stared at him blankly, my hand pressed to my throat.

He made a dissatisfied noise and ran a hand through his hair. "That wasn't a yes, which means if you can't go, I need to." He winced, adjusting something below his belt. My face flamed as I realized his body had reacted to mine. "Think on it," he said as he walked to the door.

"Wait," I said, finally finding an ounce of sense. When his shoulders tensed, I fumbled to clarify. "I mean, I was just wondering—why would you do that with a human?"

His laugh was low and tempting. "We aren't all Osric." His eyes trailed over me. "And you looked delicious."

The door closed behind him, leaving me trembling and alone.

I WENT TO THE ANTECHAMBER OF BLOOD HOUSE IMMEDIATELY afterwards, despite the arousal that still heated my body. Thankfully, that cold, dark room served to cool my ardor, and within a few minutes I was breathing normally, even if I hadn't yet comprehended what had happened.

He'd kissed me. Drustan had kissed me. With his mouth. On my mouth. It had been . . .

I forced my racing thoughts to still when I heard footsteps in the corridor.

Kallen's gaze found me instantly when he appeared in the archway.

"Can everyone in Void House see in the dark?" I asked as he entered the room. "It hardly seems fair if Una was able to see during the Void trial."

"Only the most powerful. Una won't develop this skill until she passes the trials and earns her full magic." He stopped a few feet away. He was backlit by the red torchlight from the outside corridor, and I couldn't read his face.

"I talked to Drustan about Hector," I said.

"Oh? That was efficient."

"You said immediately."

"Given your previous definition of 'soon,' I thought it best to err on the side of caution."

I took a deep breath to settle my temper. "He says Hector is cold, calculating, and self-serving."

"Everyone knows that." Kallen sounded unbothered.

"Well, I didn't. So now I've accomplished the task you gave me, and we're done." I started to walk around him, but he caught my arm.

"We aren't. Are you certain that's all the Fire prince told you?"

If he didn't like my answers, I'd give him what he'd asked for—

though he might regret it later. "He said there were rumors Hector killed your father."

He was still for long moments, and when he answered, his voice was chilly and distant. "A common rumor. What else?"

I tried to jerk my arm away from him, and, to my surprise, he let go. "He told me Hector likes his bed partners defenseless." I spat the words, wondering what, if anything, would rouse an emotional response from this frigid faerie. "You have quite a brother."

He was in front of me so fast I didn't see him move. He gripped me as if to shake me, but his hands just flexed on my shoulders, his fingers hard through the thin fabric. His breath rasped in the still air.

Then, as if he had mastered himself, he released me and stepped away. "Thank you." His voice vibrated with some suppressed emotion. "Your next task is to tell me who Drustan meets with. What he speaks about with you and others. Anything you can tell me about his movements and opinions."

"Of course."

I had no intention of fulfilling that promise. Of the two of them, Drustan had commanded my allegiance even before that burning kiss. Now that we'd touched . . . I wouldn't betray him.

"You may leave."

I brushed past Kallen, thankful that the questioning had stopped there.

"Kenna," he said as I stepped into the corridor.

I tensed and looked back at him, although I couldn't see anything in the darkened room. "Yes?"

"You smell like smoke."

I flushed at the memory of Drustan's lips on mine and the fiery taste he'd left in my mouth. "I was near the kitchens."

As I walked away, his voice followed.

"Liar."

21

ANOTHER FORMAL DINNER WAS HELD THE NEXT WEEK. Knowing what had happened at the last one, I felt tense as I took my place among the stoic line of servants behind the candidates' table. Aidan glanced my way from several spots down, dipping his chin in acknowledgment. I smiled back, wishing we were somewhere the two of us could talk freely.

This meal was as decadent as the first. Overflowing baskets of fruit gave way to braised lamb, apple-stuffed roast duck, and creamy pies full of cheese, potatoes, and leeks. Every dish was adorned with flowers in celebration of spring. The wine was thankfully a light, translucent red, not the bloody liquid we'd drunk during the executions, and this time the servants weren't offered any of it. Pixies from Earth House darted in sinuous patterns above, periodically flinging rose petals over the assembly.

By the time dessert had concluded and no one had been butchered, I began to breathe more easily. Perhaps we had been granted a reprieve from barbarity for one night.

It was time for dancing, but the king remained seated on the dais with the house heads and Kallen, and no one dared move without his leave. Finally, Osric stood and clapped his hands. Normally he would have given a speech at this point, and I saw confused glances as Fae nobles rose from their chairs.

"Sit back down," he commanded.

The faeries sat, and a soft noise went through the room—sighs and breathed whispers, speculation no one was willing to speak aloud.

The sound cut off abruptly.

In the sudden silence, I heard the click of slow footsteps. Dread swelled in my gut, and it took all my willpower not to turn and look at whatever horrible surprise was approaching.

Pol passed me, holding a small bundle in his arms. The goat's face was as sad as I'd ever seen it, and tears glinted behind his golden spectacles. He laid his burden at the foot of the dais and backed away with bowed head.

A tiny cry split the air.

Horror crawled down my spine. A baby. There was a baby in that bundle. A small arm extended from the pile of blankets, waving a tiny fist.

"No," Drustan said, beginning to rise, but Osric motioned for silence. Drustan subsided, his face lined with rage.

Kallen, too, looked furious. His fists were clenched so tightly the knuckles looked like they would burst through his skin.

"A grave crime has been committed," King Osric said as he approached the baby. "The bloodlines of Mistei are pure. It has been this way for millennia, and you are all aware of the consequences of breaking this law. Why, then, does this sort of thing"—he flicked his fingers at the bundle—"keep happening?"

Don't kill it, I pleaded silently. I wouldn't be able to stay stoic through something that monstrous. I would surely leap at the king and try to claw his eyes out and then be executed in return.

He picked up the infant, leaving the blanket behind on the dais. He held the squirming baby beneath its armpits, displaying it to the room, and I could see that it was a boy with a wild tuft of black hair.

A keening cry rose from one of the Light House tables, and then a flash of white raced down the aisle: a lady in a diamond-studded gown who looked as if her entire world had been torn apart. She ran for the dais, but the king's guards were faster. They knocked her to her knees and stood over her with drawn swords.

"Please." Tears ran down her face as she begged. "Please, your majesty, have mercy."

The king regarded her without emotion. "Do you deny this child is born of two houses?"

"Yes, I deny it. It's a mistake. There's been a mistake."

"Thirty lashes for the lie. On top of the punishment you will soon receive for this crime."

"Please, it isn't true!"

"Thirty more for another lie."

She collapsed in a sobbing heap, head buried in her hands and shoulders shaking. When she looked up again, it was to the far side of the room where Void House's nobles sat in dark, solemn lines. "Please." She reached a hand in that direction. "Stand with me. Stand with *us*."

No one moved.

She must be reaching for the father of her child, who had lain with her but was too much of a coward to stand by her side. Hector and Kallen both stared at their court, and Kallen looked ready to do murder. Because a member of his house had been indiscreet?

No, I decided as I studied him further. Ruthless and cunning as he might be, that was the face of someone who burned with rage on behalf of the child and mother. It seemed some of the monsters of King Osric's court were more complex than I had realized.

"This child is an abomination," the king said. "It was born of Light and Void. It violates one of our most sacred rules, that each branch of magic must be kept pure." The baby wriggled in his hands and began to cry.

The lady whimpered. "It was an accident. I promise, it was an accident. Let him stay with me, my king. Please. I'll keep him far away from court. Or banish me, imprison me, do what you will—just let him live."

Her voice broke on the last word, and my heart broke with it. She knelt alone before the king, pleading for the life of her child, and it seemed neither her lover nor her house would take her side. All this time I had seen the members of Light House as villains. I hadn't thought of them as people with hearts that beat the same as mine, who loved and lost and wanted desperately to do what was right for their own, no matter who ruled them.

"Here." The king held out the baby. "Take your child from my arms."

Was he forgiving her? Showing mercy for the first time?

One look at Drustan's and Kallen's faces confirmed what I already knew. King Osric never showed mercy.

She walked hesitantly towards him. When the baby was nestled firmly in her arms, she broke down and wept, holding him close.

The king smiled and snapped his fingers.

Underfae with iridescent wings and purple skin appeared around the mother. One of them ripped the child from her arms and launched into the air, soaring over the crowd until he was lost to sight.

The lady screamed. And screamed. And screamed.

I couldn't stop the tears rolling down my cheeks. I sobbed, aware that I wasn't the only one crying. Aware, too, of Drustan and Kallen both looking at me with vastly different expressions. Drustan's was

soft and full of grief, but Kallen's was tormented—the face of someone haunted and damned by the things he'd allowed to happen.

That was what King Osric did to us. He made us witness his
atrocities, and because he held so much power, we said nothing. We
became complicit.

The remaining Underfae hadn't moved from their positions
around the lady, who had collapsed to the floor and was sobbing
uncontrollably.

"Sixty lashes for her lies," the king commanded. "And then sixty
more for her crime." Osric smiled as the Underfae muscled the faerie
up, ripped the top half of her dress open, and forced her to bend over
and brace her arms on the dais. "Rub herbs in it so the wounds scar.
Let her always have a reminder of what she has lost."

One of the Underfae uncoiled a leather flogger tipped with metal
barbs. He drew back his arm and struck.

I flinched as she screamed. Blood sprayed from her back, staining the remains of her white dress. He hit her again and again, in-
scribing cruel crimson lines into her skin. With each blow, her
natural Fae shimmer dimmed, replaced by raw, ragged wounds.

I was going to vomit. In desperation, I focused on Drustan instead. He, too, twitched with every blow, but he never looked away
from the beating. Few faces in the watching crowd showed the sick
glee I had expected, either. Some wept silently, most looked numb,
but they witnessed every lash.

Lara was gripping the edge of the table so hard it looked like it
hurt. Her face was frozen as she stared at the carnage, but then her eyes
darted to mine, and I saw grief and horror reflected in them. A silent
communication sped on the air between us, a shared cry neither of
us could let loose, and then she returned her attention to the screaming faerie, watching unblinkingly as blood splattered in ruby arcs.

I forced my gaze back, too, although the gore threatened to turn my stomach inside out. This faerie had been brave enough to stand up for her child. If she had to take this punishment, at least I could be brave enough to witness it.

There were many kinds of strength, I thought as the crowd watched the flesh stripped from the lady's back. The strength to oppose a king, the strength to love in the face of convention . . . and the strength to look at the truth, witness its horrors, and refuse to flinch.

When it was done, she lay in an unconscious, bloody heap before the dais.

"A toast!" The king raised his glass and downed the liquid, not seeming to notice that hardly anyone toasted with him.

I USHERED LARA BACK TO EARTH HOUSE AFTER THE BANQUET. WE moved quickly and silently through the stone halls, in mutual agreement without needing to say a word. As soon as we reached the Earth tunnel, its glossy wet walls dark with night, a shuddering, half-keening noise left Lara. Her shoulders curved in as she pressed a shaking hand to her belly.

My own throat was tight, and I couldn't seem to breathe properly. Now that we weren't in public where anyone might see us, the horror I'd been holding inside was rattling through me. I placed my hand against the water, feeling the cold of it curl over my fingers, imagining what it would feel like closing over my head and slithering into my lungs.

"How could he do that?" Lara asked, voice raw.

I shook my head, unable to speak just yet.

My feet didn't want to carry me the rest of the way to the house. I longed for the soil beneath my toes and the smell of green things, but Earth House had its own pressures. Princess Oriana might already be there, ready to lecture Lara about hiding her feelings better, maybe even ready to dismiss the night's events as the price of politics or a necessary lesson. The thought was sickening. If Lara made me think of a bright garden sometimes and Selwyn a bubbling spring, Oriana was ice—cold and hard, with an inner core that seemingly nothing could touch.

"It was . . ." I trailed off, unable to find a word adequate enough. "Unspeakably cruel."

"A baby," Lara said. She gripped her skirts, looking down, and I realized there was a dark stain on the satin from being near the spray of blood. "They took away her *baby*."

A bitter taste filled my mouth, but I swallowed it down. "Did you know what would happen? When you saw him brought in?"

She hesitated. "I . . . I don't know. Children of two houses have always been forbidden, everyone knows that, but I was never invited to any of the dinners until the trial season began. It was . . ." There was an even longer pause. "It was worse than I could have imagined."

"Will the mother live?" I asked quietly. There had been so much blood, more than it seemed possible for one body to contain.

"Yes," Lara said. "But will she want to?"

My eyes blurred at that. "How does anyone have children in Mistei?"

"I don't know." A tear traced down Lara's cheek, and she wiped it away. "I thought I wanted to someday, but now . . ."

Footsteps sounded behind us, the soft whisper of slippers over stone. I turned to see Princess Oriana approaching. Her head was held high, her face serene. There was blood spray on the front of her pale blue gown, too, the jagged lines like overlapping branches.

I nudged Lara's hand, and Lara immediately straightened her posture and wiped the last moisture from her cheeks before turning to face her mother.

"Why are you standing here?" Oriana asked Lara.

"I needed a moment."

Oriana's mouth twisted with disapproval. "Anyone in the house could find you here."

My jaw clenched, and I looked down so she wouldn't see my fury.

"We only stopped for a minute." Lara bit her lip, and I could see her struggling against the words that wanted to come out. Oriana watched silently—maybe sensing that Lara had more to say. "It was just a baby," she finally blurted out.

Oriana scoffed and looked towards the curve of water. "It's never *just* a baby," she said. "I thought you understood that by now."

"That was someone's child," Lara said, rushing on heedlessly. "The mother—"

"Knew the price of disobedience. And the cost of loving anything." With that, Oriana brushed past us. "I expect to see you back in the house in five minutes, Lara."

I watched her retreating back, wondering when my heart had learned so many different ways to hate.

LARA RETURNED TO THE HOUSE, BUT SHE TOLD ME I DIDN'T NEED to go with her if I didn't want to. Her gown had clasps on the side to loosen it; she could undress without me. So I returned to the public hallways, needing to burn off the furious energy that raced through my veins and made my stomach churn every time I stopped moving.

My feet took me to Fire House.

I didn't know entirely why. I considered the question as I rested in an alcove and stared at the wall of flame from a safe distance. Perhaps it was because Drustan had shown grief tonight. Perhaps because he had kissed me. Perhaps because he was a friend who did not need my services—he welcomed my aid but hardly needed it—and sought to speak with me anyway.

I sank to the floor and sat there for hours, watching the dancing flame. Periodically faeries came and went, the curtain of fire parting around them, but few spared a glance for me. The mood was somber, and soon no one passed through the fire at all. It was an early night for everyone as the Fae sought refuge in their house territories, the only places the king could not touch.

If I had my own house, I would never come out. I would keep my people safe in there. It would be small compared to Mistei, but surely it would be better than living in constant fear.

I drifted asleep in that alcove, and when I awoke, Drustan stood over me. He drew me to my feet, and I followed him silently to the room where we had kissed. He closed the door, and again an orange glow painted it, locking us in. He strode to the desk, leaning against it with his back to me. The muscles on his arms were stark beneath his sleeveless tunic and flames flickered above his fingers, casting a hot shimmer in the air.

I took a few hesitant steps towards him. "Are you all right?"

"No."

I sank onto one of the only pieces of furniture in the room, a red-and-yellow striped couch. "What will happen to the baby?"

He made a rough noise. "It's a changeling now. It will be sent to the human world, exchanged for an infant, and left to grow old and die alone."

Changelings were real? They were a myth in the human realm. Supposedly those Fae babies masquerading as human children grew up strange, magical, and malevolent, a joke played on humans to remind us faeries still existed. No one I knew had ever encountered one.

"Why?"

Drustan still didn't face me. His fingers drummed on the desk. "A long time ago," he said, "for that's how these stories always start, the Fae of Mistei were weaker, but each individual had the powers of all six houses in varying amounts. No one can verify this, of course. No one is alive who remembers it, and there are Fae who have lived a very, very long time. It's part of our lore, though, so perhaps there's some truth to it.

"The Fae realized that if they took lovers with magical abilities similar to theirs, they could enhance the powers that were strongest in their family lines. They began breeding for strength. Eventually we reached the result you see today: six houses, now five, each specializing in one branch of magic: Earth, Fire, Light, Void, Illusion, and Blood. Our identities became defined by our powers. Our houses separated and stopped sharing information."

He shook his head, looking down at the fire licking over his hands. "The problem with such a coldhearted breeding plan is that it does not account for love. And once a society is as divided as the Fae are, there's no place for a child with the magic of two houses. The children of two worlds, as they were once called, were ostracized, turned into servants, or kept within house walls. They became changelings at the beginning of King Osric's rule."

I wondered how many children had suffered just because they'd been born into a world that valued power over love. "Why only then?"

"Because Osric is a tyrant," he snapped, the flames at his fingers shooting higher, "and it's to his advantage to keep us separate and ensure we don't form alliances. A child of Light and Void . . . Can you imagine if a bond started forming between those houses? They've been enemies ever since Osric first took the throne with Light's support. One child might not make a difference, but if interbreeding were to continue . . ."

"The houses might start making alliances."

He nodded. "King Osric rules by might, and his strength has been bolstered by Light's unwavering support. Were that to falter, or were the other houses to strike a deal, the king might find himself with another rebellion on his hands."

So much pain. So many lives lost and futures stolen. "Why send the babies to the human world, though?"

"Osric probably thought it was a crueler punishment than killing them. That child will die either way—separated from the Fae, he cannot undertake the trials and gain immortality. This way the parents know their child is being raised in poverty by filthy humans. The boy will live a short, miserable life and die alone."

"Filthy humans," I echoed, stung by the words.

Drustan turned to look at me at last. His face was carved in grave, tired lines. "That is how Osric thinks."

I sighed, releasing my anger towards him. "So human babies are brought here in exchange." That explained the servants who had no memories of life in the sun. "And the Fae cut out their tongues and put them to work as soon as they are able, and no one cares about their lives or deaths."

"Kenna . . ." He reached for me, but I turned away, pressing the heels of my palms into my eyes.

"How can he rip children from their parents?" Despite my best efforts, tears leaked out from beneath my hands, dripping down my cheeks. "Not just faerie parents, but human ones as well. Those children were loved."

My words were vehement, and I recognized dimly that part of my despair stemmed from the fact that my father hadn't loved me in that way—had left rather than carry that burden of love. It was a self-ish reason to grieve, but my emotions had tangled with the past and the present so thoroughly I could barely separate the threads. I had never belonged in Tumbledown, but I didn't belong here, either, and the humans imprisoned below didn't belong here, and the faeries who spent their entire lives in the human world, feeling alienated and never knowing why, didn't belong there . . .

Strong hands gripped my shoulders and turned me around. "Thank you," Drustan said vehemently. He kissed away the tears on one cheek, his lips hot against my damp skin. "Thank you for your anger."

"Why?" I dashed the remaining tears from my cheeks. "Why do you care so much?"

"I'm not a monster."

"You know what I mean."

After a heavy pause, he stepped away from me. "I had a friend." The words were halting. "My closest friend, a lady from Fire House named Mildritha. We grew up together, and truthfully, I always wanted her to be more than just a friend. But after centuries of saying she preferred her independence, she fell in love with someone else. She fell in love with the young heir to Earth House."

The realization hit me like a lightning bolt. "Leo." Lara's missing brother.

Drustan nodded. "He was quite a sight, with that golden hair and the confidence of ten warriors. Mildritha fell in love with him and he with her. Eventually, it became clear she was carrying a child."

My throat felt thick. "The king found out."

"He did. Before Mildritha gave birth, she was whipped in front of everyone." Pain twisted Drustan's face. "No protest would sway the king. And Leo . . . He was good. He stood with her, was punished by her side. Knowing what would happen after she gave birth, he was desperate to get her and the baby away." His throat bobbed. "He died trying to find a way through Osric's wards at the bottom of the hill."

A noise left me, a soft *oh* of shared grief.

"After the birth, Mildritha's child was taken from her," Drustan said. "Not even a week later, she killed herself."

More tears slipped down my cheeks as the story reached its tragic, inevitable end. Tears for Drustan and the loss of his friend. For the faerie child abandoned to grow up alone and the human child forced into servitude. For Mildritha and Leo's doomed love, and for Lara and the brother she'd lost. I wrapped Drustan in my arms and hugged him tightly. After a hesitant moment, as if he were unused to being comforted, he embraced me back.

"Have you ever tried to find the baby?" I asked, the words muffled against his shoulder.

"The king will never allow me beyond the wards. The only faeries allowed through are his minions, or sometimes visitors from other courts. I've thought about seeking aid from one of them, but it's too risky."

"Other courts?" I looked up at him in surprise. "They come here?"

He dipped down, pressing a soft kiss to my lips. The salt of my tears mixed with his smoky, spicy flavor. "Yes. Some will visit for Beltane and the Fire trial."

My throat ached. "Are the other courts better than this one?"

"Each court is unique. Some are crueler, if you can imagine that."

I couldn't. "But some are kinder?"

"Yes." He kissed my temple. "Some are kinder."

I stroked his face, and he turned into the caress to nuzzle my palm. "Maybe someday this one will be kinder, too."

22

THE FINAL EVENT BEFORE THE FIRE TRIAL WAS A PICNIC. IT seemed strangely innocuous compared to everything I'd experienced so far, yet there I was, basket in hand, following Lara out into a warm spring day.

I laid out a blanket, placed plates of food on the grass, and retreated beneath a nearby tree to stand with Aidan.

"Do the Fae normally go aboveground this often?" I asked. This sunny slope was still part of a larger prison, but it provided an illusion of freedom.

"No," he said. "Trial years are special. The major festivals are always held aboveground, but events like this wouldn't normally happen."

While I had chosen a patch of shade, Aidan stood beneath a gap between the branches, lifting his face to the sun. His eyes were closed in bliss.

I smiled at him. "You look happy."

"Fire faeries like heat."

"What's it like inside Fire House?"

He sighed contentedly. "Very warm and very dramatic. The furnishings are every shade of flame, and there are torches everywhere. There are hot baths fed by underground springs and piles of pillows in every room, so you can always feel warm and relaxed. Some rooms are even carpeted in fire. The whole place flickers and glows, and aromatic smoke fills the hallways." His tone was dreamy as he painted the picture.

"That does sound dramatic." The hot baths and piles of pillows would be nice, but I couldn't imagine preferring carpets of fire to Earth House's soothing ambience.

Aidan winked. "Someone's always drinking or fucking in a corner, too."

I wondered how often that someone was Drustan. Frequently, no doubt. I suppressed a stab of jealousy. He was a prince, and even if he weren't, just because we'd kissed didn't make him mine.

I heard a snap and realized Lara and the candidates seated around her were staring at me. I headed in her direction as Aidan whispered, "Good luck."

I curtsied when I reached Lara's side. "Yes, my lady?"

She wouldn't quite meet my eyes. "Here she is," she announced to the group. Gytha, Talfryn, Una, Karissa, and Markas examined me with interest.

My senses went on alert, like an animal realizing predators were nearby. Why were they staring at me?

"Your pet is so small." Karissa tittered behind her hand. "Like a child."

I resisted the urge to roll my eyes. I was short, yes, but not that short. *Short* had been a minor inconvenience in the human world, but it seemed to be an insult among the statuesque Fae.

"Ugly, too," Gytha said. "Like a little goblin."

Gytha, Karissa, and Markas laughed.

It was foolish to feel stung by the words, especially when I knew they weren't true. Gytha and Karissa were just playing some game designed to humiliate Lara.

Una studied me with keen dark eyes. The Void lady had been one of the most successful candidates so far, and more than one servant was betting on her success. She was dressed more simply than the other candidates, per usual, in a loose-fitting black linen sheath dress. "Have you ever seen a goblin, Gytha?" she asked. "Somehow I doubt it."

"Why would you doubt me?"

Una's smile dripped with wicked poison. "Because I can't imagine you having the courage to visit the Nasties."

More laughs followed this assertion. Gytha glared at Una, but the Void lady remained unruffled, so Gytha returned her attention to me. "Her hair is like a bramble patch. I'm shocked the king would give you such an atrocious-looking servant, Lara."

Lara still wouldn't meet my eyes. She shrugged.

My stomach sank further with each new taunt, and my resolution not to compare Lara with Anya faltered. Anya had never stood by when a friend was in need.

"He knows the servant reflects the master." The voice behind me announced the arrival of Garrick. I kept my spine straight as the Light candidate approached. I could feel him behind me, a heavy tingle that raised the hairs on my neck. "They say you're a beauty, Lara. Perhaps the king meant to reflect other parts of your personality."

Talfryn shot to his feet. "Lady Lara's personality is as beautiful as her face."

"Talfryn," Lara said quietly.

"It's true." Talfryn stood firm. "I won't allow anyone to demean the heir to my house."

Garrick laughed, and I jerked as one of his fingers traced the back of my neck beneath my upswept hair. "You don't stand a chance, Talfryn. Sit down before I maim you."

Talfryn, to his credit, remained standing.

Markas, who had become Garrick's frequent ally in cruelty, stood and joined Garrick. Now both of them were behind me. Tempting as it was to turn and spit in their faces, that wasn't my role here, and it would reflect poorly on Lara and probably yield terrible consequences. I held still despite the tense energy racing through me and commanding me to run.

"Sit down," Lara ordered Talfryn, undoubtedly trying to defuse the situation. At last, he sat.

Garrick didn't remove his hand, though. Instead, his finger trailed down my spine to my waist. My skin crawled at the too-intimate contact. "She's scrawny, too."

"Garrick," Una said in bored, icy tones. "Is this meant to be entertainment? It's very dull."

"I'm just trying to solve a puzzle. Here we have a beautiful Noble Fae lady, who Talfryn maintains is as beautiful on the inside as she is on the outside, and here we have her scrawny human servant. Perhaps her beauty is hidden, hmm?"

He gripped my collar and pulled.

The fabric resisted, choking me. I coughed, hands flying to my neck, but the stitches began to give way beneath his strength. My dress split down the shoulder seam.

"Stop it, Garrick." Lara reached out an ineffectual hand.

Markas laughed, and then he was attacking the other side of my dress. He yanked on a sleeve, sending me stumbling. The dress ripped entirely on Garrick's side, the front falling loose. I scrambled to cover myself. I was wearing a chemise, but faerie undergarments were whisper-thin and hid little.

The dagger armlet hummed frantically, its top edge now mere inches from Garrick's fingers. A few more tugs on my sleeve and it would be revealed. I struggled to escape, but Markas's arm looped around my waist, holding me still as Garrick circled in front.

Kill, the dagger whispered. *Drink*.

"Stop it." Lara had risen at last and was pulling on Garrick's arm. Defending me, but it was too little, too late.

Garrick laughed and ripped the hanging flap of the dress down to my waist. My sweat-dampened chemise stuck to my skin, the fabric translucent. I flushed. No man had ever seen me in this state of undress.

"What do you think?" He gripped the neck of my chemise as I fought to shield myself. "Do humans have some hidden beauty underneath their clothes?"

Kill. To my horror, the dagger began creeping up my arm, ready to strike.

No. You can't kill him. If the dagger killed him, I would certainly be put to death.

Punish, it said, and punishing sounded perfect, but if anyone realized I carried a weapon, it would be taken away. I couldn't afford to lose it now.

Garrick knocked my arms away and ripped my chemise down the front. I cried out, kicking at him as I tried to cover myself, but Markas gripped my wrists and forced my arms behind my back. My breasts were exposed to the entire picnic. Faeries watched from nearby blankets, curious about the commotion. My cheeks burned and my heart raced with a potent mixture of hatred and terror.

"Shall I continue?" Garrick shrugged off Lara's hand as she tried to stop him again.

Hit him, I silently begged, but Lara was still too meek to attack a fellow candidate. She pleaded with him while he laughed and gripped the fabric at my waist, preparing to tear my final shield away from me.

The dagger began slithering down my arm towards Markas's imprisoning fists, singing a melody of hatred in my head. *Punish. Punish. Punish.*

"Stop this." A new, thunderous voice joined the mix.

Markas released me instantly. Seconds later, Garrick stepped back as well. I covered myself, struggling to pull the torn parts of my gown back together before turning around.

Lord Kallen stood a few feet away, as still as a wildcat about to pounce. His dark eyes burned with the promise of violence. "What is the meaning of this?" he asked in the coldest, most terrifying tone I'd heard from him yet.

I stumbled back, holding my torn dress tight to my chest.

"A mere game." Garrick spread his hands innocently.

Una moved to her brother's side and whispered in his ear. When she was done, Kallen looked even more murderous.

"The human is off-limits," Kallen said. "She belongs to Earth House."

Garrick had the nerve to laugh. "She's a human. Why does it matter? She's worthless."

Kallen moved so quickly I didn't see more than a black-and-silver blur before his sword rested at Garrick's throat. "Think carefully before you question my orders."

A speck of night appeared in the air beside Garrick, the size of a coin but swiftly growing. Garrick yelped, but he couldn't retreat from the killing darkness or he'd sever his own throat on Kallen's sword. "You can't kill me," he said, bravado turning to bluster.

Kallen smiled, slow and awful. "Oh, believe me, I can."

The blackness grew, pressing closer and closer to Garrick's sleeve.

"Forgive my impudence, Lord Kallen," Garrick blurted. "I didn't mean to question your orders."

Kallen didn't move. "You apologize for questioning my orders—yet you do not regret assaulting a servant from another house?"

Beads of sweat formed on Garrick's forehead as the hole inched closer. "Lady Lara, forgive my insult to your house."

No apology to me, of course. I glared at Garrick, wishing him dead. The dagger hummed in agreement.

"What is your response, Lady Lara?"

Lara looked between us with wide eyes. "Just—don't let it happen again."

I winced at the tepid response, once again feeling the sting of betrayal. Lara, my mistress, my *friend*, had let this happen. She could have stopped it, and she hadn't.

The Void magic vanished, and Kallen sheathed his sword. He snapped his fingers at me. "Come."

I bristled at once again being called like a dog, but I had no choice. I walked towards him as steadily as I could, holding my dress in place and trying to conceal my shaking.

"Where are you taking her?" Lara made eye contact with me at last, an apology written on her face. I ignored it.

"I will escort her back to Earth House. Una's handmaiden can serve you."

Garrick's hostile eyes followed as the Void lord led me underground.

"ARE YOU WELL?" KALLEN ASKED ONCE WE HAD DESCENDED SEVeral levels.

I struggled against the angry words that wanted to burst out of me. The dagger still hummed against my skin, egging me on. *Punish. Rage. Hate. Kill.* In the end, I was too unsettled to maintain any pretense of calm. "Of course I'm not," I spat.

"I'm sorry for what Garrick did." I couldn't read his face anymore; his fury had faded into stillness. Perhaps it had all been for show. "It was unacceptable."

"Because I belong to Earth House, right? Because it's illegal to mishandle someone else's property." When he didn't respond, I kept goading him. "I'm not anyone's property, you know."

"In Mistei you are. That's how the system works."

"Well, maybe it shouldn't work like that." I stalked by his side, unwilling to trail behind like a lost puppy. "Maybe this court needs to be taught a lesson." The dagger echoed my thoughts as it took a tiny sip of my blood, as if soothing its own violent impulses. I welcomed the small sting—it grounded me in my body, gave form to my rage.

Kallen gripped my arm and pulled me into a small, mostly bare room. A shimmering, translucent black curtain fell over the door, just like the wards I'd seen Drustan cast. "Never say anything like that again."

"Why not?" I demanded as I clutched the dress tightly to my chest. Somewhere deep down I knew why not, but rage ruled me. Fury pumped through my veins, filling me with restless energy that needed an outlet. If I couldn't express it in an argument with him, I would scream until my voice went hoarse.

Kallen's eyes burned with some intense, unfathomable emotion, but his face was as still as if it had been carved from stone. What did this cold, mysterious faerie feel? I got the sense sometimes that his eyes were openings to a very deep pit, and some terrible beast lurked at the bottom.

"Do you want to live?" he asked.

"Yes, but that doesn't mean—"

"It does. This is the world you live in, and if you want to survive long enough to change it, then you have to play by its rules."

Change it? Kallen had the ear of the king; why would he want to change anything? I scoffed. "Why don't you just report me to King Osric? Betray me the way you did that noble from Void House when he spoke treason? Isn't that your job, to be the king's loyal dog?"

Something awful had gotten into me. The words fell into the air like a hammer against an anvil. I pressed a hand to my mouth as if I could push them back in, but it was too late.

Kallen looked taken aback—and then furious. "I don't tell the king about you because you are useful," he bit out, and I cringed at his sharp tone. "You're positioned in a house whose allegiance would make all the difference in an uprising. Since most faeries don't notice humans, you can move freely. All of this makes you worth saving—so long as you continue providing me with information."

So I was only worth saving because I made a good spy. I tasted his bitter truth—and rejected it. "I'm worth saving anyway. I'm not your puppet."

Kallen spun and paced to the wall. He raised a fist, and at first I thought he was going to strike the stone, but instead he rested his hand against it, bowing his head.

My breaths sounded excruciatingly loud in the silence.

"What has Drustan told you lately?" he finally asked.

A ragged laugh burst out of me. "That's it?" I wasn't sure what else I had expected. More angry words? For him to banish me to rot with the other humans? Why did I even want this confrontation with one of the most dangerous faeries in Mistei to continue? But my anger wouldn't let me back down, and the dagger on my arm reveled in that rage, rippling against my skin.

Kallen was suddenly in my face, his hard body mere inches from mine. I raised my chin, unwilling to retreat. I still held my dress in place with one hand, and with every breath, my knuckles barely brushed his chest. His gaze lingered on my mouth before dropping to the hand clenched at my breast. "Are you looking for a fight?" His voice was so soft I wouldn't have been able to hear him if I'd been standing only a few feet farther away.

"No." The statement came out breathier than I had intended.

"I think you are. The question is, why?"

Why, indeed? I didn't understand myself.

We stood together, two adversaries locked in silent combat, until finally he stepped back. "Tell me about Drustan."

The breath whooshed out of me at Kallen's retreat. "He hasn't told me anything of note."

"I don't care if you think it's of note or not."

Clearly I had to say something or Kallen would never leave me alone. "He told me about the changelings."

"Why? What did he tell you about them?"

"I had questions after the dinner. He told me why the babies are sent away."

"And what are Drustan's feelings about changelings?"

Drustan had been devastated as he'd recalled the fate of his closest friend and her child. "I don't know. I assume he finds it cruel."

"As you do." His gaze took in all of me, as if he could see down to the root of my soul.

"Yes," I said honestly. "I'm just a human, though."

We studied each other, and I wondered again what he thought and felt. If Hector wanted to take the throne, would Kallen support him? Or did he only support his own well-being and thus the well-being of the king?

I was still feeling bold. "What do you think about the changelings?"

Kallen looked away. "That will be all."

I couldn't let it go. He'd taken all my anger so far without throwing me to Osric and his executioners—he could take this, too. "Are you saying you don't care?" A muscle ticked in his jaw, but he didn't reply, so I pressed on. "That child will never know his mother. The human baby who replaces him will suffer. Do you truly not have a problem with that?"

"I can't afford to have a problem with that," he said. "None of us can."

I wanted to call him a monster for refusing to care about the helpless. That wasn't entirely true, though, was it? I'd been helpless today, and he had saved me.

His phrasing struck me as significant. *I can't afford to have a problem with that*, he'd said. Not *I don't have a problem with it*.

Remembering Garrick's hands on me, the tearing sound of my dress and the brush of air against my bare skin, I wondered how much worse it would have gotten if Kallen hadn't intervened. I was useful to him alive, but why should it matter to him if I were humiliated or hurt? Why stop Garrick and Markas at all?

The King's Vengeance wouldn't—*shouldn't*—care.

"Why did you do it?" I asked, my tone softer than it had been before. A weapon partially sheathed.

"Do what?"

It didn't sound like a real question, though. His eyes flicked between mine, then dropped to where my hand still clutched my torn dress together.

"Save me. It can't have just been because I'm useful."

He looked at me for a seemingly endless stretch of time. Midnight-blue eyes, inscrutable expression. Tension in his jaw . . . and everywhere else, I realized. Like he was perpetually ready for some unknown calamity. Like he was . . . waiting.

"No," he finally said. "It wasn't." Then he swallowed. "Do you wish I hadn't?"

Maybe the room was shifting. Maybe I was dizzy from stress. I felt like I was sinking slowly into the bog, my foot having found something that looked like clover but wasn't, and a shadow underneath was reaching up to gently pull me under.

Kallen wasn't telling me why, but he had given an answer all the same. And strangest of all was that he almost looked unsure. Like he was afraid of what I might say.

Fae misdirection, probably. The urge to play with his prey. Lord Kallen probably didn't feel enough to fear anything.

Still . . .

I cleared my throat. "I suppose I should thank you."

At that, the hint of uncertainty in his expression fled, and his lips quirked slightly. "And are you going to?"

I wrestled with my own tongue for a few seconds. "Thank you," I finally managed to say.

In response, he inclined his head.

Uncomfortable with my own gratitude, I took a deep breath. "Very well. I'm leaving."

"You are to continue sharing any and all information with me," he said. "Especially when it relates to Prince Drustan, and especially if it relates to any rumors of rebellion, unrest, or negative sentiment against the king."

An odd stab of disappointment went through me as I realized we were right back where we had started. "Of course." *Not.*

My hand was on the door handle when I remembered something from that terrible night when the king had ripped a baby from its mother's arms. The child's father was from Void House. "The changeling. You didn't . . . Were you the one who told King Osric about him?"

"No," he said instantly. Vehemently. "But I'll find out who did. And believe me when I say the father has been punished for his failure."

What failure? Abandoning his lover and infant in their time of need? Or siring a child in the first place?

I wouldn't ask, though. Not when I'd already pushed so hard and miraculously come out unscathed. I nodded and slipped out, leaving Kallen behind.

◎◎◎◎◎◎

LARA KNOCKED ON MY DOOR LATE THAT NIGHT.

I rubbed sleep from my eyes and padded to the door between our rooms. My stomach sank at the thought of seeing her, but I opened it anyway.

She wore a filmy white nightgown and her braid was uneven—because I had refused to tend to her before bedtime. Her eyes were reddened.

"Can I come in?" she asked in a small voice.

I stepped aside and silently ushered her into the room.

She looked around, taking in the simple surroundings before sitting gingerly on my bed. "It shouldn't have gone on that long."

"It shouldn't have gone on at all," I snapped. "A responsible mistress wouldn't have let that happen to her property. A *friend* wouldn't have let that happen."

Lara winced at my harsh words. Her fingers clenched in her gown, crushing the delicate fabric. "I know. I'm so sorry."

I sighed and sat beside her. "Even if you're sorry, it still hurts."

"I know." Her hand covered mine. "I've never known how to stand up for myself, so I've never really thought about standing up for other people. I didn't know what to do."

My throat ached. "You could have made him stop. Yelled at him. Hit him. Anything."

"I'm not a fighter. Not like you. I don't have that in me." Her mouth quirked in a lopsided smile, but I saw the sheen of tears in her eyes. "You would have been a better Noble Fae than me."

Would I? I didn't think so. Not if being Fae meant being callous and calculating. Not if it meant hurting the people around me. "I'm not Fae. You are. You're the heir to Earth House and a candidate in the trials. You have to be strong."

Those watery brown eyes met mine. "How?"

"I don't know. Practice, I suppose."

"I'm afraid."

"So am I. It doesn't matter, though. We have to be strong. And you have to be even stronger than me, because so many depend on you. *I* depend on you."

She nodded and squeezed my hand before releasing it. She dashed the tears from her eyes. "I'll try."

It was all I could ask. I nodded, swallowing the lump in my throat as she rose and walked to the door.

"You aren't property," she said over her shoulder. "I—I don't know how to have a friend. I've never really had one before. But I'll keep trying."

She left before the first tears fell into my lap.

23

BELTANE ARRIVED IN A FLURRY OF RED AND ORANGE.
The hallways were draped in flame-colored gossamer,
and all the torches glowed crimson. Incense spiced the air, and I
grew lightheaded from the smoke. Every heady breath sent the complex scent of fire, sex, and cinnamon spinning through my lungs.

In honor of Fire House, everyone was adorned in radiant flame-colored hues or the black and gray of smoke. Lara shone in a scarlet
satin gown that faded to orange at the sleeves and hem. Her hair was
covered by a net of gold studded with rubies, I'd painted her lips red
to match her dress, and her eyes were highlighted with ebony liner
and gold powder.

Even I looked intense in a simple iron-gray dress, my dark hair
unbound and curling, my lips red and eyes outlined in gold. Fire
House's drama had infected us all; everywhere I looked faeries drank
and laughed and kissed in the hallways, hands roaming indecently.

"Beltane is our wildest celebration," Alodie had told me that
morning. "The Fae revere pleasure, and no house more so than Fire
House. You'll see a lot of scandalous things today."

I maintained a calm facade, but truthfully, I was shocked. I'd never seen couples embracing so wantonly in public. The bonfire this evening was said to be even wilder—what would I see then?

I wasn't supposed to attend the masked bonfire revelry—the Noble Fae would grow so uninhibited that the gaze of servants was prohibited—but the nature of the trial would supposedly be announced there, so Oriana had found a way to sneak me in. For the last week, faerie visitors had been arriving from other courts, which meant strangers would attend the celebration. I would wear a fine gown for the first time in my life, cover my face with a mask, and keep an eye on Lara, with the goal of protecting her and helping her once the nature of the Fire trial was revealed. With so many visitors attending, no one would think twice if they didn't recognize me.

We still didn't know what the trial would involve. Aidan refused to tell me anything, although he swore I needn't worry—it wouldn't be difficult to succeed, so long as Lara followed her instincts.

We passed a cluster of visiting faeries on the way to a formal luncheon, half of whom wore moon-shaped stone pendants and half of whom had silver bangles at their wrists. Lara inclined her head graciously while I did my best to remain invisible as I drank in the sight of them.

They were beautiful, as all Noble Fae were. A few were around my height, while others towered over even Lara. The only other difference I could see between them and the courtiers of Mistei was their attire. Regardless of gender, the visitors wore sheer, scandalous sweeps of fabric that left little to the imagination: red or black gauze gathered with ribbons or banded with leather or chains. I could see their nipples and the dark shading of their pubic areas through the gossamer.

After we had reached a sufficient distance away, I leaned in to whisper to Lara. "Where are they from?"

"The ones with stone pendants are from the ice halls in the north of Grimveld. The ones wearing silver are from Elsmere."

"Elsmere?" There was that place-name again.

"A Fae city in the south of Lindwic. Grimveld was named after their Fae, but Lindwic was not."

Lindwic was south of Grimveld and southwest of Enterra, across the mountains. Their fibercrafts were unparalleled, and it was one of the countries I'd dreamed of traveling to as a trader. I hadn't realized they had their own Fae enclave, but the southern forests were rumored to be wild and nigh impassable, and magic thrived in the hidden places of the world.

Mistei's faeries mingled with the visitors as we made our way towards the luncheon, and I spotted Kallen leaning against a wall and speaking with a lady from Elsmere. She was around my height but much more voluptuous—a fact made clear by the nearly transparent gray draperies she wore. Her hair was a dark red-brown and her eyes were blue as the summer sky as she looked up at Kallen. His head was bent over hers, his mouth near her ear.

A Beltane flirtation? Kallen hardly seemed the type.

As if my thoughts had summoned his attention, his eyes shifted to me. Then he cupped the lady's elbow and turned her away, guiding her towards Fire House.

Kallen is always whispering in ears at these events, Drustan had said. I'd told Kallen about Elsmere's rumored change in leadership, and here the Void lord was, arm in arm with a faerie from that very kingdom.

"You look anxious," Lara said.

I forced my eyes away from Kallen's tall frame and my mind away from worries about what he might do with the information I'd provided. "I just can't believe how revealing those outfits are," I said, gesturing towards a group of Grimveld Fae in sheer black.

"Right?" Lara cast me a thrilled glance. "I want one."

"I don't." To have that much of my body exposed to the public? No, thank you.

Lara laughed. "I forgot how prudish humans are."

"Even you look prudish compared to them." I'd never thought Osric's shining, dangerous court would look tame, but the attire I'd seen today had been beyond my wildest imaginings.

"They're just getting in the spirit early. My dress tonight will be just as revealing. So will yours."

I grimaced. "Do we have to?"

"It's part of the tradition. All adult Noble Fae put on their most scandalous outfits and meet around the bonfire at sunset. They jump over the fire, and after that it's like they go mad. I've never seen it before, but I hear it's completely uninhibited. Dancing, drinking, fighting, sex . . ."

"Would you . . . you know . . ." I trailed off, blushing too hard to finish the sentence.

"Have sex with someone?" Lara considered the question thoughtfully. "I don't know. Not everyone does, but it's encouraged. I just don't have anyone I want to be with right now."

An image of Drustan rose in my mind, but I immediately banished it. I wouldn't be jumping over the fire because I was Lara's bodyguard and assistant. Drustan would, though. What if he went wild and slept with someone right in front of me?

A sting of jealousy told me how foolish I'd grown over him. He was attractive and kind to me, but he was still a prince and I was a servant. Whatever his reasons for kissing me, it would be absurd to assume he wanted me more than he wanted anyone else.

I couldn't keep my eyes off him at lunch, though. We were in the same room the first Fire event had been held in. The king thankfully wasn't present, so Drustan reigned over the room from a seat at the high table, sharing laughs and boasts with the nobility around him. He gleamed in a red velvet tunic slashed to reveal hints of gold and jet.

Aidan caught me gawking at Drustan, but for once he didn't tease me about it. He couldn't, considering how intensely he was studying Edric. The Fire candidate's golden shirt was unlaced, revealing a large slice of muscled chest, and rubies sparkled in the dark cloud of his hair. He was already drunk on Fire House's spicy red wine, and he roared with laughter at every joke, tossing his head back with abandon.

I nudged Aidan. "Are you all right?"

He smiled at me, but there was no joy in it. "Of course."

Like me, he hadn't been invited to the gathering tonight. Unlike me, he would stay underground, enjoying a night of revelry in the mirrored ballroom with the other servants.

"Are you worried what Edric will do?" I finally voiced the suspicion that had been growing for weeks.

Aidan scowled at me. "Of course not."

I waited with raised eyebrows.

Aidan winced. "Maybe a little."

Compassion filled me. "He might not do anything."

"Oh, he will. Edric loves pleasure, and anything less than pure hedonism would be an insult to the Shards."

"And you? Will you do anything?"

Aidan shrugged. "Maybe, maybe not. Edric's never attended the bonfire before, but every year I attend the servant revels. It depends on who's available."

Both Edric and Aidan might take lovers tonight, but it didn't seem like Aidan would truly enjoy it. "Do you think he knows how you feel?" I asked.

Aidan laughed bitterly. "A wise lord should always know what his people want."

"But does—"

Aidan shook his head, cutting me off. "This is tradition. It means nothing."

We were silent for the rest of the lunch.

Once the Noble Fae started drinking in earnest, Lara dismissed me so I could prepare for the celebration. I curtsied and left, secretly relieved to get away from the boisterous clamor.

Somehow I wasn't surprised when Drustan caught up to me at the base of the ramp.

"Prince." I curtsied deeply. "May I be of assistance?"

He looked sinfully delicious today, his hair shining bright as the torches and his eyes flickering with reflected flame. He wasn't smiling, though. "We haven't spoken since after that dinner," he said.

"Lara has kept me busy."

"I confided in you that night. I want to make sure those confidences are safe."

My heart jumped into my throat. Did he know I'd been talking to Kallen? "They're safe."

Those gray eyes were too perceptive. "I have a lot of enemies, Kenna."

"You do?" I don't know why I asked—it wasn't like I didn't know someone plotting revolution would be unpopular in certain circles.

"I do. So when I heard you left that picnic with Kallen and then stopped for a chat . . . you have to understand my concern."

I went cold. Plenty of people had seen Kallen escort me away, but I hadn't realized we'd been seen entering that room for a private conversation. At least his wards would have prevented eavesdropping. "He asked about you," I admitted. "After he broke up the fight. He asked what we talk about."

Drustan didn't blink. "And what did you tell him?"

"I told him I asked you about the changelings and that you

explained what they were. That was all. He thinks you take an interest in me because you bet on me at the winter solstice." The boundary between lies and truths grew blurrier the longer I spent with the Fae.

"Are you sure that's all?" The foreign chill in his eyes and the warning in his voice made me shiver. I was finally seeing a glimpse of Drustan the ruler.

"Yes." I kept my head high, willing him to trust me. "I had to say something, but please believe I would never betray you."

He nodded, and just like that the ice melted, leaving only flame behind. "I do believe you. And I'm sorry about what happened at the picnic. I wish I'd been there to knock Garrick on his ass. Remember, though—Kallen is extremely dangerous. It doesn't matter what he told you or whether or not he saved you. He's a snake."

"I understand."

He started to turn away. "I have to return to the party."

I touched his sleeve before he could go. "What's the fourth trial?" It was my last chance to find out.

He laughed. "Tired of subtlety, I see. You should be careful—you wouldn't want anyone to think you're cheating."

I leaned in, emboldened. "You already know I'm cheating. Just a hint?"

His eyes gleamed, and he backed me towards the wall. The stone hit my shoulder blades, and I watched, breathless, as he kept approaching. He stopped mere inches away, his hot breath rushing over my lips. "I suggest you stop thinking about the trial and start focusing on enjoying your first Beltane," he said. "It's the Fae's one opportunity for freedom."

He truly wasn't going to tell me about the trial. I suppressed my disappointment. "Freedom from what?"

"Everything. Morality. Restraint. Thought." He traced a finger down my neck, and I shivered. "You haven't seen the Fae truly come undone. I wish you could be at the bonfire—it would be an exquisite experience."

We locked eyes for long seconds. Would he kiss me again? I wet my lips, hoping for it, even though I knew the danger of being discovered with him.

"Don't tempt me," he whispered. "I'm already on the edge. You don't know what you'd be unleashing."

I shuddered as he left. I didn't know . . . but I wanted desperately to find out.

$$\textcircled{a}\textcircled{a}\textcircled{a}\textcircled{a}\textcircled{a}\textcircled{a}$$

I RAN OVER THE RULES FOR THE BONFIRE WITH LARA LATE THAT afternoon. If I was going to be her chaperone, I would take my duties seriously. "Have fun, but if you get uncomfortable, pretend to pass out from too much alcohol. I'll watch over you. Plenty of people will be having sex, and Alodie told me the fire is spelled to prevent conception, so there are no rules about who can sleep with whom—you might get advances from anyone. You don't have to say yes, though. Only do what you're comfortable with."

Lara rolled her eyes. "You're growing overprotective. Good to know about the contraceptive fire, though—although honestly it might not matter, depending on who I end up with." She had told me she was interested in all genders, and her last romance—more of a friendly sex arrangement, from the sound of it—had been with another Earth lady.

I had wondered about the contraception spell until I'd realized it was probably intended to prevent interbreeding between houses. Beltane was an ancient tradition, as ancient as any the Fae celebrated, and logic and reason had no part in it. Since the ceremony couldn't be changed, the king had chosen to prevent unintended consequences.

Lara spun in a circle. "How do I look?"

I bit my lip, suddenly jealous. She looked incredible, like she'd been wrapped in smoke. Her filmy dress barely reached the tops of her knees, and the entire stomach panel was missing, revealing smooth skin. It was held in place by wicked leather straps that wound around her chest and neck. Her mask was black enamel encrusted with rubies.

"You look perfect. You'll win dozens of hearts, I'm sure."

She gave me a knowing look. "It isn't about the hearts."

For a moment I wished I could truly join in the revelry rather than standing watch. That I could let go and feel unabashed pleasure with the rest of them. I'd never gone beyond kissing or been seen fully unclothed. What would it be like to dance naked in the moonlight? To feel a hard body on top of me, inside me?

"Put on your dress," Lara said, snapping me out of my reverie. "I want to see it."

I returned to my chambers, where the dress hung in the bathroom. Could I call it a dress when it came in two pieces? I hadn't quite believed it was an outfit when I'd first pulled it out of the wardrobe. I'd tried to put it back, but no matter how many times I opened the doors, the wardrobe had presented me with the same thing.

I shimmied into it, fixing the clasps in place before attacking my hair with oil and a wide-toothed comb. I had already done my makeup, painting my lips crimson and lining my eyes in black pigment that swept out in wings to my temples. I finished my preparations by dusting every inch of exposed skin with glittering golden powder that transformed me from a human playing dress-up into a mysterious foreign faerie.

When I returned to Lara, her jaw dropped. She clapped her hands in glee. "Amazing!"

I twirled, then immediately stopped when my skirt billowed up. "I feel naked," I confessed.

"You look perfect."

The fabric was a deep wine red. Thankfully, it wasn't transparent, but there was very little of it—just a small flutter of a skirt and a tight band around my breasts. Golden chains fell from a collar around my neck, connecting to the top. After some trial and error, the dagger had transformed into a hair clip, considering my near nudity. It held up half of my hair while the rest tumbled to my waist.

With a mask of garnet lace covering the entire top half of my face, I truly looked like one of the Fae.

"This outfit is brilliant." Lara flicked a chain and smiled. "It's definitely not a style you see in Mistei, even at Beltane. Everyone will assume you're visiting from far away."

Whether I had the confidence to carry it off remained to be seen.

We padded out together, both barefoot in preparation for the revelry. Lara exited through the water tunnel, but I took a back route through the catacombs, emerging in a little-used corridor on one of the levels where guests were housed. As I joined the throng heading for the stairs, no one looked at me suspiciously, although several faeries appraised me with lust in their eyes. I did my best to smile flirtatiously, but inside I felt flustered.

We emerged just as the sun kissed the horizon and began its final descent. The sky was painted in violent colors that reflected the bonfire already blazing on the grassy slope. I made my way to the refreshment table and grabbed a glass of wine. The rich, spicy liquid burned on the way down.

Deep, echoing drumbeats sounded from beyond the bonfire, and faeries were already moving in time with that relentless rhythm.

Some were plastered together, their sweaty bodies writhing in tandem, but others spun wildly or quaffed cups of wine, their masked faces tipped up towards the distant stars.

The wine loosened my muscles, and heat pooled in my belly as couples groped each other all around me. I wished I was one of them, that I had an outlet for the restless need that filled me. I took another deep gulp of wine instead.

I hadn't seen Drustan so far—perhaps he had already joined the faeries who writhed in twos and threes and more all over the hilltop.

A cry of lust split the air. I followed the sound, then stared, mesmerized, as a half-naked faerie male pounded into the lady who writhed beneath him. Her breasts bounced with each hard thrust, and my own nipples tightened in response.

I'd never seen anyone have sex before.

It was wild. Primal. Thrilling. My heart thundered as I imagined it was me lying in the grass instead, with Drustan on top of me, curtains of copper hair falling around me and sticking to my damp skin as he thrust inside me again and again and again . . .

Another fire roared to life beside the bonfire. This one was smaller, with unnaturally dark red flames that reached to waist height. A faerie jumped over it, and a cheer went up from the watching crowd.

As if a dam had burst, the Noble Fae surged towards the fire, jumping in a continuous stream. The drums grew louder. Chanting and wailing rose to accompany them, an eerie cadence that echoed in my bones and commanded me to dance.

I resisted, watching for Lara. She waited at the end of the line, shoulders tight with tension. She glanced at me for reassurance, and I smiled in encouragement.

I was surprised to recognize Kallen only a few places ahead of her in line. He wore a filmy black shirt studded with jewels that winked like stars around the moon of the opal brooch, and his trousers were far tighter than normal. His mask was only a small band of dark cloth, and excitement burned on his face as he took a deep swallow of wine, threw the goblet to the ground, and leapt over the fire.

The second he landed on the other side, he spun towards the nearest faerie and punched him.

I gasped, hands flying to my mouth, but the other faerie just laughed and threw a punch in return. Others joined in eagerly, until the fight became an outright brawl. Two faeries from Grimveld leapt over the fire before joining the mayhem, as did the lady from Elsmere I'd seen Kallen speaking with earlier—she moved faster than seemed possible, tackling an Illusion faerie as she shouted a battle cry to the sky. I caught one more glimpse of Kallen's face before he went down under a well-placed kick. He was grinning with exhilaration.

It's the Fae's one opportunity for freedom, Drustan had told me.

I'd assumed he meant sexual freedom, since that was what I'd heard about the most from Lara and Aidan, but it was far more than that. The Fae were succumbing to every instinct, both joyous and violent, as they gave in to their darkest desires.

The vicious thrill on Kallen's face gave me shivers. He was normally so controlled. Was this violence what hid beneath the surface?

It was Lara's turn. Her skirt flared around her as she gracefully cleared the fire. When she landed, she stiffened as if in shock, then looked down at her hands.

I began making my way towards her, worried about what that expression meant. Had she hurt herself?

Lara laughed, high and wild, and launched herself at the faerie next to her. Her nails raked a bloody trail down his face, and then she slapped him—hard. He was so drunk he fell to the ground with a groan, but as she twirled away, he raised a pleading hand after her.

I reached her side. "Are you well?"

I barely dodged the punch she threw at me.

"Oh!" she exclaimed, recognizing who had approached her. "Oh, Kenna, it's the most wonderful feeling. The fire spoke to me. It told me to be strong." She laughed again, merry as pealing bells. "Don't worry about me—I'm going to be absolutely fine."

She pranced towards the dancing, turning in sensuous circles until someone approached her. When he reached out to touch her, she punched him, knocking him flat. Everyone around them laughed, including her victim, who wiped blood from his rapidly healing nose and grinned up at her. Lara dropped to her knees, straddling him. She met my eyes one more time, shooing me away with a smile before focusing on her prey again. She kissed him hard and deep, then punched him again.

I kept an eye on her, but Lara did seem perfectly fine. She moved from faerie to faerie, alternating between dancing, kissing, and starting fights. She didn't disappear to have sex with anyone, but by the bliss on her face, I guessed that she didn't even want to. It seemed this was Lara's secret fantasy—a world in which she could dance wildly and commit violence with no repercussions, in which she could be as strong as she'd always wanted to be.

I kept my distance, understanding she had no immediate use for me. Eventually I realized she wouldn't need me at all, so I returned to the refreshment table and downed another glass. The drums tugged at me as the wine breathed its spicy song into my veins, and before I knew it, I was dancing, too, my arms raised high, my head tilted back towards the stars. They were barely visible through the billowing smoke, but I smiled at them anyway. Those bright constellations were my old friends.

A hand grabbed my arm.

I turned and saw a face I didn't recognize, an unknown faerie with long brown hair and a cheerful grin beneath his yellow mask. He gripped my hips. "Let's dance," he breathed against my lips. His breath was laced with alcohol.

I held him off with a hand on his chest. "Maybe later."

He blinked at me, clearly befuddled. "You didn't jump."

"Uh," I responded eloquently. Apparently my discipline had aroused suspicion.

"She didn't jump," he announced to the crowd around us.

"Jump," they began chanting as he pushed me towards the flames. "Jump, jump, jump!"

"First visit to Mistei?" he asked, noticing my hesitation. I nodded. "I'll go again so you can see there's nothing to worry about." He released me and leapt over the fire to cheers.

Then others were pushing me forward, still chanting. I took a deep breath and started running, fear and excitement mingling. The fire's heat licked against my bared skin. What if I didn't jump high enough?

Then I was soaring through the air just above the flames.

Time stopped.

I hung, suspended in a shower of embers as still and bright as the stars above. One bent leg stretched out before me and one behind, and my skirt had ridden almost all the way up to my waist.

Heat consumed me.

What do you want? the fire asked.

My heart spoke for me without any input from my mind. *To be loved. To be touched. To be free.* I yearned for it with every piece of me, the desire as strong as any hunger or thirst I'd ever felt.

Then do it.

The embers resumed their dance through the air, and I landed gracefully on the other side, my bare feet skimming over the grass. Exhilaration raced through me, and I laughed wildly as the crowd cheered.

I saw him then.

There, dancing near the bonfire in black leather and a shirt that hung open all the way to his navel, revealing ripples of muscle. Drustan froze in place as he saw me. His eyes were bright as silver coins behind his onyx mask.

My feet carried me towards him. His mouth hung slack as his gaze wandered over me, cataloging every inch of bared skin.

Without hesitation, I gripped his face in my hands, stood on my toes, and kissed him.

His arms snapped around me like a trap. My breasts were crushed against his chest, the nipples hard beneath the fabric. I groaned and writhed against him, sucking his tongue deep into my mouth.

"Kenna," he breathed.

He picked me up, never separating his lips from mine. I wrapped my legs around his waist, too out of my mind with desire to care if my body was exposed to the world. He strode away from the revelry, kissing me deeply, one hand supporting my bottom and one on my upper back, fisted in my loose hair.

We descended the hill until the drumbeats grew distant, until there were no more moans around us, and then he knelt, my body still entwined with his. My back hit the grass, and I arched, rubbing my aching core against him as his hands came down on either side of my head. He rolled his hips into me, catching my cry in his mouth as pleasure sizzled through me.

He broke away to bite the skin at the juncture of my neck and shoulder, just below my golden collar. I jerked against him.

"Little cheater," he accused.

I moaned. "I didn't hear anything about the trial." Maybe the announcement would happen later tonight.

His hand coasted down the golden chains until his palm rested on my breast. "Do you care about the trial?" He delicately squeezed a nipple through the fabric.

"No." I writhed, wanting him to do it again, to do it harder. "More."

He chuckled and gripped the other breast, pinching my nipple until I cried out and rocked against him. "Good."

A wall of flame rose around us. I jolted, startled, but the heat wasn't uncomfortable and the fire didn't spread. He was granting us privacy, I realized. A safe space to be as uninhibited and wild as we wanted.

Let me have this, I told the dagger in my hair with my last sane thought. It didn't respond, but somehow I knew it wouldn't drink blood tonight, even if Drustan accidentally touched it. Tonight, pure Fae magic coursed through me along with my arousal, and it was good and right.

My hands raced over Drustan, ripping at his shirt. I was desperate to touch him, to bare all that hot skin. He swore as I tore the shirt to shreds, then pulled back to rip the remaining tatters off. He gripped my throat with a strong hand, and I arched at the domineering gesture, but his clever fingers were working at the clasp. Within seconds the collar had been unhooked from my neck, and then he pulled the top off. The skirt soon followed, and then the scrap of underwear.

He sat back and stared. I should have been abashed, but I wasn't. I laid my arms over my head and arched my back, presenting my breasts to him. He sucked in a harsh breath, then dropped to take my nipple into his mouth.

I gripped his hair as he suckled, blind to anything but the fire and the stars and the pleasure.

"What did you want?" I asked as his mouth traveled to my other breast. "What did the fire show you?"

He bit down, and my body clenched in response. "The power to break all the rules," he murmured against my skin. "To have anything I want without limits."

Then his mouth was coasting from my breasts to my navel. One of his hands began a slow ascent from my knee, inching ever closer to the place where I was empty and aching.

"Oh, please," I panted as his tongue teased above and his fingers played below. "Please touch me."

No one had ever touched me down there but myself. I knew what he'd find—I was wet for him, wetter than I'd ever been in my life.

His fingers finally reached my core. I choked on a shout, closing my eyes in bliss as those hot fingers played. When they moved up to the apex of my sex and the sensitive spot that would make me climax if he touched it long and hard enough, I moaned.

He rubbed small, unrelenting circles until I was writhing beneath him. My hands ripped through his hair, tugging on him, begging him to give me what I needed. "Please."

He chuckled, and his fingers retreated as he shifted his body lower.

I groaned, reaching down to force his hand back to my sex, then froze as I felt the wet sweep of his tongue against me.

"What—" I started to say, but then he licked me again, and the question turned into a gasp. My knees drew up around him, my thighs brushing the strong muscles of his arms. He settled in, looping one arm around my leg. The other hand returned to stroke my entrance, and then one long finger was pushing inside.

I cried out. My body clenched around that finger as his tongue raced over me, sending me higher and higher until my vision darkened and I shook all over.

When I came back to earth, he still didn't stop. One finger became two as he worked my body, preparing me, seeing how much I could take. I made a soft noise of discomfort, squeezing my legs tight around him before forcing them to relax.

"Have you done this before?" he murmured against me.

"No," I admitted. "But I want it."

He set back in even more hungrily, driving me harder, circling my sensitive clitoris until I spasmed beneath him again.

"Please." The hoarse whisper was all I could manage. *Let me feel this*, I wanted to say. *Give me everything.*

He rose, wiping his mouth on the back of his hand before settling his hips between my thighs. He dipped down to kiss me, and then I felt the nudge of his thick erection. He pushed, stretching me slowly.

There was pain, but it faded quickly. All I could feel was the heat of his body, the iron solidness of him inside. I'd never imagined sex would feel like this: this overwhelming sensation of being full of him, of being a part of him as he was a part of me.

He pushed again, and I gasped as he seated himself fully. He stroked my hair out of my face, kissing each temple before dropping a long, lingering kiss against my lips.

I wound my arms around him and tucked my feet against his calves, kissing him back with all the passion in my soul. This was incredible. Perfect. Everything I'd been missing, and I'd never even known it.

Then he started to move.

Long, rolling thrusts that drew cries from my throat and made me rake my nails down his back, desperate to claim him as he was claiming me. I was drowning in the sensations, the slick slide of his body as he conquered mine. He clenched a fist in my hair, holding me in place as his tongue plunged deep into my mouth in time with the rhythm of his body.

Flame licked over his hair and skin, racing tendrils that tickled when they brushed against me but didn't hurt. His body was so hot I wanted to melt into him. That heat was echoed inside where he moved, slow and steady and strong.

His pace quickened. I shouted something then, some nonsensical combination of words. I leaned up and bit him, my teeth seizing the strong muscle of his shoulder. He jerked and grunted, losing the controlled evenness of his thrusts as I sank greedy teeth and nails into him, as I wrapped my legs around his waist and urged him on with writhing undulations of my hips. He pounded into me, as out of control as I was, his sweat dropping to my forehead to mingle with mine as the fire roared around us.

He gave a few more hard thrusts and shook, holding himself deep inside as he trembled and gasped. I held him tightly, tears springing to my eyes at the intimacy.

I thought we were done then, but Drustan drew back and dropped a hand between my thighs to coax another climax out of me. I screamed, tears trailing down my cheeks as I closed my eyes, my entire body vibrating with release, my soul practically soaring into the sky.

I'd never felt so free.

24

I WOKE COVERED IN DEW. DROPLETS BEADED IN MY HAIR AND eyelashes and made my bare skin prickle with cold. I shifted and winced at the soreness between my legs.

Oh.

I pushed myself into a sitting position and looked around. It was just after dawn, and light gilded the forms of sleeping, naked faeries all up and down the slope. A blackened circle of grass was all that remained of the fiery boundary Drustan had raised last night.

He lay beside me, one arm flung over his head, chest rising and falling slowly. His eyes twitched beneath his lids as he dreamed.

I raked my gaze over his bare chest and then his bare lower half. I hadn't seen that part of him clearly last night. In the daylight it looked soft and small, nothing like the hard intrusion of the night before. I knew something of male anatomy, but curiosity burned through me—if I were to wake him and arouse him again, what would it look like under the light of the rising sun?

Temptation called, but I couldn't afford to find out.

I staggered to my feet and hunted for my skirt and top. While I could stumble into Earth House later than normal without arousing suspicion, the longer I stayed out here, the more likely it was I would be caught. Firelight and the mask still tied to my face had given me an aura of mystery in the darkness, but in the bright light of day, with the glittering powder washed from my body by dew and sweat, I probably looked very human indeed.

I cast one last, lingering glance at Drustan before hurrying away.

As I descended back into the claustrophobic confines of Mistei, my mind grew sharper, the fog of sleep and wine beginning to fade.

I had slept with Drustan.

Drustan, the Fire prince. One of the five most powerful faeries in the kingdom. I had taken him into my body with barely any conversation beforehand. I had moaned and scratched him and gone utterly out of my mind with lust.

My face heated at the recollection. Would he judge me for what I'd done?

I pushed the ashamed thoughts down. Did I judge him for what he'd done? No. He'd lost all inhibitions, and it had been beautiful. The only reason I doubted myself was because I was thinking in human terms. I was remembering the Elder's staid, judgmental sermons, rather than trusting myself and my instincts.

The dagger stirred in my hair, a gentle warning that someone was approaching. Luckily, a door to the catacombs glittered nearby, and I slipped inside.

My body ached in unfamiliar ways as I descended a set of narrow stone steps.

I wasn't a virgin anymore.

The realization didn't feel as profound as I'd thought it would. Virginity would have mattered if I'd ever wanted to marry a man from my village, but what use did it have here? I'd never really wanted to marry, anyway. Human men had always been so . . . dull. Controlling and small-minded.

I remembered Drustan's hot hands, the flicker of fire over his skin, the spicy taste of his tongue in my mouth.

I didn't regret it.

I was nervous about facing him again, though. I cringed to remember how I'd scratched and bitten him like an animal, although he hadn't seemed to mind. He'd even thrown his head back in ecstasy later that night, on the second time we'd joined. I'd left a purpling mark on his shoulder where my teeth had sunk in. With his healing powers, it had faded quickly, but in that moment I'd felt fierce, primal, and possessive. *You are mine*, that bite had proclaimed.

He wasn't mine, though. Maybe when it was just the two of us in a circle of flame on a night devoted to pure hedonism, but not in real life. He was a prince and I was a servant. He was Noble Fae and I was human. He had power; I did not.

Oh, but if I did have power, the things I would do . . .

Back in my room, I changed into a nightgown, removed my makeup, and dragged a comb through the tangle my hair had become after hours of Drustan gripping it. As I finished, I heard movement in the other room.

I knocked softly on Lara's door.

"Come in."

She was lying in bed, also in a nightgown, smiling dazedly at the ceiling. I exclaimed when I saw the bruises peppering her skin. Her left eye was swollen nearly shut.

I rushed to her side. "What happened? I can bring a compress."

She batted my hands away. "I'm fine." She sounded happier and more relaxed than I'd ever heard her. "Did you have fun? I lost track of you."

She didn't know I'd slept with Drustan. I thanked the stars for that. "I did," I said as casually as I could manage. "I danced and drank until dawn. What about you?"

She stretched and winced at the motion. "It was incredible. I fought and drank and shouted . . . and I kissed so many people, and then I hit every single one of them." She giggled. "They hit me back, but I always won."

"That doesn't sound fun." I studied the bruises. "Maybe we can take revenge on the ones who hurt you."

It was the kind of thing I would have said to Anya if someone had been cruel to her, but back then my revenge would have been a small prank or some sort of public humiliation. I was startled to realize that now I was thinking in terms of actual violence. Had living among the Fae changed me, or had this viciousness always been within me?

"No." She struggled to sit upright against her pillows. "It was what I wanted. It was what *they* wanted. Kenna, I've never felt so powerful in my life. I could do anything last night."

She was beaming, so I hesitantly smiled back. "Did the fire tell you to hit people? You said it told you to be strong."

Her eyes went dreamy and distant. "It was the strangest thing. Time seemed to stand still while I was jumping, and then something— maybe the Fire Shard, who knows—asked me what I wanted, and somehow the answer was there. I was tired of being weak. So it told me to be strong and take what I wanted."

The power to break all the rules, Drustan had panted in my ear when I'd asked what the fire had shown him. *To have anything I want without limits.*

My deepest desire had been to be loved and touched—to be valued. To feel free at last after an upbringing in poverty and my recent months as a servant. To take what I wanted, just like Drustan and Lara.

I took her hand, gentling my grip when I realized her knuckles were bruised. She would heal soon—not as fast as Drustan, but definitely faster than me. "I'm happy you got what you wanted," I said, and I meant it.

THE CANDIDATES MET FOR A LATE LUNCH TO CURE THEIR HANG-overs. Lara had felt fine after eating a hearty breakfast, but Edric and Karissa looked nauseated. I hadn't seen what any of the other candidates had done, since I'd been too busy keeping an eye on Lara and then experiencing my own darkest fantasy.

I blinked hard, trying to keep my eyes open. I'd slept for a few hours that morning, but it hadn't been nearly enough.

Aidan cast me an amused glance. "Did you have fun last night?"

I smiled nonchalantly. "Yes. Just stayed up too late drinking."

"You know, I didn't see you at the servants' gathering last night. Where were you?"

"I went to a smaller party." *A party of two*, I thought, and suppressed the urge to giggle. Goodness, I was tired.

Aidan raised his eyebrows. "That's the face of a woman with a secret."

"It was nothing special."

"Darling, I hate to tell you, but that means he didn't do a very good job."

I couldn't help it. I snorted with laughter and had to clap a hand over my mouth and nose to contain the sound.

Aidan grinned. "So? Who was it?"

"I don't know what you mean," I said, still trying to repress my giggles. "All I did was drink."

"Sure." Aidan rolled his eyes. "Whatever you say."

"And you? Did you . . . meet anyone?"

His face shadowed, and I immediately regretted the question. "No. I just drank."

Was he parroting my words or telling the truth? I couldn't pry deeper without inviting him to interrogate me as well. I glanced at Edric, wondering what the Fire candidate had done last night.

"Oh, he did." Aidan had caught my glance.

"I thought you weren't a mind reader."

"I only read desires, darling, which is why I know you have a secret." He winked. "No, I speak purely as someone who recognizes when a friend is prying where they have no business."

A friend. Something inside me warmed at the words. "I'm just curious."

"And you must think me a fool. Keep prying, though. I think I like the sympathy."

I heard the edge of pain beneath the humor, so I squeezed his hand. "Whenever you want to talk, I'll listen."

"I share when you share."

"So never."

We both laughed.

The doors to the dining room opened. I glanced up, and my stomach tumbled as if I were falling.

Drustan.

He looked sleepy, but somehow his heavy lids only increased his charisma. He was sex incarnate in a carmine shirt that opened to mid-breastbone. My cheeks burned and my heart increased its frantic pace as his eyes swept the room and finally landed on me.

"No," Aidan whispered, sounding utterly scandalized. "Kenna, you absolute witch, tell me everything."

I ignored him.

Drustan's eyes traced down my body and up again. He gave me

a slow, lazy smile that made my stomach turn over, and then his tongue darted to the corner of his lips; a small, careless gesture, but I knew what it meant.

"Great Shards." Aidan sounded like he was about to pass out.

"Candidates." Drustan turned his attention to them. "Did you enjoy your first taste of Fire House's favorite holiday?"

Murmured assents and nodding heads met the question, although a few winced and rubbed their temples as if the motion had worsened their headaches.

"When will the trial happen?" Una asked. "I thought the announcement was supposed to be last night."

"It already happened." Drustan winked.

The uproar that followed was almost comical.

"What do you mean, it already happened?"

"Did we pass?"

"Oh, Shards, I'm going to be sick."

Garrick stood, planting his hands on the table and pinning Drustan with an angry glare. "We weren't told the rules."

"What was the test?" Karissa looked terrified. She traded concerned glances with Talfryn, which surprised me; apparently the two worst performers had formed a bond, despite their initial hostility. He, too, looked petrified at the thought of failing whatever the test had been.

I frowned, considering what I'd seen. What could the trial have been? There hadn't been any announcement . . .

But the fire had been magical, and it had given everyone who jumped over it a very clear command. The trial had been dedicated to hedonism. If the candidates hadn't succumbed to their wildest desires . . .

Drustan confirmed my suspicion. "The fire told you what to do. A true Noble Fae values pleasure and instinct as much as anything else. If you showed the fire you were capable of seizing what you wanted, you succeeded."

That sounded like an extremely easy test considering my experience last night, but I was surprised to see dismay on a few faces. Talfryn looked devastated, although Karissa was suddenly smug. Wilfrid, the male Void candidate, looked anxious, as much as he ever let emotion show through his habitual reserve. Then, to my surprise, I noticed Una sitting stone-still, alarm evident in her stiff shoulders and widened eyes.

Was it a coincidence two of the three failures had come from Void House? They supposedly embraced chaos, but every Void faerie I'd met, including Hector and Kallen, most often exhibited a demeanor of cold control. It didn't make sense. All the other houses I could summarize in a few words, but Void had proven contradictory and opaque.

I almost smacked my forehead. Contradictory and opaque. Just another way to say chaotic and dark. Perhaps I understood them after all, as much as I ever would.

"Enjoy your meal." Drustan exited without another glance in my direction.

I exhaled, my shoulders drooping as he left. Should I be relieved he hadn't acknowledged me again? Or upset? I had no idea how women behaved in these situations.

I refocused on the tables, where the candidates were hotly debating exactly how much commitment to hedonism they'd needed to show and whether or not it had been fair of Fire House to test them without sharing the rules.

"I suppose you don't need to worry," Garrick told Lara. "I saw you last night. You were attacking faeries like an animal—when you weren't sucking on their tongues." The words were stinging, clearly meant to humiliate.

Lara met my eyes across the room, then lifted her chin. "I did. And I would do it again. Are you jealous, Garrick? Maybe you want me to hit you, too."

Gytha and Karissa crowed in delight, and Edric clapped Lara on the shoulder. She met Garrick's gaze defiantly, with no shame on her face.

I had never been prouder.

25

I RAN INTO TRIANA LATER THAT DAY.

She was struggling under the weight of a large basket of fabric, so I offered to help. "What is this?" I signed once we'd delivered it to one of the sewing workshops.

"Dresses from Light House," she replied slowly. I was getting better at the language, but I wasn't nearly as advanced as Triana was. Her hands fluttered like birds whenever she spoke with Maude, but she simplified her sentences for me. "Lady wore them once. Now rags."

"What a waste," I said, signing "waste" along with the spoken words. Because the Fae lived forever, they did anything to avoid being bored, even if it meant discarding something after one use.

The thought made me uneasy. Was that what Drustan saw in me? A novel experience? A way to avoid boredom?

I forced my thoughts away from self-doubt. Whatever his reasons for sleeping with me, it had happened. Worrying wouldn't change anything.

"What have you been doing lately?" I asked, doing my best to sign at least part of the question. Other than the simplest phrases, I still needed to use verbal speech to make my full meaning known, but hopefully I'd soon be able to convey more complex thoughts.

"Seamstress. I sewed before."

Before the brothel, she meant. Tension had crept into her expression. She seemed happier than when we'd first met, but I wondered if the mental wounds would ever heal.

Which reminded me of something I'd wanted to ask her for a while now. "I'm so sorry to ask this, but can you tell me where the king's brothel is?"

"Why?"

"I need to see it. Maybe someday I can do something to help the other people there."

"You can't," she signed emphatically. "It's dangerous."

"Please." The idea of that brothel kept haunting me. I wanted to know how many humans needed help.

She sighed before replying with reluctant fingers. "Down the stairs near the quartz room."

The quartz room was a popular gathering place near the throne room—it made sense King Osric would want his pleasures easily accessible. The corridors around it were always populated by Noble Fae, which meant it would be hard to sneak down the staircase without being noticed. Now that I knew roughly where it was, though, I could try to find the brothel via the tunnels.

I touched my fingers to my chin and extended them towards her. "Thank you." I hesitated. "How are you feeling?" It was a feeble question, one that didn't come close to articulating what I wanted to know. Had she recovered from the trauma? Was recovery even possible? I was still plagued by nightmares of my mother wasting away, Anya dying, and the terror of fleeing from the Nasties. It made me feel weak when people like Triana, who had been hurt far worse, woke up every day and went about their business as if nothing had happened.

"It's hard. But getting better." Her lips trembled as she smiled, and I hugged her, in awe of her quiet strength.

I EXPLORED THE CATACOMBS NEAR THE THRONE ROOM THAT night, searching for the brothel. My stomach churned with anxiety, but I had to see it. Since my own introduction to sex, I kept remembering what Drustan had said about Hector—that he liked his bed partners defenseless.

The thought filled me with rage.

The dagger tightened on my arm, reflecting my anger back at me. *Hungry.*

It had taken small bites out of me on occasion, so it wasn't completely starving, but the amount of blood it was drinking clearly wasn't enough. A visceral memory welled up of the Nasty I'd stabbed in the eye. That blood had been acidic against my skin, but in this imagining it was delicious and peppery, leaving an alcoholic burn in my mouth.

I rejected the fantasy and the lust for blood that came with it. *Stop that,* I thought. It was the dagger's memory, mixed with mine. I shuddered at the joy it had felt during that act of horrible violence.

Then feed me.

You'll just drain things dry. I don't want to kill anyone else.

I won't. Unless we have to. I was starving then. If I wasn't starving, I would drink slower. Take less.

You drink from me all the time.

Only small amounts. You do not offer more.

I didn't think I'd ever explicitly offered *any*, but then again, I hadn't stopped it. *You could kill me by accident*, I told it as I found a narrow staircase and began making my way downward.

Bonded. Can't kill you. Won't.

The dagger's hunger burned in my own gut now, distracting me from the task at hand. I sat on the steps, considering my options.

This was a serious problem. If I didn't feed the dagger more blood, it would get hungrier and hungrier until I needed to defend myself against someone, at which point it would lose control and kill. It might even kill if someone brushed against it by accident. But if I fed it too much of my blood, I could die—unless it was telling the truth about being unable to kill me.

I didn't want to murder anyone, and I couldn't risk the dagger attacking one of the Noble Fae. Which meant I needed to start giving it more blood.

What if I just left the dagger somewhere and walked away? I hadn't known it was homicidal when I'd first picked it up. True, it was good to be able to defend myself, but wouldn't an ordinary kitchen knife work just as well?

Its affront echoed through our bond. I didn't know how closely it could track my thoughts, but it certainly picked up on intentions. *Bonded*, it repeated. The metal coiled even tighter around my arm.

I sighed and rubbed my eyes. I believed it. I could sense through our strange connection that the dagger always needed a master, and that its time under the bog had been torturous. It hadn't parted from its past owner willingly, and now it wouldn't be parted from me.

She didn't part from me willingly, either, the dagger replied.

Who was your last mistress? I asked, curious, but the dagger didn't respond.

Enough of this. Either I trusted it to protect me or I didn't. "Fine," I said out loud.

The dagger eagerly ran down my arm like liquid and solidified in my hand. I looked at the blade, took a deep breath, and cut a shallow slice in my forearm away from any major veins.

Blood welled around the wound and vanished into the blade just as quickly. There was a tugging sensation as it drank even more.

"Enough," I said.

The dagger stopped drinking reluctantly. I tore a strip of fabric from the bottom of my dress and wrapped it around the cut.

As it resettled into its familiar position as a circlet around my arm, I considered again how I'd found it. *How did you survive in the bog for so long without blood?*

Pain. Emptiness. Waiting. A kind of nightmarish sleep, the blurred impressions it shared with me implied.

Waiting for what?

Someone to touch me.

Me. I shivered at how close to death I had come. *Why didn't you kill me when I touched you? You must have been starving.*

You rescued me, and I was no longer bonded to a mistress. The first drop of blood I tasted after her death bound us.

How did your mistress die?

Again no response, but I felt its sorrow.

I stared sightlessly into the darkness, wondering exactly what this creature was, the dagger that was alive and yet not alive, that hungered and raged and yet was capable of affection for a long-dead mistress.

Do you have a name? I thought suddenly.

Caedo.

Many famous weapons had names, like Painbringer or Lightning, but this felt more personal. Like I'd finally learned the name of a mysterious acquaintance, a name it had owned since birth and maybe even chosen itself.

I was struck by an idea and nearly hit my forehead at the obviousness of it. *Can you drink animal blood?*

Yes.

Had I truly never considered this before? *I'll collect some from the kitchens so you can feed more regularly.*

I hadn't expected the gratitude that emanated from Caedo, nor its contentment as it wound its way up to perch in my hair as a smooth silver headband. It was fond of me, I realized.

The solution to the problem of the killer dagger was much easier than I had expected it to be. I didn't have to starve it, mutilate myself, or let it kill anyone. I could steal pig's and lamb's blood from the kitchen and keep it fed and content, and there would be no need to fear it anymore.

I huffed a laugh. I'd assumed nothing could be simple, so I'd overlooked an easy answer. The gash on my arm would no doubt leave a scar. It would be a reminder that not everything had to be difficult, and that sometimes the solutions to my problems were right under my nose.

I FOUND THE KING'S BROTHEL.

It was down several winding staircases and past a section of maze-like tunnels. The noises were what let me know I was in the right place.

Wild sounds of pleasure, horrible sounds of pain. Laughter. Screams. I clenched my fists and squeezed my eyes shut, trying to suppress the nausea and terror.

There weren't any peepholes in the walls, but a ladder led up to a narrow crawl space. The floor was dotted with tiny holes that allowed me to peer into the rooms below.

I crawled as noiselessly as I could over chambers decked with satin, velvet, and silk. They contained enormous beds, piles of cushions, and red gossamer curtains. The floor was swirling white-and-black marble, and the walls were carved with figures of faeries, humans, and even Nasties engaged in sexual encounters. A few of the rooms were empty, but most weren't. A variety of scenes played out below in flashes of skin, ranging from the sensual to the horrifying.

Triana had told me not everyone in service in the king's brothel was unwilling. Some chose this life because they valued the money or the touch, and they could quit when they wished. Some were exclusive to certain patrons and didn't have to serve anyone who inquired. I had no issues with that type of work in general, so long as the choice was theirs.

That wasn't the case for all, though. Some Underfae served to work off debts or as a punishment for past transgressions against the Noble Fae, and there were humans like Triana who had been abducted for their beauty. Like the rest of the human servants, they were provided nothing more than housing, food, and clothing. Despite seeing no payment themselves, they fetched a high price. There was a certain type of sadistic faerie who enjoyed inflicting suffering and found delight in the abuse of power, and in King Osric's favored brothel, that desire was of course catered to without regard for morality or decency. The unwillingness of their victims was the point.

The unwilling were easy to identify. Horror and hate filled me as I memorized faces: both the faces of the victims and the faces of the Noble Fae abusing them. If I ever encountered one of those monsters in a hallway alone, they would not survive the meeting, consequences be damned.

Caedo tightened around my bicep, echoing the urge to kill.

Tears filled my eyes as I passed some of the worst displays, but I forced myself to keep going. I needed to memorize the layout of the rooms, note any exits. Triana had said there were sixty in service here and roughly a quarter of them had been forced into that service. Maybe I could take those fifteen people with me if I escaped. And surely Drustan would release them if he took the throne.

Not every scene was cruel, or even sexual, though. I paused to watch, surprised, as a Light lady cuddled fully clothed with a contented-looking female sprite in one room; in the next, a winged Underfae laughed and teased his client and was rewarded with kisses.

Not all the Fae were monsters. But too many of them were.

Of the obviously unwilling, I counted seven humans and three Underfae before I reached the final, most elaborate room. It was decorated in purple and white, with opalescent gossamer instead of red. I knew what this was. Triana had told me King Osric kept a special room for his "pets"—the unlucky human women he claimed exclusive access to.

Triana said they never lasted long.

A naked woman knelt on an enormous four-poster bed with violet sheets. Her hands were cuffed behind her back, and a black bag covered her head, cinched tightly at the neck. The fabric clung to her nose and mouth with each sharp, desperate-sounding breath.

My hand flew to my mouth, and I retched silently. Ritualistic scars covered the pale skin of her back and arms. A few were old, but most were various shades of pink that indicated she was in the early stages of healing. The cruel swirls looked like filigree, a design that would have been beautiful as a tattoo but was horrifying carved into her flesh.

The door opened. White-blond hair gleamed in the candlelight as King Osric stepped into the room. Hate surged into me, hotter and more vicious than I'd known myself capable of before arriving in Mistei.

"There you are, my beautiful pet."

The woman stiffened at the king's voice.

"No one else would consider you beautiful anymore, of course," he continued, "but I think there's something so elegant in suffering." He laughed, a musical sound that contrasted sharply with the violence expressed in his victim's skin.

He pulled a small, hooked blade from his belt. "Let's begin."

He knelt on the bed behind her, gently trailing a hand over her back before he sank the tip of his knife into her forearm. She flinched.

I forced myself to watch as he carved a delicate design into her skin. Blood poured from the wound, sinking into the purple sheets. I felt ready to vomit, but the woman didn't move from her kneeling position, although her body shook and occasional whimpers escaped. The skin beneath her metal cuffs was red and blistered.

"I prefer it when they beg." Osric started a new design. "Tears, pleas, screaming . . ."

She didn't respond.

He laughed. "You're special for more than one reason. No one's ever lasted this long, you know. Maybe I like this better after all."

The pain must have grown to be too much, because at last she squirmed and tried to pull away. Osric shoved her face-down on the bed and inscribed a spiral next to her shoulder blade. Her faint cries were muffled by the sheets.

How much more suffering could she take? How much blood could she lose and still survive?

Osric surveyed the pain he'd wrought with a bright smile. Then his hand moved to his belt.

I couldn't watch anymore. I crawled away, my eyes blurred with tears and my stomach on the verge of revolt.

I lay shaking in the corridor below the crawl space for a long time. I vomited twice, unable to get the image of Osric and his victim out of my head. Triana had said it was horrific, but I'd never imagined anything like that monstrous cruelty. I imagined stabbing my knife into King Osric's chest, straight into his heart.

Yes, Caedo hissed in my mind. It, too, was agitated. Now that I'd lost my fear of the dagger, I could sense more complex emotions behind its ever-present hunger. It hated the king, too, but the violence committed in that room hadn't roused its bloodlust, though I didn't understand why.

Not like that, the dagger told me. I saw glimpses of battles, blood taken from enemies. Memories of killing in outright conflict. *Never like that.*

I forced myself to my feet. It was late, but I didn't want to return to Earth House. Didn't want to lie awake in bed reliving tonight's nightmare over and over.

What if there was still a way out? What if the tunnels led beyond Mistei? I hadn't found any exits yet, but I hadn't been in this part of the catacombs before. I would walk for miles if I had to—anything to find a way to save the people in that silk-shrouded prison.

I walked and walked until my feet ached. This path was long and straight with regular offshoots. I didn't follow any of those, choosing instead to explore as far in one direction as I could.

At last I felt a change in the air, a sharp tingle that made the hair on my arms stand up. Caedo vibrated in warning, and I stopped. Was there something—or someone—here? It nipped at my arm, and suddenly I could see a glittering wall of light farther down the corridor. The dagger had given me temporary faerie sight, as it had in the bog. I approached the light gingerly, knowing without the dagger telling me that this was a powerful ward.

The dagger sent an image into my mind: a shimmering white curtain spreading through the rock and dirt around us, curving away into an impossible distance. An impenetrable wall surrounding the entirety of Mistei, not just the aboveground entrances.

Frustrated, I cut off a piece of my hair and threw it at the ward, wanting to see what would happen. The curl sizzled and vanished in a puff of smoke.

My frustration was replaced by defeat. It had been a foolish hope—that I could somehow walk far enough to get out of Mistei without being stopped. That there was some hole in the king's defenses. If that were the case, wouldn't some of the Noble Fae have managed to escape by now? Wouldn't Drustan have managed it, if not for himself, then for the lady he'd loved? He didn't know about the tunnels, but Oriana did. If she had been able to offer her children freedom and prevent Leo from dying, wouldn't she have done it?

My dreams of freedom turned to smoke, too. I forced myself to face the brutal truth: I would be a servant forever, spending the rest of my life underground. I would age and eventually die down here.

Unless King Osric could be overthrown, and new, better leadership could take over.

In a way, the death of my hope for escape was a relief—it was one less worry, one less thing to focus on. All my rage and energy could go towards a different cause.

I had only two goals now. Making sure Lara survived the trials . . . and helping Drustan rebel against the king.

26

LARA'S GOOD MOOD CONTINUED LONG AFTER HER BRUISES from the Fire trial had faded. The next trial was Earth's, she told me, and she already knew what it was. "It's the magic test. We're going to be sent aboveground to a forest about an hour away."

I looked up in surprise from the pile of cosmetics in front of me. "Won't the wards stop you?"

"Oh, the ones on the main hill above the throne room? No. We'll be underground for most of the journey. The forest we'll be in is also surrounded by wards, though, so we won't be able to leave."

I thought I understood how the wards around Mistei were set up now. One enormous bowl bounded the entire city from the surface to deep underground, and smaller circles surrounded every entrance to the hilltops and forests above, sprouting like mushrooms. That way no one could tunnel out and no one could escape during the few events that took place aboveground.

"So how will the forest test you?"

"We have to use magic to survive for a week with no supplies. It should be easy."

I looked at Lara skeptically. "Have you ever been outdoors for more than a few hours?"

"No, but I'll be fine."

Earth's control over soil, plants, and water was ideally suited to this challenge, but Lara only wielded a small amount of power. It wouldn't be enough. "Can you hunt for food?" I asked. "Build a shelter? How will you stay warm at night?" Even though it was late spring and the weather was warming, the nights would be chilly.

She waved a dismissive hand. "I'll build a fire for warmth."

"And how will you do that?"

She opened her mouth, then closed it again. "I don't know yet. But I can call up water from the ground, and maybe I can make vines sprout with fruit to eat." She didn't sound entirely sure about that. "I'll figure the rest out."

"What if there are predators in the woods?" I pressed.

"I'll fight them."

"With your bare hands?"

"Why are you being so awful?" she snapped.

"She has a point," a voice said from behind us.

I hadn't heard Oriana come in, but the princess leaned against the door with her arms folded, studying us.

I curtsied, but Lara just scowled. "I'll be fine."

"The king just added another constraint to the test." Oriana's normally composed face was drawn tight with tension.

"Can he do that?" Lara asked. "I thought the tests were determined by the Shards."

"The basics of them, yes. But the king can add little . . . surprises . . . if he wishes." The princess's tone indicated this would not be a pleasant surprise, and my worry grew. "He's decided it'll be more entertaining if the contestants are allowed to kill each other."

"What?" Lara and I demanded in unison.

Oriana's expression was grim. "It isn't against the spirit of the trials, since some contestants might die anyway."

Lara flinched at this reminder. "Well, I'll just avoid everyone, then. I'll make a . . . a burrow or something."

"He's going to encourage the candidates to hunt each other, Lara."

This was very bad. The Illusion candidates couldn't weave full illusions yet, but they could disguise themselves well enough to blend in with their surroundings. Lara might not even sense them approaching. Garrick was a formidable fighter, and he'd taken a strong dislike to her. What if he tracked her down?

Lara looked petrified. "What will I do?"

Oriana switched her gaze to me. "Can you hunt?"

"Yes, my princess." It had been a required skill growing up outside the village with no consistent source of funds.

"You made it through the bog. Could you survive outside for a week with no supplies?"

"Yes." I knew how to build a fire and construct a shelter, how to identify edible plants, and how to find safe drinking water by digging a hole next to a river so the water would seep in and the soil would filter out impurities.

"Then we'll use you," Oriana said. "We'll smuggle you into the forest and you'll spend the week with Lara."

My stomach felt tight, and cold dread prickled over my skin. A week in the wilderness with a pampered Fae lady who possessed very few survival skills sounded awful even before I considered the fact we might be murdered at any moment. "What if one of the candidates sees me?" I asked. "And wait, is the king casting an illusion so people can watch, the way he did in the bog?"

"The Earth Shard is the sole judge and won't allow outside viewers," Oriana said. "Much to the king's dismay, of course. He wanted to see any deaths in detail. In terms of the other candidates, we can dress you as a tree nymph so anyone who catches a glimpse of you will assume you're supposed to be there. You must do everything in your power not to be seen, though."

"Are there nymphs in the forest?" Lara asked, surprised.

"Not normally, but the king is letting a few woodland Underfae out for this test. He says it will make the trial more realistic if they interact with or sabotage candidates." Oriana paused, lips compressing. "And there will be Nasties. Flesh-eating ones."

"Shards," Lara breathed.

Oriana's composure was legendary, but even she wasn't made of stone. Her brow creased with worry as she looked between me and her only daughter. "It won't be easy. Start preparing now."

Lara and I lapsed into silence after she left, contemplating the terrifying prospect of a week in the woods surrounded by enemies.

I taught Lara everything I knew over the following days. She would need to find shelter first, either near a water source or somewhere she could summon water. She would need to disguise her shelter to prevent other candidates from spotting it, so a burrow might actually be a good idea. She would need to disguise herself, too, which meant looking as much like her surroundings as possible. Green and brown clothes, and then she was to smear every inch of exposed skin with mud.

She looked increasingly horrified at each new piece of information. "Mud?" she squeaked.

"It'll disguise your scent as well. Some of the Nasties might be able to smell you otherwise."

"They'll definitely smell me if I'm covered in *mud*."

We decided on a plan. I would hunt, while Lara would find water and plants using her magic. I would, of course, verify that the plants were actually edible. Since neither of us wanted a confrontation, we would do our best to stay hidden for the entirety of the test rather than trying to prove ourselves against the other candidates. Osric's bloodthirsty whims weren't worth dying for.

It was a decent plan . . . so why did I have a creeping feeling this was about to go very badly?

27

I VISITED THE BROTHEL AGAIN A WEEK BEFORE THE EARTH trial.

I hadn't wanted to return, but something I'd overheard at lunch had set me on this course. Drustan had been conferring with a Light lord, a tall, slender faerie with dark hair and blue eyes who I vaguely remembered seeing Drustan speak with at the first lunch of the trial season. "They have a wonderfully flexible girl down there, Lothar," he'd said, not seeming to care that I was standing only ten feet away in the line of servants. "You should try her out."

My entire body had flushed with hurt and a horrible, burning anger. There was only one thing he could be talking about.

"I'm intrigued," Lothar had replied. "I'll join you tonight."

So there I was, lying in the crawl space above the brothel and waiting for Drustan to appear.

My rage had burned hot all day, and Caedo pulsed around my arm with echoed fury. How could Drustan complain about Hector's habits and then visit the brothel himself? Yes, many were willing, but even if Drustan was visiting one of those, to callously say so in front of me had hurt. And if he planned to choose one of the others . . .

No. He wouldn't. Surely I would have sensed if he was that kind of monster.

Still, a sick thought haunted me, whispering doubts in my mind. What if sleeping with me had given him a taste for the forbidden and this was the next step in taking anything he wanted, without limits?

Caedo hummed, feeding me images of metal sliding into flesh and the wet spill of blood.

We need to wait, I told it. *See the truth first.*

I didn't know why I needed to see this. Maybe to convince myself Drustan wasn't worth the longing I'd poured into the thought of him, the longing I still felt through my jealousy and rage. If he did this, even if his companion was willing, I would fill that space that ached for him with hatred instead.

I ignored the sights and sounds below as best I could, waiting for long hours as I crawled back and forth. At last he appeared, walking smiling into one of the bedrooms with Lothar. The human woman who had escorted them in bowed and left.

An orange ward flickered to life on the door.

"It needs to happen soon," Drustan said without preamble.

"Agreed," Lothar said. "When, though? Osric is well guarded."

Shock hit me like a hammer. They weren't here to have sex; they were here to discuss the rebellion! Fury faded into dizzy relief as I recognized the shrewdness of the plan. Drustan needed to meet with his coconspirators somewhere, and he was a notorious hedonist. Who would suspect that a coup was being plotted in the brothel, especially since Drustan had been joined by a representative of Light House?

This finally solved one mystery—the identity of the male faerie

Drustan had met with in the library, one of two figures wearing pastel clothing. I hadn't thought it was possible Drustan had Light allies, but here was the proof. Lothar's name sounded familiar—who exactly was he, and who had been the third faerie in the library that day?

"After the trials," Drustan said. "Once we know which of the candidates will succeed. They're young and can be swayed to our side."

"Makes sense."

They were really going to do it. My heart thundered so loudly it was a wonder they didn't hear it through the ceiling.

"I'll tell Dallaida," Drustan said.

Wait, the Queen of the Nasties? Had he used the information I'd given him and decided to recruit her, or had they already formed an alliance? It would explain where he'd been that day he'd emerged from the lower levels with a scratch on his face—the Nasties were known for their claws.

Drustan's web of conspiracy spread far wider than I had guessed.

"You think she can be relied upon?"

"She hates Osric. She's eager to end him, and the Nasties are the only ones who can."

The words didn't make sense at first. Why would the Nasties be able to harm Osric? Even if they hadn't been forbidden from visiting the Noble Fae levels, the wards had been renewed at the spring equinox. No one in Mistei could harm the king—not a prince, not a lady, not a human in service to a house.

Except . . . I sucked in a quiet breath, realization hitting. The protective ward in the throne room was written in the blood of Earth, Fire, Void, Light, and Illusion—but the Nasties were no longer part of those houses. They might have sworn fealty to Blood House long ago, but no house head existed anymore to contribute to that ward.

Drustan planned to have the Nasties—those gruesome, overlooked, shunned creatures the Noble Fae on the upper levels had
relegated to the realm of nightmares and stories—slay the king
for him.

It was brilliant.

"My soldiers will protect the right flank, then," Lothar said.
"You still want to do it in the throne room? He's the only one who
can cast magic there, so we'll be limited to swords."

"That's why it's the best place. He won't expect it, and his troops
will be limited to weapons, too."

That was part of the warding spell, I remembered Alodie telling
me when I'd asked for more details about it. The ward protected the
king's safety throughout Mistei, but he'd also arranged for a secondary prohibition against any use of the other four houses' magic in the
throne room. That chamber was the heart of his empire, and he
wanted his power there to be absolute.

Now Drustan would use the king's hubris as another weapon
against him. So clever, so daring . . . so very dangerous.

"We'll need to work out the best way to get our combined forces
in without attracting notice," Lothar said.

"We have time." Drustan studied Lothar speculatively. "You'll
likely be standing closest to Roland."

Lothar sneered. "You think I'll lose my nerve?"

"I have to consider all possibilities."

"I'd do anything to remove my brother from power."

Lothar was the younger brother of the Light prince. Would this
awful court never stop surprising me with its twisted histories and
betrayals? Now I remembered where I'd heard his name—when
Markas and Karissa had been discussing Garrick's claims that he
was the new heir to Light House.

I could understand why Lothar wanted to overthrow Osric,

though. If Drustan ruled Mistei, Lothar could become Prince of Light and a favorite of the new king—so long as he murdered Roland before Garrick could be named heir instead.

The fact that this was my first thought, not that Lothar would do it for the good of Mistei alone, was concerning. I was thinking more like the Fae every day.

"Very well," Drustan said. "Let's tackle the issue of troop movements next, and do let me know if Gweneira hears any more of her intriguing whispers." He frowned. "We should meet again soon. Hector has been making overtures to a few members of my house, and I don't like how cozy Kallen was with the Elsmere delegation, either."

"One game, many players," Lothar said. "Hector's intent is clear, but Kallen's motivations are as murky as ever. Does he cultivate Elsmere for his brother or for Osric?"

Drustan grunted. "He's the king's creature first and foremost."

I felt a prick of guilt. I was the reason Kallen had heard about a leadership change in Elsmere. If he was cultivating them as allies for Osric, it was partially my fault.

"Still," Lothar said. "If Void were to gain the support of outsiders, they wouldn't be constrained by the wards, either. And if they get to Osric first . . ."

"Don't worry too much about it," Drustan said. "Elsmere won't be back in numbers until Samhain anyway. We'll have made our move by then."

My breath came fast with excitement, and I curled my fingers against the grate. The rebellion had suddenly gone from conjecture to something tangible. The next step was figuring out exactly how I could help.

The meeting concluded soon after that, and I began shimmying backwards. My dress caught under my shin, and my foot scraped against the stone as I adjusted. I froze.

"What was that?" Lothar asked.

There was nothing but silence below for a few tense moments. I held my breath, not daring to move a single muscle.

"Probably just a rat crawling in the walls," Drustan said, but he sounded on edge. "I've been assured that this room is completely secure, and nothing should be able to penetrate the ward on the door."

Except he hadn't warded the ceiling, which he hopefully never realized.

I waited for a long time after they left, too afraid to move when someone might be lingering outside. When the room remained empty, I made my escape.

"KENNA."

I was rushing to the human levels to pick up a fabric delivery for Earth House. I turned at the summons, and my heart lurched.

Drustan stood behind me, looking uncharacteristically solemn.

I flushed at the sight of him. We hadn't spoken a word to each other since we'd been intimate, but the heat painting my cheeks wasn't all from awkwardness and desire. I was afraid, too—afraid he'd somehow learned it had been me hiding in the ceiling and not a rat.

I curtsied. "Prince Drustan."

"I have a message for Lady Lara." He gestured for me to follow.

He took me to the room near Fire House where we had first kissed. Once he shut the door, a curtain of shimmering orange covered every surface—including the ceiling.

He spun almost violently, gripping my shoulders in hard hands. I cried out, fear coursing through me at the sudden hostility in his expression.

"You heard," he accused.

I shook my head. "I—I don't know—"

"Don't lie to me." He punctuated the words with a shake. "I smelled you last night."

"S-smelled me?"

"In the brothel. You always wear the same honeysuckle perfume. I thought it was a coincidence at first, but you were eavesdropping, weren't you?"

Betrayed by my ever-growing affection for cosmetics. I shook my head and opened my mouth, but he jostled me again. "I like you, Kenna, but this is a matter that could mean life or death for thousands of faeries and humans." His voice dropped in pitch, becoming half growl. "Think very carefully before you lie to me again."

My breaths jammed together in my throat. He was threatening me. This man I'd lain with only a few weeks ago was threatening me.

I forced myself to take a deep breath, reaching for reason. I'd only known Drustan for a few months. King Osric had ruled for eight hundred tyrannical years, and this was the first true chance to stop him. Of course Drustan's cause was more important than me.

"I was there," I admitted.

He released me and ran a hand over his face, exhaling raggedly. "How?"

I couldn't tell him about the catacombs. "I followed you."

"Why?"

"I heard you talking at lunch." I hated how jealous the admission made me sound; how jealous I had been. "I couldn't believe you were visiting the brothel after everything you'd said about Hector hurting defenseless people."

"Kenna, you're going to get yourself killed if you continue to act this recklessly." He paced away while I struggled not to point out that the only danger I'd been in was from him. "How did you hear? The rooms are soundproof, and I warded the door."

This would be tricky. "There are passages between the walls from a long time ago."

He spat out a curse. "Of course. Some ancient ruler probably wanted to blackmail their subjects. How did you find out about them?" His eyes pinned me in place. I saw the intelligence behind them, the shrewd mind assessing whether or not I spoke truth.

"I heard a rumor."

He laughed, and it wasn't a kind sound. "From who?"

"From the Nasties. I went down there again to talk to some of them." It was a lie, but what else could I say? If the Noble Fae knew about any secret tunnels, Drustan would have been caught long before this.

"Why did you go back down there?"

I attempted to look contrite. "I shouldn't have, but I still wanted to find out more about the Blood trial. A few of the Nasties looked sympathetic last time, so I thought if I stayed away from Dallaida's palace . . ."

He didn't look like he entirely believed me. "And they just told you about the passages?"

"They seemed to know a lot about what happens on the upper levels, and I asked how they knew. They said there are hollow walls all over Mistei where it's possible to hide and listen in." Close enough to the truth to sound convincing, but far enough away that I wasn't betraying Earth House. "Their favorite place to listen is the brothel, and they told me where that entrance was."

He swore and ran his hands through his hair. "I'm never meeting anyone there again. Dallaida probably knows far more than is safe."

I didn't want her denying the story I was spinning, so I hedged.

"I don't know. The ones I spoke with weren't particularly sympathetic to her. Not all of the Nasties are united."

"Of course they aren't. They're vermin and monsters, constantly clawing to get ahead." Drustan slumped against the desk, studying me with weary eyes. "What am I going to do with you, Kenna?"

"Let me help you." I sank to my knees, clasping my hands at my chest. The subservient position chafed, but I needed him to know I was on his side and wouldn't ever hurt his cause. "I didn't know you were holding a meeting there. I was just . . ."

"Just what?"

I hated what I was about to say even more than I hated being on my knees. "Jealous."

He sighed and pulled me to my feet, rubbing his hands up and down my arms. "Jealousy is a very human emotion, Kenna."

I winced. "I know."

I waited in the ensuing silence, dreading whatever truth was about to be aired between us.

The angry tension in his face finally dissipated, bringing back the person I recognized. "I'll admit," he said, "if our roles had been reversed, I would have hated the thought of you going to another, too."

My heart fluttered. "You would?"

He stroked my cheek, and I leaned into the caress. "I've had to make a lot of hard choices over the years. Threaten people I don't want to threaten. Make bargains I never wanted to make. Everything I do is to create a better life for everyone in Mistei—humans and faeries alike. Do you believe me?"

I nodded.

"I can't afford to be distracted by my own desires. But when I look at you . . ." He exhaled. "Shards, Kenna, you've gotten under my skin somehow. It's dangerous. For both of us."

We stood only inches apart. I tilted my head back, my eyelids drooping as his hot breath brushed over my mouth. "I don't care."

He smiled tightly. "Sometimes I don't, either. That's exactly why it's dangerous."

"Is that why you haven't spoken to me since Beltane?"

"You haven't spoken to me, either."

The accusation was absurd. "Because I'm a servant. There's no reason for me to speak to you in public unprompted."

"You do so many things you shouldn't, Kenna. Why stop at that?"

It was a fair point. I blushed, remembering some of those things I shouldn't have done. I tried to move away, but his hands tightened, keeping me near him. "What are you thinking about?" he asked.

"Nothing."

"Liar."

I took a deep breath and steeled myself. We had to talk about the particulars sometime. "Beltane."

His fingers flexed on my shoulders, and the heat emanating from him intensified. "I haven't stopped thinking about Beltane since it happened."

"It was nice," I choked out.

"Nice?" His eyebrows shot up. "You certainly know how to make me feel secure in my performance."

"More than nice."

He laughed. "It was intense. Earth-shattering. Wild. Primal. There are about a thousand adjectives that would describe it better than 'nice.'"

"I enjoyed it." My face felt like it was on fire. Maybe his magic was consuming me, burning me up from the inside out.

He growled and hoisted me into the air. I gasped as he carried me to the wall and pinned me against it. "I'm going to get you to admit just how good it was." He rucked my skirts up, giving me the freedom to wrap my legs around his waist. I moaned as his erection came into contact with my core.

"How will you do that?" I asked breathlessly.

In response, he rolled his hips into mine. My eyes slid shut in pleasure, and I arched into him, gripping his shoulders as I ground against him.

"There it is. Your passion is incredible."

I opened my eyes. He truly did look awestruck as he stared at me. Had the Fae grown so jaded they didn't get lost in sex? It was still new to me, though, and I wanted more of it.

I fisted my hands in his hair to hold him in place, then captured his lips with mine, plunging my tongue into his mouth. He grunted in surprise, and then he was kissing me back passionately, his mouth moving like a flickering flame, his body pressing me against the wall until all I could feel was the stone behind me and his hardness in front.

I gasped as he broke free from the kiss and bit my neck. He ran his tongue up my skin, tasting me, then closed his teeth over the front of my throat. As if he were a wolf, and I his prey.

I wanted to be his prey.

He spun, carrying me across the room to the couch. He dropped me, and before I could sit up, he was there, shoving my skirts up to my waist, ripping off my undergarments before his mouth found me, hot and wet.

I cried out, and the protective ward rippled as the sound hit it. By the time he slipped a finger inside me, I was more than ready to take him into my body, but there was something I wanted to do first.

I shoved him off me. He fell back on his knees, looking bemused as I struggled upright and sank onto the floor facing him. "Stand up," I commanded.

His breath quickened as he obeyed. I tore his trousers open, shoving them to his ankles and stripping off his undergarments. His cock rose in front of me, thick and beautiful. Strong veins twined up the side, and the head glistened with a trace of liquid.

I leaned in and sucked him into my mouth.

He shouted, throwing his head back as his hands fisted in my hair. His skin tasted salty and decadent, the odor of exotic spices he always gave off concentrated in this secret place. I tongued and sucked, making up for whatever I didn't know about technique with unbridled enthusiasm. His hips jerked, and he gripped my hair as if I were the only solid thing in a spinning world.

"Stop," he gasped.

I drew back reluctantly, giving him a final lick before rising.

Drustan's face was feral with lust. He bared his teeth and grabbed me, shoving me until I was bent over the arm of the couch. He tossed my skirts up, then moved behind me and kicked my legs open.

I gripped the cushion as his hands coasted up my legs. When two of his fingers thrust into me, I moaned, shoving my hips back.

"You're ready."

I nodded, panting.

"There's no contraceptive fire this time," he said, fingers pressing a secret spot that made me let out a guttural noise.

It was something I'd considered after Beltane. I'd dreamed of fucking Drustan again, but I wasn't sure if I wanted children now or ever, and Mistei certainly wasn't the place to risk having a mixed human-faerie child. I struggled for words as he continued stroking me. "There's—a special tea. To prevent that." Aidan—ever delighted and nosy about this development—had informed me about the option, which was a common one in Mistei, and Maude had thankfully known how to brew it. She'd raised an eyebrow but refrained from asking questions about why I suddenly needed it, just pressing the packet of herbs into my hand with an instruction to brew the tea at the same time every morning.

Drustan grunted. "Good. Still, I'll be careful."

He removed his fingers. For one excruciating moment I felt nothing, and then the broad head of his cock fitted into me. He filled me with a relentless stroke.

I muffled my scream with my hand, biting down at the intensity of the pleasure.

He didn't pause to let me adjust but thrust into me hard and fast, gripping my hips. I took it greedily, even when he went so deep it was almost painful. In that moment he owned me.

He bent over me, bracing his hands beside my head as his rhythm increased. Soon he was pounding into me, and my cries of pleasure could no longer be contained by my hand.

Drustan withdrew abruptly. I shuddered, then gasped as his fingers pressed hard against my clit. I convulsed, my vision exploding into a million stars.

I sagged over the arm of the couch, unable to move even to right my clothing or face him. His ragged breathing was loud in the silence. When I finally lifted my cheek from the cushion, I saw him lying on the carpet, his dazed eyes fixed on the ceiling. He'd finished in his hand.

My legs wobbled as I sank onto the floor next to him.

"See?" he said in a ragged voice. "More than nice."

I chuckled and buried my face in his side. "I'm not sure. Maybe you should try to convince me again."

DRUSTAN AND I STAYED IN THAT ROOM FOR HOURS. EVENTUALLY, though, we needed to leave.

My fingers trembled as I struggled to button my dress.

"Let me." Drustan took over, although his hands didn't work much better than mine. He looked disheveled, his normally sleek hair tangled around his shoulders, his skin gleaming with sweat. His fine white shirt was torn, and one of the buttons on his trousers had been ripped off.

I was just as bedraggled. My dress was, thankfully, intact, but it was streaked with sweat, and my hair was a rat's nest. I patted it gingerly, wincing at the thought of how much combing it would take to untangle.

It had been worth it, though.

Drustan and I stared at each other once we were both dressed. The dazed look in his eyes suddenly struck me as funny, and I clapped a hand to my mouth, suppressing a giggle.

"What are you laughing at?"

"I honestly have no idea."

He shook his head. "I think I figured out what it is."

"What's making me laugh?"

"No. Why it's so different with you."

It was different with me? I couldn't imagine how many people he'd had sex with over the years. "Why?"

"You make me feel young again."

With his smooth skin, bright eyes, and muscular frame, it was sometimes easy to forget how old Drustan was. Now, though, I felt the gap between us as something monumental. He had lived for *centuries*. I had only lived for two decades.

I didn't know what to say in response, so I just stared, taking him in.

He smiled. "Come on, you need to get back to Earth House." As I walked towards the door, he seemed to remember something. "Wait. Earlier, you said you wanted to help. More than you're helping now, I assume?"

Did sleeping with him and occasionally feeding him small pieces of information even count as helping his cause? I nodded, feeling a tingle of excitement.

"You know everything now. I wish you didn't, but I can't take back what you heard. That means if you help, you are part of the conspiracy." His gray eyes were serious now. "Which means if we fail, you will pay the same price the rest of us will."

A worse price would be spending the rest of my life a servant to King Osric's cruel court. "I know."

Drustan hesitated, then nodded. "We have all of Fire House and approximately a quarter of Light House on our side. We have Dallaida and the Nasties she controls, but she's notoriously volatile and ultimately serves her own interests. In contrast, Osric has all of Illusion House, most of Light House, and the begrudging allegiance of everyone too afraid to stand against him. He has wards protecting him. He's one of the most powerful faeries ever born and controls legendarily brutal soldiers. Even with everyone we've gathered against him, it isn't an even fight."

Put that way, it didn't sound nearly as promising as I'd hoped. "What can I do?"

"I need allies. Specifically, I need Earth House."

I shook my head. "They're neutral. Nothing will change that."

"They are *historically* neutral," Drustan corrected. "That doesn't mean it needs to continue. You have the ears of Princess Oriana and Lady Lara, and I know they aren't content with the way things are. The pieces are there; all we need to do is change Oriana's mind."

"How will I even explain to Princess Oriana that I've been working with you? She'll see it as a betrayal."

"Don't go directly to Oriana. Don't tell anyone outright what you've been doing. But if you can, see if Lara is open to the idea of different leadership. If so, I can take it from there."

"I'll try." For him. "What about Void House?"

He grimaced. "Hector wants the throne and is supposedly pre-paring for his own coup, although how he plans to hang on to power without internal allies, I have no idea. I still hope he can eventually be swayed, but right now I'm assuming everyone in Void House is our enemy until proven otherwise."

Enemies everywhere. I thought of the consequences for Earth House should I succeed in bringing them into this. "What exactly happened to Blood House after the last uprising?"

Dread passed over his face, an echo of past tragedies. "I suppose you know enough already," he said. "But, Kenna, you can never re-peat this. Never. We're safe within my wards, but your life would be in danger if you mentioned this anywhere else."

I nodded in acknowledgment.

"Blood House controlled things of the flesh," he said. "As a re-sult, they were both warriors and healers. They could be brutal and unyielding, but above everything else, they valued strength and hon-esty. They were the opposite of Illusion in that way—Illusion spins lies and dreams, while Blood cared about what was true and tangi-ble. Of course, this meant Blood and Illusion despised each other."

Healers? With a name like Blood House, I'd assumed they were all vicious killers.

"When Osric took the throne," Drustan continued, "no one stopped him. He hadn't revealed his true nature yet, and he was the strongest of the Fae. It was only after he started executing dissenters that the Fae realized what he was. Void, Fire, and Blood were the only houses brave enough to stand against him. An alliance was formed, and civil war broke out."

I listened raptly. Here at last was information about one of the greatest mysteries of Mistei: the missing house no one was allowed to speak of.

"Osric was still vulnerable to harm at the time. He hadn't yet learned how to create the warding spell you witnessed at the spring equinox, and he hadn't trapped everyone underground yet, although most of the population lived in Mistei anyway. So the rebellion had real hope that they would win. It began with assassinations and skirmishes in close quarters, progressed to larger battles, and then eventually the two armies met on a field of combat deep underground."

"Underground?"

"There's a cavern so vast you can't see one end when standing at the other." His hand moved across the air as if tracing the image in his mind. "Nothing was being accomplished with skirmishes, so everything was gambled on one battle. Light and Illusion against Fire, Blood, and Void, with Earth abstaining."

"Illusion won."

"Correct." Drustan's hand dropped to his side. "Despite our superior numbers, despite our planning, Osric's forces were too brutal, his illusions too disorienting. His ruthlessness knew no bounds. He even slaughtered children to distract the faeries fighting in our lines. Eventually the battle was lost."

He had been born after the war, but he spoke as if he had been there. "Your family fought in that battle."

"They did."

"How did they survive? Why didn't Osric put them all to death?"

"Osric is as clever as he is cruel," Drustan said bitterly. "He wanted to ensure Mistei remained powerful should outside threats arise, and he knew the houses needed strong leadership to prevent further unrest. So he gave each house head a choice. Swear eternal fealty to him—or watch their houses be destroyed. The leaders of Fire and Void capitulated, trading honor for the well-being of their families and subjects. Princess Cordelia of Blood House did not."

"She sacrificed all of her people?" The thought was horrifying. There were *thousands* who lived in or supported Earth House.

"I don't think she truly believed Osric could do it. But either way, the entirety of Blood House agreed with her. They would live or die with their honor intact." Drustan shook his head. "Osric let Princess Cordelia return to her house, undoubtedly knowing she would try to help her people escape. When they streamed out through a hidden exit they thought only the Blood nobles knew about, Osric's forces were there. The princess was slain trying to help her children across the bog to the mortal lands. Osric then forced his way into the house through the back entrance to kill anyone left who wouldn't bow to him."

It must have been carnage on an unimaginable scale. "Did anyone bow to him?"

"The Nasties, of course." Drustan smiled grimly. "Blood had kept them like feral pets for centuries, but they were never truly equal. They weren't willing to die for the Blood princess's mistake. So the king made them swear fealty and then sent them far below, where he wouldn't have to look at them. Then he forbade anyone from mentioning the crimes of Blood House again. If anyone had overheard what I'd just told you, we'd both be put to death."

Put to death merely for speaking the truth. Osric hadn't just murdered the princess and her heirs—he'd killed the servants, the Underfae, even children and babies too young to know what was happening. He'd massacred one-sixth of the population of Mistei in a single night.

"If you want to know whether he'd do it again," Drustan said, "the answer is yes."

"So Earth House could be destroyed." Then it would be Lara and Selwyn with their throats cut. Alodie with a sword through her gut. Earth's children lying in piles, their blood staining the pools and streams red.

"Yes. I won't lie to you about that. But the alternative is to keep things as they are—and they may get even worse soon. It's rumored Osric is researching ways to invade each house's territory. He got lucky with Blood's secret exit, but now he wants the ability to go wherever he pleases. Plant spies in every house to listen for dissent. If that happens, not a single place in Mistei will be safe from him."

The stakes of Drustan's war were unimaginable. All those lives hanging in the balance—but how many more would be lost if this revolution never happened at all?

I thought of the brothel, of the humans with missing tongues, of the public executions and the warded exits and the countless babies stolen from their parents because a certain kind of love was unacceptable. People would keep dying. They would spend their lives underground, living in fear, and their descendants would never know any different.

Earth House wasn't mine to sway—but that didn't mean it couldn't be swayed.

I swallowed my trepidation and nodded. "I'll talk to Lara."

28

I DREAMED ABOUT ANYA.

She was laughing at me, her hair shining like some rare metal in the sun, her smile so infectious it made me laugh, too.

When I woke in the middle of the night, the sound of her laughter remained.

No, not laughter. Crying.

I knocked softly on Lara's door before opening it.

She sat up in bed, hastily wiping her tears away.

"What's wrong?" I asked softly.

She sniffled. "I'm afraid."

How far we had come, that she could admit that to me without hesitation. I sat beside her and stroked her hair. "Of the trial?"

"I don't want to be hunted. What if they find me? What if Garrick kills me?"

"I won't let him."

"But even if I live, what if I don't do well enough and the Shards decide I'm not worthy? I don't want to lose my power. I don't want to die." Her voice broke on the words.

"You won't die," I said. "You've been doing well in the trials. And Princess Oriana would still love you if you didn't have your power."

She shook her head, and the tail of her long braid whispered against the sheets. "You don't understand. The Noble Fae hate weakness. No one who loses their powers has ever been welcomed back."

"Truly?" How awful. "Your mother is different, though. She's not as cruel as the others."

"Maybe. I don't know." She sighed. "I want to go for a walk. Come with me?"

I nodded and grabbed my cloak, fastening it over my nightgown before sliding my feet into warm slippers.

Lara led me to the end of the hallway, but rather than descending the stairs, she pressed a knot in the wood. A hidden panel slid open, and I followed her into a stairwell. When the door shut behind us, it was pitch black. I followed her upward, keeping my hand against the cool stone wall. Eventually faint light filtered down, and I could see Lara standing just below a flat, glass-like ceiling.

"Stay right next to me." She touched the ceiling, which slid away to reveal more steps. They were wet, as were the smooth walls on either side when my hands brushed over them—a boundary of water, just like the corridor leading into the house.

"Can anyone from Earth House get up here?" I asked.

"No, only the ruling family and whoever we allow. The magic knows."

We soon reached the lake's surface, where the stairs ended at a series of flat rocks that formed a path to a tiny tree-dotted island.

Earth House had a secret back entrance—just like Blood House. I shivered at the thought of King Osric finding his way inside.

On the island, we sat on the grass and looked up. The moon was bright, almost full, and the stars shone like ice and crystal. There was simply no substitute for the night sky, no matter how much magic the Fae used to recreate it.

"I come here when I'm sad," Lara said. "Selwyn does, too. Oriana forbade us from doing it, but sometimes we just have to."

"Do you come here a lot?"

"No. If I came here more often . . . I don't know." She grabbed a small stone and tossed it into the lake, watching the ripples spread. "I worry it would stop being special. Or that it would become so important to me that I'd never be able to enjoy anything underground again."

"I think I understand." The bog had been that way for me, though I'd seized every possible moment to walk its hidden paths. I'd felt free there, no longer constrained by the miserable facts of my life outside its borders. It had brought me to Mistei and stolen Anya, too, but that was the way of things. You could love something and still have it hurt you.

I told her about the bog then: the rich, earthy scent, the feel of peat moss beneath my toes, the collection of mundane but well-loved objects taken from beneath its murky waters.

She looked at me with compassion. "I'm sorry you lost your collection."

My eyes prickled. "Thank you." Of everything I'd lost, that seemed the most trivial, but I missed it all the same.

The darkened night, whispering wind, and isolation seemed to invite secrets. Maybe if Mistei changed, Lara could come here without fearing that the freedom would make her life underground even less tolerable in comparison.

"Do you ever wish things were different?" I asked.

Lara laughed. "Only constantly. I can't wait for the trials to be over."

"Not like that." I bit my lip. "Like, really different."

"What do you mean?"

"Do you ever wish the borders were open, or that someone else was in charge?" The words were risky, skirting on treason, but Lara was my friend. Besides, what use was I to the rebellion if I wasn't willing to put my safety on the line?

She looked around as if checking to see if anyone was eavesdropping, then lowered her voice. "Don't say things like that."

"There's no one here. I'm just curious. What if there was a better version of Mistei where everyone was free and happy?"

She huffed. "You sound like Selwyn."

"I do?"

"He's always going on about how much he wants to change things." She plucked a piece of grass, splitting it with a fingernail. "Honestly, it worries me. If he talks like that outside Earth House, he won't live long."

Her matter-of-fact tone pained me. "It shouldn't be like that. People should be allowed to say what they feel."

"You don't understand."

"I do. Or at least, I see what it's like for all of you. What if Earth House stopped being neutral, though? What if you stood up for yourselves?"

"Hush!" She clapped a hand over my mouth. "We're within Earth territory, but still—never, ever say something like that out loud again." She removed her hand gingerly, as if afraid I'd start screaming treason at the top of my lungs.

"Help me understand," I begged. "Tell me why neutrality is so important."

"Earth House's power comes from its neutrality. We were advisors to queens and kings and arbiters of disputes. Everyone respected us."

"It's not like that now, though."

She shredded another piece of grass. "No. But if Earth House stays neutral, it doesn't matter how much the others mock us. We'll survive no matter what."

Maybe their current neutrality was in the name of safety . . . or maybe they never took a stand because they never wanted to be on the wrong side of history. Either way it felt cowardly, but I didn't dare say that. I wouldn't push her any further tonight. "Thank you for telling me," I said. "There's so much I still don't understand about your world."

We talked about other things then: our childhoods, our dreams, the people we'd known. Hours later when we rose to go in, she held out her closed fist. "Here, take this." She dropped something into my cupped palm.

It was one of the ornamental buttons from her dressing gown, an emerald pine tree with a golden trunk. There was a broken thread where it had been ripped free. "Did you tear it on something?" I asked.

"It's for you."

I looked up, puzzled. "I don't understand."

Lara smiled, radiant as the moon. "It's the first item in your new collection."

29

As the earth trial drew near, I became increasingly aware of another ticking clock. I hadn't provided Kallen with any information lately. In fact, I hadn't spoken a single word to him or come anywhere near him since the day of the picnic, when he'd saved me from Garrick and Markas.

The memory of our confrontation still confused me. Why had I taken out my rage on him, of all people? Why hadn't I been able to control myself? He was dangerous. He could have had me killed for arguing with him . . . yet he hadn't.

I wondered if he would someday, once I'd outlived my usefulness as a spy.

I didn't want Kallen coming to find me again, complaining that I hadn't been forthcoming with information, so the night before the trial, I went to Blood House. As I waited in the dark antechamber, I reflected on what Drustan had told me. The empty room no longer seemed eerie or menacing. Instead, the still air felt mournful.

Somewhere beyond this room, families had once laughed and thrived. Children had run and played, just as they did in Earth

House. And the faeries who had lived here hadn't just been fighters; they had been healers as well.

I'd expected Blood House to be more sinister, considering the ominous name and the mystery shrouding it. I'd envisioned a cave populated by murderers who consumed the blood of the innocent and powered their dark magic with human sacrifice. Instead, the citizens of Blood House had been proud and honest, and they had been willing to die rather than submit to a tyrant.

It reminded me of how wrong I'd been about Caedo. I'd taken the dagger's bloodlust for evil, but it had simply been overwhelmed by deep, painful hunger. It couldn't help the way it had been forged, and now that I'd begun regularly feeding it animal blood, its violent urges had mostly ceased.

Few things in Mistei were exactly as they seemed. Blood House had been as noble as Illusion was corrupt. My dagger had begun showing restraint. A faerie prince could lust after a human. Even Lara had come to show more depth than I'd ever expected from her.

Caedo quivered against my arm, letting me know someone was approaching.

Here was another faerie who wasn't quite as he seemed. The merciless King's Vengeance, who had shown mercy to a mere human. Kallen slipped into the antechamber, a swift shadow I wouldn't have noticed if I hadn't been looking for him. "I'm surprised you came," he said, casting a shimmering obsidian ward over the entrance.

"I'm trying to be a better spy." I approached, wishing I could see his face. "It's very unsettling knowing you can see in the dark when I can't."

He sighed. "Light your torch."

This part of Mistei grew dark at night, with some wall torches extinguished and others burning so low they were nearly embers, so I'd tucked a small, unlit torch into my belt next to a pouch containing a tinderbox in case more illumination was needed. Of course Kallen had noticed it—he seemed to notice everything about me. "You aren't worried someone will realize we're here?"

"No one will come anywhere near without me sensing them. I cast shadows in the hallway. I'll know as soon as they're disrupted."

He had so many strange powers, and the ones he'd told me about probably only scratched the surface.

I lit the torch and raised it. The firelight caught on the sharp angles of his face, throwing his expression into relief. To my surprise, Kallen didn't seem as impassive as normal. He looked downright weary.

"So?" he prompted. "What was so important you pulled me away from my house in the dead of night?"

"It's not the dead of night."

"I'm waiting."

I sighed. "I wanted to let you know that I'm trying to collect information for you, but I'm not having much luck. Honestly, the only thing I heard about any sort of unrest is a rumor that Void House is planning an uprising."

I'd practiced my lies until they sounded as natural as possible. I had two purposes tonight: to fulfill my end of the bargain with Kallen without giving away any information about Drustan's coup attempt, and to learn whatever I could about Void's plans.

"Who told you that?" When I didn't immediately answer, his lips quirked. "Drustan, no doubt. I know you two talk with startling frequency."

I ignored the implication that my interactions with Drustan were out of the ordinary. "Is it true?"

"Did he tell you anything else?"

I blew out an annoyed breath. "He told me a little more about the old rebellion. Fire and Void House used to be allies. What happened?"

At first I thought he wouldn't answer. "It's complicated," he said at last. "Five hundred years have passed since the war, and alliances change over time. It doesn't help that I serve the king. Fire plays at fealty, but they don't truly mean it."

"Why do you serve him?" I was genuinely curious. "Your brother barely goes to court at all."

He studied me as if trying to peer inside my head and discern the nature of my thoughts. "No one asks me about myself. Or about Hector, for that matter. They're all afraid to."

"Or you aren't very interesting," I said, then immediately wanted to slap myself. Why did I keep antagonizing him?

To my surprise, he chuckled. It sounded rusty, as if he hadn't laughed in a very long time. "No one taunts me, either. They're afraid of what the king's dog might do to them."

At the reminder of what I'd said to him, I lowered my gaze. "I'm sorry I called you that." The apology was at least a tiny bit genuine, if only because I regretted endangering my life by goading him. "I was furious at the situation."

"I'm over three hundred years old," he said dryly. "I collect secrets for a living. I think I understand why people lash out."

I looked up, startled by this strange, softer side of him. I'd planned to soothe his temper tonight and work my way into his good graces, but he didn't seem like he had any temper to soothe. Again I noticed the faint melancholy on his face, the shadows under his eyes. Something was bothering Kallen, but I knew better than to ask what.

"So? How did you start serving the king?" I asked.

He was silent for a long time. "It was part of the price for my house's continuing survival."

"What do you mean?"

"My father was the only member of our family who survived the rebellion," he said. "His consort, all his children . . . gone. He bowed to the king in the end, and to reward Void for returning to the fold, his life was spared. But that wasn't enough for the king."

The ominous words seemed to crawl down my spine. Nothing was ever enough for King Osric.

"My father took a new consort," Kallen continued, "and Hector was born shortly after the war. He became the heir, of course. When I was born, the king insisted I serve him, instead. This would ensure Void House's ongoing loyalty."

That sounded like Kallen had been a hostage, rather than a volunteer. "Do you enjoy it?" I asked. "Being the King's Vengeance?"

Again he let out a startled chuckle. "Does anyone enjoy anything down here?"

It was a profoundly sad question, but I couldn't deny the truth of it. "Why doesn't Fire House have anyone serving the king so closely?" Why had Void been the only one to pay that price?

"The previous Fire prince didn't have any children after Drustan, and Drustan has no heirs, either. There's no spare."

How uncomfortable to be seen as a spare. A second choice, good only for leverage. "So Fire resents Void because you are loyal to the king."

Kallen smiled.

"Are you loyal to the king?" I prompted.

"You're very persistent. I serve my king and love my house, as all good Fae must. Why are you so curious about this?"

Because I was curious about everything, and Kallen was proving to be a strange sort of mystery. "I'm just trying to understand how everything fits together. Why are you asking me for information about Drustan when the rumors of rebellion are about Void House?

I won't know what information is most helpful unless I know your motivations."

"A tidy argument. However, I have never asked you to bring me only the information you deem most helpful. I have asked you to tell me everything. So what else do you have for me?"

I scrambled for something else to say. "Earth House is determined to stay neutral." No surprise there. "They are unaware of any unrest, as far as I know."

"So Earth House is still neutral, Void House is supposedly plotting against the king, and you are now better educated in the history of Mistei. Is that it?"

Put like that, my information did not sound at all worthy of getting him out of bed. I nodded hesitantly.

He inclined his head. "Thank you for coming as soon as you felt you had something to share. My interests remain the same. Keep focusing on Drustan's activities, including anyone you see him meeting with. Tell me anything you learn, even if it seems trivial. Listen closely for any mention of unrest."

He left, but I remained in the antechamber, puzzling through the interaction. Had he actually thanked me? I'd been expecting a fiery confrontation, but apparently me taking the initiative to see him had mollified him, or else he'd just been in a bad mood during our previous meetings.

There was another possibility, though. A spymaster must know plenty of ways to make his sources talk. Perhaps he was seeing how I responded to various approaches. He'd clearly already figured out that my curiosity about Mistei needed to be appeased at least a little bit, which explained his willingness to answer some of my questions. Now his politeness had defused any rude words I could have said. Not that I had been planning on rudeness, but my temper occasionally got the best of me.

His melancholy, polite demeanor tonight made me more uneasy than the cold mask did. A cruel faerie was something I understood. An angry faerie was likewise simple. I knew what both types wanted and what they were capable of doing to get it.

Kallen had proven himself more complicated, from grieving the changeling to saving me from Garrick to his downright civil behavior tonight. The last thing I wanted was for one of my most confusing enemies to become even more complex—or worse yet, sympathetic.

30

L ARA DEPARTED FOR THE EARTH TRIAL JUST BEFORE DAWN. I couldn't follow her because no one was allowed to see where the candidates went. The location had been kept secret to prevent cheating; all the candidates knew was that they'd be spending a week outdoors. They would learn the rules once they reached the forest. Survive for seven days, using magic to do so. The hunting of other candidates was encouraged. And for the first time in these trials, killing another candidate was allowed.

Lara would get as far away from the others as she could, cover her scent with mud, and seek shelter. I would follow that night and find her using the same trilling call we'd used in the labyrinth.

Which left an entire day to worry about how she was faring.

Somewhat unnervingly, Princess Oriana came to supervise my preparations late that afternoon. She sat in my desk chair, staring at me while I picked through the wardrobe.

I scowled at the tree nymph outfit it offered me. "No."

"You need to blend in," Oriana said.

"With all due respect, my princess, this is not the way to do it."

The outfit, if it could be termed that, consisted of a tiny, ragged skirt and two triangles of fabric to cover my breasts. It was worse than my Beltane costume. "I'll die of exposure before I can help Lara."

She sighed. "Humans are so fragile."

"Can I wear something similar to what Lara's wearing?" Dappled brown-and-green trousers, a matching long-sleeved shirt, and sturdy shoes, with a fur-lined cloak for warmth. "If I smear my face with mud and put twigs and leaves in my hair, I'll probably look like some kind of Nasty."

Her assessing glance told me she was imagining it and found the idea of me passing as a Nasty all too plausible. "Very well. Just know this: if your identity is discovered, you will die before you ever leave that forest."

My skin prickled. "I understand, my princess."

She left after that, and I completed my preparations in silence.

Alodie came to find me right before sunset. I'd just finished eating a hearty meal, knowing it might be my last for some time. The asrai led me through the catacombs for over an hour, stopping at last before a simple staircase that led directly into the forest. After a quick hug for luck, she was gone.

The staircase ended inside a hollow tree. I waited, listening for movement outside, but I couldn't hear anything but the whisper of wind. I eased open a door in the trunk and emerged into a night-dark forest.

Alodie had told me a stream ran near the hidden door. I followed a faint trickling sound to an ice-cold ribbon of water barely the width of my palm. I dug into the mud at the stream's edge, shuddering at the chill as I smeared it over my face, hands, clothes, and hair. I topped the wet, sticky mass of my hair with twigs and leaves and then moved quickly through the woods, emitting a trill every few minutes to see if Lara was nearby.

The task felt daunting. She had promised to head east, but it might take hours to come within earshot, and in that time any number of monsters might find me. The candidates would be keeping an eye out for suspicious movements. They might kill me on sight, whether or not they knew who or what I was.

I walked for a long time, checking the stars whenever the canopy opened to confirm I was heading in the right direction. Once something hissed in the underbrush, but it quieted after I passed. Another time I heard voices ahead of me—two of the candidates conferring together. I froze against a tree as Garrick and Markas passed not ten feet from my position.

"We'll start tomorrow," Garrick murmured, and then they moved on.

I didn't need to wonder what would start tomorrow. They'd clearly formed an alliance and would be eager to eliminate the competition. Lara, as one of the most successful candidates, would be a high-priority target.

Hours later, a faint call finally floated through the air to answer mine. The moon was high overhead, the sky the velvet black of the small hours of the morning, and I was so tired I wanted to collapse into the nearest bush. I stumbled towards the sound, calling out again after a few minutes. This time the answer came from much closer.

I was almost on top of Lara when I found her.

"Kenna." Her whisper stopped me in my tracks. The dirt at my feet shifted as a trapdoor rose to reveal the top half of her face.

I wriggled into the hole beside her. It had been carved into the ground below a fallen tree trunk, a few feet tall but just wide enough for two people to lie side by side. When Lara dropped the door covering the entrance, it was pitch black. "No fire?" I whispered.

"N-no." Her teeth chattered. "I tried to light one earlier, but it didn't work."

It was so late—and so dark—that there was no point in trying to fix anything tonight. "We'll figure it out in the morning."

We huddled together for warmth. It was strange at first, having someone so close to me, but soon I stopped caring. It was incredibly cold now that I'd stopped moving. We combined our cloaks into one blanket and clutched each other like sisters until I finally fell into a restless sleep.

⊙⊙⊙⊙⊙⊙

I WOKE NATURALLY AT SUNRISE, EVEN THOUGH NO LIGHT PENE-trated our shelter. My body was used to the schedule, and when I lifted the trapdoor the tiniest amount, I saw the woods bathed in the delicate gold of a new morning.

Knowing animals would also be out at dawn, I headed into the forest to hunt. Caedo took its favorite form, that of a lethal dagger, and its anticipation of the hunt mingled with mine until my heart pounded in time with the pulsing vibrations from its hilt. It felt strangely good to be out in the wilderness again, dependent only on myself for sustenance.

I moved carefully, staying low to the ground. My cloak was still in the hole, both to keep Lara warm and so the fabric wouldn't hamper my movements, and with my mud-spattered garments I blended in well with the surroundings. Flakes of dried mud fluttered to the ground in my wake; I'd need to reapply my disguise later.

In a clearing ahead, two glowing green lights drifted at eye level.

I watched them from behind a tree. They looked like pixies, although it was hard to see any details beyond their small size and glow. Pixies were harmless, but I didn't take any chances.

A movement in the underbrush piqued their interest. One of them dove, and moments later a high-pitched screech announced the death of some small creature. The other pixie joined the first, and when they rose into the air again, a dead rabbit hung between them.

Their features came clear as they flew past. Their faces had the same delicate shape as a pixie's, but their mouths were gaping maws that took up the entire bottom half. Blood dripped from needle-sharp teeth and claws. Their bodies were covered in scales, their wings membranous and tipped with talons.

These weren't Underfae, then, but Nasties, some ravenous variant on a pixie that could probably rip my throat out in an instant. I had been right to hide.

Once I was certain they were gone, I explored the clearing. Often one animal meant more in the immediate vicinity, and I found signs that animals came this way frequently: trampled dirt, snapped twigs, and clumps of fur snagged on bushes. I found a hiding spot and waited.

Eventually my patience was rewarded. Another rabbit appeared, its twitching nose skating over leaves and grass.

I struck, and blood splattered across the leaves.

This would keep us fed today, and I didn't want to leave Lara alone for much longer, so I returned to the shelter. Along the way I spotted an imp with pointed ears and antlers foraging for mushrooms—one of the Underfae who had been let out to sabotage candidates. Imps were notoriously acquisitive, so we'd need to keep our belongings secured. I waited behind a bush until the waist-high creature gathered his treats and moved on.

Lara stirred when I opened the trapdoor. It was cleverly constructed, a latticework of tightly woven branches covered in mud that fit neatly over the burrow she'd carved into the earth.

"This is nice," I said, peering into the shelter. I'd felt its dimensions last night, but I hadn't seen the small pool of water at the far end. She must have summoned it from the ground.

Lara gave me a speaking look. She hadn't applied mud to her face the way I had, though a smear of dirt crossed one cheek. "This is horrible."

"It'll be over soon. Come on, let's have breakfast."

It was much easier to build a fire with Lara's help. She saved me endless digging by using her magic to carve two holes: a larger one and a small one next to it that joined the first pit at the base. The larger hole would conceal the fire and the smaller hole would ensure it continued to receive air as it burned, rather than smothering beneath the soil. I lit it using a hand-drilling technique my mother had taught me.

I thought of her smiling eyes and calloused hands, the soft lift of her voice as she'd taught me survival skills and as much of her herbcraft as I had the patience for. She would probably have seen this ordeal as a great honor—her only child, chosen to aid the Noble Fae.

"What are you thinking about?" Lara asked.

I started. I'd been staring into the flames for long minutes. "My mother. When I was little she taught me how to build a fire."

Lara nodded, and I was grateful when she didn't push any further.

I skinned the rabbit and skewered it on a stick while Lara watched, looking queasy. Soon we were eating hot, succulent meat.

"This is good," Lara said in surprise. Juice dribbled down her chin, and she winced as she wiped it away. "Disgusting, though."

"I love eating something I just caught. It tastes better knowing the work that went into it."

"I'm trying not to think about how cute it was before you killed it."

"Oh, please. You eat meat all the time."

"Yes, but normally I don't see the process it undergoes before reaching my plate."

I looked at her curiously. "Do you never visit the kitchens?"

"No. Oriana doesn't want us mingling too much with the Underfae."

Typical Noble Fae snobbery. "Selwyn visits sometimes."

"Why am I not surprised? I'm sure he feels very noble about visiting the servants."

"He's quite egalitarian."

"It's easy for him to support equality when he's still benefiting from being a lord. I wonder if he would actually enjoy a world where everyone was equal." She traced patterns in the dirt with a stick—a rabbit, a fire, two little figures. "Leo was the same."

She rarely spoke about her older brother. "He wanted everyone to be equal?"

"For the most part. He still wanted to be a lord, but he wanted to use that influence to make everyone's lives better. He wanted to unite the houses and abolish human servitude."

And then he had fallen in love with a lady from another house and risked everything to be with her. "I'm sorry you never met him."

"Everyone tells me how charming and brave he was. He would have been a wonderful prince eventually."

Instead, Lara was the heir. "You'll be a wonderful princess."

She shook her head. "Let's get back inside. I don't want anyone to see us."

We'd evidently reached the limits of her comfort speaking about her family and her future. I couldn't blame her. I felt the same about my own personal tragedies. I, too, had a voice that taunted me in the middle of the night, one that said I was so worthless my father had abandoned me, so useless I didn't even make a good servant, and so unlikable I'd only had one friend growing up, a friend I hadn't been able to save . . .

We left a few embers smoldering to make it easier to start a fire the next time we needed one. Then Lara and I crawled back underground to wait.

We waited for days. That was our strategy—hide from the more violent candidates, use her magic and my hunting skills to source food and water, and emerge unscathed at the end of the week. What I hadn't anticipated, though, was how boring the waiting would become. By the second day we were snapping at each other, by the third our heartfelt conversations had become arguments, and by the fourth we barely spoke. On the fifth day the rabbit-roasting spit—along with half a rabbit—went missing, courtesy of an imp Lara spotted hurrying away with its prize, and we had a fierce, whispered fight about who should have been watching more closely. By the sixth day I couldn't stand the thought of spending one more second trapped in a foul hole in the ground with her.

"I'm going hunting," I snapped.

"You already hunted this morning."

"I don't care. I'm hunting again."

"Don't let anyone see you," she called after me. I repressed the urge to make a rude gesture over my shoulder. As if I wasn't aware of the situation.

Instead of hunting, I explored, heading farther away from our tiny camp than I had dared to before. I was caked in so many layers of stinking mud that my skin felt like tree bark. It itched horrendously, and I resented Lara even more for refusing to apply the same level of disguise.

Voices sounded ahead.

I took cover in a small thicket, pressing myself low to the ground. It was Markas and Garrick again, conferring in whispers. My stomach dropped when they came into view.

They were both spattered with blood.

"I can't wait to see Hector's face." Garrick grinned savagely. "I'll be sure to let everyone know it was Light House who did it."

"And Illusion," Markas protested.

"You helped, but I struck the final blow."

Their voices dwindled, and I lost sight of them. I lay there for long minutes, my pulse pounding frantically.

Who had they killed?

It could only be Una or Wilfrid. I didn't know Wilfrid well—he mostly kept to himself—but he had seemed pleasant enough. I respected Una, and it hadn't escaped my notice that she had tried to stop Markas and Garrick from hurting me.

Maybe Garrick had taken his revenge.

I retraced the path the two faeries had taken, following footprints and breaks in the foliage. Maybe it wasn't too late to help whoever they had attacked.

I soon realized there was nothing I could do.

Wilfrid lay in the middle of a clearing in an enormous pool of blood, his blank eyes fixed on the sky. A tree branch protruded from his gut. He'd been stabbed with it, and by the look of the wound, Garrick had deliberately moved the wood to widen the hole.

I bent over, struggling not to vomit up precious food. It was a gruesome way to die. The bruises and cuts on his face and hands indicated this hadn't been a quick killing. He had fought.

Drink.

I recoiled from Caedo's suggestion. "No." The notion was abhorrent. Wilfrid's blood was still cooling, and the dagger wanted to feed on him like some carrion bird.

He will not feel it. Caedo was growing restless after days of nothing but small amounts of rabbit or squirrel blood.

"I don't care whether or not he feels it. It's wrong."

Hungry.

"One more day," I said through gritted teeth. "Then I'll get you more animal blood."

The dagger's hunger itched at the back of my brain. Maybe I should have let it feed, but I had discovered one of my limits. It was one thing to drink the blood of an enemy in battle. It was another to desecrate a corpse.

I wanted to bury the body or burn it—something to ease the throbbing grief and rage in my chest. I had hardly known Wilfrid, but he hadn't deserved this. In the end, though, I left him where he was, staring blindly at the clouds. Let the other faeries see what had been done to him. Let them know how he had died and who was responsible for the brutality. Some would see the killing as a mark of strength, but hopefully more would be outraged.

What would this do to Void's supposed alliance with Light and Illusion? Would Hector take revenge? Where would Kallen's allegiance fall if the king praised Garrick for the kill?

I left the clearing, and when I saw where Garrick and Markas's path split off from mine, I hesitated. Where were they now, and who were they hurting? I couldn't stand the thought of sitting in the dark while they hunted for their next victim, so I changed direction and began tracking them, stealthy as any forest predator. Maybe I could warn whoever they came for next.

I almost didn't see their camp.

Markas couldn't cast complex illusions or make things disappear yet, but he could disguise them. Their lean-to blended in so well with the surrounding woods that I had to blink a few times to understand why the trees in that area looked slightly off.

I didn't hear any sounds, but a fire still smoked nearby. Beside it was a crystal Garrick must have used to concentrate his light powers into a beam hot enough to burn.

Struck by an urge to commit violence, I darted to the campfire, pulled out a partially burned log, and laid the flaming wood at the base of the lean-to. It caught quickly, fire licking up the bark and branches while sap hissed and popped.

No one came out screaming, and the fire burned merrily until the entire structure had collapsed into smoking rubble.

I hoped they had kept their supplies in there.

If they weren't in the shelter, they must be hunting for other candidates. What if they found Lara? Markas could make her eyes play tricks on her, and Garrick would be impervious to any magic she tried to use against him. They would beat her easily in a physical conflict.

Growing more and more nervous, I carved a path through the trees, moving quickly.

I was back in familiar territory when I heard Lara scream.

I FORCED MYSELF TO SLOW MY FRANTIC PACE AND MOVE SILENTLY as I approached our campsite. If I had any hope of helping her, I needed the element of surprise.

Lara stood in the middle of the clearing, wielding a flaming branch like a club. Before her, Garrick and Markas exchanged amused glances.

"Get back," she said.

"Are you going to burn us?" Markas asked. "You aren't Edric. It won't work."

A hole opened beneath Markas's feet and he stumbled into it, cursing. Another opened beneath Garrick, but he was faster.

"Clever," Garrick said. "Not clever enough, though. I saw your tracks in the woods earlier."

Lara hadn't been in the woods; I had. Which meant I hadn't been nearly as stealthy as I'd thought.

Another hole opened, but this one was shallow, and Garrick righted himself quickly.

Lara's magic wasn't infinite. I had to do something.

Garrick held a branch he'd carved into a sharp point. He meant to kill her the same way he had killed Wilfrid. He nodded at Markas.

Markas raised his hands, and Lara blinked as if confused and swatted at something in front of her. Garrick used her momentary distraction to begin circling behind her. She would be trapped between them in seconds.

I picked up a rock and threw it as hard as I could.

It grazed Garrick's leg, rather than his head where I'd actually aimed, but it was enough to distract him. His eyes found me almost immediately. "What is that?"

I hunched over and hissed, doing my best to look like a monster and not a mud-spattered human. I picked up another rock.

"Tree nymph?" Markas asked doubtfully.

"Have you ever seen a nymph? They look a lot better than that."

Lara's eyes pleaded with me. *Save me.*

I would try.

A light flashed and I staggered back, blinking to clear the afterimage from my vision. Caedo practically screamed in my mind, and I barely had enough time to leap out of the way as Garrick's sharpened branch whistled through the air. It would have skewered me if I'd been any slower.

I threw the rock, and this time he was close enough that it hit him squarely in the face, sending him staggering back for a few precious seconds. I sprinted around the edge of the clearing. Maybe I could keep him distracted long enough for Lara to fight off Markas.

Lara charged at the Illusion faerie with a bloodthirsty scream.

Markas's eyes widened as her branch crashed into his temple. Sparks and ash flew as the wood snapped, and Markas collapsed in a boneless heap.

"Kill him," I shouted, but Lara just stared at his unconscious form.

Garrick laughed loudly. "The human. Now I recognize your pathetic servant. Have you been cheating, Lara?"

I reached Lara's side. "You have to kill him. He'll wake up eventually."

She didn't move.

Blood trickled from a cut on Garrick's forehead, and although he was still smiling, anger burned in his eyes as he approached. "I'll kill the human first. Then I'll decide if I want to kill you now or wait to have King Osric do it in front of everyone."

"Stay back." I held Caedo between us.

"Knives are also cheating. Do you even know how to use that?"

Hungry.

"Perhaps we can strike a deal, Lara," Garrick said. "Once the human is dead, I might be persuaded to forget what I saw." He raked a lascivious gaze over her body.

"He won't," I told Lara.

"Like I'm an idiot," she replied.

Garrick pulled his arm back with lightning quickness and threw the branch like a spear.

I knocked Lara to the ground, and the wood sliced across my arm, digging through mud and skin. Blood welled up and dripped to the soil below.

Garrick ran towards us. Lara was struggling to her feet, I was bleeding, and Garrick had pulled a smaller sharpened stick from somewhere . . .

Cold wrath filled me, combining with the dagger's bloodlust to form something cruel and hungry. I felt the vibration of Garrick's thundering steps through the soles of my feet. He was targeting Lara again, discounting me as a threat because I was a mere human, even though I was the only one wielding a real weapon. I let him fly past and lunge for Lara . . .

Then stabbed him in the back.

Hurt.

I did it again. Garrick fell to the ground, the stick clattering out of his fist. His eyes widened in shock as I plunged the knife into his abdomen.

Punish.

I twisted it as he had twisted the branch in Wilfrid's gut. He screamed, high and sharp.

Kill.

I dragged the blade across his throat. His blood pumped out, flowing down his neck and chest and turning the soil to mud. He convulsed, staring at me in horror.

Drink.

Yes, the dagger could drink this time. It had let me strike Garrick several times when it could have drained him dry in an instant. It had allowed me to fulfill a need for revenge that had been locked away inside me, a bloodlust so powerful and raw I hadn't recognized it against the background of my familiar mental landscape. Now I welcomed the rage and power, the sick joy, and as Garrick's life drained away, I placed Caedo against his throat.

The blood was gone in moments.

All of it, even the blood staining the soil. Every bit of that red flow was sucked into the groove in the center of the blade until Garrick lay still, pale, and cold.

The burning rage drained out of me and was replaced with a numb sort of shock. Lara stared at me, her eyes wide with terror. Not just because of Garrick, I realized. Because of me.

Markas groaned, and Lara's eyes shot to him. "We have to go before he wakes up." She gingerly reached for my hand to pull me to my feet.

Kill, Caedo said.

No. I was starting to shake. I couldn't stop staring at Garrick's body.

I'd murdered someone.

It didn't matter that he was a faerie and an enemy. I'd never killed anything but animals or Nasties before. Worse, I'd never killed with such murderous joy in my heart. How much of that bliss had come from Caedo?

How much had come from me?

I followed Lara blindly through the woods. We stayed away from trails and waded through streams to disguise our tracks. Finally we came to a halt beside a fallen tree. It was enormous, with a tangle of exposed roots large enough for both of us to hide within. I edged between two roots, settling into a seated position on a patch of decaying wood.

We breathed hard for several minutes, staring out at the forest.

"You killed him," Lara said.

My stomach cramped. "I did."

"What is that knife?"

Caedo hummed in my hand, pleased. I looked down at the dark red jewel, still glowing faintly from the blood it had consumed. "I don't know. I found it one day."

"Kenna . . . you looked like you enjoyed it."

I dropped my head, pressing the heel of my palm against my eye. My arm stung at the motion; I'd forgotten about the wound. My sleeve was blood-soaked and muddy. "It was awful, but there was so much energy running through me . . ." I trailed off. It was impossible to explain.

She laid her hand on my knee. "I think I understand." Her face was drawn, but she no longer looked afraid of me. "I felt like that on Beltane. I was hurting people and knew it was bad, but I was also glad."

"I feel horrible."

"He was going to kill us."

"I know. And I would do it again. I just . . . I think I'm going to see him dying in every nightmare I ever have."

There was no talk of hunting or lighting a fire that night. Lara summoned a small amount of water for us to drink and then we sat together, shivering.

The forest was louder than I'd realized. We'd been shielded from its sounds by the earthen walls of our shelter. Out here, I was aware of every owl's cry, of the wind through the trees and unknown creatures rustling in the bushes. A few times I saw something long and low slink by, but we held still and whatever it was moved on. Dancing green lights began glittering in the trees. It was beautiful, like watching fireflies, but I knew what they were.

I didn't dream about Garrick because I didn't sleep. Eventually Lara's head drifted onto my shoulder, but I kept watch the entire night.

At last the sky began to lighten. Dawn, my old friend. I watched the sky turn purple, then rosy, then blue.

I nudged Lara awake. "We did it."

It was the seventh day.

THE RESULTS OF THE TRIAL WERE ANNOUNCED AT DINNER THAT night.

I had bathed and then slept for a few thankfully dreamless hours before waking up to prepare. It had taken ages to restore myself to something resembling presentable, and even then the face that greeted me in the mirror was haggard and haunted. A different person than the one who had left.

The contestants' table was set for six.

I watched anxiously as they filed in and took their seats. Talfryn and Edric were there, thankfully. Markas and Karissa sat together, although Markas didn't speak to her or even look up from his plate. The last to arrive was Una.

Garrick, Gytha, and Wilfrid were all dead.

This was a more intimate gathering than the state dinners; only the candidates and a small delegation from each house attended. The Light and Void contingents glared at each other, and Prince Roland gripped his fork as if he wanted to stab someone with it.

Garrick had been his nephew. Somehow I'd forgotten that.

At the high table, Kallen stared broodingly at his meal, looking up frequently to check on Una. With Wilfrid's death, he must have realized how close he had come to losing another member of his family. As if he felt my stare, he glanced in my direction.

I didn't look away. For once I wished he could hear what I was thinking. *I'm sorry about Wilfrid. Sorry I couldn't stop it.*

Perhaps he understood, because he nodded slightly.

At the other end of the table, Drustan didn't look concerned or sorrowful, but I supposed he had no need to be. He would have considered all three dead candidates enemies. His smile struck me as vulgar, though. How could he smile when three young lives had been lost? When I'd taken a life so recently?

He couldn't know what I'd done, of course. No one but Lara would ever know. Still, it felt as if my world had changed overnight, deeply and profoundly, while everyone else had stayed the same.

King Osric made a toast. "To the six remaining candidates. Each of them survived, hopefully while using enough magic to please the Earth Shard." He grinned. "And some of them used enough violence to please me."

A few faeries stiffened at the callous words. Roland took a deep swallow of wine.

"Garrick would have taken the honor for slaying Wilfrid, but alas, he is no longer with us. That death will be claimed by Markas instead. Stand, Markas."

The Illusion candidate did, but he kept his gaze fixed on his meal. I wondered if he could feel Void House's hostile stares and knew exactly how much of a target he had just become.

"Gytha was slain on the last night as well. Stand, Una."

The last remaining Void candidate stood, her face a blank mask.

"I hear you killed Gytha in retaliation for the attack on Wilfrid."

"Yes, your majesty."

"One death apiece to Void and Illusion House. Let us drink to our two killers."

Roland frowned and whispered in the king's ear. After the room had finished drinking, Osric spoke again. "I have been asked why I did not announce who took the honor of slaying Garrick. Unfortunately, I cannot." He paused for dramatic effect. "He was killed by something else entirely."

Agitated questions filled the air, and Osric smiled with the glee of an actor leading his audience through a carefully planned scene. "We don't know which creature did it, but we know how they did it. He was stabbed and drained completely of blood."

The room went deathly silent. Even Kallen looked shocked at the revelation.

"That's not possible," Roland said.

"Nevertheless, it's true. The mystery is, who or what did it, and why did they copy Blood House's favorite killing technique?"

The forbidden name fell like a stone into a still pond, sending ripples through the assembled Fae. Nothing was forbidden to King Osric, though.

"It was a Nasty, there's no doubt about that," he continued. "Markas says he saw one of them before it happened."

Thank goodness Markas had fallen unconscious before Garrick had revealed my identity.

"A Nasty trying to honor Blood House?" Roland asked, stumbling slightly over the taboo name. "It's plausible."

"We let out quite a few of the Nasties for the trial. It seems one was holding a grudge."

"How would they drain him, though? Any weapons capable of that were destroyed."

My skin prickled. I knew what this was leading to.

"There are many blood-drinking creatures deep underground." Osric sounded enchanted by the thought. "The knife marks on his body were probably a diversion to cover up how it really fed. It was a foolish choice. The Nasty should have known no one but a Noble Fae from Blood House would have been able to wield a weapon like that."

Not true. Caedo tightened affectionately around my arm. *They are fools.*

They certainly were.

Caedo had chosen me as its new mistress after the last one died. Would it have been able to do so if any Blood faeries still lived, or had it only turned to a human because the entire house was dead? And who, exactly, had dropped the knife in the bog?

Who was your last owner? I asked.

The rightful ruler of Mistei, of course.

I blinked, confused. *Osric?*

No. The dagger's hatred for Osric pulsed in my blood. *My mistress*

would have been queen if she'd won the war. Instead she died a prin-
cess, and now I am all that remains.

My breath caught. This wasn't just a mystical dagger. It had been one of the most important weapons in a war fought centuries ago. Caedo had belonged to Princess Cordelia of Blood House, leader of the rebellion, who had refused to bow to a tyrant and had died with her people instead.

And now I, Kenna the human servant, no one special from an unremarkable town, a cheater who had just killed one of the Noble Fae, wielded it.

31

WHEN I WOKE THE NEXT MORNING, A RED FEATHER HAD been pushed beneath the door that separated my room from Lara's.

I ran my fingers along its silky surface, wondering why Lara had put it there. Then I turned it over and smiled. The number two had been shakily written on it in eyeliner. The second object for my collection.

I placed it beside the first in my desk drawer, tracing my fingers over it reverently.

All those years I had wondered which of my relics and oddities had belonged to the Fae, and now here I was, receiving gifts from a faerie. It didn't replace everything I had lost—but perhaps I could start again.

Now that the Earth trial was over, I finally had time to complete a task I'd been thinking about since Lara had brought me to her secret island. I conversed with Caedo as I left Earth House. Some final barrier had given way between us with Garrick's death, and conversation had become as easy as breathing.

The realization wasn't comforting.

Why did you want me to kill Garrick? I asked.

You wanted to kill Garrick.

No. I had to kill him. That's different.

Is it?

I scowled, and a passing Underfae took one look at my face and skittered away. I couldn't shake the feeling that what I'd done clung to me like a foul stench.

I didn't want to.

The metal thrummed in irritation. *If you hadn't wanted to, you wouldn't have done it.*

Just because you're some ancient, bloodthirsty relic doesn't mean everyone thinks like you.

Just because you're human doesn't mean you have to be dishonest with yourself.

Ridiculous. *You made me enjoy it.* That was what disturbed me most of all. When I'd stabbed Garrick, the horror had been tainted with pleasure.

Did I?

I refused to dignify that with an answer.

I found Drustan in the quartz room, near the entrance to the brothel. He sat on a crystalline couch with a smiling Fire lady on his knee. She was gorgeous, with curling burgundy hair and bronze skin, and she looked infatuated with him. As if that weren't enough, Drustan was grinning suggestively at a Light lady across the room while more giggling ladies looked on.

I lurked in the hallway, feeling the burn of jealousy.

I had no claim on him, but the sight of him with those beautiful ladies made me want to rip their hair out. I wanted to shove them away from him, slap him, and then kiss him so hard and deep he'd forget everything but the taste of me.

He glanced at the doorway, and I schooled my expression into something I hoped resembled boredom. I walked on, hoping he would take the hint.

He caught up with me when I was almost to our secret room just outside Fire House. Strange, that I thought of it as *our* room now. It was his room. I had no claim on that, either.

"Well?" he asked, casting a ward on the room for secrecy.

"I'm sorry to interrupt." I aimed for indifferent—and failed utterly. The words came out icy.

His brows rose. "Then why did you?"

My face grew hot. I briefly considered storming out, but that would have been petty and cowardly. My bruised ego didn't matter; the important thing was saving Mistei from King Osric's tyranny. "I have information for you. A potential ally."

"Oh? Tell me more, my sweet Kenna."

I lifted my chin, still determined to project nonchalance. "Lara doesn't support breaking neutrality, but Selwyn might."

"Selwyn? He's a child."

"He's not that young. He'll undertake the trials in a few years. Lara says he talks about wanting all Fae to be equal. He wants to change things." I felt guilty about sharing Lara's confidences, but this was about more than our friendship. Besides, if Selwyn truly wanted to change Mistei, shouldn't he have the chance?

Drustan's eyes grew distant as he contemplated possibilities. "All this time wondering how to push Earth House away from neutrality, and I hadn't even considered him."

"He won't speak for all of Earth House. Oriana has been committed to neutrality for a long time, and Lara is afraid to defy her mother or the king. But maybe Selwyn could help sway them to your cause—far better than I could."

"I'll talk to him. However cold she may seem, Oriana loves him. He could be a convincing voice in our favor."

I didn't show it, but I was proud he'd listened to my suggestion. "I'll let you know if I hear anything else."

His voice stopped me halfway to the door. "Leaving so soon?"

I took a deep breath and faced him. "Why would I stay? I told you what I needed to. Besides, you don't want to keep your companions waiting."

He laughed outright, and my cheeks burned hotter. "Why, Kenna, I believe you're jealous again."

"Why would I be?"

He stalked towards me. "Because you want me."

My heart pounded frantically, but I looked him up and down, then shrugged dismissively. "I suppose you do amuse."

This time his laugh echoed off the walls. He grabbed me by the upper arms and pulled me towards him. "This is a novel experience."

"What is?" I was struggling to maintain my composure, but the nearness of him, the *heat* . . .

"Being an object of jealousy. The Fae don't often feel it. We live for so long that it's hard to hold on to any strong emotion. Humans feel so intensely, though." His voice roughened. "It's intoxicating."

"I'm not jealous."

"You saw me with others, and now you're being cold to me."

"I'm not cold. I just have places to be."

He ran his hands up and down my arms, raising goose bumps beneath the thick fabric. "Would it help if I told you I only woo the ladies to gain their loyalty? To bring them to my side?"

Was that what he was doing? Using his charm to gain allies? "I'd still have places to be."

His hands roved lower, over my back and down to grip my buttocks. A shudder went through me as he yanked me into him, his hips pressing firmly against mine. His hard length pressed against my lower belly. "I like it when you're cold," he whispered. "But I like it better when you burn."

Then we were kissing desperately—like starving people at a feast, like drowning people gasping for air. I laced my fingers through his long hair and tugged so hard his lips briefly broke from mine. He grunted. "There's the fire." His lips crashed into mine again.

I bit him.

He pushed me against the nearest wall, his hand dipping between my legs. I cried out at the sensation, even muted as it was by the heavy dress and undergarments that separated us.

"I want to eat you up," he said.

I challenged him with my eyes. "Then do it."

There was a long, tense pause, and flames shifted in his gray irises as he considered it. I expected him to grab me, to carry me to the couch or even take me on the floor . . . but he stepped away.

"I have a meeting," he said, still breathing rapidly. "An important one. But the things I'm going to do to you next time . . ."

My stomach tumbled, finding the precipice before my mind fully caught on. He was going to leave me like this?

I wouldn't show him my dismay. What would that do but prove my jealousy? "Then you'd better impress me next time, Fire prince."

32

OVER THE NEXT FEW WEEKS I DIDN'T HEAR ANY MORE about Drustan's efforts to convince Selwyn to join him. The Fire prince did keep his promise, though. We met in our room every few days, and every time he made me burn.

The rest of my time was spent accompanying Lara to events and carrying out my normal duties. No one knew what the Blood trial would be, since there was no house head to direct the proceedings, so spying wouldn't do me any good. The Blood Shard itself would somehow guide the candidates.

It gave me shivers to think about exactly how powerful the Shards must be. They were supposedly just cold stone infused with magic, but how could a magical stone grant visions? How could it run a trial? No wonder the Fae worshipped the Shards as if they were gods, the same way humans worshipped the Fae.

At night, during my stillest, darkest moments, I thought about Garrick. His murder had been justified, but I couldn't forget how it had felt. The blade had slid into him so smoothly before I'd twisted it like some kind of torturer. I'd *enjoyed* it when he'd stared at me with such awful fear. I'd never seen that look in someone's eyes before. It had made me feel powerful.

Caedo remained silent on those nights, letting me struggle with my guilt alone. It couldn't feel guilt, I reminded myself when I grew bitter over the dagger's continued silence. Whatever powered its strange consciousness felt no conflict and would gladly kill again.

In a way, my guilt made me feel better. I wasn't a monster.

Soon the summer solstice arrived, the final holiday before the Blood trial. Mirrors had been hung in the hallways, reflecting the torchlight until every corridor gleamed as brilliantly as the midday sun. Mixed in with the mirrors were milky crystals and ropes of diamonds. The holiday was sacred to Light House, so the ceremony was held in their aboveground courtyard. It was sunny and warm, a perfect blue-vaulted summer day. The broken glass from the trial had been swept away, and the marble had been polished until it shone white as the clouds. A circle of enormous crystal standing stones ringed a marble block in the center.

I fetched wine for Lara and myself, and we drank together at the edge of the courtyard, watching the proceedings with interest. Lara had never been invited before, so she didn't know what to expect, either.

The wine was nearly clear, tinged with the faintest hint of gold. I'd expected it to fill me with the fuzzy pleasure other Fae wines had, but instead it seemed to focus me. My vision sharpened and my heartbeats calmed, and rather than feeling arousal, as I had with Fire's wine, or happiness, as I had with Earth's, cold anger began building in my chest.

As the rest of the white-clad gathering drank, the smiles around me disappeared and talking dwindled to a minimum. By the time Prince Roland strode to the center of the circle of stones, the tension had escalated so much that a cold sweat broke out on my forehead.

"Welcome," Roland said. He held a crystalline dagger in one

hand. "The summer solstice, the longest day of the year, gives us the opportunity to cast light into the darkest corners. Only by facing our crimes can we be cleansed."

That didn't sound good.

King Osric watched from a throne at the edge of the courtyard, and his smile was even more unsettling than the tense frowns around me. He clapped his hands. "Let the punishments begin."

I heard the distinctive clink of chains as a line of faeries began making their way through the crowd. They were led by a guard I remembered from previous executions, an enormous winged Underfae with milky eyes and smooth golden skin where his mouth should have been. He held one end of a long chain, and his other hand wielded an axe.

The mix of Underfae and human prisoners were clothed in gray rags. Their hands were cuffed to the chain, and they shuffled past with bowed heads. When the first prisoner reached the edge of the standing stones, the line stopped and the prisoners knelt. I flinched when the guard lifted his axe and brought it down on the length of chain separating the first prisoner from the second.

"Rise," Roland commanded.

The prisoner staggered to her feet. She was human, with a gaunt frame and tangled brown hair that reminded me far too much of mine and my mother's. She couldn't have been more than sixteen years old, but she looked at Roland with deadened, world-weary eyes. Her torn rags revealed a back lined with scars.

"You are accused of attempting to escape from your duties. Do you wish to confess?" He must know the girl couldn't speak. When she stayed silent, he snapped his fingers. "Very well."

The guard shoved her to her knees before the marble block, and she rested her head on it. This time when the axe came down, her head tumbled after it.

I bit my lip, struggling not to cry out as blood dripped down the block and pooled beneath her limp body. Two Light sylphs with long fingers and filmy wings dragged the corpse away. A streak of red painted the ground behind them.

Something was wrong with my response to the execution. I knew it was terrible, but my emotions were muted; even my shock felt distant. Somehow the wine had separated me from my emotional core.

Roland snapped, and the guard released the second prisoner, a short Underfae. He was similar in appearance to Aidan, although his pitch-black skin and star-flecked eyes indicated he was a Void sprite.

"You are accused of stealing a jewel from a visiting faerie. Do you wish to confess?"

"I didn't do it, my prince." The words were faint, as if he himself no longer believed his protestations.

The guard shoved him to his knees before the block and forced his hand onto the stone. The sprite tried to jerk away, but a sylph pinned the arm down. The axe dropped, removing the sprite's hand. He screamed as blood pumped from the stump.

I glanced towards the Void delegation, wondering how Kallen felt about one of his people being punished by Light House. He stared broodingly at the sprite as he was dragged away, looking calm enough—except for the hand clenched at his side. It was strange and somehow wrong to see him dressed in a cloud-white tunic. His night-dark hair and midnight eyes didn't fit the attire, and I had the uneasy feeling of watching a predator dressed in the skin of some less dangerous animal.

The punishments and executions continued.

The criminals were thieves, runaways, and those who had disrespected the Noble Fae. Those heard speaking ill of the Noble Fae had their tongues removed with Roland's crystal knife, and any caught trying to spy on a neighboring house had their eyes gouged out. Underfae healed better than humans, but the wounds were grievous; they would be maimed for the remainder of their lives. Soon the marble floor between the stones was covered in blood, but the punishments continued unabated.

The only break came an hour later, when everyone in attendance received another glass of wine. Every sip soothed and focused me until I could see the grain of the marble, the facets of the crystal knife, and every stray drop of blood. My sense of horror was even more removed, and for a while I watched the executions and mutilations with calm righteousness.

Yes, they deserved this punishment.

After the Underfae and humans were done, five Noble Fae prisoners were brought forward. I wondered if they were about to have parts removed, too. Even fully immortal Noble Fae weren't able to regenerate pieces of themselves entirely; Lara had told me that if a limb was reattached, the wound could stitch itself together, but there would be no creating something from nothing.

Roland's blade sparkled in the sunlight. A sneer touched his lips as the first Noble Fae lady was brought forward. "Nelda of Earth House, you are accused of speaking ill of King Osric. Do you wish to confess?"

Nelda shook her head.

I hadn't seen her around Earth House before. Then again, there were many Noble Fae I had never met. I glanced at Lara. "Do you know her?"

"A minor noble. No one of import. Oriana will be furious, though." Her voice was distant and unconcerned.

The guard led Nelda into the circle, but instead of pushing her to her knees, he left her standing before the altar. Both Roland and the guard retreated behind the stones. When Roland raised his arms, the crystals began to glow. He was channeling sunlight into them, and with every second that passed, the light intensified. Beams shot inward from each crystal, meeting in the center.

Nelda screamed.

The flash was blinding. When the sparks in my vision cleared, Nelda lay crumpled on the ground. An enormous, smoking hole had been burned all the way through her torso.

They dragged her corpse away, and the next Noble Fae was brought forward.

Each of them had spoken ill of the king. Each was executed in the same manner. Roland was demonstrating his magic for once, not just his martial skills.

The summer air smelled of copper and burning flesh. Everything about this was wrong, from Lara's calm face to the blood soaking the courtyard, but even that awareness felt distant. A glass wall had been erected around my heart, and the part of me that wanted to scream and rage at the cruelty was trapped behind it.

I closed my eyes and took a deep breath in through my nose. Almost over. It was almost over.

The final faerie was led forward, and this one I recognized. It was the Fire lady who had been sitting in Drustan's lap in the quartz room. Her burgundy hair was tangled, her skin was streaked with dirt and sweat, and she was crying.

"Edlyn of Fire House, you are accused of plotting against the king and encouraging rebellion."

Murmurs rose from the watching Fae, but Drustan seemed unconcerned, his muscled arms crossed over his simple white tunic.

"Do you wish to confess?" Roland asked.

"Yes." Edlyn fell to her knees. "Please, I beg you. I didn't know . . ."

"Didn't know what?"

"Will you spare me if I tell you the truth?" She directed the question to King Osric.

"That depends on what you say."

Edlyn glanced at Drustan guiltily. "The Fire prince commanded me to talk to the Illusion ladies. I had no choice."

The murmurs increased. Drustan cocked an eyebrow, looking distantly amused.

Alarm stirred in my chest, rattling the bars of the cage that held my emotions prisoner. It would be fine, I told myself. Drustan was a prince, and it would be his word against Edlyn's.

The fear didn't leave, though. It swelled until my composure began to crack and the horror of the situation trickled back in. My skin felt clammy and cold despite the warmth of the day. The spilled blood looked so very red in the sunshine—a greedy sea of death, and the tide was still coming in.

"Why did he tell you to do that?" Roland asked Edlyn, sending Drustan a hard look.

"He said we needed to know how loyal the king's house was, and if any of them seemed inclined to rebel."

"When did this conversation with Drustan occur?"

"The day after the Earth trial concluded, near the quartz room." She clasped her hands at her chest. "Please, your majesty. I had no choice."

"It would seem not," Osric said. There was a long pause as Edlyn's shoulders slumped in relief. "Of course, that is the response of a coward. You could have chosen to inform me of Prince Drustan's commands before carrying them out."

Edlyn started crying again. "He's my prince."

"And I am your *king*. Your loyalty is to me above all." Osric drummed his fingers on the arms of his chair. "Let us test the truth of your story." He motioned to Roland, who faced the Fire nobles.

"Prince Drustan of Fire House," Roland said. "You are accused of plotting against the king and encouraging rebellion."

Panic finally broke through the glass wall raised by the wine, and my callousness shattered with it. I watched, hands twisting in my skirts, as Drustan walked to the center of the stones to stand beside Edlyn, who still knelt in supplication. He was wearing a rapier with a golden hilt that sparked like flame in the sunshine, and my heart hammered as he unbuckled the sword belt and laid it on the ground. A gesture of surrender? Then he straightened and held out his arms as he faced the throne. "Is this how a prince is treated, your majesty? Subject to judgment on the word of an insignificant noblewoman?"

"It is damning testimony," Osric said, narrowing his eyes. There was a shimmering around him, an eerie warping of the air above his tapping fingers. "What reason would she have to lie?"

"She's a coward who's afraid for her life." The words cracked through the air like a whip, and Edlyn flinched. "As to why she would try to implicate me specifically," Drustan continued, casting her a scornful look, "I presume it's because I haven't visited her bed recently. She's been feeling slighted."

Edlyn was his lover?

"No," she whimpered. "You told me to do it."

Drustan ignored her, returning his focus to Prince Roland and King Osric.

"She told us when and where you spoke." Roland clearly doubted Drustan's explanation.

"She lied. I was never alone with her. Lady Gweneira of Light House was there at the time and can attest to this, and my servants can attest to my whereabouts before and after that meeting."

The Light lady he'd flirted with that day stepped forward. She was serenely beautiful, with a willowy frame and brown hair cut close to her scalp—an unusually short hairstyle for the Fae, but one that suited her. Her posture was impeccable as she curtsied low before the king. "It's true, my king. I was there. We spoke only of the trials and the latest fashions."

Roland and Osric looked taken aback by the testimony from the Light lady, but the sound of her voice was familiar. At last I knew who the third conspirator had been in the library that day. Lady Gweneira of Light House was working with Drustan and Lothar.

Edlyn looked between Drustan and Gweneira in disbelief. "She's lying!"

"Silence," Roland commanded. He looked at Osric, and for once he seemed troubled. "Lady Gweneira is my cousin," he told the king. "Her reputation is impeccable, and she has never lied to me."

Oh, if only he knew.

Gweneira lowered her lashes coyly. "Thank you, cousin. You should also know that Lady Edlyn has a reputation among the ladies for being . . . unstable." With that damning testimony, she returned to her position in the crowd.

"You bitch!" Edlyn screamed after her. Roland cuffed her, knocking her fully to the ground. Blood trickled from a cut on her temple.

Roland resumed questioning Drustan, although there was doubt on his face. "Even if she's lying about the conversation, why would she have plotted against the king without your approval?"

Drustan shrugged. "Because she's a fool? Because she dislikes being a minor lady and craves more power? Who can understand the motivations of criminals?"

"She's one of your nobles. You are responsible for her crimes."

"Am I responsible for every female who makes an unwise choice out of jealousy?"

The callous words made me stiffen. At his feet, Edlyn began crying louder. I shoved away my pity for her. She had brought this on herself by betraying the rebellion.

"I've been fucking someone else recently," Drustan continued, "and Edlyn didn't enjoy second place. I'm not surprised she lashed out. She's always been insecure."

My stomach churned. That was me he was speaking so coldly of *fucking*.

Only one faerie glanced at me, and this one had a trace of pity in his expression. Kallen. I shouldn't have been surprised that he knew. I met his eyes, forcing myself to look indifferent.

He looked away.

Drustan had to act like this, I told myself. He was in danger of losing his life and the future of his entire cause. He had to play the bored prince, the kind of person who would sleep with Edlyn and then insult her while she wept at his feet, who would move from lover to lover with no thought for their feelings. Better that than for Osric to see what he truly was.

"Edlyn is known for being overly emotional, your majesty." The voice came, surprisingly, from Edric. The Fire candidate stepped forward and bowed. "No one in Fire House would be surprised to hear that she betrayed Drustan out of spite."

"She betrayed *me*," King Osric said.

"I did not mean to give offense, my king. She betrayed you first and Drustan second when she tried to implicate him in her crimes. I would pledge my very life on Drustan's loyalty and honor. He would not have done this." Other Fire faeries murmured agreement.

Roland and Osric were wavering in the face of so much opposition. "Very well," Osric finally said. "Prince Drustan, the accusation is rescinded. For now."

I exhaled in relief as Drustan bowed. "I live to serve you, my king." He picked up his sword and strode out of the killing circle.

He didn't glance back at Edlyn, not even when Osric motioned for Roland to execute her. She screamed, and when the flash of light faded, she lay with a hole in her chest, her empty eyes staring after the Fire prince.

WE WERE FORCED TO REMAIN IN THE COURTYARD AFTER Drustan's pardon, drinking wine—normal red wine this time—and casually conversing as if we weren't all standing in a lake of blood. By the time Lara and I were able to slip away just before sunset, the hem of my white skirt was stained crimson.

Lara went straight home, but I was too restless and angry to follow. I paced the hallways in my blood-stiffened dress, clenching my fists so hard my bones hurt.

Perhaps I was hoping Drustan would find me.

The fifth time I passed the ramp that led to Fire House, he was there, leaning against the wall. He hadn't removed his solstice clothes, and his red hair was stark against the snowy cloth. He held out his hand, and despite my anger and hurt, I took it.

Once in our warded room, we separated. He paced to the desk, and I sank onto the couch.

"I regret that you had to see that." He poured two glasses of wine from a decanter he found in a drawer, and I took mine in silence. "You have to understand . . ."

"What?" The wine was a welcome warmth in my throat. It was tempting to drain the glass and ask for another, but no. Dulling this moment would be running from it, and I'd drunk enough that day.

"I have been planning this rebellion for *decades*," Drustan said. Flame crackled at his fingers. "Decades of alliances and research and plotting, and then to have it undone in the final weeks by one of my allies . . ." He shook his head, and the flame vanished. "I had to say whatever would convince them to look away from me."

"I do understand." I played with the folds of my gown, wincing as the stiff hem scraped against my blood-crusted slippers. "But Edlyn . . . You mocked her. You said she was jealous and overly emotional."

Like me.

Drustan didn't seem to register the parallels. He shrugged. "She was. We used to sleep together; that part was true. She didn't appreciate my neglect."

I bit my lip. "The things you said about her were cruel." I could still hear her crying and that last, horrible scream.

"What she did was worse." He sank to his knees in front of me, eyes and voice growing fervent. "Kenna, this rebellion carries the hopes of thousands. She would have ruined it to save her own life. She would have condemned us all to death." He tucked a piece of hair behind my ear. "I'm not afraid to die for this. No one who works with me closely is. But I refuse to die before I've had a chance to make a difference."

I nodded, my eyes burning.

He kissed me softly. "You're braver than Edlyn ever was," he murmured against my lips.

I frowned. "That's not what—"

But he was kissing me hungrily, and I succumbed to the pleasure, as I always did. I gripped his shoulders, pulling him between my legs, wrapping my limbs around him as if I could make him part of me, as if I could keep him safe with nothing but my own flesh.

Later, while he moved within me, while I clawed his back and cried out in pleasure, I let myself imagine it. Just him and me, safe and healthy, living proudly together in a world no longer ruled by King Osric.

That was worth any sacrifice.

33

THE NIGHT BEFORE THE BLOOD TRIAL, THE KING HELD A BALL.
This ballroom was hewn out of obsidian and dotted with
gemstones. I'd never seen so many jewels in one room; they caught
the torchlight in a writhing rainbow of color that matched the swirling couples below.

I watched from a balcony with a few of the other servants. This
was a more intimate affair, and servants weren't allowed on the dance
floor. Many of the Underfae had taken the night off, but Aidan and
I had chosen to watch the spectacle instead.

He leaned against the railing, staring gloomily at Edric as the handsome Fire candidate danced with a succession of partners, both male
and female. "He looks wonderful, doesn't he?" Aidan asked dourly.

"He does." Edric wore a cloth of gold tunic with a short cape
crafted from links of variegated metal, each one fashioned to look
like a flame.

"And he was very brave at the solstice."

I chuckled, although the memory of the solstice was still painful.
"Why do you sound so sad about how handsome and brave he is?"

Aidan traced the balcony railing with an ash-gray fingertip. "Because it's hard to see something you want every day and know you'll never have it."

My laughter died. I couldn't pass judgment on that.

My gaze inevitably strayed to Drustan. He, too, looked incredible in a copper ensemble that matched his hair. The torchlight highlighted his athletic movements as he turned lady after lady in smooth circles across the floor.

"Your prince is handsome, too," Aidan said.

My fingers clenched around the railing. "I know."

We hadn't been together since the evening of the solstice. More than a week without seeing or touching him. He hadn't sought me out, but I hadn't sought him out, either.

"He mentioned you."

"What?"

"At the solstice. At least, I assume that was you."

"Oh." The *fucking* comment. "I assume so." Did I really know that he'd been speaking about me, though? How could I expect loyalty from a prince who only spent time with me behind closed doors, who would never be able to love me in the open?

Who might never love me at all?

"How did you feel about it?" Aidan tried to sound nonchalant, but I saw the concern in his eyes and was grateful for it.

I squeezed his hand. "Let's just say I can empathize with your mood tonight."

We watched for hours, until Edric kissed a beautiful Fae lady. Aidan left quickly after that.

When the clock struck midnight, I was the only servant still watching. I didn't want to go back to Earth House and lie awake in bed worrying about what would happen tomorrow. Better to stand here watching with pride as Lara accepted dance after dance. She had been a success throughout the trials, and the Noble Fae were finally taking notice. I was happy for her, even though it made me sad to think that no one would ever know what I'd done. What I'd sacrificed, whom I'd *killed*, to help my friend win.

Footsteps sounded behind me.

I expected it to be one of the Underfae, so I was shocked when I turned and saw Kallen. He wore midnight silk flecked with diamond stars, and a thin silver band circled his head, contrasting sharply with his black hair.

"Hello," he said.

I blinked at him as he joined me at the rail and rested his elbows against it, more casual than I'd ever seen him. "Hello," I hesitantly replied. "Are you here for information? I don't have any."

He shook his head. "Not tonight."

"Then why are you here?" He should have been dancing below, as he had earlier. He'd moved like quicksilver across the floor, light-footed and elegant.

"I find balls dull."

"That's no reason to spend time with a servant, much less a human."

He made a humming noise. "'Much less' isn't any kind of term for you, Kenna."

What did that mean? Typical faerie nonsense, but my skin flushed hot for reasons I didn't want to examine. "Won't you be missed? What if someone looks up here and sees you?" Interacting with servants was hardly a popular activity for the Noble Fae outside of the spring equinox celebrations. Except for Drustan, of course, who did whatever he wanted to.

Only in empty hallways and warded rooms, though, a small voice in my mind said. *He hasn't looked up once tonight.*

My eyes fell to Drustan again—who was holding a blushing Earth lady far too close as he whispered in her ear. Jealousy surged in my breast, hot and stinging.

"No one misses me," Kallen said.

The words startled me, and I ripped my attention away from Drustan and focused on the dark faerie at my side. "That can't be true." Surely at least other members of his house cared for him.

"How could it not be true?" He shrugged, a subtle, resigned movement. "No one even wants to *look* too closely at me, lest I murder them or betray them to the king. Half the court is convinced I can hear their whispers on the night air."

I bit my lower lip, recalling the way he was able to disappear into shadow. "Can you?"

His mouth twitched at that. "Only if those whispers reach the ears of one of my sources."

Sources like me. I tried not to hate myself too much for it.

"Well, I'm looking at you," I told him, letting my gaze linger on his face, then the broad stretch of his shoulders under black silk. A deadly faerie. A beautiful one, too, but then all the Fae were.

"You do seem to lack a sense of self-preservation, yes."

"I'm still alive, aren't I?"

"You are," he acknowledged. "Somehow."

"I'll try not to be offended by you saying 'somehow.'"

He was still facing the gathering below, elbows on the railing, but his face tipped towards me at that. A lock of black hair slid over his shoulder, and I had the irrational thought that his hair looked soft. His lips parted, but he didn't say anything. I wondered if I'd annoyed him with my flippancy, for daring to speak to him like we were any sort of equals. "It's interesting," he replied at last.

"That I'm alive?" It was suddenly hard to form words. The way he was staring at me was . . . I didn't know what it was.

"That you *look*. That I—" He bit down on the rest of that sentence, then shook his head. "The danger in looking at the wrong people, Kenna, is that sometimes they want to look back."

Uneasiness crawled over my skin. I was so aware of him—of his height and the taut strength of his body, of the infinite and unknowable depths of his eyes. Of the stillness and the threat of him, of the bodies in his past and the blood in his future.

Of the way he looked almost . . . sad.

"Am I the wrong person in this scenario, or are you?" I somehow managed to ask, heart fluttering like a trapped rabbit's.

Now he looked startled. "Are you—" He broke the words off, then made a soft noise I couldn't interpret. "What a strange woman you are."

The statement was so absurd it broke through the uneasy tension that had been building in my gut. Of everyone in Mistei, I had to be the least strange. "How flattering," I said dryly, shifting on my feet and trying to shake off the lingering feeling of . . . whatever it was. I still didn't understand why we were having this conversation, and I didn't like not knowing. "So why seek out such a strange woman? Why not keep spinning your web down below, cultivating the rest of your sources?"

He scrutinized the dance floor, a small furrow etched between his brows. "I told you. Balls are dull."

"You dance well, though." Exceedingly well. I'd found myself watching him more than once, noticing the way he moved with liquid grace.

He met my eyes again, and now I saw exhaustion in those midnight-blue pools. "Dancing well doesn't mean I enjoy it."

"Perhaps you need better partners." I nodded at the faeries below. "They're all so restrained. In the human world . . ." I trailed off, biting my lip.

"What about the human world?" His gaze was solid and steady, encouraging me to continue.

"Dancing is more exuberant. Everyone ends up sweaty and laughing by the end of it. No one down there wants to sweat."

"How succinctly you summarize the difference between the Fae and humans."

I studied him curiously. I'd made what I'd thought was a horrible bargain with him, but he hadn't been nearly as terrible as I'd expected. He hadn't pushed me that hard or demanded as much as he could have.

He'd been oddly honest with me already tonight—as honest as the Fae ever were with their insinuations and partial truths—so I decided to see what else this enigmatic faerie would share. "Why haven't you been crueler to me?" I asked softly. He winced, and I was so startled by that small sign of hurt that I laid a palm on his sleeve. "I don't mean it like that. It's just that you're the King's Vengeance. You could do anything to get what you want. You could torture me or threaten me or beat me, and the king would approve of everything you did. Why haven't you?"

He studied my hand on his sleeve, then lifted his gaze to meet mine. "You saw the solstice punishments."

"I did."

"Every solstice I'm reminded of a fundamental truth. Act like your enemy long enough, and you become them."

"I don't understand. What enemy?"

He shook his head, dark hair brushing his shoulders. "It isn't important."

"No, I think it is." His arm was warm beneath my palm, the heat of him sinking into me through the thin silk of his shirt. A more natural warmth than Drustan's magical fire.

There was a long pause while Kallen looked at me like he was weighing questions and possibilities. "Roland thinks he's justified no matter what he does," he finally said. "So do all the Fae. So do I, most of the time. But not everything is justified."

I squeezed his arm, strangely moved by the confession. To my surprise, he rested his other hand on top of mine. His palm was warm and calloused.

"You don't want to hurt people," I said wonderingly.

"You don't have to sound so surprised."

"I'm not surprised, just . . ." I hesitated. "All right, surprised."

He barked out a laugh. "I appreciate your bluntness."

"I'm not surprised about you, specifically." I grimaced as he raised his eyebrows. "All right, maybe about you, specifically. But I've seen very little compassion in Mistei. By all accounts you're a heartless spy and murderer, capable of any crime on behalf of the king."

"And by all accounts humans are ignorant, dirty, worthless creatures." I bristled, and he smiled. "Does that make it true?"

"Fair point."

We stared at each other, caught in a moment that felt oddly fragile.

I don't know why I did what I did next. All I knew was that it felt right.

I faced him fully, dropping my hand from his arm. His own palm slid away from mine reluctantly. "I think you need to learn how humans dance."

His brows shot up. "Do I?"

"Yes."

"Why is that?"

"Because balls bore you, and they shouldn't bore anyone." If I were free, I would love to be twirling down there. "Besides, this dirty human knows a few tricks that might surprise you."

He let out another rusty chuckle. When I moved away from the railing, out of sight of anyone who might happen to look up from below, he followed, pacing after me with slow, considered intent. A shiver skated down my spine. This was some sort of madness, probably, but I raised my arms in a dancing frame and smiled when he clasped me close.

"What step should we do?" His hand flexed on my waist.

"I'm going to teach you something new."

And I did, teaching him a rollicking dance I'd always loved. It wasn't dignified or elegant, but it was fun. We spun madly, and as he threw his head back and finally laughed freely, I laughed with him.

34

THE NEXT MORNING, I DRESSED LARA IN A BLOODRED ROBE.
"It's tradition," she explained as I fixed a single ruby on a golden chain around her neck. "Everyone wears red the day of this trial."

"There's no one left to care if you wear red. Why not wear what you want?"

"You don't understand."

I did, though. For all their restlessness and obsession with change and stimulation, the Fae were tied to their traditions.

Someone knocked on the door. "Come in," Lara called.

Alodie entered holding a wooden box in her pale blue hands. "I found this by my bed," she explained in a dazed voice. "I know I have to give it to you, but I don't know why."

Lara took the box. "It's all right. It must be part of the trial."

We studied the box after Alodie left. It was roughly the size of my hand and had been carved with depictions of weaponry between the twining branches of a tree. The wood was worn almost smooth, as if it had been handled for centuries.

"What are you supposed to do?"

Lara examined it. "I'm not sure." She pried at the lid, then yelped, sucking her finger. "It's sharp."

I ran my finger over the seam, looking closely at the box. A tiny thorn popped out and stabbed into my skin. "I suppose we'll need to figure out how to open it."

We tried for long minutes, but nothing seemed to unlock it, and we were cut by minuscule thorns every time we touched it. The box drank our blood as quickly as it appeared.

This is like your magic, I thought at Caedo, but the dagger didn't respond.

It was evident this was some kind of puzzle box, but how were we supposed to open it? There was nothing on the surface but the tree and the weapons: no lock, and nothing to dig my fingers into.

I started pressing instead, ignoring the small pinpricks of pain. I crowed with glee when one of the daggers compressed into the surface. Something within the box clicked, and the lid popped open.

Inside was a small dagger, a silver cup, and a note.

Fill the cup with blood at the Blood Tree. Water it well.

Lara frowned at the note. "That sounds bad."

"What's the Blood Tree?"

"It's this ancient tree at the entrance to Blood House. They tried to cut it down after the rebellion, and then they burned it, but nothing worked."

"Sounds like you have to cut yourself there, fill the cup, and feed the tree your blood."

Lara made a face. "I don't want to."

"You have to. People will be watching, which means I can't help you this time."

She stared at the knife as if it were a serpent ready to bite.

Seconds ticked by, and I sighed. This wouldn't go well if Lara couldn't cut herself. "You have to fill the cup there," I said, "but maybe we can collect some blood in advance so it won't be so bad."

I found a vial that would fit behind a bracelet hidden beneath Lara's sleeve. Once she began the ritual, she'd be able to combine it with the blood she drew at the tree, which meant she wouldn't need to cut as deeply as the other candidates.

I handed her the dagger so she could start filling the vial, but Lara didn't take it. She still looked petrified.

Perhaps I could help in this trial after all—I was certainly used to giving up my blood to Caedo. "It's not so bad. See?" I dragged it lightly across my own forearm, well away from any prominent veins. Blood dripped into the vial as I tried not to wince at the sting. "I'll help you fill it."

She gritted her teeth and cut into her arm. Together we squeezed the wounds, yelping in pain as the vial slowly filled. We bandaged ourselves after, with Lara hiding the cut under her billowing sleeve. Then we attached the vial to Lara's bracelet and headed for Blood House.

For once, the corridor leading to the forgotten house was well lit. I almost didn't recognize the entrance when we reached it; I was used to a pitch-black room, and today the space was flooded with light.

Dismal light, though. The torches burned a gloomy red, flickering over the checkered floor. At the end of the antechamber I finally saw the elaborately carved archway that led to Blood House. We passed under it and entered a large hall with the same checkered black-and-white floor. Every inch of the gray stone walls had been carved with depictions of Noble Fae, Underfae, and Nasties. They seemed to crawl with life as the torchlight cast dancing shadows over them.

An enormous tree stood in the center of the hall. Its trunk was so wide at least six people would need to link hands to measure around it, and its branches reached towards the far-distant ceiling. It had no leaves, yet I sensed the tree was very much alive. Beyond the tree was a large metal door covered in protruding spikes; probably the entrance to the house proper, and not something I wanted to get anywhere near. Caedo hummed contentedly in my mind as we approached, pleased to be home.

I joined the other servants at the back of the room, but Lara took her place in the line of candidates facing the tree. Soon all six were there. They knelt as one and sliced into their hands, letting the blood drip into the cups laid before them. Lara flinched at the cut, but she managed the opening of the vial in her bracelet expertly—it was only because I knew what she'd done that I could tell the flow of blood into her cup was more substantial than her fresh wound merited.

Once the cups were full, the candidates rose and poured their blood onto the gnarled roots rising from the tiled floor.

My vision went dark.

I stiffened, wondering if the torches had been extinguished, but then a faint ruby glow filled the space. The tree's branches were now covered with crimson leaves and the room was otherwise empty—the candidates and servants were gone.

Look, the tree whispered.

I was back in the hut I'd grown up in. It was just before dawn, and my nose was pressed against the cold glass of the window. I could see my father's back retreating down the narrow path behind our home. He looked over his shoulder, but when he saw me waving a tiny hand, all he did was turn around and keep walking. Something in my chest seemed to break.

I was in the village, hunkering behind the tailor's shop as a pack of other children threw stones at me. My forehead started bleeding, and the pain made me furious. I threw the rocks back at them and screamed as they ran. When I hit one of the girls in the head, I laughed.

I was fighting boys in the Tumbledown schoolyard, no longer willing to wait until rocks were thrown. They pulled my hair and punched me, but I punched harder, and besides, I bit. The parents called me a wild animal when they came to retrieve my latest victim. *"She's half feral." "She shouldn't be allowed near the other children."*

I was thirteen years old and desperately hungry and angry. When my mother tried to teach me herbcraft, I told her the work was boring and I'd rather be a trader. That I'd rather be rich and free than poor like her—poor like she'd forced both of us to be.

I was shouting at the teenage boys who harassed Anya, then jumping on one who had groped her. I wrapped my arms around his neck and bit his ear while he shrieked and tried to shake me off. *"Anya's guard bitch,"* they called me that day, and the name stuck.

I was staring at my reflection in a pond with the angst and fury of adolescence, wishing I was dead so the villagers who looked down on me would feel the guilt they deserved. Wishing *they* were dead. Wishing all of us were dead.

I was throwing a rock through the window of a woman who mocked my mother for being unable to keep a husband.

Smacking the first boy who tried to kiss me.

Bickering with Anya about our families.

I was lying awake late one difficult night towards the end of my mother's illness, resenting her for the time spent caring for her and the worries that piled up and the coins that left my hands faster than I could earn them.

I was scowling and shouting and hating and lying and wishing harm on those around me. Every foul thing I'd ever done, every dark thought I'd ever had, churned up in front of me before spinning away into the darkness. Between each flash of vision I saw the tree, ancient and waiting.

It had tasted my blood, I realized dimly through the torrent of memories. I'd just wanted to help Lara fill her cup, and now the tree was punishing me with my failings.

I was wailing after my mother died, screaming at the unseen Fae for failing her. Hating them and hating the faith that had made my mother turn her face to the window instead of to me in her final moments, that had made her look for a rescue that was never coming.

I was running in terror across the bog, listening to women dying behind me, and when I turned, only empty air remained where my best friend had been.

I was wielding a dagger and threatening to kill the first Nasty I'd ever seen while it dug its claws into my ankle. I was cutting into other Nasties as they hunted me through the lowest levels of Mistei, killing them without hesitation because it had come down to them or me, and I had chosen me.

I was baring my teeth at Kallen, wanting to hit him to make up for my humiliation at Garrick's hands.

I was slicing into my skin to feed Caedo.

I was scratching Drustan during sex, overwhelmed with a primal rage and lust I didn't know how else to express.

I was twisting the knife in Garrick's gut, smiling as he stared up at me in terror. His blood was hot on my palms. His throat gaped open in front of me, and for a terrible moment I felt joy.

Look, the tree said, and the memories cleared. A small woman with wildly curling hair stood facing me, one hand on the rough bark. It was me, but I was baring my teeth, and blood ran from my hands and pooled at my feet, so much blood . . . the blood I had shed and would shed, the blood I was capable of shedding.

Look.

I looked. Every wound had been torn open inside of me all at once, and what I'd learned from it was how small and terrible and violent I could be.

Are you sorry?

I stared at the bloody apparition that represented my darkest self. Was I? Sorry for the fighting, for the well of rage I pulled from so easily, for the deaths I had delivered?

For hurting my mother and Anya—yes. For the rest of it? I paused, thinking. *No. I won't apologize for defending myself or my friends.*

That wasn't the entire truth, though, was it?

I regret enjoying it, I admitted, knowing the tree understood I was speaking about Garrick.

Did you enjoy it? The tree seemed genuinely curious.

Yes.

You enjoyed it, or Caedo did?

Both. Seeing my past laid out in front of me and feeling the visceral pain beneath the images, I'd been confronted with a dark truth about myself. *I enjoyed getting revenge. I enjoyed making Garrick afraid of me. It was only for a moment, but I felt it.*

It was both awful and freeing to admit my crime to the Blood Tree, to speak the truth I had known all along. I couldn't blame Caedo for my violent impulses. I couldn't pretend my reactions had been beyond my control. All I could do was face who I was and refuse to look away.

My bloody twin vanished. The tree's branches were bare once more, and the room was filled with faeries.

I blinked, wondering if this was another hallucination, but nothing else happened. The candidates stared at the tree with wide eyes. Were they, too, reliving their past crimes? Or was the test something else entirely, and the tree had punished me for feeding it my blood?

Lara sagged to the floor. I rushed to her side, but she held me off with an outstretched hand and wobbled back to her feet. "I think it's over," she said in a dazed voice. One by one the other candidates stirred, stumbling or twitching as they returned to their bodies. All of them looked haunted by whatever they'd seen.

The magical energy that had filled the space drained away, and we were left standing in a dusty room before an ancient, silent tree.

The trial was over.

ALL LARA WOULD TELL ME IN THE FOLLOWING DAYS WAS THAT she'd seen ugly visions. I pressed for more details, but she refused, saying she didn't want to think about it.

"I don't know," she admitted when I asked if she thought she had passed the test. "It asked me if I was sorry for . . . well, the bad things it showed me. I said I was. I think it was pleased, but how would I know?"

The tree had been pleased? Had it been testing whether the candidates could feel remorse? I supposed that counted as strength of character. It seemed unlikely for the Fae, but then again, Blood House had once been full of healers, and they'd chosen death over bowing to a tyrant. It would make sense for the Shard to seek out the trait its house had once had in abundance.

It was a good thing I wasn't the one being tested.

I visited Triana and Maude soon after, bringing a pot of vegetable soup with me. Triana pulled me aside after our sign language lesson. "Are you nervous?" she asked.

"About what?" I signed in response.

"The trial result. If your lady fails . . ."

She didn't need to complete the sentence. As Oriana had once promised, if Lara failed, I would die or become one of the lowest servants. "She won't."

Triana didn't look confident about that assertion. "Be safe."

"Of course. Are you well?"

"I worry. You are my friend."

I smiled, touched by her concern. "And you are mine." I switched to speaking aloud when I couldn't think how to sign the rest. "You're very kind, but I can take care of myself. Save your worries for yourself and the people around you."

Her mouth twisted, and she rubbed a palm over the soft stubble of her growing hair before speaking again. "There's a new girl today."

I tried to puzzle out what she meant. New girl . . . "You mean you're getting a new girl from the brothel?"

Triana's eyes were sad, and she signed the confirmation near her heart. "Yes."

"You'll take good care of her. You're a strong woman. Focus on helping her heal, and I promise I'll be safe."

A tear traced down her cheek as she hugged me, and I marveled at her strength and compassion. Seeing the new girl would remind her of everything she'd suffered, yet in the midst of that emotional turmoil she'd found the time to tell me she cared for me and that I should be safe. Because we were friends.

I reflected on that as I returned upstairs. Anya had been my only friend in the human world. Somehow in a little over six months in Mistei, I'd made more: Lara, Aidan, Triana, Maude, Alodie. And that dance with Kallen, the way we'd laughed . . . It had felt like discovering solid ground in a bog where I'd only encountered treacherous mud before. Perhaps given time we could have become friends, though Drustan's rebellion would come before that could ever happen, sometime during the months between the end of the trials and Samhain.

I supposed Drustan, too, could be counted as a friend, but something in me rebelled at the thought. He had become so much more, even if I'd never let him know how much he meant to me.

I stopped walking.

What if I told him?

The encounter with the Blood Tree had been cathartic. It felt like my emotional wounds had been ripped open, drained of infection, and rebandaged in order to heal properly. Facing the truth had been difficult, but I'd been sleeping better ever since.

What if I faced this truth, too? I cared for Drustan and wanted to be with him openly and proudly. Or rather, for *us* to be with each other. In the new world he would build, we should be able to.

I was going to tell him. Not tonight—there was too much preparation to do for the final ball announcing the results tomorrow night—but after that, I would corner him in our secret room, clasp his face in my hands, and tell him exactly what I wanted.

35

LARA'S BALL GOWN WAS A MASTERPIECE.

Delicate evergreen skirts floated over a thick froth of petticoats that rustled with every step. The dress had been embroidered with tiny trees and animals, an entire forest in miniature. Sparkling sapphires highlighted hidden ponds, and rubies and diamonds formed clusters of wildflowers. Her train was a waterfall of blue silk that flowed behind her as she walked.

I'd outdone myself with her hair, too. I eyed the elaborate braided updo with satisfaction. It had taken six months, but I'd finally become an expert at hair and cosmetics. I'd never suspected I had it in me to be pleased by such a stereotypically feminine skill, but there it was. I was proud.

Lara smiled at me in the mirror, but I could tell she was nervous. "You look wonderful," I assured her.

"But will I be judged wonderful?"

I sank to my knees in front of her, and my blue skirts pooled around me. I wore the inverse of her colors—my gown was light and airy, the blue skirt covered by a shimmering overlay that made the color beneath ripple like water. Dark green shapes sprouted at random like islands in a mighty river. I'd never felt finer.

I gripped her hands, looking up at her with respect and affection. "You will succeed. You passed every test."

"Only because you helped me."

"That doesn't matter. The only thing that matters is the result."

"Kenna . . ." She chewed her lip and looked down at our clasped hands. "I wouldn't have succeeded without you."

"I think you would have. You're stronger than you realize."

"But what if you hadn't been here? What if I had tried and failed? Sometimes I wonder if I deserve to win."

Deserve to live, she meant. "You deserve everything," I said fiercely. "You're not like the others, but that's not a bad thing. You're kind. You have heart. Faeries like Garrick and Markas do well in competitions, but they don't make the world a better place. You will." Once King Osric was overthrown, there would be room for Lara's compassion.

"You're a good friend." She squeezed my hands before releasing them. "Oh, before I forget—I have something for you."

I was astounded when she pulled an enormous emerald pendant from her drawer and pressed it into my hand. "I can't take this. It's too precious. I'm just a servant."

"You're not just a servant, and if you give it back I'll throw it in the fire. Just take it."

The stone was perfect, a round cut with beveled edges that glittered in the light. On the back of the ornate gold setting, four simple words were inscribed: *For my best friend.*

The jewel blurred behind a veil of tears. "Thank you."

"Oh, stop it." She looked towards the ceiling and pressed her fingers just below her eyes as if willing her own tears to stay at bay. "You'll make me cry, and then you'll have to reapply my makeup and we'll be late for dinner."

I laughed and slipped the jewel into a hidden pocket in my skirts. Someday I'd wear it proudly so all the world could see.

Best friend. I hadn't called anyone that since Anya had died. I still mourned her, but life had moved on anyway. I'd met new people and experienced unimaginable things, and somehow, in a court suffocated by fear and oppression, I had found another best friend for my aching heart to love.

⊚⊚⊚⊚⊚⊚

THE BALL WAS HELD IN THE THRONE ROOM BECAUSE THE SHARDS were too precious to gather together anywhere besides the heavily warded space. It was an exclusive event—only the candidates and the most important families from each house attended. The house heads and Kallen sat on the dais near King Osric, clad in their most radiant attire. The assembly below shone just as brightly, with jewels sparkling from hair, ears, fingers, and the scabbards of ornamental swords.

I barely managed to restrain myself from gaping at the opulence. Glass orbs containing dancing pixies floated overhead and more pixies performed aerial tricks, so many of them that the air shimmered like a hive of bees. Gauze-clad sylphs and asrai twirled between fire jugglers. Even the silver walls rippled with magic, like captured rainbows trying to break free.

Then Osric raised his hands, and the room went away.

We were in the middle of a grassy field, surrounded by the hum of insects and the chirp of birds. Snowcapped peaks rose in the distance, and flowers bobbed their heavy heads at my feet. The smell was heady in my nostrils, and the sun sank warm into my skin.

The sky transitioned from dawn to midday to dusk to night so quickly I only had a few moments to appreciate the beauty of each. When the night sky was darkest, explosions of color and light burst against it in radiant starbursts. Each pop was met with cheers, and as the sparks fell to earth, they chimed like glass.

The world flipped. I was standing on a cloud, and the ground hung high above me, a far-distant patchwork ceiling. Then I was falling, the wind whipping at my face as I stifled a scream. Right when it seemed I would bash my head against the sharp rocks below, the vision changed.

We were deep underwater, standing on a silvery seabed in the middle of a kelp forest. Currents eddied around me as schools of glittering fish flirted with my fingers. The shadow of something enormous passing overhead blotted out the distant sun.

When the light returned, we were back in the throne room.

My heart raced. I knew Illusion's powers could force others to see and hear things that weren't there, but I had never imagined how real the visions would seem. How I would *feel* them, too.

Aidan chuckled at my expression. "I'd say you get used to it, but you don't."

After the demonstration, the music began, an unearthly symphony played by unseen musicians. Aidan and I watched the dancing, quietly gossiping and admiring Edric's and Lara's elegance.

As the ball stretched on, though, I felt more and more unsettled. It seemed cruel to make the candidates wait so long for the results. If I felt sick with nerves, Lara must feel so much worse, though no one would know it looking at her. Aidan kept tugging at the collar of his orange velvet tunic, fidgeting with his own worry.

Osric finally clapped his hands just before midnight, making my breath catch and my heart launch into a more frantic pace. All movement stopped as the Fae faced the king. "Bring the Shards," he commanded.

At last I would see the stones the Fae worshipped, the most magical artifacts in the world.

The moment the Shards entered the room, carried by the house heads and a few nobles, the air grew charged with power. My skin tingled, and a faint vibration thrummed against the soles of my feet.

The hand-sized stones were beautiful. They were smooth on one side and jagged on the other, as if they had been struck from the same large orb, but the power roiling within each crystal differed wildly. Flames licked up the inside of Drustan's Shard, while a maelstrom of water, leaves, and dirt swirled in Oriana's. The Void and Light Shards were inky black and blazing bright, and the Shard an Illusion lady carried was flooded with shimmering rainbows. The final Shard was a deep, liquid red. The Illusion lord carrying it winced with every step, and blood poured down his palms.

He is not meant to hold it, Caedo said.

Apparently, like every other Blood artifact I'd encountered so far, the Shard bit.

The bearers placed the Shards in six golden stands that ringed the center of the room. When the last one was placed, each crystal began to glow, and then light shot from them and collided at the center of the circle. A force thumped into my chest as the beams met, and my hair blew in a sudden wind. Where the six beams had joined, a whirling cyclone of magic stretched from floor to ceiling.

A reverent hush fell as Osric began speaking. "Long ago, there was a great war between the gods of another world, far past the stars. When it was done, there were none left but six, all injured and dying. To protect the memory of their world, these gods bound their magic into pieces of crystal. These Shards fell from the stars to our earth, and when they landed, the magic burst free to create a new world. The magic chose the Fae, drawn by our beauty and strength, and so six houses were formed to honor the six types of power."

The loss of the sixth house felt tangible and wrong, like a gaping hole in the universe. That bloodred light tangled with the rest, but nothing anchored it in this room.

"Now the Shards determine which faeries are worthy of power, which aren't, and which deserve only death," the king said. "These are the three fates that await our candidates today."

Sweat beaded Lara's hairline, and her fingers were clenched in her skirts, rumpling the gorgeous embroidery.

"Stand before me, candidates," Osric commanded.

The six surviving candidates faced him in a line, the maelstrom of power at their backs. Their hair and clothes shifted in a mystical wind.

"You will enter the combined magic one at a time. When you emerge on the other side, you will either be immortal . . . or dead. If you live, you will possess magic . . . or not. Mistei has no use for the weak." Osric clapped his hands. "Let the judgment begin."

The candidates had lined up in order of where they'd been sitting: Markas, Karissa, Edric, Talfryn, Lara, and Una. Markas stared at the magic nervously and didn't move an inch.

Una cast him a judgmental look before speaking. "I'll go first." She walked confidently into the circle of Shards, and the whirlwind grew stronger, the colors brighter. Without hesitating, she entered the churning column of magic. She emerged less than a second later, smiling. Kallen had risen to his feet to watch, and when she lifted her hands to show the shadows coiling around them, he grinned and collapsed back into his seat.

"Una has been found worthy," the king announced. "May you bring honor to Void House and my kingdom."

The dark magic wisped away once Una stepped out of the circle— presumably her power was now subject to the wards protecting the throne room. As she joined a group of applauding Void nobles,

Markas took a deep breath and stepped forward. The maelstrom intensified as he disappeared within it, and I found myself hoping he wouldn't emerge.

He walked out, laughing as opalescent light shimmered around him. I suppressed my disappointment as the king repeated the exhortation to bring honor to his house and to the kingdom.

Maybe everyone passed and the entire trial season was the Shards' idea of a joke. Markas had performed well on most of the tests but not all, and even Una had likely failed the Fire trial.

Cheered by the success of the others, Karissa tossed her red hair, winked at Talfryn, and walked into the magic with a smile. Moments later, she emerged, but something was wrong. Her limbs were loose, her eyes vacant. She collapsed to the floor and didn't move again.

Silence fell.

Osric snapped, and Pol rushed forward to examine her. The king's steward shook his head.

They didn't move Karissa's corpse. She looked so small and alone there on the floor, with her body curled and her hands beside her head as if she were sleeping. The swirling magic behind her no longer seemed beautiful but brutal.

Edric must have been terrified, but he stepped forward boldly and bowed to the king before entering the magic. It held him longer than it had the others, and Aidan gripped my hand when he failed to reappear within a few seconds. I squeezed his hand, knowing no comfort would be enough should Edric fail.

Then Edric emerged, grinning. A crown of flame hovered above his head.

"Oh, thank the Shards," Aidan muttered, leaning heavily on me.

Talfryn was next. Lara touched his shoulder before he left, smiling in encouragement, but he didn't smile back. He faced the maelstrom grimly, like a prisoner who had been condemned. I recognized that look from when I'd slain Garrick—the horrible realization that death was inevitable. He and Karissa had performed similarly; he must know that if she had failed, so would he.

He pressed a hand to his chest, on top of three embroidered birds that circled his heart. Then he stood tall, took a deep breath, and walked into the magic with more courage than I had ever seen anyone display.

His corpse fell out, landing half on top of Karissa. Their eyes stared blindly at each other.

Where did the Fae think they went after death? Did they believe in an afterlife? I had never believed in one, but now I found myself praying to the Shards that Talfryn would end up somewhere better than this.

Lara was the only one left. Tears glittered in her eyes as she stared at the two corpses. Talfryn had been her champion and a friend.

I held my breath as she steeled herself, but before she could step forward, Pol hurried to the king's side and whispered in his ear.

"What?" Osric demanded.

Pol whispered again, and Osric's face turned white with rage. "Bring it."

Lara still hesitated before him, but Osric barely seemed to see her. He tapped his fingers on the arms of his throne, visibly seething.

Pol returned bearing a burlap sack.

One look at it and I knew whatever was inside would be unpleasant. It was dripping, leaving a trail of red spatters behind.

"I have been betrayed." The room seemed to shudder with Osric's rage, and I flinched, worried the ceiling would come down. It couldn't, I reminded myself. It was only an illusion. "My guards apprehended soldiers on their way here."

Gasps met this pronouncement. Kallen shot to his feet, staring at the bloody sack with a burning expression I couldn't identify.

Drustan remained as nonchalant as ever, but his knuckles were white on the arms of his chair.

My heart tripped in my chest. Had Drustan decided to start the revolution now, or was this something else? Why wouldn't he have warned me? He'd said he'd take action after the trials were over so they could recruit the successful candidates, but I'd been thinking weeks after, not *immediately*.

Osric gestured to Pol, and the steward upended the sack. A severed head tumbled out.

It belonged to Lothar, Roland's younger brother and Drustan's coconspirator.

I gagged at the gruesome sight, feeling an accompanying surge of panic. Drustan's rebellion was truly happening tonight. Or it would have happened tonight, but something had gone terribly wrong.

Roland gaped. "What is the meaning of this?"

"It seems you and your brother betrayed the throne," Osric said in vicious, biting tones. "He was leading a squadron of Light soldiers in this direction."

"No. It isn't possible." At Osric's implacable look, Roland dropped to his knees. "My king, I have always been loyal to you. You know this. If Lothar truly has plotted against you, then he has brought everlasting shame to our house."

"Be silent. We will speak of this later."

Roland retreated, still staring at the severed head.

I dared a glance at Drustan, who no longer looked quite so calm. Exactly how many soldiers had Lothar been leading? What did this mean for the attack he had planned?

"Ten other traitors were supporting him," Pol said, "all low-ranking nobles from either Fire or Light House. Each led a squadron of twenty-five Underfae. All have been slain."

Two hundred and sixty of Drustan's troops massacred. The loss was staggering. My heart sank at the bleak expression that settled on his face.

He had lost.

He had lost before he had begun, because even with Nasties willing to attack the king, the soldiers had been needed to protect them. Now if the Nasties appeared at all it would be to a room full of Osric's soldiers, with any element of surprise long gone. Illusion reinforcements were already filing in, bristling with steel.

Osric turned slowly to Drustan, and a howling void filled my chest. No, not him. I couldn't lose this passionate, enigmatic prince who had admired me for my very humanity. I watched numbly as two soldiers shoved Drustan to his knees before the throne. His sheathed sword still hung from his belt, but it would be useless against Osric. The maelstrom whirled behind him, faster and faster, as if furious with what he had done.

Lara had stepped aside and stood watching from the edge of the crowd, looking frightened. She hadn't yet faced the Shards' judgment. By the time she did, the floor would be stained with Drustan's blood, and all my hopes for a better world would be dead with him.

"You were often seen in Lothar's company," Osric said with chilling fury. "You enjoyed visiting the brothel together, didn't you?"

"We did, but I was not aware of his treason." Drustan sounded remarkably collected.

"How can you claim that? You were frequently seen with him, you have already been accused of treason once, and half of the fighters slain tonight belonged to Fire House. You are guilty."

"Please, your majesty. Listen to me. You already know Lady Edlyn was plotting against you; perhaps she was working with Lothar. She must have known that if he was caught, suspicion would fall on me."

"This is ridiculous." The voice belonged to Prince Hector, who now stood at Kallen's side. Cruel glee shone in the slash of his smile.

"There have been rumors about you for years, Drustan. Do you truly think we'll believe that sniveling fool Edlyn was capable of plotting a revolution?"

"Only a fool would try to attack the king," Drustan shot back. "And my own blood is in the ward that protects him."

"Silence," Osric commanded. His fist slammed onto the arm of his throne. "Prince Drustan, my patience with you has reached an end. Unless you can provide me with tangible proof that you haven't plotted against me, you will be put to death."

Please, no.

"I promise I'll prove it," Drustan said. "Just give me time."

Hector smirked and muttered something to Kallen before stalking off. Kallen kept watching Drustan, his expression perfectly blank.

"You will prove it now or you will die."

An axe-wielding executioner stepped forward, and Drustan glanced around wildly. "I know of another traitor."

What? My mind was racing frantically; I couldn't think who he meant. Was he using this opportunity to eliminate some unknown enemy?

"I found out today and meant to tell you in private," he continued, "but you have forced my hand."

Osric raised a skeptical brow. "Go on."

"I overheard Lord Selwyn of Earth House speaking with his manservant about overthrowing you."

Drustan's words hit like a punch. I barely heard Lara's cry past the buzzing in my ears.

No.

Please, no.

I stared at Drustan, at his handsome face and lying mouth. At the person I'd cared for, the one I thought I'd known.

I had told Drustan about Selwyn's sympathies. I had encouraged him to speak with the teenager, and Drustan undoubtedly had. And now . . .

Drustan had betrayed him to save his own life.

Whatever happened to Selwyn would be my fault.

"He's a child," Osric said dismissively. His rings glittered as he tapped his fingers in a restless cadence, eyes narrowed on Drustan. "His house is neutral."

"He is close to adulthood and well-known for sympathizing with servants. And he's been seen with Lothar recently."

Osric looked to Kallen for confirmation. Kallen clenched his jaw and nodded with obvious reluctance.

Princess Oriana approached the throne. She cast Drustan a look of burning hatred before facing the king. "Your majesty, my son would never do this. Please—"

"Silence. Have him brought here. We will let the boy speak for himself."

We waited for long minutes while Oriana's servants went to fetch Selwyn. There was nothing else to be done. If Oriana refused to bring him, it would seem like confirmation of his guilt.

Lara kept looking at me, but I couldn't meet her eyes.

When Selwyn arrived, he was dressed in a simple blue tunic adorned with his signature yellow rose, and his golden-brown hair was mussed. He glanced around warily.

"Step forward," Osric commanded.

Selwyn joined his mother, jolting as he noticed Drustan still kneeling on the floor. I winced. He hadn't yet learned how to hide his feelings or lie convincingly. If he really had been working with Drustan . . .

"You have been accused of treason," King Osric said.

Selwyn paled. "I—I don't know what you're talking about, your majesty."

"You were heard plotting to overthrow my rule. You were seen consorting with Lothar." The king gestured at the severed head, and Selwyn jumped as if only now seeing it. He looked like he might be sick. "Do you deny it?"

"I spoke with him, but not about anything treasonous."

"You're a sixteen-year-old boy. What reason would you have for meeting with a lord of Light House?"

"He was kind to me." The words sounded almost like a question. "We liked the same books."

I closed my eyes in despair. Selwyn would never succeed with such a feeble defense.

"Lothar hated reading," Roland said grimly from the king's side.

"Oh." Selwyn flushed. "Well, uh, I didn't realize—"

"Lothar implicated you before he died," the king lied.

So clever, and so cruel. If Selwyn was guilty, he would assume the king knew everything and the game was over.

Selwyn's ragged breaths were loud in the still air. He looked at Lara with frightened eyes. She clasped her hands to her chest as if pleading with him to deny it.

Selwyn nodded once, then threw his shoulders back and faced the king again. "I did plot with Lothar." His voice quavered. "But my mother and sister were ignorant of it."

"No!" Lara dropped to her knees. "No, please . . ."

My eyes stung. Selwyn had surrendered to the king, but not for his own sake or to plead for clemency. He had confessed to spare his mother and sister any punishment.

"How long have you been plotting against the king?" Roland demanded.

"Since before the summer solstice." With every word Selwyn's voice grew stronger.

"Who else did you plot with?"

He didn't even glance at Drustan. "No one. Lothar approached me. He wanted me to rally Earth troops to fight in an uprising."

Tears streaked down my cheeks and spattered on the bodice of my fine gown. This sweet, noble boy had done what Drustan could not. He had sacrificed himself for the sake of his family and allies.

Drustan didn't even look ashamed as he watched the drama from his position on the floor. In that instant the love I felt for him twisted in my chest, warping into something horrid and hateful. Drustan had chosen his own life above everything else, and now a true idealist would pay the price.

I had been a fool.

The king continued to question Selwyn. How did they plan to defeat the wards? Did Lothar have assistance? Had Selwyn gathered any troops?

Selwyn answered with remarkable composure. Lothar had an unknown plan to remove the wards around the king, and he had been working with a dead Fire lady. Selwyn had failed to gain support within Earth House and had finally told Lothar he wouldn't be able to help. Since the massacred troops had belonged to Fire and Light, he undoubtedly spoke the truth, which meant he was about to be convicted on intention alone.

The king asked one final question. "Do you regret it?"

It was similar to what the Blood Tree had asked me, but I felt certain Selwyn would answer differently than I had. He would tell the king he did regret it and beg for forgiveness. Perhaps, since he was a child and had failed to rally support, he would be allowed to live.

Selwyn looked the king directly in the eye. "No."

Surprised exclamations filled the air. Lara keened from her position slumped on the floor, but Oriana seemed frozen, as if encased in ice by her tragedy.

"Why not?" Again the room seemed to shudder as Osric's anger blew through it.

"Because you are cruel. Because you are unjust. Because everyone in Mistei deserves to be free, from the Noble Fae to the humans." Selwyn's eyes burned with conviction, and his cheeks reddened as he spoke the traitorous words. "And even if I won't see it, I'm happy to know you will not rule forever."

King Osric snapped his fingers, and a guard shoved Selwyn to the floor so hard his head cracked against the marble.

As the executioner raised his axe, the king stood. "Wait."

The entire room held its breath as Osric approached the supine figure. He prodded Selwyn with his toe, and the boy flinched.

"I don't want to execute him the normal way." The words were precise, cutting. "I want him annihilated. I want him undone by the realm he claims to love." Osric's hands shimmered with magic as he pulled Selwyn to his feet and shoved him backwards towards the whirling cyclone of magic. "Let the Shards rip him to pieces," the king said, voice rising. "Let them tear his life from him. It's what a traitor deserves."

Selwyn stood inches from the killing vortex, sweating and trembling as his fear made itself known at last. He had been so brave, so good, and as he looked at Lara and his mother one last time, I sobbed out loud, unable to keep it in any longer.

Then the king gestured, and Selwyn's hands flew up to protect his face from something unseen. He stepped back.

It was hard to describe the sound the vortex made when he fell into it. A screeching like claws on glass, perhaps, or like the dead crying for release from their icy tombs. The sound of plans gone horribly wrong as the Shards protested the presence of someone who did not belong there.

Selwyn collapsed on the other side, his wide brown eyes staring sightlessly at the ceiling.

Lara screamed.

I collapsed, sobbing for Selwyn and the loss of someone truly good, and, more selfishly, for what I had done to him and the revelation that the prince I'd cared for had been capable of this violence. Not by his hand but by his words, just as my words had damned Selwyn and, by extension, my best friend.

Hard hands grabbed me, and I was dragged to my feet and thrown to the floor before the throne. Disoriented, I shoved myself up, wiping away tears as I tried to see what was happening. A hard boot hit my back and pinned me to the black marble. In my peripheral vision I saw another gleaming silver boot—one of the king's guards.

"It's fascinating how deeply your daughter and her pet mourn, Oriana," the king purred. I fought despair as I noticed Lara pinned to the ground as well. Her tear-flooded eyes met mine.

"My son said Lara wasn't involved." Oriana sounded preternaturally calm. How was she not raging and clawing out the eyes of everyone who had done this to her child?

Then again, we all fought with the weapons we had.

"Your son was a liar and a traitor."

"Lara is incapable of something like this. She's too weak." The words were harsh, but I understood why Oriana had said them. Better to belittle her only daughter than lose her altogether.

"And yet she performed better in the trials than anyone but Una," Osric said. "I begin to think Earth House is more duplicitous than I ever suspected."

The guard gripped my hair and dragged me to my knees. I bit my lip, ignoring the stinging pain in my scalp.

"I do not believe these two were involved," Drustan said. He knelt a few feet away from me, but I couldn't read anything in his expression.

Osric turned on him. "And how would you know? Unless you have more familiarity with the traitors' plans than you pretend."

Drustan's mouth opened, then closed. At last he replied. "Oriana is right. Lara is weak. Her handmaiden had to help her through the trials."

The blood drained from my face. I stared at Drustan, reeling at this final betrayal. For it was a betrayal, no matter what his intentions were. Perhaps he meant to save us from being executed as traitors, but even if he succeeded, Lara would be ridiculed for the rest of her life, and I . . .

I would still be killed.

That had been Oriana's promise, the same promise the Noble Fae gave to every human who entered Mistei. The ground would swallow us up, and we would never emerge from this hell again.

"How do you know this?" Osric asked.

"I sensed a token on the handmaiden after the Void trial, stolen while she aided Lara through the labyrinth. I pitied the girl, so I did not report her, but she undoubtedly continued helping her mistress."

Osric's shining black boots clicked against the stone as he approached. I kept my gaze on his knees, not daring to look at that awful, powerful face. "Did you help your mistress, human?"

I didn't respond.

The guard fisted my hair and forced my gaze up. "Did you help her?" Osric repeated, his irises swirling with magic.

"No, your majesty," I said.

Osric laughed. "You deny the word of a prince?"

"I deny any word but my own."

"What filth." Osric looked at me with utter contempt. "Throw her in."

"Wait," Lara cried.

The king turned on her. "Perhaps you would enjoy going first? As you wish. Let's see what the rewards of cheating are."

I trembled in the guard's grip as Lara was dragged towards the column of magic. She had succeeded in every trial, which meant she would still be found worthy. Then what would the king say?

The guards pushed her in.

The maelstrom swirled as it had for every other candidate, but Lara stayed inside it for a long time. Too long.

At last, the veil of power parted, and she stepped through.

I clapped my hands to my mouth, tears springing to my eyes at the sight of her standing whole and healthy in front of me. She had succeeded.

Something was wrong, though. She was frowning at her hands. Then her face crumpled, and I understood.

Her magic was gone.

"You have been judged unworthy," King Osric said with the delight of a spider winding silk around its prey. "Princess Oriana, what do you say to this revelation about your daughter?"

Oriana stood rigid, as if the slightest movement would shatter her. "She is no longer my daughter."

There was a storm where my heart had once been, a swirling tempest of pain that battered me from the inside out. Lara had been right about her mother, and we had all been so very, very wrong about what was needed to pass the trials.

Osric's smile was oily and foul. "I'm sure I'll find some use for her."

"Mother?" Lara reached out a shaking hand, but Oriana turned away.

As Lara stumbled into the crowd, Osric returned to his throne. "Throw the human in. Let her die for what she did."

"Your majesty," Kallen said, "she was undoubtedly only acting on orders—"

"Silence!" Osric still seethed with rage. Tonight had been the most substantial challenge to his power in centuries, and even though Lothar and the soldiers were dead, even though Selwyn was dead, even though Lara had lost her powers, it wasn't enough. The king would have blood from anyone he could, and no words of reason could sway him.

I met Kallen's eyes, silently thanking him for defending me when no one else had. As the guards dragged me past Drustan, I looked at him, too. His gray eyes were unreadable. Either he felt nothing or he was concealing his feelings to protect himself yet again.

I didn't care. I let him see my rage and contempt, and I didn't look away until he dropped his gaze.

Then I was standing before a rainbow-hued cyclone. From this close I could hear singing, an impossibly beautiful melody that would be the last thing I ever heard.

They pushed me in.

I STOOD IN THE MIDDLE OF A TEMPEST.

The thunderclouds were of every hue imaginable, and the lightning streaking down sent crackling reverberations through my chest. I breathed in energy and exhaled my own soul. I started to dissolve, my body ripped to shreds by the howling wind.

You cheated. The piercing voice wasn't male or female but somehow both, with echoes beneath it as if a chorus chimed in agreement. I felt flayed alive as an unknown entity peered into my mind, raking sharp talons through the memories of everything I'd done. *You did not abide by the rules.*

Another voice spoke, this one female, dark, and pulsing. *She followed the rules. She passed each trial.* The dagger on my disintegrating arm thrummed in time with every word.

She was not supposed to compete. This voice crackled like flame.

It was the Shards, I realized with an agonized, grieving wonder. The Shards were discussing me.

She had no choice, the throbbing female voice responded. The Blood Shard.

I agree. The lilting words sounded like the babbling of a stream over tumbled rocks as Earth came to my defense.

Of course you agree, the first voice argued. Based on the pain that chorus caused in my mind, I wondered if it was Illusion speaking. *You wanted the other one to succeed as well.*

And I accepted the group decision, Earth said. *The lady had a choice. This one did not.*

Not only didn't she choose, but she performed better than her lady. I shuddered at the sound of this Shard: male and deep, with a cold edge that spoke of nightmares. The churning clouds pulsed black as it spoke.

I say no, Illusion said.

I say yes, Blood replied.

She did not wield magic during the Earth trial.

She did. She carries Blood House's most sacred artifact. The magic did not come from her, but she did wield it.

She is not a part of your house, the Fire Shard interjected.

I claim her.

At the Blood Shard's firm words, the others paused.

I say yes, Earth said.

No, Fire replied. *This is foolishness.*

It's time, Blood said. *The balance must be restored. That will be her task.*

More silence as the Shards considered. Then the deep, chilling voice of Void spoke. *Blood is correct. The balance has been gone for too long. I say yes.*

My body was disintegrating further with every second that passed. I didn't feel pain, just a strange sense of being stretched too thin. Soon the pressure would grow too great, and I would snap. The broken pieces of me would vanish into the storm, and I would no longer exist.

It is an interesting debate, a final voice interjected. Light, who spoke with ringing clarity. *If she had been a candidate and cheated, we would have rejected her. But she was not. She participated because she had to, and because she cared for her friend.*

Caring is irrelevant, Fire sneered.

Not always, Light replied. *In this case it shows great courage.*

I could barely comprehend the conversation anymore. My mind was drifting further from my body. Lightning struck in front of me, but my vision was dimming, and all I saw was a faint flicker.

For a moment I felt relief. Soon I would be free from Mistei, and it wouldn't hurt at all. I would drift away and become another scrap of cloud on the wind.

Then I remembered Lara. She was still out there and in pain. She had not been released. They were all still out there—thousands of faeries and humans suffering under an evil so great I had never imagined its like. I would be free, but what if they never were?

I wanted to stay.

You feel that? Blood asked, her tone triumphant.

I do, Light responded. *And so the decision is made. I say yes.* I felt that great, echoing presence focus on me. *Kenna Heron, you have been found worthy. Take this gift and restore the balance.*

The wind swept me away, and I saw no more.

36

I WOKE WITH MY HEAD ON SOMETHING SOFT.

I rubbed my cheek against it, trying to determine what it was. A pillow? But no, the rest of my body was sprawled on cold stone.

I opened my eyes a crack. Rich brown velvet stretched in front of me, culminating in . . . a hand.

I was lying on Talfryn's corpse.

My head spun. What had happened? I stayed still despite my revulsion, keeping my eyes slitted open the barest amount and listening to the room around me.

It seemed not much time had passed. Oriana was stalking away, her mouth set in a grim line. Osric sat on the throne, laughing as he accepted a glass of wine. Beside him, Kallen stared at me, looking shaken.

The king gestured, and Drustan rose to his feet. "You have proven yourself loyal, Prince Drustan. If there should be a third incident, though . . ."

Drustan bowed. "There won't be, now that the true traitors have been rooted out." He returned to stand with the members of his house, and he didn't look at me even once.

Osric clapped his hands. "Bring the entertainment!"

A group of nearly naked Underfae and humans flooded in. Some of them posed artfully, displaying their bodies, but others trembled, standing with slumped shoulders and bowed heads.

"The trial season has concluded, and the strongest have survived. These are my offerings to you. Use them as you see fit."

Triana was there, I realized with horror, dressed in a diaphanous purple robe and visibly shaking as a Fae lady approached her. My rage increased as revelers began groping the nearest servants, then boiled over as Osric leered at a collection of terrified-looking humans. Triana and the others had been freed from the brothel. They should not have to descend into this hell again.

I couldn't move, though. The Fae would see that I was alive, and the next time they tried to execute me would certainly be more successful.

The Shards were taken away as the drinking and carousing began.

Osric summoned one of the human women. Her head was freshly shaven, and the taupe gauze wrapped around her breasts and hips hid none of the elaborate, curving scars and fresh scabs that covered her body. It was the new girl, I realized sickly. The one Triana had greeted yesterday, no doubt reassuring her that she was safe at last. Instead she was here, once again about to be subjected to the king's cruelty. She kept her head lowered as Osric settled her on his lap and began stroking his hand up the inside of her thigh.

I could just hear his next words. "You thought you were free, didn't you?" He pinched her leg, and she mumbled something in response. Apparently he had decided not to remove her tongue yet. He laughed gleefully. "Oh, it's too funny."

Nausea churned through me at his sadism, and as it did, my veins pulsed with something hot and angry. I stilled, reaching for the sensation again.

Liquid heat poured through me, as if my blood sparked with fireworks.

Caedo quivered against my arm, radiating pure joy.

What's happening? I asked the dagger.

You passed.

What do you mean?

You have power now.

My fingers throbbed with energy. I felt full to bursting with that strange fire. *What power?*

You are Blood House reborn.

I finally comprehended what I'd heard in the vortex. The Shards had given me the powers of Blood House because I had undertaken all the trials by Lara's side, aided by the dagger's magic. Now that hungry energy pulsed through me, linking the dagger closer to me than ever before. We were inextricably bound, fueled by the same heat.

What did this mean?

Was I immortal now, too?

Yes, Caedo said.

My mind spun. It was too much to contemplate.

I opened my eyes a bit wider, wondering when someone would come to remove the bodies and discover that I was, in fact, alive.

Then I saw the face of the woman perched on Osric's knee, and the world fell away.

My whimper was muffled by Talfryn's velvet tunic. I stared, wondering if my eyes or my memory had failed me. But no, it was definitely her, the same heart-shaped face and hazel eyes I had known almost my entire life.

Anya.

She was thin and haggard now, and the scars Osric had carved into her twined over her entire body. Her right cheek was marred by a narrow spiral of raised skin, and her neck trickled blood from a new injury. Her eyes were flat, her posture slumped. It was as if she had retreated inside of herself, as if she didn't even feel Osric touching her.

That was why she had disappeared in the bog without me noticing. She hadn't drowned or been eaten by the Nasties. She had been abducted by the king's minions because she was beautiful. Because he wanted her.

I almost surged to my feet, but before I could do more than stiffen, I heard screams from outside the throne room.

A servant burst in. "Nasties," she panted, pointing at the door.

Seconds later, a tide of monsters surged through.

They flapped, crawled, and slithered, hundreds of them, ranging from a huge golden snake to the horned swordsmen I'd faced before. They shouted and howled in glee as they began clawing and chewing their way through the assembled Noble Fae.

I was scrambling to my feet, desperate to save Anya and find Lara, when a group of soldiers clad in the livery of Fire House burst in through a different door and immediately engaged Osric's guards.

The rebellion was happening after all, and apparently not all of Drustan's forces had been slain. He drew his own sword and lunged at Roland as his troops poured into the room.

A loud creaking sound echoed through the space as the trapdoor in the middle of the throne room opened. Dozens of faeries in Earth House livery poured out from the hidden tunnel I'd once explored on the way to the brothel.

Selwyn had lied.

With his final words, with his grueling confession, he had lied. Not only to protect his family, but to preserve this. The final attack, made possible by his secret golden key. The end of Earth House's neutrality. He had died knowing the revolution would go on without him.

I hoped he was watching from the afterlife and smiling.

No one noticed me crouching next to three corpses. Noble Fae fought Underfae while the Nasties battled their way forward, trying desperately to reach the king. He wasn't warded against them, only against the five houses . . .

My heart thumped hard in my chest.

Five houses.

I'd seen the ritual, had watched as the wards were renewed with the blood of Fire, Light, Void, Illusion, and Earth. There had been no need to ward against Blood, because Blood House no longer existed.

Now it did.

Caedo slithered down my arm, forming a perfectly sharp dagger in my hand as I stood and stalked towards the head of the room, where Osric shouted orders from behind his throne. I couldn't see Anya anymore, but I would find her later. There was a death to claim first.

Someone stepped into my path. I looked up into shocked midnight-blue eyes.

"You're alive," Kallen whispered. His controlled mask had fallen away, and there was a strange, intense emotion on his face as he reached a trembling hand to cup my cheek.

Dark crimson power coiled in wisps over my skin, and I saw the moment he realized what I had become. He swallowed.

"Move." I needed to get to the king.

His sword flashed, and I flinched—but he was blocking a blade that had been slicing towards me from behind. My attacker's weapon went spinning to the ground, and then Kallen plunged his sword through the heart of the Light House soldier who had tried to kill me.

It was the second time I'd seen him murder someone in this

room, but this time he was anything but calm. He was breathing hard, and his eyes burned with rage. And he'd done it . . . for me.

"Go," he said roughly, tearing the opal brooch from his tunic and flinging it to the ground. "And good luck."

I didn't question his actions; there would be time for that later. I continued towards the dais, where Osric still cowered. Before me, Illusion and Light soldiers clashed with Fire and Earth rebels. Blood painted the floor, making the footing slick, but I darted through the chaos with ease. My small stature had become an asset at last.

More soldiers poured in, these ones clad in Void black. They approached the Earth troops . . . and fell in beside them, fighting together against the king's forces.

Drustan had been right about Void House plotting its own coup. Perhaps they hadn't meant for it to happen like this, but here they were, ready to kill. And there Kallen was, stabbing his sword through Roland's chest while Drustan retreated from the Light prince's latest blow. For a moment the two of them stared at each other. Then Drustan nodded, and they began fighting back to back.

I still burned with rage at Drustan, but now I understood what I hadn't before. He'd known there were more Fire and Earth troops. He'd known the Nasties awaited the signal to attack. Perhaps he had saved his own life from selfishness . . . but perhaps he had saved it because he'd known he would be needed when the battle finally broke.

I still didn't think I could forgive him.

Something flashed in my peripheral vision. An axe, slicing towards my head. I wouldn't be fast enough to dodge. If only he were slower . . .

Then, miraculously, he was. The soldier's arm descended sluggishly as his eyes gradually widened in shock.

Blood magic affected bodies. Which meant *I* affected bodies.

I willed him to stop entirely, and he did. Garnet power raced over my skin as I focused on guard after guard, willing each one to stop fighting so rebels could dive in for the kill.

Soon I was all alone at the back wall a mere twenty feet from the king's dais. He stood behind his throne, flanked by two guards, but though he didn't carry a sword, his upraised hand was weapon enough. Any rebels who charged him grew disoriented, stumbling towards death. The throne room was warded against the use of all magic except his—and mine.

The Nasties were getting closer, but I couldn't wait for them to reach the king. With every second more rebels were slain by the combined Illusion and Light forces.

I summoned the full, roaring strength of my new magic and willed his guards to stop.

They froze with swords still raised. Osric continued casting illusions, unaware his protectors were no longer capable of movement. I sprinted towards him, praying he wouldn't hear my footfalls.

I leapt onto the dais and stabbed the guards one by one as Caedo sang in my mind. The dagger feasted, and the drained bodies crumpled silently. I was just behind Osric now, my nose nearly touching his brocaded ivory tunic. He smelled like sickly sweet death.

I reached around him and slit his throat.

Osric collapsed beside the throne, clamping a hand onto the gushing wound. Each pulse of his heart sent more blood pouring over his fingers. His stunned violet eyes met mine. For the first time in months of cruelty and suffering, he looked horrified.

I smiled down at him.

A brutal, vicious joy slid through my veins, intensifying with every spurt of blood. Osric tried to stand again, but I grabbed my skirt with my free hand, lifting the gauzy fabric so I could kick him in the chest. He fell onto his back with a gurgling cry.

Someone screamed.

The fighting stilled as all eyes went to the throne—to me, standing over King Osric as he writhed and choked. The king was still stanching the flow of blood with one hand, but he raised the other towards me. His fingers were trembling.

Then he disappeared.

I gasped, alarm jolting through me as I looked frantically around the now-empty dais. Could he teleport? Where and how—

Feel, Caedo said in my mind, interrupting my spiraling thoughts. *Don't look.*

Dark red power still wisped over my hand, curling around the hilt of the dagger and playing with my fingers. It pulsed, drawing my attention to the beat of my heart. I became aware of other hearts pounding in the room, a chorus I somehow heard without hearing as a new sense came alive.

A rapid, shallow patter came from near my feet, slowly moving away. King Osric's heart, pumping out his dwindling life as he tried to crawl to safety. Weakened as he was, he'd still been able to cast an illusion.

As my eyes tracked the path Osric had taken, my new magical awareness brushing against the pool of blood he had disguised, I noticed Anya curled up in the corner of the room, just off the dais. Her terrified eyes met mine.

I raised my knife towards her in grim salute, then stalked after Osric. My boot hit his invisible leg, and I crouched to drive the dagger into his gut. The king's body flickered back into existence as he screamed.

"For Anya," I said, twisting the knife in his intestines. Caedo sucked in a deep mouthful of the welling blood, but not all of it—neither of us wanted the king's suffering to be over yet.

Light's and Illusion's forces were trying to cut their way towards the throne, but the combined might of Fire, Earth, Void, and the Nasties stopped them. And some soldiers had stopped on their own, blades sagging as they watched the violence unfolding on the dais, their faces reflecting an array of grief, horror, shock . . . and hope.

Hope was an empty dream, or so I'd believed for most of my life. I'd let myself feel it again with Drustan, placing my fragile faith in his courage and nobility, in his heroism, in the power and resources a mere human would never be able to wield. Inventing a story that, in the end, he hadn't been able to live up to.

Maybe that sort of hope was empty. But this kind? The kind I could force with my own two hands, with a blade sliding into my victim's flesh, with a cry of furious joy on my lips?

This was better.

I stabbed Osric on the right side of his chest, the dagger breaking ribs to puncture his lung. "For Mistei," I called out as he convulsed.

There was blood everywhere. It pooled on the dais and saturated the king's tunic and glittered on my exposed skin like the most treasured rubies. A drop trickled down my cheek to the corner of my mouth, and I licked it away. Shivering, incandescent energy filled me as I swallowed. It was like wine, but better—rich and complex, addictive not only in the taste but in the fear reflected in the king's face as I swallowed.

I leaned in, meeting Osric's shocked, pain-filled violet eyes. "For me," I whispered.

Then I stabbed him in the heart.

Caedo drank this time, deep and long. I almost couldn't tell where the dagger ended and I began; as Caedo took its fill, I felt sated, too. Like the blood was settling into my stomach and giving me new life.

The king's pale flesh turned white and waxen. He jerked and fell still.

I heard a sound that wasn't a sound, a pop of air I felt in my chest. The wards on the floor shimmered and then dissipated.

As I stood over Osric's corpse, the Nasties nearest me stared with awe on their scaled and brutal faces. Soon a band of them had surrounded the dais with their backs to me. Protecting me, I realized.

The battle didn't last much longer. Illusion's troops fell into chaos and most of Light's troops fled, and then the throne room was populated with rebels and survivors, with prisoners and the dead.

Drustan was staring at me from the same spot where he had knelt not even an hour before. His sword dripped.

For one gratifying moment, he looked afraid.

WITH THE SLAUGHTER OVER, FAERIES MOVED AROUND THE ROOM, conferring with one another, wiping their weapons clean, or covering the dead with sheets. The corpses would be disposed of according to each house's tradition, though I wasn't sure what would happen to the fallen Nasties, who lay uncovered. Was that by preference? Or was even their sacrifice deemed unworthy of the Noble Fae's respect? Their own queen hadn't even come to support them—another ruler content to let others pay the price of her politics.

Low wails sounded from a few faeries who grieved over the fallen, while others were loud and boisterous in their victory. Drustan grinned exultantly at one of his generals while Hector watched from the edge of the room, arms crossed and expression unreadable. Kallen whispered in his brother's ear, though his eyes were fixed on me. He wasn't the only one watching, and as the battle rage drained out of me, I grew uncomfortable under the weight of so many stares.

No one moved to cover King Osric's corpse. He gazed at the ceiling with empty eyes, sunken-cheeked and pale as bone. Caedo purred in my mind, gorged on blood, and its heavy, sated contentment seemed to fill my own gut. I looked down at the sharp steel in my hand, feeling strangely like I didn't belong in my own body.

That was my hand that slew King Osric. The tyrant was dead because of me.

Do you regret it? The voice in my head was familiar, though it seemed to come from a further distance than it had during my time in the maelstrom. The Blood Shard, speaking to me as I now realized it had during the trial.

No, I thought, too disoriented to even question how or why the Shard was communicating with me. I didn't feel guilty for murdering Osric and never would.

I had enjoyed it in a sick, primal way, but I couldn't seem to summon up guilt for that, either. Looking down at Caedo, I felt the strangest wish that some of the king's blood remained for me to lick off the blade.

A soft sob caught my attention, familiar despite the distance and time. I turned my back on King Osric, searching out the person who had made that sound.

Anya was curled up on her side, body shaking.

"Anya!" As I hurried over, Caedo liquified and swirled around my arm, becoming jewelry once more.

Anya flinched and raised a hand to shield her face when I crouched next to her. "No, no . . ."

Her shaved head had contours I'd never realized existed. The dips and divots seemed strange to my eyes, like a truth I'd known all my life had suddenly shifted to reveal more facets. The puckered pink scars looked even more gruesome close-up, and there was a scab over her ear where the shaving razor hadn't been wielded carefully enough.

My heart ached. "It's me," I said, tears flooding my eyes. She seemed so small and frail, a wisp of the person I'd known. "Anya, it's Kenna. I'm here."

She shook her head, refusing to look at me. Her eyes were fixed straight ahead, but I got the sense she wasn't truly seeing anything. "Not real," she whispered. "You're not real."

"I am."

"It's a lie," she said, still staring at the far wall. "You're just tormenting me."

"What?" I touched her shoulder lightly, but she cried out as if I had hurt her, so I yanked my hand away. "Please, Anya," I begged. "Look at me."

She shook her head again. "I won't believe it," she said, voice growing as dead as her eyes. "You can't trick me anymore."

Comprehension hit, and it felt like my rib cage had cracked open. She thought I was an illusion. She'd been Osric's special "pet," and he'd tormented her in more ways than I could imagine.

"Oh, Anya," I said softly. "I'm so sorry. About what he did. That I wasn't there to save you." The tears slid down my cheeks now, salty grief collecting at the corners of my lips. "I'm so sorry." My voice broke on the last word.

"Just take what you're here for," she said dully.

Her entire body was trembling, and her eyes had gone totally unfocused. I looked around as if the answer to this tragedy could be found in this bloodstained chamber. It couldn't, but an Underfae was walking nearby with an armful of sheets. I took one, then gently draped it over Anya. It felt wrong to cover her with a burial shroud, but I wanted her to be warm, so I tucked it around her, taking care to leave her face, neck, and hands free. She was alive. This wasn't an ending.

"You're safe," I whispered. "Osric is dead."

Her eyelids flickered, but she still didn't look at me. Her fingers curled around the edges of the sheet, pulling it closer.

"I'll leave you alone for a bit." It was agony to abandon her now that we'd been reunited, but she wasn't going to believe me yet, and there were things to do. Conversations to have, plans to make before I could take her somewhere safe.

Lara approached then. The hem of her green gown was soaked in blood, and her hands were clasped tightly at her waist. There was a haunted quality to her expression. "Kenna?" she asked hesitantly. "How—how is this possible? How are you alive?"

Another friend hurt. Another one damaged by Fae cruelty.

"I'll tell you everything later," I said, standing on shaking legs. "This is . . ." I trailed off as Anya curled into herself again at the sound of my voice. "My friend," I murmured. "From the bog. She wasn't dead after all."

Lara didn't look like she was processing my words. "Oh," was all she said.

Lara had just lost her brother, her magic, her mother, her house. I reached out to touch her elbow, and she didn't react at all. Her eyes were red-rimmed, her face blotchy from prolonged crying.

"I'm so sorry—" I started to say, but Lara shook her head sharply. "No," she said, voice rough. "Not here."

"All right." I swallowed the words of grief and rage that wanted to pour out. "Later, then. When we're back . . ." I trailed off, not knowing what to promise. Where were we supposed to go? Not back home, certainly. Princess Oriana had denounced her. She was no longer a lady of Earth House, and I was no longer a servant.

Anya made a low, miserable noise. "Not real," she whispered.

Lara stirred at the sound and looked down at Anya. "I can have someone guard her," she said. Then fresh grief washed over her face. "Or . . . no, I can't. Not anymore."

Someone approached then, a familiar figure with the palest blue skin and eyes that swam with grief. "I'll find people to guard her,"

Alodie said, voice hushed. "To guard all of you." She curtsied to Lara. "My lady."

Lara looked surprised and touched by the asrai's offer. "Thank you, Alodie," she said, voice rough. "I—thank you. But Oriana won't want you to do anything for me anymore. Or for Kenna."

"Then for the human," Alodie said, turning her wet eyes to me. "If you want it, I can at least do that."

I nodded, nearly crying at this offer of friendship and fidelity. "Her name is Anya," I said softly. "And thank you."

Alodie nodded, then glided away to retrieve a pair of Earth Underfae. They moved into position on either side of Anya where she lay curled on the floor, guarding her in silence. Alodie rested a hand on Lara's arm for a lingering moment before moving back into the throng to continue caring for the wounded.

Lara and I stared at each other. "I don't know what to do," she said.

"I don't, either."

We weren't welcome in Earth House. We probably weren't welcome anywhere.

Caedo curled tighter around my arm. *You have a new home*, it said. *You can take them with you.*

It took me a moment to understand. *To Blood House?*

A thrum of acknowledgment. *You are Blood reborn.*

I was only barely beginning to understand what that meant. But if it meant there was shelter for my friends and me, that was enough for tonight.

A familiar voice came from the center of the room. "Citizens of Mistei," Drustan called out. "Gather round."

My shoulders instinctively stiffened.

Everyone turned to face him, conversation dying. He raised his hands, beckoning people closer. Soon the survivors were gathered in a loose circle facing him. Lara stayed by my side, but no one else seemed to want to get too near. Even the small group of Nasties who had dedicated themselves to preserving my safety remained a healthy distance away, glancing at me nervously.

"Tonight has been hard and bloody," Drustan said. "But we have prevailed."

A ragged cheer greeted his words.

I felt a painful thickness in my throat as I took in Drustan's handsome, determined face. Blood arced across his cheek and stained his tunic, and his hair was tangled from the fighting. With a sword sheathed at his hip, he looked like the noble, courageous hero of my dreams.

His revolution had saved us all. And he'd betrayed Selwyn and sacrificed me to make sure of it.

"The king is dead," Drustan said. "We're free."

More cheers sounded.

I met Kallen's eyes across the circle, where he stood among a group of Void nobles. He raised an eyebrow, and one corner of my mouth lifted in sardonic acknowledgment. *The king is dead*, indeed. The king had been killed. By me.

"Fellow citizens of Mistei," Drustan pronounced, his voice echoing off the blood-spattered walls, "we have the chance to create a new life. A new court. We will open our doors to the world again. We will live where and how we choose. We will *love* who we choose." His eyes finally found mine, but I stared back at him stonily.

Love meant different things to us.

As Drustan looked at me with a horrible, complex longing in his eyes, I was excruciatingly aware of the human woman curled under a burial shroud behind me, her head pressed into her knees as she rocked silently. One day Anya would heal. I would do anything to see it happen.

That was what love was. Not just romantic love, but any type of love. It was caring so much for another person that you would do anything to see them happy and whole.

Drustan looked away from me at last. "My friends, I have been planning this moment for decades." His smile was both triumphant and gracious; I should have known all that charisma would make him a remarkable orator. "It has taken many of us working together in secret to make it come about. It has required great sacrifice. At the next feast we will raise a glass to each and every one of the fallen in gratitude for what they have done. But first, we have rebuilding to do."

Hector pushed to the front of the crowd beside Kallen. His long hair was matted with gore, and there was a healing cut on the side of his neck. I realized now where he had gone during Drustan's interrogation: to rally the Void troops, in the hopes that something might happen after all and they could join the fight.

"The first item," Drustan said, "is to choose a new ruler."

Hector and Kallen exchanged a glance. A wave of cynicism washed over me. I knew exactly who Drustan would suggest, and while once I would have thought it a wonderful thing, I was no longer so sure. Ruthlessness needed to be tempered with mercy, and he hadn't displayed much mercy lately.

"I suppose you want to be king," Hector said.

"I would be honored to be king." Drustan pressed a hand to his chest. "After all, I have sacrificed for years to make this happen. But for us to overcome Osric's poisonous legacy, the houses must choose together." He turned in a circle, arms outstretched. "My friends, I humbly offer to be your king, if you will accept me. If any other candidates wish to nominate themselves, please do so now." He clearly didn't expect anyone else to, since he was unquestionably the leader of the rebellion.

Hector stepped forward. "The eloquent Fire prince isn't the only one who has been working to overthrow Osric. I have been preparing with my house in secret, and we were happy to lend our aid today."

"You never allied with me," Drustan said with sharp-edged friendliness.

"I knew what would happen to your allies. After all, we witnessed what happened to Lord Selwyn."

Lara made a soft, grief-stricken noise.

"He pledged his troops," Hector continued. "He stood by your side, and you betrayed him. You gave him up to Osric, and then he died for you."

Uneasy conversation rose throughout the hall as Drustan's cheeks reddened. "You know nothing of it," he said. "We discussed this possibility. The boy was willing to give his life."

"Was he? I heard he seemed surprised when he was brought in."

"He was an excellent actor."

"So a sixteen-year-old boy well-known for his soft heart agreed to die just so you might survive to be king?"

Lara sobbed loudly. I wanted to hug her, but what right had I to offer comfort? I had sent Selwyn to Drustan and thus to his death.

"The boy was an idealist," Drustan said. "As am I."

"I don't see idealism," Hector sneered. "I see opportunism."

"If you had worked with me these last decades instead of seeking ways to undermine me, perhaps you would see differently."

"I was working with outside forces. Elsmere is Void House's ally now; under my direction, they would have struck Osric at Samhain."

So what Lothar had speculated in the brothel was true—Drustan had found a way around the king's ward with the Nasties, but Void had been working on its own plan to kill Osric. I looked at Kallen again, trying to read his stoic expression. He'd been speaking with

Elsmere's faeries at Beltane—possibly as a direct consequence of the information I'd provided—but he'd presumably been balancing schemes on top of schemes, an array of possibilities and alliances to cultivate. Playing the king's spy while plotting to end him was a more dangerous and complicated game than I could imagine.

"Is Elsmere Void's ally or Mistei's ally?" Drustan asked. "And how convenient for you that my people paid the price before you had to put any proof behind these bold claims."

"Enough." The snapped command came, surprisingly, from Princess Oriana. Her golden hair had come undone, but there was no blood on her dress. She had not fought. Not for the rebellion, not for Mistei . . . not for her daughter.

I hated her for it.

"This bickering is pointless," she said. "Light and Illusion will regroup and present a new candidate for the throne. Either you come to an agreement of some kind, or the entire court will fracture."

"I will be king," Hector said.

Drustan stalked forward until they stood only inches apart. "No, you won't. Oriana, who do you support?" His tone implied Oriana's choice should be easy, that she should choose the prince her son had given his life to help.

"Earth House remains neutral."

Lara stiffened. I understood the feeling. Selwyn had died for this cause, had sacrificed himself to end the rule of a tyrant, but his mother still refused to participate in the battle?

"What?" Drustan turned on her. "Your son stood beside me."

"And died beside you." There the bitterness was, seeping through her cool facade. "Regardless, I will not throw away millennia of heritage because of personal sentiment. Earth House remains neutral."

Hector smirked. "So Void supports me, Fire supports you, and Earth stays neutral. That leaves us evenly split."

"Not quite." Drustan's eyes found me in the crowd, and my heart sank. "You may not have noticed, Hector, but if you were near the front of the fighting, you would have seen that Kenna was the one who slew the king."

"I saw." Hector barely glanced at me.

"Why was she able to approach him?"

"Because she's human."

Drustan shook his head. "Human, but sworn to Earth House. As a servant, she shouldn't have been able to hurt him. And as a human, she shouldn't have survived the Shards at all."

As if recalling my execution, Hector frowned and studied me.

"Kenna," Drustan said, "show them your power."

The secret would be out soon enough anyway. I raised my hand, and bloodred light shimmered over it. Gasps and exclamations sounded as faeries backed even farther away from me. I clenched my jaw and focused on Drustan. *Don't move*, I thought at him, putting all my will behind it. I imagined that simmering, liquid power stretching towards him and looping crimson bands around his arms and chest.

His eyes widened in surprise, and I could see him straining against invisible bonds. He was far more powerful than the guards I'd frozen and broke through my hold quickly. "Very good," he said through gritted teeth. "The Shards declared Kenna worthy and gifted her with the powers of Blood House."

"Impossible," Hector said, so I sent a tendril of magic his way as well. My head spun as I imagined him motionless; the rush of power felt foreign and tiring to wield.

When Hector broke free, he looked even paler than normal.

"That means Kenna is now Princess of Blood House," Drustan said. "She gets to decide who her house will support."

I blinked. Princess? That hadn't been part of my bargain with the

Shards, had it? But if no one else existed in Blood House . . . I supposed I was princess by default.

"She has a house of one," Hector said dryly, and I had to admit it was a reasonable argument.

"The Shards gave her that power. They must have meant for her to use it. So tell us, Kenna—who do you support as king?"

I stared at Drustan, at that grin full of secrets, at those warm gray eyes, at his outstretched hand. A month ago that look would have sent me running into his arms, and I knew he expected it to have the same effect now. I had been wildly jealous over him, after all. I had betrayed Lara's confidence for him. I had slain the king to support his rebellion, even after he had directly caused my near death. Why shouldn't he assume that I would support him?

He still didn't understand humans. Or perhaps he simply didn't understand me.

"Blood House abstains until you prove any of you are worthy to rule."

Gasps went around the room. Drustan looked as if I'd slapped him, while Hector smirked. Even Lara glanced at me askance, and Kallen's jaw had dropped in outright shock.

"What more proof could you possibly need?" Drustan asked tightly. "My revolution has freed us all."

My eyes fell on Anya, still shivering in a ball in the corner. "Not all," I said, feeling the stab of grief and fury again. "You've made it clear you know how to scheme and kill, but what do you have to offer when the violence is done?" I gestured around the room at the sheet-covered corpses, all those who had fought or died for him: Noble Fae, Underfae, Nasties, humans. "Their blood is barely cool and all you can think of is your crown."

My latest words sent the gathering into an uproar. Faeries were shouting over one another, expressing various opinions about

Drustan's virtues, Hector's power, and how a human upstart could dare question the wisdom of the Noble Fae.

"Someone has to take power now," Drustan said. The warmth in those eyes had turned to cold ash so quickly—but his fire had never truly burned for me, had it? "Light and Illusion will regroup, and soon. We need a leader."

It was probably true, but I couldn't bring myself to give him or anyone else the throne right now. I'd thought I'd known Drustan before this bloody night, but he'd proven that vision of him to be a naïve, love-addled fantasy. How could I throw my trust behind him, knowing how long tyrants could last in Mistei?

The Blood Shard had claimed me, given me its magic. I still didn't understand why or how to fully use that power or what balance I was meant to restore, but obediently following whatever path the Noble Fae set out for me couldn't be what the Shards had hoped for. Besides, Drustan had proven he would sacrifice anyone for his cause.

Maybe he was right to. Maybe that was what revolutions needed. But what came after the revolution?

"How will you liberate the humans?" I asked. "And the Under-fae, will they have a say in your new court? What rights will you give them, or do they have no purpose except to serve you?" Belatedly I glanced at the Nasties who had protected me earlier. A large golden snake stared at me from three solemn green eyes. "And the Nasties, what of them? They helped bring you this victory."

Drustan stalked towards me. "Have you lost your mind?" he demanded. "Now isn't the time to be discussing any of that." The snake slithered in front of me, baring razor-sharp fangs, and Drustan stopped. "We can discuss this later," he said, holding up his hands as if trying to placate both me and the snake. "Once my rule is established."

"If we aren't unified from the start, how is this different from Osric's rule? You said you wanted a new world where everyone is free and equal. Prove it."

We locked eyes, frozen between hate and love, passion and betrayal.

Drustan turned away. "Perhaps Princess Kenna needs to learn more Fae history before making such proclamations." The words were laced with condemnation. "But it's been a tumultuous night, and she is obviously not thinking clearly. I move for the house heads to reconvene tomorrow, when tempers have cooled and everyone is prepared to treat this matter seriously."

"My position will be the same," I informed his back. He stiffened but didn't face me again.

"As will mine." Hector studied me with a mixture of calculation and respect. "If Princess Kenna wants proof of who is most worthy to rule, then I will provide it."

"Light and Illusion will attack," Drustan said. "As soon as they regroup, they'll want to reclaim the throne."

Hector shrugged. "Let them. I'm willing to fight."

"As am I. But if your stance towards being king should change, let me know." Drustan stalked past me, staying out of striking range of my new snake guardian. As he passed, he murmured, "If you wanted another war, congratulations. This is how you get one."

Then he was gone, and I was left staring at an empty doorway.

The gathering broke up after that, and the Fae stumbled away to care for their wounded, dispose of bodies, and come to terms with what had happened. Alodie left with the rest of the Earth contingent, casting me a worried glance over her shoulder. Eventually even the Nasties slithered away, presumably to report to their queen.

The throne room was still and quiet. Osric's corpse lay uncovered on the dais, waiting for someone to decide what to do with him. I inhaled the lingering scent of death, wondering what to do with myself.

Caedo crooned an inviting song in my mind, sending vibrations into my arm. *Home*, it sighed.

Blood House awaited, but how would I even get inside? And what would I do once I got there? I was a princess with no court and no allies.

Except that wasn't entirely true. Two people remained in the hall with me after everyone else had gone. Anya still rocked in her corner, and Lara stood silently beside her.

"I—I don't know what to say," I told Lara. "I'm sorry about everything. About Selwyn. About the Shards."

Lara's eyes were reddened, her dress was torn, and her hair tumbled in a wild tangle to her waist. She looked the complete opposite of the spoiled lady I'd met six months ago. "Thank you."

We kept staring at each other.

"This may sound strange," I said, "but do you want to—"

"Yes," she interrupted. "Whatever it is, yes."

I laughed through the sob that caught in my throat. "You don't even know what I'm going to ask you."

"It doesn't matter. You're my friend."

Tears poured down my face as I pulled her into a tight hug. I cried into her shoulder, and she wept into my hair.

"What I was going to say," I said when we finally separated, "is that you are welcome to become a lady of Blood House. I don't know if it works like that or not, but you will always have a place to stay with me."

Her pride must have stung at this reversal in our fortunes, but she nodded. "I would be honored."

"Can you help me with . . ." I gestured at Anya, whose gaze was still blank. By every power in me, the old stubbornness and the new, strange magic, I would help her get well again.

"Yes," Lara said. "Always."

We managed to get Anya to her feet, supporting her between us. She went without much resistance, seeming to have retreated somewhere deep inside herself. As I adjusted my arm around her waist, I thought about the twists of life that had brought the three of us here. So much fear, so much pain. The future stretched before us, as uncertain as it was terrifying.

But hope was what we made it. I wasn't going to wait for someone else to create that future for me. I was going to seize it with my own two hands, then carve it into a shape I wanted.

I lifted my chin, took a deep breath, then walked with my two closest friends towards Blood House and a new life.

ACKNOWLEDGMENTS

Thank you to all the wonderful people who have made this book possible. Cindy Hwang, my amazing editor—thank you for seeing the potential in this story. It's an honor to work with you, and I'm grateful for your enthusiastic support and excellent notes. Thank you also to the incredible Penguin Random House team: Jessica Mangicaro, Kaila Mundel-Hill, Stephanie Felty, Elizabeth Vinson, Stacy Edwards, Jennifer Sale, Daniel Brount, Tawanna Sullivan, and everyone else who helped make this book a reality. For the UK edition, thank you to Áine Feeney, Javerya Iqbal, Jenna Petts, and the entire Gollancz team.

Jessica Watterson—you are the best agent an author could hope for. Thank you for your support, kindness, and amazing publishing brain, as well as for your excellent notes on this book. I'm so lucky to be your client and a member of the SDLA family!

The cover for this book is so gorgeous I cried when I saw it. Thank you to Erion Makuo for that fiercely beautiful illustration of Kenna and to Katie Anderson for the design and art direction.

This book has had a long path to publication, and I want to thank everyone who has been a part of that process. Sarah Tarkoff and Angela Serranzana—thank you for being my first beta readers and giving wonderful feedback. Can you believe this book is being published at last? Thank you to Celia Winter for giving notes on the first few chapters, to Victoria Ramsey for helping workshop the back cover copy, and to Jenna Levine for letting me ramble infinitely in your DMs. Thank you also to the friends and family members who have supported me along the way to this moment. Mom and Dad, Steve and Mahina, and the entire extended family—what a wonderful group of people you are. I love you all and wouldn't be here without you.

Fancy Drunk Lady Book Club! You get the dedication on this one because you have been such a source of joy over the last decade. Thank you for your friendship and for filling my life with good conversation, good food, and good books, even when I have to join the meetings via video. And here's to the adventures of Valkyrie Jones, paranormal investigator extraordinaire.

To the Berkletes, Words Are Hard, and the SDLA Sisters—thank you for the insight, the commiseration, the creativity, and the joy you bring. I would be much more of an anxious wreck than I already am if it weren't for your steadfast and cheerful support. Thank you as well to the authors who read this book early and gave kind blurbs.

I am so grateful to the booksellers and librarians who have supported both Glimmer Falls and this new series. And to Village Books in particular—thank you for the preorder campaigns, the signing events, the Chuckanut Radio Hour, and all the good you do for our community.

And to the readers—you are the reason for everything. Thank you so much for picking up this book. May your lives be full of magic and beautiful stories.

Photo by Mahina Hawley Photography

SARAH HAWLEY lives in the Pacific Northwest, where her hobbies include rambling through the woods and appreciating fictional villains. She has an MA in archaeology and has excavated at an Inca site in Chile, a Bronze Age palace in Turkey, and a medieval abbey in England. When not dreaming up whimsical love stories, she can be found reading, dancing, or cuddling her two cats.